Praise for _____

"Strong characters and positive yet realistic relationships."

Booklist

"If you are due for a visit to Hope Harbor, *Sandcastle Inn* has an opening just for you! This is such a delightful setting, and the multidimensional characters that Irene Hannon so skillfully writes just add to the engaging dynamic."

Reading Is My Superpower

"*Sandcastle Inn* is like hearing a testimony and coming to the belief that there is still hope, even amid uncertainties."

Interviews & Reviews

Praise for *Windswept Way*

"Hannon's nuanced character development and snappy pacing make this tale of second chances a pure delight. Readers will eagerly turn pages until the satisfying close."

Publishers Weekly

"Hannon, who has long been viewed as a successful writer of Christian thrillers, proves she can excel in the contemporary romance genre as well."

Library Journal

"Another warm, satisfying Hope Harbor novel."

Booklist

"*Windswept Way* is a wonderfully entertaining, impressively original, wholesome romance."

Midwest Book Reviews

Praise for *Sea Glass Cottage*

"Hannon hits the right notes of romance and comfort in this winning story."

Booklist

"Set in a charming town with inhabitants who are just as charming, the Christian romance novel *Sea Glass Cottage* is a sweet story of second chances."

Foreword Reviews

"Hannon's characters glow with life in *Sea Glass Cottage*."

Evangelical Church Library Association

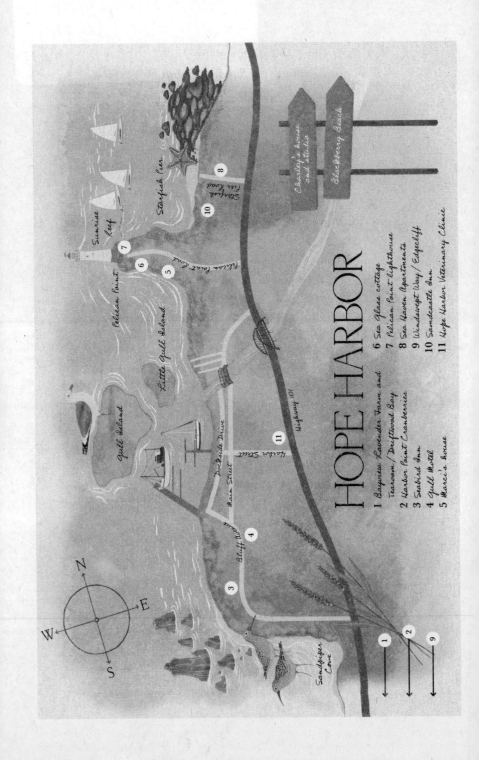

HOPE HARBOR

1 Bayview Lavender Farm and
  Tearoom / Driftwood Bay
2 Harbor Point Cranberries
3 Seabird Inn
4 Gull Motel
5 Marci's house
6 Sea Glass cottage
7 Pelican Point lighthouse
8 Sea Haven Apartments
9 Windswept Way / Edgecliff
10 Sandcastle Inn
11 Hope Harbor Veterinary Clinic

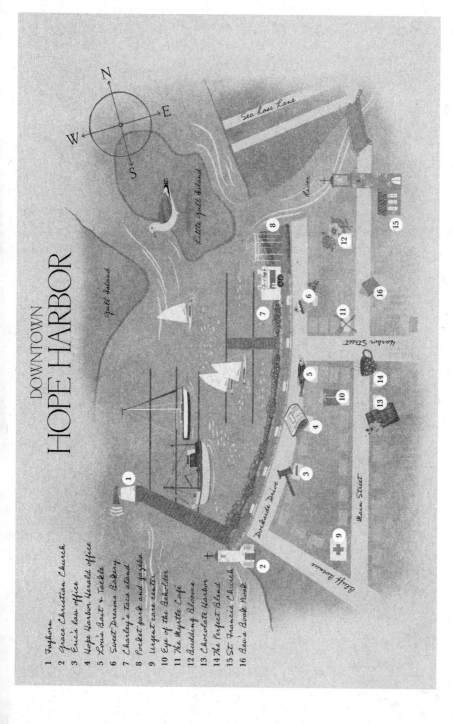

Sunrise Reef

Books by Irene Hannon

HEROES OF QUANTICO
Against All Odds
An Eye for an Eye
In Harm's Way

GUARDIANS OF JUSTICE
Fatal Judgment
Deadly Pursuit
Lethal Legacy

PRIVATE JUSTICE
Vanished
Trapped
Deceived

MEN OF VALOR
Buried Secrets
Thin Ice
Tangled Webs

CODE OF HONOR
Dangerous Illusions
Hidden Peril
Dark Ambitions

TRIPLE THREAT
Point of Danger
Labyrinth of Lies
Body of Evidence

UNDAUNTED COURAGE
Into the Fire
Over the Edge

HOPE HARBOR
Hope Harbor
Sea Rose Lane
Sandpiper Cove
Pelican Point
Driftwood Bay
Starfish Pier
Blackberry Beach
Sea Glass Cottage
Windswept Way
Sandcastle Inn
Sunrise Reef

STANDALONE NOVELS
That Certain Summer
One Perfect Spring

Sunrise Reef

A Hope Harbor Novel

IRENE HANNON

Revell

a division of Baker Publishing Group
Grand Rapids, Michigan

Published by Revell
a division of Baker Publishing Group
Grand Rapids, Michigan
RevellBooks.com

Printed in the United States of America

Library of Congress Cataloging-in-Publication Data
Names: Hannon, Irene, author.
Title: Sunrise reef / Irene Hannon.
Description: Grand Rapids, Michigan : Revell, a division of Baker Publishing
    Group, 2025. | Series: A Hope Harbor Novel
Identifiers: LCCN 2024035114 | ISBN 9780800741938 (paper) | ISBN 9780800746766
    (casebound) | ISBN 9781493448661 (ebook)
Subjects: LCGFT: Romance fiction. | Christian fiction. | Novels.
Classification: LCC PS3558.A4793 S86 2025 | DDC 813/.54—dc23/eng/20240802
LC record available at https://lccn.loc.gov/2024035114

This book is a work of fiction. Names, characters, places, and incidents are the product of the author's imagination or are used fictitiously. Any resemblance to actual events, locales, or persons, living or dead, is coincidental.

Photo illustration by Anton Markous.

Emojis are from the open-source library OpenMoji (https://openmoji.org/) under the Creative Commons license CC BY-SA 4.0 (https://creativecommons.org/licenses/by -sa/4.0/legalcode).

Baker Publishing Group publications use paper produced from sustainable forestry practices and post-consumer waste whenever possible.

25 26 27 28 29 30 31   7 6 5 4 3 2 1

To Shep Hermann—

A gracious man with a heart for God,
who celebrated life . . .
and who shared his little piece of paradise with us.

We will be forever grateful
for his kindness and generosity,
and will always treasure our magical days
at his beautiful home by the sea.

Though he now dwells in his eternal home,
he continues to inspire all those
whose lives he touched—and enriched.

Rest in peace, Shep.

1

· ·

Was something burning?

Bren Ryan stopped reading the instructions on the tube of hair dye in her hand, destined for use later today, and frowned at her reflection in the bathroom mirror. Sniffed.

A faint acrid odor with a hint of fishiness prickled her nose.

Not quite a burn smell but close. And definitely worth investigating.

Leaving the dye on the vanity, she followed the scent, wincing as another slash of lightning strobed through the sky outside the window, followed by a boom of bone-jarring thunder.

Man, this was bizarre weather. Squalls on the Oregon coast were supposed to be confined to the winter months. They never ushered in August—especially storms that went on for hours. Besides, even in the winter, torrential rain and high winds were far more common than lightning and thunder.

Whatever the cause of this uncharacteristic outburst from Mother Nature, it was certainly a dramatic beginning to her thirtieth birthday.

And perhaps it was also an omen that her decision to create a birthday resolution to-do list and shake things up a bit during this new decade of her life was sound.

The smell intensified as she approached the kitchen, and she paused on the threshold. Gave the room a slow scan.

Everything appeared to be normal.

Could the unpleasant odor be coming from outside?

Bren crossed to the window above the sink, pushed it higher than the scant inch she'd left it cracked, and leaned over. Inhaled.

The air outside was damp but fresh.

This was weird.

She straightened up and swiveled back toward the room.

Where could the smell be—

Wait.

Was that *smoke* coiling out of the electrical socket at the end of the counter?

Heart stuttering, she dashed across the room and got up close and personal with the plate over the outlet.

The thin, vaporous wisps sinuously twisting from the prong slots were, indeed, smoke.

Which meant there was a fire inside the wall—or at the very least, smoldering wires or insulation that could soon morph into a fire unless she acted fast.

Bren grabbed her phone off the charger on the counter and tapped in 911.

After a crisp greeting, the efficient dispatcher elicited all the pertinent details and moved on to instructions. "Your fire department has been alerted. You should vacate the house and take shelter from the storm someplace safe until the crew arrives."

Bren glanced out the window toward the driveway, where rain continued to pummel her older-model Kia as dawn gave way to day. "I could wait in my car."

"A structure would be preferable. Is there a neighbor who could provide shelter?"

The older couple in the next house down the road would take

her in if she showed up on their doorstep, but they never got up until after eight. Why ruin their morning too?

"No."

"In that case, go ahead and move to your vehicle. I'll stay on the line until you're secure."

"Thanks."

Bren slid her phone into her purse, unlocked her car with the remote, pulled on the bright yellow slicker that always hung by the back door, and scurried through the rain.

Once she was behind the wheel, she put the phone back to her ear. "I'm in the car."

"Stay there until the fire crew arrives."

"Got it."

As the dispatcher severed the connection, Bren checked the time. Six twelve.

No way was she going to make it to work in eighteen minutes. She'd be lucky to get to The Perfect Blend when the shop opened at seven, let alone early enough to help with prep and setup. Who knew how long it would take for Hope Harbor's volunteer fire department to arrive?

Dang.

From the day Zach Garrett had given her one of the two barista jobs in his new coffee shop three years ago, she'd never once missed a shift or shown up late. Reliability, punctuality, and diligence had been hallmarks of her employment.

Two of those were about to take a hit.

Sighing, she put in a call to Zach and peered at her tiny rental house through the rivulets of water sluicing down her windshield.

As milestone birthdays went, this one wasn't off to an auspicious start.

Hopefully it wasn't a preview of the year to come.

"Morning, Bren. What's up?"

At Zach's chipper greeting, Bren massaged her temple and gave him the bad news. "But I'll get there as fast as I can."

"Hey, no worries. I'll manage." His tone transitioned from upbeat to concerned. "Is there anything I can do to help?"

Her throat pinched.

Zach might be her boss, but he was also her friend. As were so many of the people in her adopted town, all of whom were more like family than the blood relations she'd left behind in Kentucky long ago.

"Thank you for asking, but at this point it's all in the hands of the fire department. I'm hoping the damage is minor and a quick fix will take care of it."

"Keep me in the loop."

"Will do. I'll get there as fast as I can."

"Like I said, I've got it covered. Nobody will get too bent out of shape if they have to wait an extra minute or two for their drink."

That was true—and another reason she'd fallen in love with this town.

"Thanks again, Zach."

"No thanks necessary. I'll see you when I see you."

Bren ended the call, set the cell on the seat beside her, and tapped a finger on the steering wheel as she waited for help to arrive, keeping an eye on her watch.

Five minutes later, a fire engine appeared down the road, the siren increasing in volume until the truck stopped in front of the house.

Not bad for a volunteer operation.

Flipping up the hood on her slicker, she opened her door and prepared to brief whoever was in charge.

The man who approached as she alighted got straight to business. After peppering her with clipped questions, he trotted off to confer with the members of the crew, who descended on her house with various pieces of equipment.

Including an ax.

Her stomach kinked as she slid back behind the wheel.

That wasn't promising.

Nor was the muffled pounding that seeped through the frame walls minutes later, audible from inside her car.

When the man in charge reappeared and strode toward her, the grim set of his mouth telegraphed imminent bad news.

Bracing, Bren exited the car again, sans hood. At least the driving rain had stopped and the storm seemed to be dissipating. "What's the verdict?"

"You have an electrical fire inside the walls. Good thing you have a sensitive nose. Most people don't detect those until there's significant damage."

"Are you saying the problem is minor?" *Please let that be the case!*

"There's no visible damage, but it's hard to say what's on the other side of the drywall. It could take us a while to verify the fire hasn't spread. The wiring in the house should have been replaced years ago."

At the hint of censure in his inflection, she straightened her shoulders. "For the record, I'm a tenant, not the owner. I don't know anything about the mechanics of the house." Except that lights did tend to flicker randomly, and several of the outlets were finicky. But every house had its quirks, right?

"Understood." His manner softened. "If you'll give me the owner's contact information, I'll apprise them of the situation. At minimum, drywall repair and wiring updates will be needed."

In other words, she'd be living in a construction zone for the foreseeable future.

Oh, joy.

She passed on her landlord's phone number and surveyed the house. "Do you want me to hang around? I'm already late for work."

"No. We could be here another hour or two."

"Then I'll head out. If you'd lock the door from the inside and pull it shut as you leave, I'd appreciate it."

"No problem."

While he got back to business, Bren started the car, pointed it toward The Perfect Blend . . . and tried to look on the bright side.

It wasn't as if the house had actually caught fire. All of her personal possessions were safe. And if she had to live with drywall dust for a while, that was manageable. The house would still be a big step up from most of the places she'd called home over the past twelve years.

Eight minutes later, she hustled through the door of The Perfect Blend to find a long line stretching from the counter.

Zach's expression shifted from surprise to relief the instant he spotted her. "I didn't expect to see you this fast."

"There was nothing for me to do at the house." She stashed her shoulder bag under the counter and put on her apron as she gave him a quick briefing.

"What a mess—and on your birthday, no less." He grimaced as he wiped the nozzle on the espresso machine.

"I've had worse birthdays."

"Yeah?" He eyed her as he plated a piece of cranberry nut cake for the espresso customer.

Whoops.

Only Bev at the bookstore knew any details about her younger years. And Charley Lopez, the town sage and taco-making artist who always had uncanny insights, had discerned a number of facts. Other than that, she'd zipped it. Why dwell on a past she'd left behind, or let it pollute the fresh start she'd made here three years ago?

Bren pushed up the corners of her mouth. "Ancient history. On the plus side, I caught the fire early." She turned toward the next customer in line, ending the exchange with her boss. "Morning, Fred. The usual?"

"Not today." A fan of lines appeared at the corners of Fred Ward's eyes as he winked at her and tucked the latest edition of the *Hope Harbor Herald* under his arm. "Charley finally convinced me to try the Mexican coffee he's always raving about.

I decided to broaden my horizons. Don't want to get stuck in a rut, you know."

"I hear you. One café de olla coming up."

The silver-haired man cocked his head. "What's this about a fire at your place? Couldn't help overhearing while I waited in line."

No point in being reticent about the incident. Few happenings of note slid under the radar in this tiny community, and a fire—or almost-fire—would be big news. Everyone would hear about it within hours.

"I'm hoping I caught it before too much damage was done." She gave him an abbreviated recap of her morning as she prepared his drink, popped in a cinnamon stick, and snapped on the lid. "Here you go. Enjoy."

"I expect I will. Charley's never steered me wrong."

He wandered over to one of the tables clustered around the freestanding fireplace in the center of the shop and settled in for his every-other-Wednesday perusal of the *Herald*—an activity he'd indulged in like clockwork since the opening week of the shop, often with his wife by his side . . . until she'd died last year.

Pressure built in Bren's throat as Fred took a tentative sip of his brew.

No surprise he'd become a regular fixture here several days a week now that Helen was gone. The Perfect Blend was a haven of warmth and welcome for all who ventured inside, staff and customers alike.

For the next hour, she was too busy filling orders to worry about what was happening at the house. But when her cell began to vibrate with a call from her landlord as the morning rush subsided, her pulse picked up.

Angling toward Zach, she lifted her phone. "I need to take this."

"Go ahead. I'll handle the counter." He shifted his attention to the customer who'd pushed through the front door.

Moving off to the side, she greeted her landlord, who gave her the bad news fast.

"I'm at the house, Bren. The fire department is finishing up. I'm sorry, but I don't think the place will be habitable for at least the next month. I'm going to have to tear out all the wiring, so the electricity will be shut off. There are also sizable holes in the walls that will have to be repaired. There could be other damage too."

Dang again.

It appeared this birthday was going to be a total bust.

But bemoaning her misfortune wasn't going to solve her housing dilemma. She'd just have to book a room at the Gull Motel until she came up with a plan.

"Okay. I'll find somewhere else to stay for the duration. Can I get inside later today to pack up my clothes and personal items?"

"Yes. I cleared that with the fire crew. I'll keep you apprised of the progress on the repairs and get you back in as soon as it's practical and safe."

"Thanks. Do they have any idea how the fire started?"

"Their theory is that energy from a lightning strike nearby entered the house through wires or pipes that extend outside the structure. Or it could have come in through the meter and moved to the electrical panel. They said a whole-house surge protection device would have prevented that, but storms like the one we had today are rare. I never thought it was necessary to install one." He expelled a breath. "This wasn't my lucky day, I guess."

Hers, either.

But she left that unsaid.

As they ended the call, Zach finished with his customer and joined her. "That didn't sound reassuring."

"It wasn't." She filled him in. Swiped a cloth over a coffee stain on the counter. "I never expected to end up homeless on my birthday."

Although it wouldn't be the first time.

Another piece of information she didn't intend to share with anyone—her boss included.

"What a bummer. Maybe you could—"

"Excuse me. May I interrupt?"

She swiveled toward Fred, who stood on the other side of the counter, his folded newspaper under his arm.

"I wasn't eavesdropping, but I picked up the gist of your plight. If you need a temporary place to stay, you're welcome to use my guest cottage."

She arched her eyebrows. "I thought you rented that out to vacationers."

"Used to. Haven't had much interest in doing that without Helen. She was always the more sociable half of our partnership. She could chat up guests like nobody's business." His smile held a hint of melancholy. "Anyway, the cottage is sitting there empty. I expect it's dusty, but the plumbing and electricity are in tip-top shape."

Bren wiped her palms down her apron, vision misting at the man's kindness.

Nice as his offer was, though, she couldn't afford the rates tourists paid for private cottages in this picturesque town during high season. The Gull Motel would have to do until she lined up a place in the same price range as her present lodging.

"I appreciate that, Fred, but my budget won't accommodate an extended stay at the kind of prices your usual guests paid."

"You're not a usual guest. You're a Hope Harbor resident. That makes you a neighbor. Since the place isn't generating income anymore, you're welcome to use it free of charge."

She did a double take.

Seriously? He was willing to let her stay in his cottage gratis? Amazing.

Yet tempted as she was to accept his generous offer, she shook her head. "I couldn't do that. It wouldn't be fair."

Fred studied her. Pursed his lips. "Do you mind telling me your current rent?"

"No." She gave him the monthly amount.

"For how many rooms?"

"Four."

"The cottage only has two. A living room/kitchen combo and a bedroom. You can pay me half what you're paying your current landlord. We can break it down into weekly payments to give you flexibility on the length of your stay."

Her jaw dropped.

Was this for real?

"Take the deal, Bren." Zach grinned and gave her a shoulder bump before he moved away to assist another customer. "Never look a gift horse in the mouth."

Bren bit her lip.

Taking handouts didn't sit well. And this was a handout, no question about it. When Fred rented the cottage to tourists, he no doubt charged the monthly amount he'd quoted her for a mere handful of nights.

"Don't overthink it, my dear." Fred's mouth bowed. "Helen would be happy to see the cottage occupied again, and she was all about extending a helping hand to those in need. Let me do this for you in her memory."

Smart strategy to position it as a favor to *him*.

And since he'd put it that way, maybe she should think of his out-of-the-blue offer as a birthday gift on this day that had otherwise been totally unbirthdaylike.

"If you're certain, then I accept."

"Wonderful. Come by whenever you like later today, and I'll give you the key." With a courtly dip of his head, he strolled across the shop and exited.

As the door closed behind him, Bren went back to work, heart lighter, spirits buoyed.

See? Even on an otherwise bad day, there was goodness to be found.

And there was yet more goodness after the shop closed at one o'clock and a dozen of her friends from Hope Harbor spilled out of the back room bearing brownies from Sweet Dreams Bakery and tacos from Charley's stand to help her celebrate her milestone birthday.

Warmth bubbled up inside her as they all indulged in a hug fest.

This was why she'd settled here. Put down roots.

Maybe she didn't earn a lot of money working as a barista. Maybe she didn't live in a plush house like the one of her youth. Maybe a carefully vetted special someone to share her life with wasn't in the cards for her.

But look at her friend at Bev's Book Nook. The bookshop owner lived a simple life too—on her own terms, with no apparent regret about the lack of romance in her life. She was a role model, for sure.

And as Bren gathered up her things, thanked everyone for coming to her surprise party, and set off for her house to pack up the items she'd need for the next few weeks, she made a resolution.

In this new decade of her life, she was going to embrace her solo life and put to rest the insidious, romantic daydreams that crept up on occasion. Banish once and for all any illusions about happily ever after.

Because as she knew firsthand, illusions could lead to nightmares.

2

What a disaster this day had been.

Heaving a sigh, Noah Ward parked his rental car, cut his lights, and surveyed the dark windows of his parents' Hope Harbor retirement home.

Arriving on the cusp of midnight hadn't been in his plans. Nor had multiple flight delays or leaving the car charger for his phone back in St. Louis.

And at this hour of the night, it was too late to rouse his father with a knock on the front door.

Too bad his cell had died hours ago. Otherwise, he could have called ahead and avoided this predicament. But he could rack out in the empty cottage behind the house, get a decent night's sleep, then alert Dad to his presence in the morning. An unfamiliar car parked a house away shouldn't raise any concerns if his father rose early and glanced out the front window.

Noah slid from behind the wheel, stretched, and retrieved his overnight bag from the back seat. His larger suitcase could stay in the trunk until morning.

After locking the car, he fished around in his pocket and pulled out the keys his father had given him when he and Mom bought this place a decade ago. It was a shame the demands of his CPA job had kept him too busy to pay more than an occasional fast visit here. The little seaside town was appealing, and it was easy to understand why his parents had been charmed by it on the vacations they'd taken here prior to making a permanent move from the Midwest.

But it was far less hassle to send them tickets to St. Louis a couple of times a year. That way, he could work during the day while they visited with longtime friends, then spend the evenings with them. It had been a fine arrangement.

Until Mom died, and Dad decided he was done traveling.

Noah maneuvered around the corner of the house in the dark, trying not to trip on the stepping stones. He didn't need a face-plant to cap off his journey, even if that would be a fitting end to this miserable day.

Nor had he needed this trip, just as the second quarter financial reporting was ramping up.

But how else was he supposed to get a read on a father who wasn't a texter, caller, or emailer, like Mom had been? Dad's heart scare a couple of months ago may not have caused any serious long-term damage, but it had been a wake-up call. What if a major health issue *did* arise? Who would Dad be able to call on for help out here?

Brow crimped, Noah pushed through the gate under the arbor that led to the backyard.

It was far more sensible for his father to move back to St. Louis, where he had friends and a son who could lend a hand if necessary.

Convincing Dad of that would be a challenge, however. One best tackled in person, without forewarning. If he'd called and been up-front about the reason for this trip, his father would have insisted that he was staying put—as he'd done whenever the subject came up—and discouraged a visit. And an out-of-pattern random trip would have made Dad suspicious.

A surprise appearance had definitely been the prudent choice.

But not a surprise appearance in the middle of the night.

Noah squinted across the backyard to the cottage tucked in the corner. It was unfortunate Dad had decided to stop renting it. Talking with guests would have kept him connected to people. Without Mom to plan their social calendar and push her more introverted husband to mix and mingle, it was very possible he'd become a hermit.

On the flip side, though, a lack of reservations for the cottage could be a plus. If the place had been booked for the whole tourist season, his father would have had an excuse to put off a discussion about moving.

At the door to the cottage, Noah bent down, felt around for the lock in the darkness, and poked the key at it. Three tries later, it slid inside.

Yawning, he fumbled for the knob and pushed the door open.

It took him a few seconds to find the light switch on the wall, but once he flipped it, soft illumination flooded the room from a lamp beside the couch.

Easy to see why the compact cottage had always been in demand. Mom had had a knack for décor, and the neutral palette enlivened by splashes of accent colors created an upscale, relaxing vibe.

But he could give the place a closer scrutiny in the morning. After his marathon, problem-plagued travel day, all he wanted to do was sleep.

Bag in hand, he strode over to the bedroom door. Twisted the knob. Pushed through.

In five minutes flat, he ought to be able to—

A beam of a bright light pierced his eyes, blinding him, and he jerked to a stop. Stumbled back.

What the . . .

Before he could finish that thought, something wet hit him in the face.

In the next instant, the fires of hell rained down on him, burning his eyes, nose, mouth, and throat.

He dropped his overnight bag as his eyes slammed shut. His seared lungs balked, and he started to hack. Hard. Snot dripped from his nose.

Chest heaving, he fell to his knees as waves of pain crashed over him.

If someone was trying to kill him, they were doing a first-rate job of it.

Splaying the fingers of one hand on the floor, he groped in his pocket for his handkerchief. He had to wipe away whatever was singeing his eyeballs. ASAP.

The instant his fumbling fingers closed over the square of cloth, he yanked it out and tried to swab off whatever toxic substance was wreaking havoc.

Didn't work.

In fact, his eyes might hurt worse—if that was even possible.

"Help . . . me." The hoarse, croaked plea came out in a voice that didn't sound anywhere close to his usual baritone.

No response.

Whoever had done this to him must have a heart of stone.

Or else they'd hightailed it out of here after rendering him defenseless.

What kind of scumbag would attack an innocent man and—

Wait.

Was it possible Dad had started renting the cottage again and hadn't told him? Had he walked in on paying guests who'd assumed he was an intruder and doused him with pepper spray?

Oh, geez.

This day was going from bad to worse.

As the burning pain continued to scald his eyeballs . . . throat . . . tongue . . . skin . . . he dropped forward onto his hands and began crawling.

If whoever had sprayed him was gone, he was on his own to

find the bathroom and try to wash the noxious residue out of his eyes and off his face before this debilitating agony drove him stark raving mad.

Oh no!

After glancing at the man who was blindly scrabbling across the floor on all fours, Bren shifted her attention back to the luggage tag on the overnight bag he'd dropped after she'd greeted him with a faceful of pepper gel.

Noah Ward.

Fred's son.

A respectable CPA from St. Louis, not the intruder she'd assumed he was.

Her stomach twisted into a knot.

She'd attacked the offspring of the man who'd come to her rescue this morning.

Well, crud.

What a way to thank her benefactor.

But this wasn't her fault. Truly, it wasn't. Fred hadn't said a thing about his son coming when he'd handed her the key. And who else but an intruder would come creeping around in the middle of the night? Any reasonable person would have . . .

Noah ran into a wall. Moaned.

Oh, mercy.

The man was in severe distress.

Tempted as she was to slink away in abject mortification, she had to help him. No one with an ounce of empathy could desert someone who was in such pain. She'd have to deal later with the consequences of what she'd done.

"Um . . ." She crossed to him. "I'm sorry about this. I thought you were an intruder."

He groaned again, his breathing ragged.

A wave of panic washed over her.

Pepper gel wasn't supposed to be dangerous for most people, only big-time uncomfortable—unless you happened to have asthma.

Did Fred's son have that ailment?

"I'm so sorry. How can I help you?" She leaned down and touched his shoulder.

"Bathroom." The word was garbled but decipherable. "Water."

"Can you stand up?"

He shook his head.

"Okay. I'll guide you." She wrapped her fingers around the impressive bicep beneath his long-sleeved dress shirt and tugged him the right direction. At the doorway, she paused. "You're on the threshold."

Feeling his way forward, he entered and slowly pulled himself up in front of the sink, a maneuver that appeared to require almost superhuman effort.

No wonder cops used pepper spray as a last resort, if it could bring even this strapping, toned guy to his knees.

Bren reached past him and twisted on the tap.

After cupping his hands beneath the stream, he bent down and began throwing cold water at his face.

But was that the most effective way to mitigate the aftereffects of pepper gel?

Leaving him to his task, she went in search of her phone and googled the remedies. After skimming the instructions, she zipped to the kitchen, yanked a large pitcher from the cabinet, filled it with water, and returned to the bathroom.

Noah was still splashing water on his face.

"I'm back." She squeezed past him into the small space. "What you're doing isn't going to help much. We should irrigate your eyes. I have a pitcher of water. If you'll lean over and turn your head sideways over the sink, I'll pour the water into them."

Without a word, he followed her instructions.

Bren aimed the spout of the pitcher at the corner of one puckered eye and directed a gentle but steady stream there. "It would help if you'd open it as much as possible."

In response, he lifted a hand and pulled the lower lid down.

When the pitcher was empty, she backed off. "I'm going to get a refill for the other eye."

Without waiting for a reply, she dashed back to the kitchen and topped off the pitcher again. Followed the same procedure with his other eye.

At least he'd stopped moaning.

She repeated the drill half a dozen times in each eye until he could open them both to slits, then brought him a cup of cold water and a mug of ice chips. "If you drink the water and suck on the ice, it's supposed to reduce any burning in your mouth."

In silence, he moved to the toilet, sat on the lid, and gulped the water. Then he began sucking on the chips.

Bren tried not to gape—but man, he was a mess. His eyes were still half swollen shut and watering profusely, his face was splotchy red, and his nose was running like a faucet.

"Light's too bright." He shaded his eyes.

Right. She'd also read that pepper gel could cause light sensitivity.

After flicking off the overhead fixture, she wiped her palms down her sleep shirt. "You're supposed to get rid of your clothes and take a shower."

Continuing to suck on ice, he stripped off his dress shirt and wadded it into a ball.

The T-shirt underneath hugged a broad, muscular chest.

Bren cleared her throat and eased back as much as the confined space allowed. Unappealing as the guy was in his present condition, it was hard to ignore the well-developed pecs and abs outlined by the snug tee.

"Who are you?" He pulled off a length of toilet paper and tried to staunch the flow of mucus from his nose.

She forced herself to shift her attention from his chest to his face.

He still sounded gravelly, but thankfully his respiration had evened out. Beginning her birthday with a 911 call had been bad enough. Ending it with one would have been beyond surreal.

"Brenna Ryan—but I go by Bren. I live in Hope Harbor. There was a fire at my place this morning, so your dad offered to let me use his cottage until I can move back."

All she got in reply was a grunt.

After slurping up more ice, he stood and lurched toward the door.

She backed out of the cramped space to allow him to exit. "Listen, I'm really sorry about this."

No response as he tucked his rolled-up shirt under his arm, brushed past her, and picked up the overnight bag he'd dropped.

Halfway across the combination living, dining, and kitchen space, he hesitated. Turned. "Can I borrow your cellphone?"

"Uh . . . sure." She detoured to the kitchen, plucked her phone off the counter, and held it out to him as she veered back in his direction.

He took it, angled sideways, and tapped in a number.

Silence.

Whoever he was calling must be in bed at this late hour. Like any normal person would be.

"Dad, it's me . . . Yeah . . . Long story. I borrowed her phone." Noah tipped his head and swiped the sleeve of his T-shirt across his leaking eyes. "I'll explain later, okay? I didn't want to come into the house without alerting you to my presence . . . Yes. I'll see you in a couple of minutes."

After ending the call, Noah held out the phone, his gaze flicking to the abbreviated hem of her hot-pink sleep shirt before zipping back up. "Thanks."

"No problem." She tugged on the bottom of the silky fabric and waved a hand toward his face as she took the phone. "If I could undo the damage, I would."

"I'll survive."

True. But based on her Google search, it would take an hour or two for the effects to wear off.

"You, uh, may want to take that shower ASAP. That's what the internet says."

"Top of my list. Good night." He pivoted, strode toward the door, and pulled it shut behind him with a decisive click. As if he couldn't get away from the scene of the crime fast enough.

Who could blame him?

As quiet once more descended on the cottage, Bren drew a long, slow breath and scanned her watch.

Eleven fifty-nine.

Her birthday was almost over—and what a birthday it had been. Good stuff in the middle, for sure, but bookended by disasters.

Shoulders slumping, she flipped off the light and trudged back toward the bedroom.

If she was lucky, Fred's son would have a better perspective on the midnight attack by tomorrow morning and be content to stay in his father's house during his visit.

If she wasn't?

The younger Ward would convince Fred to let him use the cottage, and she'd be out on the street.

Wouldn't be the first time that had happened, but she'd thought those days were over.

Just went to show how foolish it was to take the status quo for granted.

She slid back beneath the covers of the bed and pulled them up to her chin. With the busy day she had planned for tomorrow—or rather, today—she needed to get a decent night's sleep.

But as she stared at the dark ceiling while the minutes ticked by and the night wore on, she faced the truth.

She wasn't going to wake up rested and refreshed and brimming with energy on the first full day of her thirtieth year.

In fact, if her run of bad luck continued, she'd end up spending it looking for another place to stay instead of ticking off items on her birthday resolution to-do list.

3

Slowly . . . cautiously . . . Noah opened one eye, then the other, as the smell of bacon teased him awake.

Everything in his parents' neat-as-a-pin guest room came into clear focus, and the intense burning that had scorched his eyes, mouth, throat, and skin last night was gone.

Thank you, God!

The long shower he'd taken after giving Dad a quick recap of his traumatic arrival had alleviated much of his distress, but given the extent of his discomfort, it wouldn't have been at all surprising if there'd been lingering effects after he woke from the exhausted slumber he'd fallen into the second his head hit the pillow.

What a relief to know his agony was nothing more than a bad memory.

Swinging his legs to the floor, he inhaled the delicious aroma wafting into the room. Mom had always been the cook in the family, but it seemed Dad had upped his game since she'd passed away.

Excellent.

Maybe he didn't have to worry as much about whether his father was eating decent meals . . . although bacon wasn't the healthiest menu choice for a man who'd had enough blockage in his LAD artery to require a stent.

Another topic for discussion during his visit—post breakfast. The loud rumble from his stomach put food at the top of his priority list.

After throwing on his clothes and giving his bristly jaw and cheeks a fast shave, he made a beeline for the kitchen.

Dad turned from the stove when he appeared, lips bowing as he gave him a once-over. "Morning. You don't look any the worse for wear. How are you feeling?"

"Back to normal, thank goodness."

"Glad to hear it. You were a mess last night."

"Thanks for the ego boost."

"Just being honest. I didn't hear any noise in your room as I passed, but I figured the smell of bacon would rouse you. You were always partial to it. Help yourself to a mug of java while I dish up the food." He motioned toward a coffee maker on the counter. "Unless you've given up caffeine."

"Never." Noah ambled over to the pot. "With the long days I put in at work, it's a vital tool of the trade."

"Still clocking those twelve-hour shifts?"

"Not always, but often."

His father shook his head while he divvied up the scrambled eggs. "Those kinds of hours would have driven me crazy. I may not have pulled in the big bucks you earn, but I was happy with a smaller paycheck, a nine-to-five job, and more time with the people I loved." He added bacon to the plates, hefting the one with the lion's share of the high-fat treat before setting it on the table. "This is yours. And speaking of people to love . . . anything new on that horizon in your world?"

An image of Candace appeared in his mind, but he expunged it at once. That memory was almost as bad as the one from last night.

"Nothing to report." He sat at the table.

"You ever going to get around to finding yourself a wife?"

Noah curbed an eye roll. Mom had been on his case about his single status since the day he turned thirty, and it appeared Dad had picked up the baton in her absence.

"I'll think about it someday." Maybe. After the memory of Candace faded. "This looks delicious."

His father took the hint and dropped the subject. "Not as delicious as your mom used to make. She could work magic with herbs and spices and eggs. But this is a big step up from my usual breakfast of oatmeal and fruit."

So Dad launched most days with a healthy meal.

Also excellent.

"It's a step up from my typical breakfast too." The energy bar or bagel he tended to gulp down in the morning filled the empty place in his stomach, if not at his table.

Noah frowned.

Where on earth had *that* errant thought come from? His single life suited him fine, thank you very much. Relationships came with too many complications. Too many expectations. Too many risks. As his experience with Candace last winter had proven.

He suppressed a shudder as his father picked up the conversation. "Remember the days we'd come home from church on Sunday and your mom would whip up a batch of those Belgian waffles you and I loved? Not to mention the special breakfasts she always made on holidays." His lips curved up. "I can still taste her poppy seed bread. You ever have any sweet treat that came close to that?"

"No. Never."

"I sure do miss that. And her."

At the sudden hint of melancholy in his father's voice, Noah reached over and touched his arm. "I do too, Dad." But not with the acute sense of loss someone would feel who'd lived with a spouse day in and day out for decades and whose world revolved around that person.

Another downside of getting involved with someone. Life

34

had enough disappointments without setting yourself up for the shattering grief his dad had to be experiencing. Losing a mom was gut-wrenching, but losing a wife you loved had to be devastating.

"I know. She was a special woman." His dad patted his hand and went back to eating. "Speaking of women, I imagine you gave Bren quite a scare last night."

"In light of her response to my appearance, I think that's a safe conclusion." He took a sip of coffee. "What's her story, anyway? She mentioned a fire at her place, but my brain was too mucked up to process much beyond that."

He continued to eat while his dad filled him in.

"So I told her she could stay until the house she rents is repaired and she's able to move back in." His father finished off his eggs as he ended his story.

"Is she paying you?"

"A modest amount."

"What's modest?" At the sum his father quoted for the monthly rate, Noah arched his eyebrows. "The income from the cottage was higher than that for less than a week when you were renting it to tourists."

"True. But I wouldn't be making anything on it at all if I hadn't offered it to Bren."

Hard to argue with that.

"Are you certain her situation is legit?"

His father's forehead puckered. "What do you mean?"

Noah broke his last piece of bacon in half as a vision of short, spiky, rainbow-hued hair materialized in his mind—one of only two details that had registered about the woman's appearance through his impaired vision.

He quashed the other image, of legs that went on forever beneath a short, silky, very bright sleep shirt, focusing instead on her psychedelic hair as he popped a piece of the bacon into his mouth.

"I mean, did you verify her story?" What if she was on the hunt for a sweet deal on housing, taking advantage of a man who'd always been a soft touch for people facing setbacks or difficulties?

"Didn't have to." Dad kept eating.

Noah set his fork down. "It wouldn't have hurt to do some due diligence. Check to make sure there really was a fire. And what do you know about her? Does she have a job? Did you ask for references? Did you run her credit?"

His father stared at him. "Good grief, Noah. This is Hope Harbor, not some big-city-crime hot spot."

"Exploitation can happen anywhere. As a number of my charitable-minded clients back home could attest, for every legitimate need there are a dozen people willing to fabricate a hard-luck tale if they can wrangle a payoff from it. There are bad apples everywhere."

"Not in Hope Harbor."

He let that pass. If his father wanted to view the world through rose-colored glasses, that was his prerogative—as long as he wasn't being bilked.

"So are you saying you don't know the answers to my questions?"

His father pushed his empty plate aside and folded his hands on the table, his expression placating. "The fire happened. Everyone in town was talking about it yesterday. Bren has been a part-time barista at The Perfect Blend for several years and is well-liked. I've known her since her first day on the job. And I didn't do a credit check because when I offered to let her use the cottage for free, she insisted on paying. We compromised on the figure I gave you. Satisfied?"

Noah chomped into the other half piece of bacon, buying himself a moment to craft a diplomatic response. "It never hurts to be careful. Besides, she looks kind of . . . different, from what I could tell with my compromised vision."

"You must mean her hair." Grinning, his father wrapped his fingers around his mug. "I have to admit that was a mite off-putting initially, but it grew on me. It's bright and cheerful and goes with her personality."

"I'll concede it's colorful, but if she had an interest in a white-collar career she'd have a struggle surviving in corporate America with that look." Especially in a traditional firm like his, where business casual meant open-necked Oxford shirts and creased trousers, and facial hair was discouraged.

"More's the pity. Fewer rules and a little less conformity in the world wouldn't be a bad thing."

Noah hiked up an eyebrow. "This from the man who always said rules were invented for a reason?"

His dad shrugged. "I still believe that, but I guess I'm more tolerant than I used to be toward people who march to the beat of a different drummer. So . . ." He leaned back. "To what do I owe this unexpected and unannounced visit?"

The same question he'd asked last night.

Noah took a sip of his coffee.

In light of his physical distress, Dad had let him dodge the query in the wee hours. But it wasn't going to be easy to put him off for long, even if tackling hard subjects on the heels of last night's trauma had about as much appeal as rainbow-hued hair.

"I was overdue for R&R, and I wanted to see you for myself after the heart incident." Perhaps a deflection tactic would redirect the conversation away from the motive for his trip. "I can't believe you didn't tell me about it until it was over."

His father waved that aside. "It was a simple problem to fix, and a simple procedure took care of it. Why would I worry you over that?"

"Because I'm your son?"

"You have too much on your plate already."

"I always have time for you, Dad."

"Nice to know. And your presence here proves that. Why didn't you tell me you were coming, though? You could have saved Bren a fright and yourself a lot of agony."

Evidently his father wasn't going to be sidetracked.

After taking a fortifying gulp of coffee, he plunged in. "I have some concerns."

"About me?"

"Yes. Hope Harbor is a long way from St. Louis—and from me and all of your friends there if you ever need any help."

"This is my home now, Son, and I have wonderful friends here, both in town and at church. They'd be a strong support system, if I ever needed it."

"It's not like having family close by, though. Or old friends."

"No. To get that, I'd have to go back to St. Louis. Is that what you're hoping to convince me to do?"

"I thought it was worth discussing."

"Nope. I don't plan to leave Hope Harbor until the good Lord calls me to my eternal home. That'll be my next move. But if you want to keep an eye on me, why don't you move here?"

Noah studied him.

While his father's manner was conversational, was there a touch of seriousness in that absurd suggestion?

"I'm assuming that's a rhetorical question."

The corners of his father's mouth tipped up. "More like wishful thinking, I suppose—but who knows? During your stay you might discover a reason to consider the idea. You couldn't find a more welcoming and agreeable place to live."

"My life and career are back in St. Louis."

"So were mine."

"You retired here. That's different."

"You want the truth? In hindsight, I wish I'd moved sooner. Why wait until you're in the homestretch of your life to live the dream?" His father stood and began clearing the table. "How long can you stay?"

Apparently the relocation discussion was over. For today, at least.

And how had his dad managed to flip the conversation on its

ear? This trip was supposed to be about a son convincing a father to move, not vice versa.

Noah drained his mug and rose too.

Despite the curve Dad had thrown him, he'd get the discussion back on track next go-round. Make it clear that moving wasn't an option for a CPA who was in line for a partnership in the not-too-distant future.

"I took two weeks off." Though if he accomplished his goal sooner, he'd cut that short. While clocking in from here every day would help him keep his finger on the pulse at the office, face time counted in his firm.

"Wonderful." His dad clapped him on the back, face alight. "I can't remember the last time I had you under my roof for such a long stretch."

Noah's conscience prickled as he carried his plate and cutlery to the sink. "My job keeps me busy."

"Understood. I'm not trying to lay a guilt trip on you. I'm just glad you're here." His father joined him at the counter. "We'll do some sightseeing together during your visit, but you should also chill on your own. You still run?"

"Yes." His daily run and weight-bench workout at home were sacrosanct. "It gives me the energy for long hours of number crunching."

"You should go for a run this morning, even if no number crunching is on your agenda. It would help clear any lingering pepper spray from your system, get you in a vacation mindset."

"That's not a bad idea—after I help you with the dishes."

"Not today." His father shooed him away. "I'll get these done in a jiffy. Then I have a board meeting to attend."

Board meeting?

That was news.

"With who?"

"Helping Hands. It's a volunteer organization that does what the name says—offers a helping hand to anyone in the community who has a need." His father squirted detergent into the sink. "It's a joint effort of the two churches in town. I thought I told you about my involvement a couple of years ago."

"It rings a vague bell." Sort of. Meaning the conversation must have taken place during the crazy busy tax season, when his mind was focused on his job to the exclusion of almost everything else.

"I'll tell you more about our work over lunch. Why don't we meet at Charley's, on the wharf, at noon? You do remember Charley's, right?"

"Of course. A man doesn't forget the best tacos he's ever eaten." In truth, they were one of his most vivid memories from his rare visits to town.

"Well said. I'll see you then."

Accepting the dismissal, Noah left his father to the dishes and retreated to the guest room to change into his running gear and contemplate his strategy going forward.

Since it was clear Dad not only loved living in Hope Harbor but was involved in local activities, the idea of him relocating could be an even harder sell than expected.

But if his father had the support system he claimed, perhaps there wasn't as much urgency to convince him to move closer. In fact, it was possible he'd be better off here.

Noah crossed to his suitcase and pulled out his running gear.

Best plan? Take a week to get the lay of the land. Then, if everything appeared to be copacetic, he might be able to return to his job faster than anticipated and leave his dad in the hands of the citizens of his adopted town.

In the meantime, he'd enjoy his stay in this seaside hamlet—and hope it held no more unpleasant surprises like the one that had greeted him minutes into his arrival last night.

4

She was going to die. Right here on the side of Pelican Point Road.

Pulse pounding, chest heaving, Bren staggered to a halt at the edge of the pavement. Leaned forward. Braced her hands on her thighs. Surveyed the intimidating incline ahead of her as she sucked in air.

Maybe she'd been a tad too ambitious on her first day of jogging. A short, flat route around town would have been far less taxing than this round-trip marathon to the lighthouse, a fair portion of which was uphill.

But good grief, she was on her feet at The Perfect Blend, moving constantly, three days a week. Shouldn't that have prepared her for a little jaunt to the headland in time to catch a view of Sunrise Reef shimmering in the early morning light?

Apparently not.

Instead, she was going to have to admit defeat and go back—walking, not running. And she'd have to rein in her ambitions. Build up to a run out to the headland and rely on her car for reef-watching excursions for the foreseeable future.

Still gasping, she straightened up and turned around . . . just as another runner rounded the bend in the road.

As she scrutinized the figure, her heart flip-flopped.

Well, crud.

Despite the sunglasses masking his features, there was no doubt about the man's identity.

It was Noah Ward, chin tipped down, pounding along the pavement with a practiced, strong stride, the bunching quadriceps in his thighs beneath his running shorts reinforcing her impression from last night of a toned, fit body.

Wiping her palms down her leggings, she gave the forested headland that was home to a number of secluded houses a desperate sweep.

Could she hide?

There. That Sitka spruce might provide coverage if she—

Noah looked up from the asphalt. Jolted to a stop. Gaped at her.

Dang.

So much for her plan to stop by Fred's house later today with a peace offering for the younger Ward from Sweet Dreams Bakery and another apology for last night's debacle. By then maybe he'd have been able to laugh off the mix-up.

Well, maybe not laugh it off, but at least recognize that her actions had been reasonable under the circumstances.

Shoving up the corners of her lips, Bren lifted a hand in greeting but stayed where she was. Her rubbery legs weren't stable enough yet for walking, and her lungs needed every second they could get to find their rhythm again.

After a few moments, Noah continued forward, his pace much slower than before. As if he too was dreading this encounter.

Bren managed to hang on to her smile as he drew close. "Good morning."

"Morning." He stopped beside her, not even breathing heavily after his uphill run. "You're Bren, right?"

"Yes."

He extended a hand. "Noah Ward. I know we've met, but last night doesn't qualify as a formal introduction."

His grip was firm as she returned his shake. "I assume your dad filled you in on my situation."

"Yes." He released her fingers.

"Listen, about the pepper gel. I'm sorry I—"

"Wait." He lifted a hand, palm forward. "I get where you were coming from. In your situation, I'd have done the same. I'm sorry I scared you."

Her tension ebbed.

His attitude was much more agreeable than she'd expected.

"I did think you were an intruder."

"Understandable. Although Dad tells me crime isn't a problem in Hope Harbor."

That was true.

But thanks to her history, even three years in this idyllic place hadn't quelled the niggling fear that the aura of goodness in Hope Harbor was nothing more than an illusion.

"It's not." She tried for a nonchalant tone. "I was a big-city girl once, though, and my self-preservation instincts are strong. How long are you staying in town?"

With his eyes hidden behind shades, it was impossible to get a visual read on his reaction to her abrupt change of subject.

"TBD." He tipped his head, brow creasing as he inspected her. "Are you okay? You seem a little flushed and winded."

She swiped off a bead of sweat inching down the side of her temple despite the cool midfifties temperature. "I'm fine."

That wasn't quite a lie. She *would* be fine as soon as her heart stopped galloping and she could breathe again.

His gaze dropped to her pristine running shoes, purchased last week to fulfill the "introduce regular exercise" resolution on her birthday list.

By contrast, his had clearly logged a ton of miles.

He folded his arms and looked past her, up the rising road. "If you're a new runner, this is an ambitious route."

No sense denying the obvious. Her clear physical distress

combined with her immaculate shoes were evidence of her novice status.

"I'm managing."

His phone pinged, and he pulled it out. Gave the screen a quick scan. "Are you on your way up or down?"

"Down." The formidable incline behind her was light-years beyond her ability at this stage. If she could get away with it, she'd return the pricey shoes and find a different physical activity to honor her birthday fitness promise to herself.

But since she was stuck with them, she'd persevere. On level ground, close to town, until she built up her stamina.

"I guess I'll see you around the house, then."

Her spirits perked up.

That sounded hopeful.

"Does that mean you're not going to want to use the cottage while you're here?"

"Not unless you're planning to leave."

"Only if I'm asked to."

"Not by me. I'm sorry about the fire at your place."

She shrugged. "A temporary setback. To be honest, the cottage is a step up from my house—and most of the places I've lived. It's no hardship to stay there."

Noah took off his sunglasses, revealing eyes the same vibrant hue as the sea off Hope Harbor on a sunny day. "Where else have you lived?"

It took several moments for his question to register as she surfaced from the intense blueness—only to get sidetracked by his unobstructed face.

Because minus the puckered eyes, red splotches, and runny nose, this guy was movie-star handsome.

As the silence lengthened, she yanked her gaze away from his, dipped her chin, and fiddled with the pull on the zipper of her windbreaker. "Quite a few places."

And that was all she intended to offer. There was no point in letting the past taint her new life in Hope Harbor. Yes, she'd let a comment slip yesterday with Zach, but that had been in the midst of a crisis situation. She had no such excuse today.

Except for cobalt eyes that had sent a tingle down her spine and temporarily short-circuited her brain.

"Well . . ." Noah lifted his phone. "I have a text to return. Don't let me hold you up."

Shoot.

He'd just derailed her plan to fiddle with her shoelaces until he disappeared from view.

She peeked toward the curve down the road that would hide her from his sight.

Would her shaky legs carry her that far without collapsing?

Unknown.

But what choice did she have?

Gritting her teeth, she lifted a hand in farewell and set off, concentrating on putting one foot in front of the other, one step at a time.

It was touch and go, but she made it.

Not until she was certain the coniferous trees would hide her from his view did she slow to a walk, her wobbly legs balking with every footfall.

It was going to be a long trek back to town.

But once she got there, she intended to take a hot bath, eat another one of the Sweet Dreams brownies the partiers at The Perfect Blend had sent home with her, then move on to the next item on her birthday resolution list.

And hope it was more successful than her first foray into running.

The view from the headland was as glorious as he remembered from his first trip to Hope Harbor almost a decade ago.

Noah slipped off his sunglasses, slid them into his pocket, and took in the scene.

The lighthouse was in far better condition than it had been on his previous visit, and a discreet, low-slung structure with vaulted windows that would frame the lighthouse from inside was tucked into the woods nearby. A special events facility, perhaps. That hadn't been here on his last trip.

But it was the vista from the headland out toward the Pacific that drew, and held, his attention.

Fists propped on hips, he surveyed the vast expanse of sea-stack-dotted water, the cerulean surface sparkling in the morning sun, ocean and sky melding at the horizon in the far distance. A pelican sailed past high overhead, its oversized orange beak vivid against the cloud-studded azure sky. Not far offshore, a sleek dolphin leapt out of the water in a graceful arc.

Noah drew in a long, slow breath.

St. Louis had its charms, but the relaxing vibe here was hard to beat.

It also made him disinclined to deal with the crisis that had dropped into his lap on the road up here.

And that was the danger of coming to a place like this. It could tempt a person to do what his dad had done and chuck the rat race. Climb off the corporate ladder and be content with a slower pace.

Which was fine if you were sixty-five.

It wasn't so fine if you were thirtysomething, with most of your working life ahead of you.

Unless you were a rainbow-haired barista who was content to make fancy drinks for a living.

But he had a different future in mind.

So while he'd chill as best he could during his stay in this idyllic spot, he wasn't going to let business slide. Meaning he should get back to town and hunker down with his laptop until he left to meet Dad at the taco stand for lunch.

After giving himself another thirty seconds to fill his lungs with the salty air and soak in the peaceful ambiance, he turned his back on the view.

Did a double take at the lean man ambling up the path toward him, his long gray ponytail topped with a Ducks baseball cap.

Wasn't that Charley Lopez? The taco-making artist?

Yeah, it was.

Strange how he'd just been thinking about Charley's tacos, only to have the man appear. At a remote lighthouse, of all places. What were the odds of that?

"Morning, Noah." Charley lifted a hand in greeting as he approached, a fan of fine lines radiating from the corners of his dark brown eyes. "Welcome back to Hope Harbor."

Noah stared at the renowned artist who moonlighted as a taco chef.

How had Charley recognized him? Other than the handful of words they'd exchanged at Mom's funeral last year, he hadn't chatted with the man at any length since his visit to the taco stand during a quick weekend trip out here for his mom's birthday four years ago.

"I can't believe you remember me."

"Some people are worth remembering. But I have to confess I ran into your father when I stopped at Sweet Dreams for a cinnamon roll this morning." Charley hefted a white bakery bag, sending a delicious aroma wafting through the air. "He mentioned you were in town. Said the two of you were coming by the stand today for lunch."

"That's the plan."

"I'll look forward to seeing you both." Charley motioned to a bench a short distance away that offered a panoramic vista of the sea. "If you'd like to linger, I'd be happy to share my cinnamon roll and the best seat in the house."

"Thanks, but I have to get back. A work issue came up that requires my attention."

"I seem to be striking out on all counts today. I offered the same deal to Bren when I saw her on the road, with the same result. I assume the two of you passed each other."

An image of the barista, with her triple-pierced ears, psychedelic-patterned leggings, and spiky hair that looked as if she'd stuck her finger in an electric socket strobed through his mind.

"Yes."

"Nice woman. It was thoughtful of your dad to give her a place to stay after the fire yesterday. A little kindness goes a long way toward smoothing rough paths and healing hearts."

Noah frowned.

Was Charley talking about the havoc the fire had caused in Bren's life—or something more?

Hard to tell from his neutral expression, although a subtle undercurrent in his inflection seemed to hint that his comment encompassed more than yesterday's incident.

But what did it matter? Bren's personal life wasn't his concern. He had plenty to deal with as it was with an aging father who lived too far away and the challenges of a demanding job.

"Dad's always been generous."

"A fine trait. And it's certainly on display with his volunteer efforts at Helping Hands. He's an outstanding board president, from what I gather."

Noah stared at the man across from him.

Dad wasn't a mere member of the board of the organization but the president?

What else didn't he know about his father's activities in Hope Harbor?

The two of them needed to have a long talk. Soon.

His phone pinged, and he pulled it out. Skimmed the text from a colleague. Stifled a sigh.

The situation at work was getting messier by the minute.

After thumbing in a fast reply, he returned the cell to his pocket. "Duty calls."

"If an urgent matter has come up, I could give you a lift

back." Charley motioned toward a parking lot at the end of the path that led to the lighthouse, where a 1957 silver Thunderbird with a white top was the sole occupant. "Bessie is at your beck and call."

The man named his car?

Noah's mouth twitched.

A little eccentric . . . but he *was* an artist.

"Thanks, but I don't want to skip my run. I'll just pick up my pace."

"In that case, you may pass Bren. She was walking kind of slow, like she was tuckered out. I offered her a lift back to town, but she said she was fine." Charley transferred his attention to two seagulls circling overhead. "Funny how often people say that when the opposite is true. Independence is an admirable trait, but it can get tangled up with pride and fear, can't it?"

Noah shifted his weight from one foot to the other.

Was that a rhetorical question, or was Charley angling for a philosophical exchange on this Thursday morning?

Fortunately, the other man motioned to the birds that had settled on the bench and changed the subject. "I don't see Floyd and Gladys up here too often."

He named birds too?

"Are you talking about the gulls?" Noah inspected the pair. The two were cuddled close together, watching the humans who shared the promontory with them.

"Yes. They're old friends."

O-kay. Definitely eccentric.

"Um . . . how do you tell them apart? They all look alike to me."

"No, they're quite distinctive if you pay attention. Like humans. Floyd, for example, has a black spot on top of his head and a nick on the right side of his beak. And he's never far from Gladys's side—especially since the webbing on her left foot was injured in the spring."

Noah peered at the birds, but if the features Charley had

mentioned were present, his eyes weren't up to the task of detecting them.

A leftover effect from the pepper gel, perhaps?

Didn't matter. Spotting seagull nuances was far less important than spotting irregularities on balance sheets—his priority for this morning.

"Well, enjoy the view." He swept a hand over the scene.

"Goes without saying." Charley focused on a spot offshore, to the right of the lighthouse. "It's a shame Bren missed Sunrise Reef this morning. It's more stunning than usual."

Noah glanced over his shoulder, toward the sea.

The sun had crested the hills to the east, gilding a string of rocky outcroppings that barely broke the surface of the cobalt expanse.

"Pretty."

"Very. It's too bad not many people notice it or bother to come up in the morning to see it at its most beautiful. I make the trip now and then. So does Bren."

Nice that the barista and Charley had time to indulge in sightseeing.

He gave his watch a discreet peek and edged toward the path. "I should get going. Sorry I can't stay to keep you company."

"No worries. Floyd and Gladys are fine companions." He adjusted his Ducks cap and continued to examine the golden rocks, his expression pensive. "Reefs are amazing, aren't they? You'd never know from looking at the surface what treasures are hidden below." After half a dozen beats, Charley turned back to him. Smiled. "See you at lunchtime."

As the man strolled toward the bench and the two seagulls hopped aside to accommodate him, Noah cocked his head.

Strange encounter. And somehow unnerving.

In fact, unnerving was an apt adjective for his first ten hours in Hope Harbor. A pepper gel attack, two encounters with a rainbow-haired woman, major opposition from his father to the idea of moving back to St. Louis, and a conversation with a philosophy-spouting taco maker who had seagulls for friends.

But once he returned to the world of numbers, he'd be back on familiar ground, where outcomes were predictable if you analyzed and crunched with precision.

Which he always did.

Noah pivoted and started back down the path, leaving the lighthouse and Charley behind as the lingering tendrils of fog evaporated in the morning sun.

It was harder to leave behind the man's comments, though. Especially the one about Bren appearing to be worn out when he'd come across her on the road.

Obviously the pepper-gel-toting barista had bitten off more than she could chew with her foray into running.

Nevertheless, she hadn't accepted a lift from Charley.

Had her pride been masquerading as independence, as the man had suggested? And what had he meant by that reference to fear?

Clamping his lips together, Noah picked up his pace.

Enough.

He was here to convince his father to move, unless he found compelling evidence of a strong support system and social network. Period. Whatever problems his dad's short-term tenant had weren't his concern.

Yet hard as he tried, the image of large, guarded hazel eyes with a distant echo of hurt in their depths refused to be erased.

5

. . . .

Bren pushed through the door of Bev's Book Nook to the tinkle of wind chimes, pausing on the threshold to give the eclectic interior a quick scan.

The two cushioned rattan wicker swivel chairs beside the flat-topped, Moroccan-motif trunk were empty, and no one was hovering in front of the popular community bulletin board that attracted a steady parade of residents.

Not that Bev Price needed gimmicks to generate traffic. With her gregarious nature and welcoming manner, people gravitated toward her like flies to honey.

"I'll be right with you."

As the owner's cheery greeting floated from the back room, Bren ambled across the shop and helped herself to a homemade gooey butter cookie from the always-stocked jar on the counter.

"Sorry to keep you waiting, but I was—"

Bev halted as she pushed through the swinging door that separated the shop from the office and stockroom. Threw out her arms and beamed a megawatt smile. "I love it!"

"Really?" Bren touched her hair. After her DIY dye job, a stylist had helped her complete the dramatic change, but it would take a while to get used to her new do.

"Yes, yes, yes!" Bev continued forward in a swirl of jasmine perfume, took her hand, and tugged her toward the jewelry case, where she positioned her in front of the mirror on the wall. "A whole new look to launch a whole new decade. Bravo to you!"

Bren examined her image.

Gone were the rainbow locks and gelled spikes she'd sported for the past four years.

In their place were fluffed, honey-brown tresses with a faint hint of her favorite color. The new style was softer. Less biker-girl flamboyant. Still too short to achieve the full effect she was after, but time would take care of that.

"The look may be new, but I'm still the same person inside."

"True. But we all grow and learn and become with every passing year. Including yours truly." Bev winked at her. "And changing things up now and then keeps life interesting. No one knows that better than me. I've lived more lives than a cat."

Bren smiled at the upbeat, energetic woman behind her in the mirror, who always brimmed with enthusiasm and a sense of adventure.

What a godsend—and inspiration—Bev had been in the nine months since the woman had moved to town and opened her shop. One glimpse at her flowing salt-and-pepper locks livened up with a vibrant swath of color—fuchsia being this month's choice—and her flamboyant attire, like today's tropical-themed caftan featuring giant birds of paradise and parrots, and it had been obvious they were kindred spirits.

The icing on the cake?

The bookshop owner was a fabulous listener, with keen insights and amazing empathy.

Bren's smile broadened.

Who could have guessed that a woman almost twice her age would end up being the best friend she'd ever had?

"I figured a milestone birthday was a good excuse to make a few changes." She smoothed back a stray lock.

"Or start a new chapter, like the sign in my display window says. It's never too late for that, either. Look at me. I'm closing in on sixty, and here I am the proud owner of a bookstore in my retirement. You never know what exciting opportunities lie ahead. And speaking of excitement, you had more than your share yesterday with that fire. I'm glad Fred stepped in and came to your rescue. You sleep okay last night in your temporary digs?"

Bren took a bite of her cookie, but the sugary treat didn't sweeten her memories of the pepper gel fiasco. "Not especially."

"I hear you." Bev gave a sympathetic nod. "It can take a while to adjust to new surroundings."

"It wasn't that."

Bev's eyebrows peaked. "Do I detect a story there?"

"Yes—and not a pleasant one."

"Uh-oh. If the arrangement with Fred isn't working out, you're welcome to hang out at my apartment until you find another place to stay. My couch isn't designed for long-term snoozing, but it'll do the job in a pinch."

Bren's throat constricted.

How had she lucked out and landed in a town with such generous, caring people?

"Thank you for that offer, but the cottage is fine. More than fine. However, I had an unexpected visitor last night."

As she told Bev the story of Noah's arrival, the bookstore owner's eyes rounded, and she eased onto a stool behind the counter. "Oh my."

"Yeah." Bren massaged the bridge of her nose. "I'm assuming it was a surprise visit, or else Fred would have told him I was staying there. But his father wasn't the only one surprised by his arrival."

"What happened wasn't your fault, though. I hope Fred's son understood that."

"I'm not sure he did last night, but when I saw him this morning on my run to the lighthouse, I didn't pick up any lingering irritation." Bren finished off her cookie.

Bev's eyebrows shot up again. "You took Pelican Point Road on day one of your new fitness regimen? I'm impressed."

"Don't be. It was an epic fail." She grimaced. "I ran out of steam long before I got to the lighthouse. The route never seemed that steep from inside my car."

Bev chuckled. "I felt the same way once on a weeklong bicycle trip I took in my younger days. I thought I was going to die half an hour in."

"I had the same thought while I was panting on the side of the road. That's how Noah found me. I tried to be cool, but he noticed my virgin shoes, did the math, and suggested the route may have been a tad too ambitious for a running newbie."

"You can work up to it, though—unless you decide running doesn't suit you. There are other ways to stay fit, you know."

"I know, but I've already invested in the shoes. I'm not giving up."

"Hurray for you. Persistence and determination pay off." Bev reached beneath the jewelry case and withdrew a small square package wrapped in bright paper. "I was going to deliver this later today. A belated birthday present. I didn't want to bring it to the party at The Perfect Blend yesterday in case any of the other guests noticed and felt awkward about arriving empty-handed." She set the package on the counter between them.

Once again, Bren's windpipe constricted. "You didn't have to do that, Bev."

"Of course I did. Thirtieth birthdays only come around once. Go ahead, open it."

Bren picked up the small package and slowly peeled off the tape. Folded back the wrapping paper. Lifted the lid on the box.

"Wow." The word came out hushed as she stared down at the beautiful teardrop earrings. "You made these, didn't you?"

"Yes. From imperial jasper. A perfect stone for you."

"They're exquisite." She let out a slow breath as she cradled the box in her palm. "But I can't take such a valuable present." At the prices Bev charged for the in-demand creations she sold online and in her shop, these would bring in a pretty penny.

"Yes, you can. You're worth it. Besides, I made them for you. They'll be gorgeous with your peridot studs."

Bren touched one of her birthstone earrings, a gift to herself on her twenty-fifth birthday.

But they hadn't cost anywhere near the price Bev could command for her work.

"Let me at least pay for the materials."

"Nonsense. A gift is a gift." Bev leaned across the counter and stroked a finger down one of the multicolored stones that glistened in the light. "I'm not a new-ager, but I wish for you all this stone represents—stability, comfort, security, strength, wholeness, and peace."

Bren's vision misted. "I don't know what to say."

A dimple appeared in the other woman's cheek. "Thank you would be appropriate."

After a moment, Bren replaced the lid and pressed the box to her chest. It was important to remember that not all generosity came with a price tag or an expectation of something in return. Like rigid conformity to a strict set of rules designed to prop up an illusion. "Thank you. For everything."

"You're welcome."

The chimes jingled, and Bren glanced around as an unfamiliar couple entered. Tourists, no doubt.

"I'll let you see to your customers." She stowed the small box in the pocket of her jacket.

"Come by again soon. I want an update on your running progress." Bev rounded the case again and pulled her into a warm hug.

"Count on it." Bren squeezed back.

On her way to the door, she stopped beside the woman who was examining a shelf of books. "You should check out the jewelry counter while you're here. It's all handmade by the owner and absolutely beautiful."

The customer smiled. "Thanks. I do have a birthday coming up." She nudged her companion.

He grinned and took her arm. "Message received. Let's see if anything catches your fancy."

While they wandered over to Bev, who led them to the jewelry case, Bren slipped out. Initiating a sale might help salve her conscience about taking such an expensive gift.

But much as she loved the earrings, the real gift had been the thought behind it.

And that was priceless.

So instead of lamenting over all that had gone wrong on her big three-oh birthday, she was going to focus on everything that had gone right—and hope Bev's wishes for her, represented by the imperial jasper earrings, came to pass in this new decade of her life.

This was the place—and he was more than ready for a potent infusion of caffeine.

Laptop in hand, Noah stopped outside The Perfect Blend to read the handwritten quote from Yogi Berra on the A-frame dry-erase board positioned near the entrance.

When you come to a fork in the road, take it.

His lips flexed.

Cute, if not definitive. A fork in the road should be carefully considered, as Robert Frost had said in one of his poems.

Although, as the poet had also noted, sometimes it was hard to know which one to take.

Noah moved aside to let a couple pass by on the sidewalk.

Fortunately, indecision had never been a problem for him. No forks had come along to tempt him from the path he'd laid out long ago, after thorough deliberation and meticulous planning.

He continued to the door of the shop and pushed through, pausing inside to give the space a once-over.

Small tables were tucked against the walls and around the free-standing fireplace in the middle, beckoning customers to linger. Poster-sized nature photos provided a restful ambiance. The soothing neutral palette beckoned.

No wonder the shop was packed.

His father's recommendation had been spot-on.

It would have been helpful if Dad had been able to join him so he could have continued his relocation campaign, but finding an empty slot on his father's packed calendar was tough. Dad had hightailed it out of the house at the crack of dawn for a standing Friday golf date with a retired mail carrier he'd befriended.

Noah blew out a breath.

Eventually he'd corner his father and have a serious discussion about a move. But for now, he may as well take advantage of the shop's peaceful, chill-out vibe while he caught up on email and got an update on yesterday's crisis at work.

Unless Dad's tenant was on duty.

Given how the air around her crackled, creating chaos rather than calm in his psyche, being in her presence would *not* be restful.

As far as he could tell, though, only two people were staffing the shop. A tall dark-haired guy who appeared to be mid- to late-thirties, and a woman with honey-brown hair farther down the counter, nothing but her back visible as she worked the espresso machine.

There were no rainbow-hued locks in sight.

Good.

The less he saw of Bren, the better. No sense putting yourself in an uncomfortable position if you could avoid it.

"Morning."

At the greeting, he shifted toward the dark-haired guy. "Good morning."

"Welcome to The Perfect Blend. Have a look at the menu and food offerings while you're in line." He motioned to the bill of fare on the wall behind him and swept a hand over the glass display case in front.

"Thanks."

As Noah joined the queue of customers, he gave the list of drinks his full attention. More variety than expected from a small-town coffee shop—including café viennois and café de olla—but it was safer to stick with the tried and true. Why take a chance on something new that could disappoint you?

"Sorry to keep you waiting. Friday mornings can be busy here, especially in the summer." The guy positioned himself in front of the register. "What would you like?"

"An Americano with an extra shot of espresso and a piece of that." He pointed to a tray containing a sweet bread.

"Excellent choice. The cranberry nut cake is from Harbor Point Cranberries south of town. For here or to go?"

"Here."

The guy behind the counter plated a slice of the loaf cake, added a fork, and set it on the counter while Noah dug out his credit card and canvassed the tables.

All of them were occupied.

But the two people at one near the fireplace were gathering up the remnants of their treat, as if preparing to leave.

The instant he finished paying, Noah pocketed his card and picked up his cake. "Thanks."

"Enjoy. Can I have a name for your drink?"

He tossed it over his shoulder as he made a beeline for the table, beating out an older couple on the same mission and avoiding eye contact with them as he staked his claim. Maybe aggressive tactics would be regarded as poor form in laid-back Hope Harbor, but as experience had taught him, tables in popular coffee shops went to customers who were observant and speedy.

After settling into his seat, he opened his laptop and took a bite of his cake while he waited for the computer to boot up.

Delicious.

If all the offerings in the case were as—

Noah frowned as he caught the brown-haired woman behind the counter watching him.

As soon as she realized he'd noticed her, she swung away, her multicolored earrings glistening in the overhead light.

He frowned.

Why would a stranger stare at him?

Except . . . as she went about her task, giving him an occasional glimpse of her profile, she seemed somehow familiar.

"Americano for Noah."

The woman's voice carried over the hum of conversation in the shop, and he peered at her as she angled sideways to place a lidded cup on the pickup counter.

Was that Bren?

No. It couldn't be.

Could it?

Maybe.

But what had happened to her rainbow hair?

Leaving his laptop and the rest of his cake behind, he rose and crossed to the counter.

The closer he got, the more certain he was of her identity.

And her greeting confirmed it.

"Hi, Noah." She offered him a smile that felt artificial. Like she was uncomfortable with this meeting too. "Did you enjoy your run to the lighthouse yesterday?"

"Um, yeah. I did. Great view." He picked up his cup. "Sorry it took me a minute to recognize you."

"No worries. I've thrown a few people for a loop today. I have to admit, I shock myself whenever I pass a mirror. This is quite a change." She patted her hair.

"Uh, yeah." Compared to her previous flamboyant look, her new image was downright sedate.

Other than a faint purple cast to the golden-brown color.

Or could the light be playing tricks on him?

He squinted at her.

Hard to tell. But from where he stood, there did seem to be a purple-hued undertone to—

"Well . . ." Bren adjusted her apron, a faint flush tinting her cheeks. "The orders are piling up. If you want cream, it's over there." She waved toward a small stand off to the side, swiveled around, and went back to work.

Oops.

His rude gaping had rattled her.

But trying to reconcile the Bren of the hot-pink sleep shirt, psychedelic leggings, and multicolored spikes with the hazel-eyed, honey-haired beauty behind the counter was a challenge. Even with that faint purple aura around her head.

Should he have complimented her on her new image . . . or would that have insulted her by suggesting he hadn't liked the old one?

Who knew?

Women were an enigma.

Noah turned away and crossed to the stand. Opened his coffee and tipped in a generous amount of half-and-half to dilute the dark brew.

This was why it was prudent to avoid interacting with eligible members of the opposite sex. Even in simple conversations, it was too easy to put your foot in your mouth, bruise feelings, or inadvertently suggest you had a deeper interest than you did and thereby create expectations and encourage assumptions that came back to bite you.

Candace being a case in point.

He retook his seat.

Speaking of assumptions . . .

Maybe Bren wasn't eligible. While she seemingly lived alone, that didn't mean there wasn't a man in her life. For all he knew, she could be engaged. Perhaps to a guy who sported a mohawk and was covered with tats.

Although that kind of dude didn't fit her new look.

Why had she changed her image, anyway? And who was the real Bren Ryan?

As questions swirled through his mind, Noah took a swig of coffee and glowered at his computer screen.

Enough about Bren. Thirty-six hours ago, he hadn't even known the woman. The only reason she kept traipsing through his brain was because people like her rarely entered his orbit—and that gave her a certain intriguing appeal.

What other explanation could there be?

But he could erase her from his mind. No problem. All he had to do was connect to the secure server at work and dive into numbers.

That, however, was easier said than done. As it turned out, The Perfect Blend was a Wi-Fi-free environment. Which was fine if you were on a vacation that allowed you to leave work behind.

He wasn't.

Tamping down his annoyance, he drummed his fingers on the table.

He could use his phone as a hot spot, but in all likelihood the connection would be slow as molasses in a town this size. Plus, it would eat up his battery.

He'd have to go back to his father's house and work there.

And maybe that would be more prudent, anyway. It was hard to focus with Bren across the room. The few times their gazes had connected had left him flustered and on edge. Not a mental state conducive to concentration.

So he finished his Americano and cranberry nut cake, packed up his computer, and exited the shop, keeping his eyes pointed straight ahead as he passed the counter.

Once outside, he filled his lungs, slowly exhaled, and walked away from The Perfect Blend, leaving thoughts of Bren behind.

Out of sight, out of mind, after all.

He hoped.

6

. . . .

Please start!

Fighting back another wave of panic, Emma Blair twisted the key in the ignition again.

Click. Click. Click.

The same dead sound she'd gotten on every previous try.

And it wasn't a battery issue. The one under the hood was only two months old.

Now what?

Clamping her fingers around the steering wheel, she inhaled a shaky breath and rested her forehead against her knuckles as rain continued to ping against the roof of the faithful Sentra that had never given her a lick of trouble, even after the odometer slipped into the six-digit range last spring.

Why, all of a sudden, had it decided to die? And why here?

But what did it matter? With the Pacific Ocean a block away, she was as far west of Nebraska as she could get anyway.

Besides, if a person had to get stuck, where better than a town with the name of Hope Harbor?

Her pay-by-the-minute flip phone began to ring, and she snatched it up from the seat beside her. Only two people had this number, and her so-called best friend was now blocked. Meaning the incoming call was one she didn't want to miss.

She put the phone to her ear. "Hey, Justin. You okay?"

"I'm hanging in." It was the same response her brother always gave. "Where are you today?"

"A small town on the Oregon coast." She flicked a look at the storefront beside her. "Outside a coffee shop."

"Wish I was with you."

"Me too." Leaving him behind had almost killed her, but distance was the best way to remove herself from that toxic environment and find a fresh start. "And you will be, as soon as I can make it happen. How's everything back there?"

"Same old, same old."

The very reason she'd left three weeks ago, the day she'd turned eighteen and reached legal age.

But at sixteen, Justin didn't have that option.

"It'll be better once you're with me."

"I know, but . . . what if there's a glitch?" A thread of fear and despair wove through his voice.

"There won't be." She put as much confidence into her response as she could muster. "Bill will be glad to have an excuse to ditch his responsibility to you."

A harsh judgment, perhaps, but she and Justin both knew it was true.

"I miss you, Em."

She watched a drop of rain trail down her windshield, pressure building behind her eyes. "I'm sorry, Justin. I just . . . I had to get out of there."

"I know it's bad here."

Yes, it was. For both of them, in different ways.

"I'll call you tomorrow, okay?"

"Yeah. Listen . . . you good on cash? The money you saved working at the bakery won't last forever."

"No worries for now." Unless her car issue was serious and put a major dent in her savings.

"If you run low, I could ask for more hours with the lawn company. Grass cutting doesn't pay a ton, but it's a steady income. And I don't spend much."

She swallowed past the lump in her throat. "I'll be fine as soon as I land somewhere."

No way was she mentioning her dead car. She'd rather skip meals and sleep in the Sentra—as she'd been doing for most of the past week to conserve cash—than take any of Justin's hard-earned nest egg. She'd only splurged one night on a bare-bones motel so she could shower and clock a decent night's sleep.

"I'm sorry Denise let you down, Em."

That made two of them.

Who knew her high school bestie would find a hot new boyfriend and turn out to be the type to renege on a promise to provide temporary housing? By text, no less, and with barely twenty-four hours' notice.

"Yeah. Me too."

"So what are you going to do?"

"Keep searching for a place to drop anchor." Which would have to be soon. She couldn't live in her car forever.

"I guess it'll be a while before you can send for me, huh?"

"The curve Denise threw me is nothing more than a temporary setback, Justin. I'm going to pick a town soon and get a job." Because until she secured steady employment and a place to live, she couldn't petition for guardianship. "Once I'm settled, Bill will be happy to turn you over to me, and the court will rubber-stamp my application. Until then, we'll talk every day."

"Okay. Love you, Em."

Emma swiped the back of her hand under her nose. "Love you too."

When the line went dead, she slowly lowered the cell to her lap as the steady rain and fog shrouded her car in a gray mist, her earlier question replaying in her mind.

Now what?

Sending a plea heavenward for a miracle, she twisted the key again.

Click. Click. Click.

Apparently no miracle was in store for her today. Her Sentra wasn't going anywhere.

At least she wasn't in the middle of nowhere. If she hadn't pulled over here to wait out the rain, the car could have died at a highway rest stop. In a town, there ought to be help close by.

Maybe someone in that coffee shop could point her in the right direction.

It was worth asking.

Because sitting here wasn't going to fix anything.

And while froufrou coffee drinks weren't in her budget, she could splurge on a small, plain java in exchange for a recommendation for an honest, reliable mechanic.

"Small coffee for Emma." As Bren set the lidded disposable cup on the pickup counter, the young woman who'd dashed in from the rain minutes before closing time moved forward to claim it.

"Thank you." After offering a timid smile, the petite brunette retreated to one of the tables by the fireplace in the almost-deserted shop.

"I think it's a wrap for the day, Bren." Zach stopped beside her. "I doubt many people are wandering around in this weather. It should be safe to start shutting down."

"Works for me." She tipped her head toward the young woman who'd had a rather lengthy exchange with Zach while he took her order at the other end of the counter. "It looked like our last customer of the day was telling you her life story."

"Not quite. But she did tell me about her car. It died out in front. She asked for a mechanic recommendation."

"I assume you referred her to Marv?"

He hitched up one side of his mouth. "Who else? He's the only game in town."

"Also a great mechanic. He patches up my Kia on a regular basis."

"The man does have a magic touch with engines." He motioned behind him. "I'll handle equipment cleanup if you want to work on the pastry case."

"You got it."

As he moved off, Bren wiped down the counter and gave the young woman another surreptitious scan.

She was using a burner-type flip phone, voice pitched low, features pinched. Calling Marv, no doubt.

Did she have sufficient funds to cover a car repair?

Hard to tell by her appearance. The jeans and long-sleeved tee she wore were low-key and nondescript, but that didn't mean anything. It could be a designer outfit that had cost a fortune, for all she knew. Unless you lived within a reasonable distance of wealthy zip codes, thrift-shop bargain hunting wasn't conducive to becoming a fashionista—if one was so inclined.

Lucky she wasn't, given her budget.

Heaving a sigh that carried across the shop, the brunette set the phone on the table and hunkered down over her coffee, hands wrapped around the cup, posture slumped. Like she was carrying the weight of the world on her shoulders.

And was that sudden glisten on her cheek a tear trailing down?

Whatever burden she was carrying, it was too heavy for someone who couldn't be much past seventeen or eighteen.

Bren wadded the rag in her fist, stomach clenching as a sense of déjà vu swept over her.

Finding yourself alone, without a friend in the world, was a bad place to be.

If this young woman was in trouble, did she have anyone to lend a helping hand?

Moving on autopilot, Bren began to empty the pastry case, wrapping the items that could be saved until tomorrow, setting aside those that couldn't, as the third mandate on her birthday resolution list strobed across her mind.

Seek out opportunities to give back for all the blessings that have come your way in Hope Harbor.

Hmm.

Was there something she could do to help this young woman? Offer a friendly ear, perhaps? Let her know someone had noticed her and cared?

The other remaining customers in the shop, an older couple at a table by the window, rose, deposited their cups in the trash, and crossed to the door.

"Sorry to linger." The man paused at the counter, his companion beside him. "We know you're ready to close, but it's hard to leave this pleasant ambiance behind. Especially in such gray, wet weather."

Bren coaxed up the corners of her mouth. "No worries. We'll be here awhile in cleanup mode. You don't have to rush out."

"Thanks, but we want to stop in at the bookstore."

"Another great place to linger on a rainy day. You'll love it there. The owner's super nice."

"That's what we heard. Thanks again for the great coffee. It was better than any chain." The man pushed through the door, opened his umbrella, and tucked the woman closer beside him as they exited into the drizzle.

When Bren angled back toward the remaining customer, the young woman's gaze skittered away after a brief second of eye contact. Then she drained her cup, slid her phone back into her pocket, and pulled out her keys.

Unless someone intervened fast, she was going to walk out the door and disappear forever.

Pulse picking up, Bren plated a cranberry scone and a piece of shortbread from Bayview Lavender Farm Tearoom. After grabbing a fork, she circled the counter and called up her friendliest smile as she approached the woman.

"Hi. My boss tells me you're having car problems. I thought a sweet treat might cheer you up a little."

The woman examined the plate, the longing in her expression at odds with her stiff, wary posture. "Um . . . thank you, but I was just getting ready to leave."

"Did you call Marv?"

"Yes. I left a message."

"If he's out helping another stranded motorist, you could have a wait. You're welcome to stay here until he arrives."

"Aren't you closing?"

"Yes, but I'll be here for another hour doing cleanup. You may as well wait inside by the fire. It would be more comfortable than sitting in your car."

The woman chewed on her lower lip. "Are you sure that wouldn't be an inconvenience?"

"Not at all."

"And your boss won't mind?"

"No." But she'd brief Zach on the situation as soon as this conversation was over. "In fact, let me get you a refill. We're about to clean out the coffee machines."

"I, uh, only paid for one cup."

"We're going to throw it out if you don't drink it. Same rule with pastries. Once they're past their expiration, out they go." Which applied to the scone on the plate she set in front of the woman, if not the shortbread. But she'd pay for that herself.

"In that case, thank you." The woman picked up the empty cup and held it out.

"I'll be back in a sec." Bren took it and returned to the prep area.

As she filled it again, Zach joined her.

"What gives with our dallying customer?"

"She isn't dallying. I invited her to stay while we clean up." She snapped on a new lid and turned to him. "I get sad vibes from her, Zach. I didn't want to send her out into the rain to wait for Marv alone in her car. And I think she may be hungry. I gave her a couple of treats from the case. I'll pay for the shortbread. It wasn't out-of-date yet."

"Nope. It's on the house. If you think she needs help and TLC, I trust your intuition. The Perfect Blend can afford an occasional gratis pastry or two for a worthy cause."

Typical Zach.

"Thanks. I'll be happy to finish the cleanup if you want to take off. Marv may not get here for an hour or two, and I don't mind hanging around and locking up."

"Are you sure? It would help if I could cut out and get a jump on dinner. We invited my aunt and her husband over tonight, and Katherine is slammed with a special truffle order for a wedding up at Edgecliff. She'll be racing to get home in time to eat with us as it is."

"She did seem a bit frazzled when I went outside for my break earlier. I saw her hustling into Chocolate Harbor carrying two shopping bags."

Zach glanced in the direction of his wife's gourmet chocolate business next door. "She was running short on favor boxes and had to dash up to a wholesale place in Coos Bay to augment her supply. If you're certain you don't mind shutting down here, I'll pop in and see if there's anything I can do to help her before I head home."

"I've got this. If nothing else, you can give her a hug for encouragement."

He grinned. "Or a little more."

Nice to find a guy who truly loved and appreciated his wife. A rarity, in her experience, but proof that not all men were selfish and domineering.

"Go." She waved him toward the door. "I'll take care of The Perfect Blend."

He ditched his apron, stowed it beneath the counter, and nodded toward the woman at the table. "If you want to send her on her way with a bag of stuff from the case, feel free."

Yep. Definitely a good guy.

"Thanks."

As Zach pushed through the front door, Bren checked on the woman. She'd finished the shortbread and had dived into the scone.

No question about it. A goody bag was going with her.

But if she was hungry . . . if she was as alone as she seemed . . . a couple of sweet treats wouldn't be enough.

Bren set the cup down, slid another piece of shortbread into a bag, then carried both items across the store.

Once again she used her friendliest smile as she put them on the table. "My boss agrees that you can stay until you deal with your car. Marv's a great mechanic, by the way. Also fair and reliable. He'll fix you up." She adjusted the strap on her apron and waved a hand toward the counter. "My boss left for the day, so I have more cleanup than usual. Why don't you relax and enjoy the fire?"

A faint shimmer appeared in the woman's irises. "Thank you."

"No problem. Are you staying in town?"

"Um . . . I don't know. It depends on what happens with my car."

In other words, she didn't have firm sleeping arrangements for tonight.

"I can recommend the Gull Motel. It's not the Ritz, but it's clean and homey. I stayed there when I first came here, until I found a place to rent."

"Do you, uh, know what they charge?"

Suspicion confirmed. Money was an issue.

"No, but I can find their number for you." She pulled out her cell and googled the motel while the woman withdrew a slip of paper and a pen from her purse.

She jotted down the information while Bren recited it. "I'll give them a call."

"If you need anything else while I'm cleaning up, let me know. I'm Bren."

After a slight hesitation, the woman responded, "I'm Emma."

"Welcome to Hope Harbor, Emma. Enjoy the sweets."

Leaving her to eat in peace, Bren returned to the counter and shifted into cleanup mode, casting occasional peeks at the young woman.

She scarfed down her food, then made one very brief phone call, likely to the motel. But her wallet remained in her purse. So unless she had her credit card data memorized, she didn't book a room.

Meaning the price must be too high, even though it was the cheapest place in town.

If she couldn't afford that, where was she going to sleep if she was stuck here while her car was being repaired?

Though that question plagued Bren as she tidied up the shop, no satisfactory answer had come to mind by the time Emma's phone finally rang.

After a brief conversation with Marv, she tucked her phone into her purse, gathered up the remnants of her snack, and stood.

Bren hung up her apron, retrieved her own purse, and circled around the counter. "Is Marv en route?"

"Yes. He said he'd be here within ten minutes." Emma surveyed the rainy scene outside the plate glass window. "If you're ready to lock up, I can wait for him in my car."

"It's drier in here. I can stay a few more minutes." Keeping her tone conversational, she pulled out her keys. "Any luck at the Gull? They can be busy during the tourist season."

"Um . . . they had a room, but I . . . I didn't budget for too many nights in hotels. And until I know what's wrong with my car, well . . ." She shrugged. "Is there, like, a youth hostel anywhere nearby?"

Money must be super tight.

And this young woman looked like she needed more TLC than a bare-bones youth hostel would provide.

"Not in Hope Harbor. You'd have to travel farther afield to find one."

Seek out opportunities to give back for all the blessings that have come your way in Hope Harbor.

Bren tightened her grip on her keys as the birthday pledge once again looped through her mind.

A worthy goal, but what more could she do for this young woman? Emma didn't come across as the type who would take a handout.

Maybe Helping Hands could find her a place to spend the night.

Or you could invite her to stay with you.

As that crazy notion ricocheted through her mind, Bren's breath hitched.

What?

Invite a stranger to share her living space?

No way.

Not happening.

She didn't know a thing about this woman. Connecting her with assistance through Helping Hands would be more prudent.

"Um . . . is there a church in town?" Emma's cheeks flushed, a strong indication she was embarrassed by her financial straits. "Sometimes they have . . . resources."

"Yes. And we also have an organization that may be able to help if you're having cash flow issues."

In either case, though, it was possible all they'd be able to provide for her was a ride to the homeless shelter in Coos Bay, where her physical needs would be taken care of for the night.

But this young woman needed more than that. Bren could feel it in her gut.

"If you could give me a number to call for either of those, I'd—"

"Wait." Pulse hammering, she took a deep breath. This could

be a huge mistake—but sometimes you had to follow your heart. "I realize we're strangers, so this may sound kind of off the wall. But I've been in my share of tough spots too. So as long as the owner of my quarters approves, you're welcome to use the sleeper sofa in the living room until Marv fixes your car." She smiled again. "And in terms of churches, I'd be happy to give you my pastor's number if you want to verify that I'm not a serial killer."

The other woman stared at her as a mixture of shock, disbelief, surprise, trepidation, and a faint hint of hope suffused her face.

She was tempted to accept. That much was clear.

The question was, would she?

7

Who was the suitcase-lugging woman—teen?—following Bren across his father's backyard?

From the table in front of the guest room window where he'd set up shop, Noah watched over the screen of his laptop as the two figures hurried through the rain toward the cottage and disappeared inside.

Did his father know his temporary tenant had invited someone to stay with her? Did their agreement include weekend guests? Or was Bren taking advantage of his father's generosity?

At the very least, his dad should know if someone else was staying overnight on his property. For insurance purposes, if nothing else.

After finishing his interrupted calculation, Noah left the problematic spreadsheet he'd been laboring over open on the screen and strode down the hall.

As he entered the kitchen, his father pushed through the door that led from the adjacent laundry room to the garage.

"It's a wet one out there. I'm glad we finished our game before the skies opened." Dad shrugged out of his jacket and hung it on a hook by the door. "Did you enjoy The Perfect Blend?"

"The coffee was fine, but I didn't stay long. They don't have Wi-Fi."

"I know. Isn't it refreshing to find a place where the only way to get wired is by drinking coffee?"

"Not if you have work to do."

"I thought you were on vacation." His father entered the kitchen and set a small, flat box on the table.

"It's a working vacation. After I had my coffee, I came back here so I could log in to the secure server at the office." He motioned toward the cottage. "Did you know your tenant invited someone to stay with her?"

His father's eyebrows arched. "No. How do *you* know?"

"I saw her arrive about ten minutes ago."

"Maybe a friend came to visit her for the weekend." His dad moseyed over to the sink and began putting away the dishes in the drainer, as if he didn't have a care in the world.

That made one of them.

"Don't you think she should have asked you first?"

"Why?"

"Because you did her a favor by offering to let her use the cottage, and she's renting it for a song. Did she give you a deposit for damages?"

His father shot him a get-real look. "Of course not. I trust her to take care of the place. If she does happen to break anything, I expect she'll offer to pay for it."

"What if she doesn't? Not everyone is honest."

"Bren is."

"How do you know?"

His father angled toward him, plate in hand. "My goodness, Noah. When did you become so cynical and suspicious?"

He shoved his hands into his pockets. "I've seen a fair amount of deceit—and situations that aren't what they seem to be—in my work." And elsewhere.

"You must have. Makes me glad I was a draftsman." Dad slid the plate into the cabinet. "You don't have to worry about Bren. We go to the same church, and she's been known to step forward if a need arises at Helping Hands. That young woman has a heart of—"

A knock sounded on the back door, and Noah swiveled toward it.

Bren was visible through the window.

"Speak of the devil . . . though that doesn't fit in her case." His father crossed the room and pulled the door open. "Are your ears burning?"

"Should they be?"

"We were just talking about you." His father hooked a thumb over his shoulder.

Bren peeked sideways. Moistened her lips as she caught sight of her pepper gel victim. "I can, uh, catch up with you later. I don't want to interrupt."

"You aren't. Come on in." His father pulled the door wide.

She stayed put. "I tried to call earlier, but no one answered."

Dad pulled out his phone. Rolled his eyes. "I forgot to take it off silent mode after my golf game. What did you need?"

"I wanted to ask if it would be okay to have someone stay with me for a few nights. If you like, I'll be happy to increase my rent for the week to cover two people."

His father sent him a smug "see what I mean?" glance before continuing his exchange with Bren. "You're welcome to have a guest. And there's no extra charge. The place is yours while you're here. Did a friend come to town for a visit?"

"No." She wiped her palms down her black slacks. "This wasn't planned. She's a customer, actually. Her car died in front of the shop, and I don't think she has the money for a hotel while she waits for it to be repaired."

Noah stared at her.

She'd taken a stranger in off the street?

Who did such a thing in this day and age?

What if this was a scam? A setup? It could even be dangerous. Why would Bren put both his father and herself into such a tricky—

"That was very kind of you." Dad's tone was warm and approving.

Noah almost choked on his spit.

How on earth could his father be on board with this crazy idea?

Someone whose brain was working needed to step in here. Fast.

"Dad." He moved forward, ignoring Bren. "Letting a stranger stay on the property may not be wise. I got a glimpse of her, and she looks very young. If she's not of legal age, you could get into trouble for—"

"She's eighteen. I asked."

As Bren spoke, Noah transferred his attention to her. "Did you see any proof?"

"She showed me her driver's license. She's from Nebraska."

"She came a long way."

"I expect she had her reasons."

"You do realize the license could be a fake."

"It's not."

"How do you know?"

"I just do, okay?" After giving him a narrow-eyed glare, she directed her next comment to his father. "If you're uncomfortable with this and want me to ask her to leave, I will. I can give her enough money for a couple of nights at the Gull. But I really think she could use some TLC, and I hate to turn someone out who's hit a rough stretch."

"A little kindness goes a long way toward smoothing rough paths and healing hearts."

As Charley's words from their meeting at the lighthouse replayed through his mind, Noah studied Bren.

Had she hit a rough stretch in the past too? Is that why she recognized the signs in the younger woman?

"What would it take for you to be comfortable with the arrangement?" His father directed the question to him.

If Dad was willing to offer concessions to appease him, he'd take full advantage of that.

"I'd feel better if law enforcement ran her through their system."

"She'd have to agree to that." Bren folded her arms, a mutinous tilt to her chin.

"Fine. Ask her. If she doesn't have anything to hide, why would she object?"

"I don't want her to think I don't trust her."

"Given the crime statistics in today's world, I don't see how she could object if you exhibit prudent caution. Blame it on me, if you want to."

His father's gaze ping-ponged between the two of them. "Practically speaking, I see Noah's point. However, I also trust your instincts, Bren. Why don't you ask if she'd mind letting the police run her license? If she agrees and it comes back clean, she's welcome to stay as long as you want to host her. If the request offends her and she decides to leave, I'll contribute toward a room at the Gull while she's waiting for her car to be fixed. Everyone agreeable to that?"

Noah mashed his lips together.

No, he was not agreeable. No one took in strangers these days, nor would any reasonable person accept such an invitation. This was a disaster waiting to—

"Yes."

As Bren responded in the affirmative, two sets of eyes swung toward him.

Blast.

If he balked, he'd come across as heartless. And this *was* his father's property. His dad could do whatever he wanted.

The wisest plan would be to go with the flow until they found out whether the woman was open to a background check.

If she refused or red flags popped up, end of story.

If she agreed and her record was clean?

He'd have to make certain Dad didn't forget to lock his doors—a habit he and Mom had begun to neglect after they moved here.

79

"I can live with that." His tone was grudging, at best.

"Problem solved." His dad turned to Bren again. "Let me know what she says. If she agrees with our plan, I'll have a chat with Lexie. That's our police chief." Dad tossed the last part of the comment over his shoulder to him.

"I'll ask her and let you know. Give me a few minutes."

"No hurry on my end."

Noah didn't say another word.

Without sparing him a glance, Bren pivoted and disappeared.

Only after his father closed the door did Noah speak. "I realize Hope Harbor is a tiny town, Dad, but bad stuff happens everywhere. Letting that stranger stay here is like picking up a hitchhiker."

"Not quite." He returned to the dish rack and continued putting away the dry plates, glasses, and silverware. "The young woman Bren took in wasn't seeking a ride—or a place to stay. Bren offered."

Noah fisted one hand on his hip and raked the fingers of the other through his hair. "What on earth would compel her to do that? Doesn't she read the paper or listen to the news?"

"I expect she does. But from what I've seen of her, she also has a caring heart." His father's mouth tipped up as he folded the dishcloth and set it on the counter. "You know what this situation reminds me of? The time you climbed that tree to rescue a kitten when you were a kid. You always had a soft spot for critters in trouble."

Noah grimaced. "That isn't a pleasant memory. If you'll recall, I got my foot stuck in a branch and the fire department had to extricate me. I also remember how that sweet kitty raked its claws down my arm before it leapt to the ground of its own accord. I still have the scars. Which reinforces my point. Sometimes trying to help backfires. Someone could get hurt here too."

"Let's see what Lexie has to say. There's leftover pizza in that box, if you're hungry." He motioned to the table.

Discussion over, apparently. At least for now.

"No, thanks. I should get back to work."

"You know what they say about all work."

"I'll find time for fun while I'm here."

But as he retraced his steps down the hall, fun was the last thing on his mind.

Even if Hope Harbor was as idyllic as everyone claimed, that didn't mean a person should wear blinders.

And whether or not Bren's unexpected houseguest was cleared by the police, he intended to keep his eyes wide open for the duration of her stay.

The owner was going to kick her out.

Twisting her fingers together, Emma reached the end of the living room in the cottage, pivoted, and paced back.

It would be hard to blame him if he wanted her to leave. In his place, she'd be nervous about a stranger on her property too.

In truth, she was more than a little nervous about *being* on the property. After all, who took a stranger into their home in this day and age—unless they had a hidden and perhaps questionable agenda?

Except Bren had offered her pastor as a reference.

She wouldn't do that if there was anything sketchy about her motivation, right?

It was possible she was a genuine Good Samaritan. A rare breed for sure, but they did exist, and—

The doorknob rattled, and a moment later Bren entered.

"Sorry. The owner's son was there, and we ended up having a longer conversation than I expected." She motioned to the couch. "Why don't we sit for a minute?"

Stomach clenching, Emma focused on the irregular grain in the hardwood floor beneath her feet as Bren moved across the room.

This was it. The woman who'd unexpectedly come to her rescue was going to tell her she had to go. She'd have to shell out the bucks for the Gull Motel for at least one night until she—

"Emma."

At Bren's soft summons, she lifted her head.

"Let's sit." Bren patted the seat beside her.

She stayed where she was. "If the owner wants me to go, you can tell me. I understand why he'd be concerned." Hard as she tried for a matter-of-fact tone, a quiver ran through her voice.

"No one's kicking you out. The decision about whether to go or stay will be up to you after we talk."

Not what she'd expected.

Maybe there was hope after all.

In silence, she walked over to the couch and perched on the edge.

"The owner was fine with the idea of you staying. His son is the one who has concerns." Bren leaned toward her, radiating empathy. "He's got a big-city, crime-conscious mindset, and he's having difficulty understanding why I would invite a woman I just met to share my living quarters."

"I can't blame him. I've been wondering the same thing."

Bren's lips flexed. "Let's just say I'm paying it forward. There was a fire at my house, and Fred offered to let me stay in this cottage until my place is habitable again." She smoothed out a wrinkle in the fabric of the couch, her expression growing more serious. "Plus, your situation struck a chord with me."

That was all she offered, but it didn't take a genius to read between the lines.

The woman sitting beside her had found herself in a bad situation once too.

Which raised a ton of questions.

But since Bren hadn't expounded on that comment, Emma confined herself to the matter at hand. "What did you mean about the choice to stay being up to me?"

She listened as Bren explained the plan.

It was hard to find fault with the request.

And what could it hurt to let the police run a background check? It wasn't as if she had anything to hide. Her record was spotless.

"I'm fine with that." She picked up her purse from the coffee table in front of the couch and extracted her wallet. "Do you want my license?"

"Let me talk to the owner first. Give me a sec." Bren pulled out her cell, had a brief conversation that involved more listening than talking, and ended the call. "He's going to contact our local police chief and explain the situation. We'll either run over to her office, or she'll swing by here."

Frowning, Emma set her purse back on the coffee table. "I'm causing you an awful lot of bother."

"No, you're not—but I do have to work this afternoon. If you'd like to explore the town, feel free. The rain seems to be over." She motioned toward the window, where a patch of blue sky was now visible among the dispersing clouds.

"I thought the coffee shop was closed for the day."

"It is. But I also do calligraphy. It started as a hobby, but the business kept growing." She stood. "There are benches on the wharf, if you want to wander down there. It's a perfect spot to—" She lifted her phone, scanned the screen, and put it to her ear. "Hi, Fred. That was fast . . . Yeah . . . We'll be here. Thanks again." She slid her cell into her pocket. "Lexie will swing by at the end of her shift. So you have what's left of the afternoon to stretch your legs and see the town. Hopefully Marv will call soon with news on your car too."

Emma rose as well. "Let me give you my cell number in case anything comes up."

After they exchanged numbers, Emma left Bren to her work.

And as she strolled down the street in the direction of the harbor and filled her lungs with the tangy salt air, a gentle peace enveloped her.

Challenges lay ahead, no question about it. The biggest one at the moment being her car repair bill.

But somehow she felt less overwhelmed and alone than she had since Mom died six months ago.

Odd, considering that she was among strangers in a strange town, her bank balance was dwindling, and she didn't have a job or a permanent place to live.

Yet as the sun peeked out, brightening the world, her heart felt lighter.

It was possible, of course, that her more upbeat attitude would be short-lived. She could wake up tomorrow feeling just as anxious and unsettled as she'd been since she'd crossed the state line in Nebraska, leaving Justin behind in the Cornhusker State.

Wouldn't it be wonderful, though, if she'd turned a corner? If a better life was ahead? If there were more people around like Bren, who were willing to take a risk and reach out to a young woman who desperately needed to know that this new adult world she'd entered wouldn't be filled with users like Bill?

And if such an outcome came to pass, it would trace its origins to the car problem that had landed her on Bren's doorstep.

She paused at the corner, checked both directions for traffic, and continued across.

Funny.

A handful of hours ago, she'd prayed for a miracle as she'd twisted the key in the ignition. When the engine didn't start, she'd assumed her request had fallen on deaf ears.

Yet what if it hadn't? What if her car issues ended up not being a disaster but a literal godsend? What if meeting Bren and getting stuck in this little town ended up being the best thing that could have happened to her?

Wishful thinking, perhaps. Fairy-tale outcomes were more often found in books than in real life.

But maybe, just this once, real life would turn out to hold a happy ending for her.

8

. . . .

"Thanks for coming by, Lexie." Bren walked the Hope Harbor police chief to the door of the cottage.

"Happy to do it." She scanned her watch. "I was going to stop in at the house, but I'm running late. Would you mind letting Fred know I was here? Adam and I promised Matt we'd both come to his baseball game tonight."

"I'll be happy to. It's never smart to disappoint a ten-year-old." Bren smiled.

Lexie angled back toward the room. "Welcome to Hope Harbor, Emma. I'm sorry about your car trouble, but I hope you enjoy your visit as much as you can under the circumstances."

"I am, thanks to Bren."

"Glad to hear it. See you around, Bren." With a lift of her hand, Lexie exited and hurried toward the corner of Fred's house.

As she disappeared around the side, Bren closed the door, pulled out her phone, and faced her houseguest. "Now that you've passed the background check with flying colors, should I assume you're staying?"

"Yes. Unless you're having second thoughts about inviting me."

"Nope." Over the past several hours, the strain in the younger woman's features had eased—validation that extending a helping hand had been a sound decision. "I'll ring Fred and let him know."

She tapped in his number, but when the call rolled to voicemail, she hesitated.

Rather than leave a message, it might be better to deliver the news in person in case he had any questions. And he was home. He'd been watering a pot of geraniums on the back porch five minutes ago.

"Change of plans. I'll run over to the house and give him the news. After I get back, I'll pop a pizza in the oven for dinner. It won't be fancy, but it'll be filling."

"You don't have to feed me. If you'll point me to a local market, I'll stock up on food for while I'm here."

Careful, Bren. Her pride's already been dinged.

"I'll tell you what. Why don't we share a pizza tonight, and if you end up staying more than a night or two, you can go with me on my next grocery run and pick up part of the tab. Deal?"

Emma chewed on her lower lip. "That doesn't seem adequate. I wish I could treat you to dinner at a restaurant."

"I like eating at home—with an occasional exception for Charley's tacos. Did you see his stand on the wharf?"

"The white food trailer with the colorful lettering, next to the tiny park?"

"That would be it."

"I noticed it from a distance, after I got a whiff of his cooking. It smelled divine."

"It is. Before you head out, we'll stop in there. You can't leave Hope Harbor without sampling Charley's tacos. They're amazing." She opened the door again. "I put a set of towels for you on the counter in the bathroom. I also put a luggage rack in the hall, next to the bathroom. And I made space in the closet in the bedroom, if there's anything you want to hang."

"I doubt I'll be here long enough to unpack but thank you."

"You're welcome. Any update from Marv while you were out walking?"

"Not yet. He told me at the coffee shop that he may not get to my car until tomorrow morning, and he's only open half a day on Saturday. So I don't know if he'll finish fixing it before he closes." Her brow pinched.

"No worries. The couch is yours as long as you need it. I'll be back in less than five minutes."

She slipped through the door and struck off across the lawn toward the house, no trace of the earlier rain lingering in the air.

But the wet grass provided tangible evidence of the downpour. And after she left the cobblestone path and trekked across the lawn to the back door, her sport shoes absorbed the beads of moisture clinging to the blades.

A change of socks would be in order as soon as she returned to the cottage.

After ascending the steps, she raised her hand to knock—only to spot Noah through the window.

Oops.

Another encounter with Fred's son today would be one too many.

A phone call would have to—

He turned from the fridge, a soda in hand. Froze when their gazes collided.

Dang.

She couldn't run off now that he'd spotted her. She'd have to pass on the news to him, if Fred wasn't available.

And maybe that was more appropriate anyway, since he was the one who'd raised the objection to Emma staying on the property.

After a few beats, he approached the door. Opened it.

He was still wearing the knife-creased slacks and long-sleeved dress shirt he'd sported earlier.

Not exactly chill-out vacation attire by her standards, but hey. To each his own.

"Is your dad around?"

"Yes, but he's on the phone dealing with a Helping Hands issue. You want me to give him a message?"

"I'd appreciate it if you'd tell him Lexie came by. There are no legal skeletons in Emma's closet. She's staying until her car is fixed."

The corners of Noah's mouth dipped south. "How long will that take?"

"I have no idea. She hasn't heard from the mechanic yet."

He set the can on the counter beside him, folded his arms, and studied her like she was a number that didn't add up on a balance sheet. "How can you be so trusting when the world is full of con artists and people who pretend to be something they're not in order to get what they want?"

As a wave of bad memories swept over her, she swallowed past the sudden sour taste on her tongue. "Emma isn't like that."

Noah's probing blue eyes narrowed, as if he was seeing more than she'd intended to reveal. "How can you be certain of that? Did she tell you her background?"

"No, but she's running from something. Escaping. Looking for a fresh start."

"How can you know that, if she hasn't shared her history?"

"Instinct. Intuition. Gut feeling." And seeing in the young woman's angst all she herself had felt twelve eternal years ago.

"Those aren't always reliable. Why don't you ask her some questions?"

"You can't force people to confide in you before they're ready. Trust has to be established first."

"You laid a pretty solid foundation for that by inviting her to stay with you."

"It was a beginning, but trust isn't built overnight. She'll probably be gone long before we get to that stage."

Faint creases dented his forehead. "What if your instincts are wrong? What if she's a user? You could get burned—or worse."

"I'll take that chance. And why should you care, anyway?"

He blinked, as if the question confused him, but rallied fast. "I care about anything that could potentially have a negative impact on my dad."

No doubt that was true.

But in the instant before he shuttered his eyes, it was clear he was also concerned about her.

Huh.

That was unexpected.

Even more unexpected?

The sudden spurt of warmth that sent a pleasant glow radiating through her.

All at once, an alarm bell began to ring in her mind.

That sort of reaction was dangerous. Letting herself develop feelings for anyone who was passing through town would be the height of foolishness.

She backed to the top of the steps before responding. "If I pick up the slightest indication that Emma's stay will have any adverse impact on your dad, I'll ask her to leave. Satisfied?"

"I guess." He frowned, his expression hard to read. Agitated, annoyed, angry—who knew? "I'll let Dad know she's staying. Have a nice evening."

With that, he shut the door.

For a long moment, Bren remained where she was while her heart did an odd quickstep. Almost like she was attracted to Mr. Oxford-shirt-wearing CPA.

Which was crazy.

She blew out a breath. Massaged her temple.

It had to be hormones. What else could it be? The man was handsome, after all. Any woman would notice his good looks and toned physique—especially one who hadn't had much romance in her life in quite a while.

Like none.

But his appeal would fade. She was too smart to let herself get all hot and bothered about a guy with no potential.

She struck off across the lawn again, more moisture seeping through her shoes as she escaped across the wet grass.

Yuck.

At this rate, her socks would be stuck like glue. She'd have to peel them off.

No big deal, though. That was a small inconvenience she could take care of in less than a minute.

Yet as she approached the cottage and glanced back at the house, she had the strangest feeling that whatever had seeped into her heart back there was going to be far harder to get rid of than clingy wet socks.

What had just happened?

From the middle of the kitchen, Noah stared at the back door as Bren's question scrolled through his mind.

Why *should* he fret over the possibility that she could get hurt or burned by her attempt to do a good deed?

It didn't make sense.

Yet despite his glib answer, the truth was the barista from The Perfect Blend had awakened his protective instincts.

And the sudden, subtle softening in her features suggested she'd not only picked up on that but liked it.

Even worse?

He'd liked it too.

Which was stupid and dangerous.

Balling his hands into fists, he began to pace.

Yes, the brief spark that had zipped between them might, under other circumstances, suggest the two of them had potential. But *current* circumstances weren't conducive to further exploration. Aside from formidable geographic issues, the two of them had nothing in common.

Bren had purple hair, for crying out loud. Her ears were triple-pierced. She wore loud colors. They were as different as two people could—

"Were you talking to someone a minute ago?" His dad entered the kitchen, phone in hand.

"Yeah." He stopped pacing. Leaned a hip against the counter. Exhaled. "Bren came by. The police cleared her guest."

"So her instincts were spot-on."

"Just because the woman's record is clean now doesn't mean it will stay clean."

"I'm not worried." His father squinted at him. "You all right?"

Noah wrapped his fingers around the edge of the counter behind him. "Sure. Why wouldn't I be?"

"Beats me, but you seem kind of tense. Rattled. Why don't you go for a walk down to the wharf? That's always relaxing."

"Aren't we eating dinner soon?"

"That was the plan, but an issue came up with Helping Hands and we're having an emergency board meeting. I'm sorry to run out on you."

"What about dinner?"

"I'll get takeout from the Myrtle. You may want to pay them a visit too. The meatloaf is delicious. Or you could finish off my leftovers from Frank's. It's the best pizza this side of the Rockies. There are also omelet and sandwich fixings in the fridge."

So much for the heart-to-heart he'd hoped to have with Dad tonight. At this rate, he'd have to schedule an appointment if he wanted to lay out his case for a move.

"I'll manage. What's on your schedule tomorrow?"

"A deck-repair project for a family going through a tough stretch. The father lost his job months ago, the wife has medical issues, and they have three young children. The deck's downright dangerous, from what I hear—especially with little kids running around. We want to get it back in safe, serviceable condition."

Noah sighed. "Do you have *any* downtime?"

"Here and there, but I like being busy. As your mom always

said, it's nourishing for the soul to be involved in the community, to make a contribution. Besides, after all the blessings I've received, it's only fair that I give something back."

As Dad's words hung in the air between them, a niggle of guilt nipped at his conscience.

He'd been blessed too. And what had he ever given back? Oh, sure, he contributed to a variety of causes. Money, not sweat equity or time, like Dad. He'd certainly never opened his home to a stranger as Bren had.

Maybe, while he was here, he could at least pitch in if someone needed help. Like the family that had hit hard times, with the shaky deck. This was supposed to be vacation, after all. He shouldn't be putting in long hours on work duties every day. A change of pace would be healthy.

"That's an admirable attitude. Could you use another pair of hands with the deck project tomorrow?"

His dad's eyebrows rose. "I don't expect you to work on vacation."

"After my run in the morning, it will be either that or number crunching. And I did come out here to see you. Not that I expected to be doing deck repairs, but if it will give us a few hours together, I'll take it."

"When you put it that way . . . the answer is yes. I do feel bad that I've had such limited time to spend with you. If I'd known you were coming, I wouldn't have booked myself up. But I hate to renege on commitments."

And it wasn't fair to ask him to in order to accommodate a son who had shown up for an impromptu, unannounced visit.

"Don't worry about it, Dad. We'll catch up."

"How about Sunday? Other than church, my day is yours."

"Consider it a date."

"I'll look forward to that." His father ambled over to the back window, moved the curtain aside, and looked toward the cottage. "Speaking of dates . . . Bren's a rare one, isn't she?"

Noah tried to make sense of that non sequitur. Failed.

"That's one way to describe her."

His father pivoted back. "You don't like her?"

"I didn't say that. She's just . . . different." He kept his tone casual as he walked to the fridge and made a pretense of examining the contents. "What do you know about her?"

"In terms of what? Background, character, hobbies, family situation, favorite color . . . love life?" At the hint of amusement in his father's voice, Noah checked on him over his shoulder.

There was a definite twinkle in his irises.

Oh brother. Non sequitur explained.

If his dad was trying to play matchmaker, however, he'd picked the wrong pairing.

Noah closed the fridge and schooled his features into a neutral mask. "Background. I wondered if a similar tough situation in her own history compelled her to reach out to Emma."

"I have no idea. I mostly know her from the coffee shop, and we have an occasional chat at church over a doughnut at the social hour after the service. But we've never delved into heavy topics or personal subject matter. Come to think of it, I don't think she's ever offered much about her past. From everything I've seen, though, she's a lovely young woman. I'm surprised she isn't married."

Noah shrugged. "Not every guy finds rainbow hair attractive."

"The rainbow is gone."

"I noticed."

"That's a start."

Noah folded his arms. "If you mean what I think you mean, no, it isn't."

His father ignored that. "If you want me to, I could do some reconnaissance on her for you."

"No, I do not want you to." At the sudden lift in his father's eyebrows, Noah dialed back his intensity. "If I want to know more, I'll ask her myself."

"*Do* you want to know more?"

He shrugged, striving for nonchalance. "Not necessarily."

"Uh-huh." His father moseyed over to the counter, pulled a glass from the cabinet, and stuck it under the water dispenser in the fridge. "I expect she'll be at church Sunday. If we stick around for doughnuts, you could have a chat with her. Or you could wander out to the cottage and strike up a conversation."

"Why would I do that?"

"I can think of a few reasons." His father lifted his glass in salute and grinned.

Okay. Time to nip this in the bud.

"Dad." He used his sternest demeanor. "Don't get any ideas."

"About what?" The exaggerated innocence in his father's countenance was almost laughable.

"You know what I'm talking about. And to be clear, I'm not in the market for a relationship. Especially here. My career is back in St. Louis."

"Careers are portable."

"Not if you're angling for a partnership."

"Is that still your goal?"

"Of course. You know that. I charted a path years ago, and I've been following it since day one."

His dad swirled the water in his glass. "Haven't you ever seen a fork in the road that tempted you to leave the straight and narrow and go exploring?"

The quote on the board in front of The Perfect Blend this morning flashed through his mind even as he shook his head. "No. It would be too easy to end up lost or in a dead end."

"Or on a mountaintop with a glorious view toward a place you never dreamed of."

"That sounds romantic in theory. In practice, it's risky."

"I suppose it can be. But you know what they say—no risk, no reward." His father examined the contents of his glass. "I'd wager Bren is a take-the-fork woman. What do you think?"

"I have no idea."

"My money also puts her in the glass-half-full camp."

Why did all roads in this conversation lead back to Bren?

"She could be." He opened the fridge again and extracted the box of leftover pizza. "You sold me on this for dinner. If it's half as tasty as you say, I may have to pay this place a visit while I'm here."

"You won't regret it." His father drained the glass, pulled his keys from his pocket, and jingled them. "I wonder what Bren and her guest are having for dinner?"

"Your guess is as good as mine."

"I bet Emma would enjoy a trip to Frank's for pizza."

"Maybe Bren will take her."

"Or you could take them both. Have a night out. Relax. Laugh."

Was his father kidding?

"I have work to do tonight, Dad."

"It will be there after dinner. And it would be a thoughtful gesture to buy them a meal. Show them both some support."

"In case I haven't made it clear, I don't support the half-baked idea of taking a stranger in, even if her record is clean." He set the pizza on a plate and put it in the microwave. "Good luck with your meeting. I'm sorry they bothered you on a Friday night."

"It's never a bother to practice the Golden Rule. Enjoy your dinner."

After setting the empty glass on the counter, his father disappeared into the laundry room. A minute later the door to the attached garage opened. Closed. A car engine turned over. The muffled rumble of the garage door signaled his departure.

Noah jabbed at the microwave buttons as peace descended in the house. Crossed to the window. Pushed aside the curtain.

Surely Dad hadn't expected him to follow through on his out-of-the-blue suggestion to invite the two women to join him for a pizza excursion. He barely knew Bren, and Emma was a total stranger.

Of course, if he *had* asked them, he could have used the

trip as an opportunity to dig for details about both of their backgrounds.

In all likelihood, however, he wouldn't have learned much. A one-time pizza outing wasn't sufficient to create the level of trust Bren claimed was required to elicit secrets or personal information.

Besides, who cared about their backgrounds? Their past, present, and future lives were no concern of his. His evening would be more profitably spent working on an analysis of the latest crisis situation at the office. The more productive he was while on vacation, the more brownie points he'd earn with his boss.

A ping from the microwave summoned him, and he grabbed his lukewarm soda from the counter. Removed his dinner. Set it on the table.

Who needed to go to Frank's when he had Frank's pizza right here?

One bite in, his father's assessment proved accurate. It was stellar pizza despite being left over. The fresh-from-the-oven version would be phenomenal.

A treat the two women in the cottage would no doubt have enjoyed after their stressful day.

But relieving their stress wasn't his responsibility. If Bren wanted to reach out to someone who was down on her luck, that was fine. He had no such obligation.

And after the weird reaction he'd had to her earlier at the back door, it would be safer to walk a wide circle around her during the remainder of his visit—especially with his matchmaker dad singing the praises of the woman with purple-hued hair every chance he got.

9

Gorgeous.

From her spot beside the lighthouse on Pelican Point, Bren smiled as the sun peeked over the hills behind her and gilded Sunrise Reef, transforming the stretched-out necklace of rocks that barely crested the cerulean surface into a shimmering gold chain worthy of a larger-than-life sea goddess.

And she had the show all to herself.

Or did she?

At a flash of movement in her peripheral vision, she looked over. Groaned.

Why hadn't Noah Ward slept late, like most people did on Saturday?

And what was he doing on Pelican Point Road again? Had this become his regular running route?

Unfortunately, that was a strong possibility. He came across as the type of guy who would establish a routine and follow it to the letter. No deviations allowed for a number-crunching, by-the-book, buttoned-up CPA.

Meaning she'd have to forgo her morning trips to Sunrise Reef until he left if she wanted to avoid the disconcerting feeling he stirred up in her whenever they were in close proximity.

On the plus side, his departure shouldn't be far off. From the occasional comments Fred had dropped about his son through the years, it sounded like he was a workaholic who'd be champing at the bit to get back to his office.

Noah lifted his gaze from the pavement. Came to an abrupt stop.

Though distance made it impossible to read his expression, his body language was clear.

He wasn't any more eager to initiate another encounter than she was.

Good.

Maybe he'd leave if she didn't encourage him to linger.

Forcing up the corners of her mouth, she lifted a hand in greeting, then swiveled back toward the reef.

A minute passed.

Two.

The tension in her shoulders began to dissipate.

She was safe. He'd taken the reprieve she'd given him and—

At the crunch of approaching footsteps on the gravel path behind her, the tension surged back.

Dang.

He hadn't left.

"Morning."

Since ignoring his greeting would be rude, she filled her lungs and slowly rotated to face him. "Good morning."

"Did you, uh, run here?" He flicked a glance at her well-broken-in everyday sport shoes.

"No. I drove." She waved toward the parking lot, tucked among the trees near the banquet center, where her Kia was the lone occupant.

"A reef-viewing visit?"

She frowned. "How did you know that?"

"Charley mentioned it. I ran into him up here on Thursday, after you and I passed on the road."

She transferred her weight from one foot to the other.

What else had Charley told him? When he'd stopped to offer her a ride, she'd been limping along like someone in the last stretch of a forced march.

Cheeks warming, she angled toward the burnished rocks. "I do like seeing the reef in the morning."

"Your guest didn't come with you?"

"I didn't want to wake her. She was dead to the world."

"At least you're not—and I mean that in a literal sense."

She swung back toward him. "Why would I be? Emma passed Lexie's background check with flying colors."

"There's a first time for everything. If she has money issues, as you seem to think, that could compel her to take desperate measures. I'd advise you to lock up any valuables."

Bren snickered. "If a heist is in her plans, she picked the wrong target. I'm not exactly rolling in jewelry or cash or electronics."

A few beats ticked by as he studied her, only the caw of a gull overhead breaking the silence.

"So what's the story on her car?" He removed his shades, giving her an up-close-and-personal view of eyes that were deeper blue than the water off the point today.

Her heart flip-flopped. Like it had during their two previous encounters.

Oh, for pity's sake. Noah wasn't even her type.

But he should be *somebody's* type.

So why wasn't he married?

Or was he? Did he have a wife or fiancée or significant other back in St. Louis who was missing him and counting the days until he—

"It wasn't a hard question." Noah cocked his head, expression quizzical.

Whoops.

Her cheeks heated up again as she tried to recall the thread of their conversation before she'd gotten sidetracked by irrelevant musings.

Oh yeah. Emma's car.

"Sorry. My mind wandered for a minute. Nothing from Marv yet. I'm hoping that's not a bad sign—for her sake."

He slipped his glasses back on. "Be careful she doesn't end up becoming the man who came to dinner."

Huh?

She peered at him. "What does that mean?"

"You know—the old Bette Davis movie."

"Bette Davis I've heard of. Not the movie."

"Sorry. I always assume everyone likes old movies as much as I do. It's a classic about a guy who comes for dinner, gets injured, and can't be moved. He wreaks havoc in the lives of everyone in the household."

"Emma isn't a havoc wreaker."

"Famous last words."

She folded her arms. "Look . . . if you're concerned about a certain barista, don't be. I don't let people take advantage of me. I'm also a decent judge of character. I can spot a phony a mile away. Emma's the real deal."

"What makes you an expert on phonies?"

"Experience." The response spilled out before she could stop it, etched with bitterness.

Of course Noah picked up on it.

"That doesn't sound like a happy story." His tone was mild, but his demeanor was somber.

She shifted her weight, waving off a persistent fly as she formulated her response. "Life isn't always happy. Everyone has encounters with unpleasant people. If we're smart, we learn from them. I bet you have a story or two of your own." Perhaps turning the tables on him would end this line of discussion.

Instead, her conjecture ended more than that.

Forehead creasing, Noah took a step back. "I should get going. I promised to help my dad this morning with a deck-repair project for a family that's down on its luck. Enjoy the view."

With that, he spun around and took off at a fast clip back down the path.

As the distance between them grew, Bren let her arms fall back to her sides.

Considering his abrupt departure, he apparently *did* have a story or two of his own. Ones he didn't want to share, any more than she wanted to spill her guts about her own background.

Fine by her. He had a right to keep his secrets.

That didn't mean she couldn't wonder why her comment had spooked him, however.

Whatever the reason, though, at least the perturbing fizz of electricity that sparked in the air whenever he was around was evaporating as fast as a Hope Harbor mist.

Now she could enjoy the reef in peace.

But when she turned back toward the sea, the gold had faded from the rocks. To make matters worse, the sun dipped behind a cloud and a shadow fell over the landscape, robbing the scene of its sparkle and life.

Kind of how the day felt now that Noah was gone.

She huffed out a breath.

How annoying was that?

Yet denying reality was senseless.

The truth was, Noah had gotten under her skin. Even though he was on the stuffy side, he also appeared to be a decent guy. Someone you could count on in a pinch, who knew how to get a job done and would always do the right thing in the end. Maybe with a dash of foot-dragging, in Emma's case, but caution wasn't always bad.

Especially in terms of men.

Noah included.

So rather than waste brainpower dissecting his character, she ought to focus on more pressing matters.

Like talking to Emma to see if she'd heard from Marv—and helping her figure out next steps if she didn't have the funds to cover whatever repairs were necessary.

"You mean you stayed in a stranger's house last night?"

As her brother's pitch rose, Emma eased the cell away from her ear and wandered toward the kitchen in the cottage to refill her coffee. "It's okay, Justin. She's very nice, and she offered to put me in touch with her pastor as a reference."

"Did you talk to him?"

"No. I got positive vibes from her, and this is a tiny town. Everybody knows everybody. She works in the coffee shop. Don't worry. It was the best solution, with my car out of commission."

"I don't like it."

"It's only temporary. I could be out of here by this afternoon."

"What if you're not? What if your car's dead?"

Her fingers tightened on the cell. "It's not dead." Or she hoped it wasn't, anyway. "Bren said I could stay until it's fixed."

"What if the repairs are expensive?"

"I have money."

"Not that much."

"Enough to fix the car."

"What if you don't have anything left for eating and sleeping?"

She tried to quash the flutter of panic in the pit of her stomach. "I'll be fine. I have to land somewhere soon, and I like this town. I might see if there are any jobs here."

"Doing what?"

"The local café may have an opening on their waitstaff."

"Oh, Em." Justin's dismay came through loud and clear across the miles. "You always wanted more than that. I remember how you used to talk about owning your own business someday."

Yeah, she had. But that was a distant dream now. Getting guardianship for Justin was her top priority.

"That could happen at some point. At the moment, I . . . oops." Her pulse picked up. "Call coming in from the garage. I'll touch base with you again tomorrow. Love you." She cut Justin off and greeted Marv.

"I came in early today to give your car a going-over, Ms. Blair. It didn't take long to find the problem. Your starter's bad."

She slid onto the stool at the counter that separated the kitchen from the living room. Braced. "How much will that set me back?"

"Somewhere in the neighborhood of $500."

Bad . . . but it could be worse. There would still be a small amount of cushion in her nest egg.

"How soon can you have it finished?"

"I'll have to source the part first. Equipment for older cars is harder to find. If I can locate what I need fast and get it here quick, I could have the starter job done by early next week. But I found other problems too. Did you notice the white smoke coming from the exhaust?"

Her stomach knotted. "No."

"Has she been idling rough?"

"Sometimes."

"That's what I figured. You've also got a bad head gasket."

As he proceeded to explain the situation in gory detail, then moved on to issues he'd found with the brakes and struts, she closed her eyes. Squeezed the bridge of her nose.

This was getting worse by the minute.

And when he gave her the estimate to remedy all the defects, she almost lost the bagel she'd eaten for breakfast.

"I'm sorry to be the bearer of bad news. I know that's a chunk of change."

No kidding.

"Yeah. Way more than I expected."

"I'll do everything I can to keep costs as low as possible, but there's a fair amount of labor involved."

She swallowed.

If she made all the repairs he'd outlined, not only would her cushion be gone, her bank account would be on fumes.

"I, uh, need to think about this."

"I understand. It's a sizeable amount to put into an older car with high mileage. I'm not trying to lose myself a job, but would you want to think about trading her in for another vehicle instead of sinking a lot of money into repairs?"

Yes, she would. But with the price of used cars and her limited financial resources, that wasn't a realistic alternative.

"No. I want to keep this one." She moistened her lips. "If you only fix the starter, would it be drivable?"

"For a while—but I wouldn't recommend it. The gasket's about to blow, and suspension problems can escalate, leading to bigger and more expensive issues down the road. The bad brakes are also a safety hazard."

She couldn't argue with anything he'd said.

"I'll tell you what. Why don't you plan to fix the starter, and I'll think about everything else over the weekend?"

"That'll work. Let me know once you make a decision."

"I will. Thanks."

After ending the call, Emma set the phone on the counter and wove her shaky fingers together. Squeezed until her knuckles whitened. Tried to quash her panic and get her muddled brain in gear.

She had to think through her options, what few there were, and talk to Bren. The other woman may have said she was welcome to stay longer if necessary, but surely Bren would get tired of the inconvenience of someone sleeping in her living room and sharing her bathroom.

Emma choked back a sob.

She ought to leave rather than take advantage of Bren's hospitality.

But short of a homeless shelter or park bench, where else could she sleep until she found a place to live? And she wouldn't be able to find a place to live until she had a job. No one would rent to her unless she had steady employment.

So priority number one was getting a job.

Expelling a shaky breath, she slid off the stool. Rubbed her damp palms down her jeans. Tried to psych herself up for the challenge ahead.

Maybe fate would be kind. Maybe, by the time she shared the bad news about her car with Bren, she'd also have a job in hand and a definite departure date to pass on so the woman who'd befriended her wouldn't have to worry that she'd inherited a permanent moocher.

If she didn't?

She'd have to put this in God's hands and hope for the best.

10

His dad was going to fall—and there wasn't a thing he could do to save him.

Heart slamming against his rib cage, Noah froze midstrike with his hammer. Sucked in a breath as his father tottered, arms flailing, on the edge of the deck that had lost its railing. Fought for air as Dad pitched over the side, out of sight.

As a word he never said strobed through his mind, he dropped his hammer, zoomed around the sawhorses that had been set up on the back lawn, and sprinted toward the deck.

The guy who'd been working beside Dad lowered himself from the four-foot-tall deck and disappeared too, while the other six volunteers converged from all directions.

As Noah flew around the deck and came to a halt, his knees went weak with relief.

Dad wasn't lying on the ground, unconscious. Instead, he was sitting up and alert. But he was cradling his right arm.

Noah dropped down beside the two men. "Did you hit your head, Dad? Are you dizzy?"

"No." His father's lips contorted into a rueful twist. "But I think I did a number on my wrist. Guess I shouldn't have tried to break my fall by stretching out my arm."

"Where's the closest hospital?"

"I don't need a hospital. The urgent care center will do."

"I'd rather take you to a hospital."

"Not necessary. Our urgent care is first-class."

"That's true." The guy next to him spoke, and Noah looked over. The police chief's husband, unless he'd mixed up the multiple introductions that had been offered upon their arrival. "The doc there worked in emergency medicine in San Francisco before he took over the center. We all go there for anything that's not life-threatening."

But what if this *was* life-threatening? What if his father had hit his head, despite his claims to the contrary?

"Help me up, Noah. We're delaying work on the deck." His father aimed a strained smile at the concerned faces gathered around them. "I'll be fine, folks. Don't let this minor incident distract you from the job we came here to do."

"I'll give you a hand." The police chief's husband—Adam?—stood, leaving Noah no choice but to follow his lead.

Between the two of them, they got his father on his feet. Adam stayed with them, flanking Dad on the other side, until they reached the car.

After assisting his father into the passenger seat, Noah closed the door and turned to the other man. "Thanks for your help."

"No problem. You could return the favor by texting me after the doc weighs in. Everyone will be wondering about Fred, and I can pass the news along."

"I'd be happy to. What's your number?" Noah pulled out his cell and tapped in the digits as the man recited them.

"Good luck at urgent care." Adam bent down to give Dad a farewell wave, then walked back to the house and disappeared around the side.

Once Noah slid behind the wheel and started the engine, he glanced toward the passenger seat.

His father's complexion had taken on a gray tinge, and the

brackets etched at the corners of his mouth suggested he was in significant pain.

Stomach clenching, Noah put the car in gear. "Can you direct me, or should I call up navigation on my phone?"

"I'll direct you. It's only five minutes away."

Noah made it in four, ignoring stop signs unless other cars were in sight despite his dad's protest that an injured wrist wasn't an emergency worth the risk of a ticket.

"Sit tight until I come around." He swung into a parking place at the center and set the brake.

"I'm not an invalid."

"Humor me, okay?"

His father gave a disgruntled sigh but complied—sort of. He remained seated but opened the door, released the seat belt, and swung his legs to the pavement while Noah circled the car. He did, however, deign to take the offered arm once it came time to stand.

"If I had to fall and injure a wrist, why did it have to be the right one?" His father made no attempt to hide his annoyance as he heaved himself to his feet.

"I'm more worried about other possible injuries. Come on." Keeping a firm grip on his arm, Noah urged him toward the door of the center.

"I don't have any other injuries."

"No offense, but I'd rather hear that from the doctor."

"Suit yourself. But I've lived in this body for seventy-five years, and I know it inside and out. Nothing's hurt but my arm."

Noah didn't argue—but he wasn't going to rest easy until he heard that verdict from the doctor.

Once inside the building, he filled out the required paperwork for his dad, then cooled his heels in the waiting area after a nurse took his father to an examining room.

As the minutes turtled by, he picked up a magazine. Set it back down. Rose and began to pace.

Hopefully his dad's injuries were confined to his wrist, as he claimed. After the heart scare, neither of them needed any more worrisome health issues to rear their ugly heads. Wrist damage, while inconvenient, would heal.

But with Mom gone, how was his father supposed to cope with a hand that wouldn't be of much use until his wrist was back in action? And if it was broken, that could take weeks.

Noah forked his fingers through his hair.

If he'd wanted an argument to bolster his case for a move back to St. Louis, this was it.

Yet it didn't solve the more immediate challenge of finding short-term help for Dad with day-to-day living if the wrist was going to be out of commission for a while.

Could he hire a home health care company to provide support during the day? Who would handle meal preparation? How would Dad get to doctor appointments and therapy? Who, besides paid help, would keep an eye on his general well-being once he was alone at the house?

As questions swirled through his mind, Noah's panic ratcheted up.

For a trip that was supposed to be at least partly a chance to chill out, this visit had been a total bust.

By the time a nurse summoned him to confer with the doctor, he was as tense as he'd been last month running interference for a client with an obnoxious guy from the IRS.

A tall, sandy-haired man in a white coat rose from a workstation in the corner as he entered the examining room. "You must be Noah."

"Guilty." He returned the man's solid grip.

"Logan West. Nice to meet you." The doctor motioned to the extra chair in the room. "Have a seat."

As Noah took it, he inspected his father, who sat in the chair adjacent to the workstation.

His color had improved, and the lines of strain in his face had eased—but the sling, and the cast on his arm, didn't bode well.

"What's the verdict?" He braced.

"Your father has a break in the distal radius." The doctor swiveled toward the computer screen on the desk and pointed to an X-ray. "It's a very common fracture. The good news is that it's extra-articular. That means it doesn't extend into the joint, which makes it simpler to treat. No surgery required." He rotated back. "The cast will stay on about six weeks, and we'll x-ray it again during the healing process to ensure everything's aligned. Once the cast is off, physical therapy will help restore function and motion. It's not a difficult injury to treat."

Noah rested his elbows on the arms of his chair and twined his fingers together. "Will he be able to use his hand while he's healing?"

"Not much. Aside from being painful, especially at the beginning, too much use can be detrimental to recovery. Wiggling fingers is encouraged, carrying things isn't."

This break was going to complicate Dad's life. Big-time.

His too.

"Were there any other injuries?"

"None that I saw in the exam I gave your dad."

"What about his head?"

"Noah." His dad scowled at him. "I told you I didn't hit my head."

"He told me that too." The doctor stepped in. "But just to be safe, I ran him through a head injury assessment protocol. He passed with flying colors."

"See?" His father arched an eyebrow at him.

"I'm glad to hear that. So how do we take care of this at home?"

"We'll send instructions with you. Ice or a cold pack on the wrist for a few days would be helpful, and propping the wrist on a pillow while sitting or lying down to keep it above the heart will reduce swelling. Over-the-counter pain medication should keep the discomfort under control."

"Should he see an orthopedic specialist?" Maybe the man across from him would be insulted by a query that could be construed as questioning his competence, but Dad's well-being came first.

If the doctor took offense at the question, he gave no indication of it. He leaned back, manner relaxed, tone conversational. "For a break like this, it shouldn't be necessary. But I always encourage patients to do what makes them most comfortable."

"I'm comfortable with your care, Logan." Dad spoke up again. "You have impressive creds and a solid track record. I haven't told this to Noah, but you're the one who suspected I had a heart issue and got me into a specialist in Coos Bay straightaway."

The doctor smiled. "I just knew to ask the right questions."

"You also have superb instincts." His dad gave the man a thumbs-up. "You ready to go, Noah?"

"Yes." He stood, but before he could extend an arm to his dad, the doctor took care of that chore.

"Thanks for the assist. And thanks for providing all of us here with first-class medical care." Dad directed that remark to the physician, then aimed a reproving glance across the room.

Brow furrowing, Noah turned to open the door.

The doctor may not have taken offense at the question that could have implied a lack of confidence in his abilities, but clearly his dad had.

Did he owe the man an apology?

"Don't do anything strenuous this afternoon, Fred." The doctor handed his father off to him.

"I won't."

Noah took his dad's arm. "When I asked about a specialist, I, uh, didn't mean to suggest that your skills weren't sufficient for this task, Doctor."

The man hitched up one side of his mouth. "No worries. This is a small town, and small towns can have difficulty attracting top talent in any field. I understand your concern. But the vibe here happens to suit me to a T. And it's Logan to the locals. We're all friends and neighbors in Hope Harbor. Call if you have any concerns. My cell number will be on the instructions waiting for you at the front desk."

A doctor who gave patients his cell number?

Where in twenty-first-century America did that happen?

Noah stayed close beside his dad as they walked down the hall, and after picking up the instructions at the desk, he settled him in the car.

Once behind the wheel, he pulled out his phone. "I promised to let Adam know the outcome."

"I sure did hate to cast a pall over the deck job today."

"No one's the worse for wear except you." After texting Adam a quick summary of the diagnosis, Noah put the car in gear.

"I'll heal. Logan took great care of me. We're blessed to have a doc of his caliber here."

"What's his story, anyway? Going from a San Francisco ER to Hope Harbor would be a seismic career shift." He pulled out of the parking lot and aimed the car toward his dad's house.

"He got guardianship of his niece after his brother was killed in the Middle East, and he didn't want to raise her in a big-city, high-rise apartment. During his search for a more family-friendly place, he found us." His father cradled his injured arm as they turned a corner. "Funny how he came here for her but ended up benefiting from the move himself."

"How so?"

"He met the love of his life. They've been married about three or four years now." As his father looked over at him, Noah caught the glance in his peripheral vision. "Isn't it interesting how life can bring us blessings when we least expect them, and sometimes in the most surprising places?"

Noah's phone vibrated in his pocket, but he ignored it. "I suppose."

"You never know where romance may lurk."

He ignored that too. "After all the excitement this morning, you should take a nap as soon as we get home."

"You're reading my mind."

The car fell silent after that, and Noah didn't attempt to prolong the conversation. If he did, his dad might return to the subject of romance—and what was the point in discussing that, when his goal for this trip was straightforward?

Namely, convince his dad to move, using today's incident as rationale.

And there was no room for romance in that agenda.

11

· ·

A job at the Myrtle Café wasn't in her future.

Shoulders slumping, Emma let the door of the eatery close behind her and slowly trudged up Main Street.

Kind and empathetic as the manager had been, if there were no openings, there were no openings.

And the Myrtle was the only restaurant in town.

After passing the coffee shop where Bren had come to her rescue, Emma paused at the tempting array of truffles in the window of the adjacent business. Inhaled the intoxicating scent that wafted out the door of Chocolate Harbor behind a departing customer. Battled the temptation to go inside and indulge in a decadent treat.

But her budget had no room for such luxuries.

She kept walking.

At the corner, she hung a right and walked until the road dead-ended at Dockside Drive, stopping to take in the scene that had soothed her yesterday.

Boats bobbed in the gentle swells of the marina that was protected by a long jetty on the left and a pair of rocky islands on the right. Overflowing planters filled with vibrant flowers were spaced along the sidewalk above the sloping pile of boulders that led down to the water. Inviting benches offered a view of the harbor, and the horizon beckoned. On the other side of the street, charming storefronts faced the sea, adorned with awnings and brimming flower boxes.

And at the end of the wide, two-block-long street that dead-ended at a river, the food trailer Bren had told her was home to Charley's tacos was parked beside a pocket park with a white gazebo.

It was picture-perfect.

Too bad she couldn't say the same about her life.

As that depressing thought settled over her like a dark, sun-snuffing cloud, Emma gritted her teeth. Straightened her posture.

An attitude adjustment was in order.

The Myrtle might not be hiring, but that didn't mean there weren't other jobs in town. She'd just have to expand her horizons. Maybe the Gull Motel had an opening for a housecleaner. Or perhaps the inn she'd seen a sign for as she drove into town could use another pair of hands. There might be a shop in town that needed a clerk.

All wasn't yet lost.

She trekked down the street, reading the signs as she went.

A law firm, a newspaper office, and a bait and tackle shop were in the mix, but none of the businesses sounded promising for someone with her limited skill set and experience.

At the corner, she stopped as the heavenly aroma from the taco stand across the street tickled her nose and set off a growl in her stomach.

She studied it from a distance, lower lip caught between her teeth.

It would be a thoughtful gesture to provide lunch for Bren today, after all the woman had done for her. A restaurant meal was out of the question, but how much could two orders of tacos set her back? And Bren wouldn't have to feed her tonight if they had a hearty lunch. The way she'd hunkered down over that pile of wedding invitations as soon as she'd gotten back from her run this morning suggested she'd be hard at it most of the day.

Another whiff of the savory aroma swirled by, and her salivary glands vaulted into overdrive.

Decision made.

Emma crossed the street and strode toward the stand.

As she approached, the customers at the serving window took their order from the guy with a long gray ponytail who was inside, then ambled down the waterfront.

"Good afternoon. Or should I say morning?" The taco man flashed her a welcoming smile, the weathered skin beside his eyes crinkling. "Sometimes the two blend together when you don't wear a watch."

"It's afternoon. Barely."

"An ideal time for tacos. One order?"

"Um . . ." She gave the area around the window a discreet perusal, but there didn't seem to be a menu—or prices—displayed. "Are there, uh, different size orders?"

"No. One size fits all at Charley's. The fish of the day is sturgeon, and there are three tacos per order."

"Do you, um, take credit cards? I don't carry much cash."

"No. There's too much plastic in the world as it is." He pointed to a Cash Only sign tucked into the far corner of the window.

She'd have to ask outright about the price.

"How much is an order?"

"That depends."

She gave him a wary look. "On what?"

"On whether you're Emma."

Her suspicion meter spiked, a tingle of unease zipping up her spine. How could this man know her name? "Uh . . ."

His smile broadened. "I ran into Bren this morning. She told me she had a houseguest who was dealing with a car problem. You fit the description she gave me."

Oh.

Her pulse slowed, and she exhaled. "Yes. I'm Emma."

"In that case, your order is on the house."

What?

"Why would you give me free tacos?"

"First order for newcomers is always complimentary. It's my way of saying welcome to Hope Harbor."

"But I don't live here. I mean, I'm looking for a job, but so far that hasn't worked out. I was hoping the Myrtle would have an opening, but they don't."

He began pulling fish fillets out of the cooler beside him. "Did you want more than one order?"

"Yes." If hers was free, she could definitely treat Bren. "Two. I'm taking lunch home for Bren."

"She'll like that." He set several fillets on the grill and began chopping an avocado. "There may be other job options in town. We have quite a few businesses here."

"All I have is a high school diploma, though."

"Not every job requires higher formal education. Sometimes experience makes up for a lack of academic credentials." He reached for a jar on the shelf by the grill and sprinkled the fillets with whatever was inside.

"I don't have much experience, either. My only job was with my stepfather's grocery chain."

"There's a market up near 101. They may need some help." He set half a dozen corn tortillas on the grill and flipped the fish. "There's a gift shop and a bookstore and a florist in town too . . . and lots of other places to try."

"I guess I'll wander through street by street." What else did she have to do while she waited for her car to be repaired? Worst case, she'd try Coos Bay up the coast once she had her wheels back. There would probably be more possibilities in a bigger town. And she could always sleep in her car again if necessary until she had enough money saved to rent a small apartment. There were rest stops scattered along 101 where overnight parking was allowed.

Charley chopped up a handful of red onions and tossed them onto the griddle next to the grill. "Can't hurt. And I have a feeling it will pay off."

"I hope so." She pulled out her wallet as he began assembling the tacos.

"Have you visited Sweet Dreams Bakery yet?"

"No." If there was a bakery in town, perhaps they were hiring. "Where is it?"

He motioned across the street. "You're almost there. They're famous in these parts for their cinnamon rolls, but if you want to pick up dessert to go with the tacos, Bren is partial to their brownies."

Shading her eyes, she shifted sideways to examine the shop. If she'd walked to Charley's on that side of the street, she would have passed by the small storefront.

Very small.

What were the odds they'd be hiring?

"Do many people work there?"

"No." Charley began wrapping the tacos in white butcher paper. "It's a mom-and-pop operation. Alice handles the front of the store and Joe does all the baking. On the rare occasion Alice is out, she finds someone to fill in behind the case. But she and Joe shut down when they go on vacation. Two weeks every year, in October, to visit their daughter and her family in Idaho. Like clockwork."

The odds they were hiring dropped from slim to minuscule.

But she could spring for a brownie if Bren liked them.

"I'll stop in before I go back to the cottage."

"You won't regret it." He slid the last taco into a brown bag and set it on the counter.

"How much do I owe you?"

"Reduced rate today. I was getting ready to close down and go to my studio, so I'm glad I was able to use the last of my sturgeon. Otherwise, it would have gone to waste."

The price he quoted seemed super low, but why question her good fortune?

She pulled out a bill and passed it over the counter. "I can't wait to try these. Bren says they're amazing."

"What a wonderful compliment." He flashed her a smile. "Please thank her for me."

"I will. And now it's off to Sweet Dreams for me."

"Indeed." After giving her a wave, he began rolling down the cover on the serving window.

She picked up the bag and started toward the bakery.

The closer she got, the more certain she was that a job query there would be a dead end. The shop was super small, the awning had faded, and the lettering in the front window needed sprucing up.

It didn't look like the kind of place that had the budget for extra help.

One step inside confirmed that conclusion.

The bakery counter and display case were on the left, and there was room for no more than a double row of customers on the right. A couple of ice cream chairs and a tiny table were squeezed into the back corner. The walls were painted a dull beige, and the offerings in the case were limited. Nothing like the elaborate treats she'd dealt with in the upscale bakery for her stepfather's small chain of high-end markets.

"Afternoon." A woman with a cheery demeanor came out of the back room. "Welcome to Sweet Dreams. What can I get for you?"

Emma pointed to the display of generously sized brownies that was front and center. "One of those, please."

"Smart choice. They're our second-best seller, next to the cinnamon rolls. But those are gone for the day, as usual." She took a brownie from the tray with a square of white bakery paper and slid it into a bag. "Anything else?"

"Not from the case, but I was wondering . . ." Emma swallowed.

"Are you by chance in need of any help in the store? I'm looking for a job."

"I wish." The woman rolled her eyes as she rang up the purchase. "Much as I'd like to have more free time, we've always run a lean ship here. Helps keep us in the black."

"I understand." Emma paid for the purchase. "I don't suppose there are any other bakeries around, are there?"

"No, but there are a couple up in Bandon. Have you had experience in a bakery?"

"Yes. I worked in one for four years at an upscale grocery store, helping the baker. He trained in France, and he taught me a lot."

"France." The woman's eyebrows rose. "That's impressive. Do you know how to make French pastries?"

"Yes. He did most of the baking, but I filled in for him while he was on vacation this spring."

"I told Joe years ago that we should upgrade, add a few fancier items to our case, but he was content with the tried and true. Not that he was qualified to make French pastries, of course. The closest we ever got to France was Paris, Missouri, years ago, to visit an aunt." She chuckled, then grew more serious. "But I wish we could tap into your skills. You might add some pizazz to our humble little shop."

Emma forced up the corners of her mouth. "It sounds like you're doing fine the way you are. I hear your cinnamon rolls are legendary."

"To tell you the truth, those and the brownies are what keep us in business. People are crazy about them. I suggested to Joe last year that maybe we should concentrate on those two items, but he said that would be too boring. And since he's the baker, he calls the shots in the back room. We did cut back a bit on the variety, though." The woman stuck out her hand. "I'm Alice, by the way."

Emma took her fingers and introduced herself.

"You new in town, honey?"

"Yes. My car broke down here. I only intended to stay as long as it took to fix it, but I like the town."

"Couldn't find a nicer place to live." Alice tipped her head. "You're the one Bren took in, aren't you?"

Good grief.

Did everyone in this town know everybody else's business?

"Yes."

"Fine young woman. You were lucky to cross paths with her."

"Trust me, I know." She picked up the bag. "Thanks for the brownie."

"You're welcome. And for the record, if we had the budget, I'd hire you in a heartbeat."

"I appreciate that. Enjoy the rest of your day."

She retraced her steps to the door and pushed through but came to a halt when a raindrop plopped onto her nose.

A quick scan of the sky revealed dark clouds surging in, blotting out the blue that had dominated the expanse earlier.

The weather here was as mercurial as Nebraska's winter storms, when snow could change to ice in the blink of an eye—and vice versa.

But water was much easier to deal with than either of those.

As she headed toward Bren's cottage, the rain intensifying with each step, Emma picked up her pace.

She'd share her job-search strikeouts with her hostess over lunch to make it clear she was actively seeking employment, then hit the streets again this afternoon. Someone in this town must need help with *something*.

And until she turned over every stone and knocked on the door of every business that offered a reasonable potential for employment, she wasn't giving up.

Because the notion of staying in this town that had welcomed her with coffee, lodging, tacos, and kindness was becoming more appealing with every hour that passed.

12

....

"Reverend Baker, you remember my son, Noah, don't you?"

As his father greeted the pastor of Grace Christian church after the Sunday service, Noah tried to focus on the minister.

It wasn't easy.

How was he supposed to concentrate when Bren was in the background, her expression animated as she chatted with an older woman who had a hot-pink swath in her salt-and-pepper hair and was wearing a multicolored tunic over lime-green pants?

He gave his father's cottage dweller a slow perusal.

Next to her companion's attire, Bren's tapered black slacks and fluffy purple sweater with yellow flecks were downright demure—and flattering. The slight purple cast to her hair even seemed sedate.

"Of course I remember him. Hello, Noah. Welcome back to Hope Harbor." The minister smiled and extended his hand.

Noah shifted away from Bren. If he couldn't block her musical laughter, he could at least erase her from view. "Thank you." He returned the man's firm clasp.

"It was a surprise visit." His father adjusted the sling on his arm, wincing slightly.

Noah frowned.

Dad ought to be home resting after the uncomfortable night he'd admitted having, as evidenced by the dark smudges in the hollows beneath his lower lashes. But missing Sunday services had always been anathema to him.

"Wonderful." Reverend Baker acknowledged the wave of a passing congregant. "How long can you stay?"

"I took two weeks of vacation." And at this point, his hopes of an early departure were diminishing by the day.

"Splendid. That should give you a chance to relax. As refreshing as long weekends or short vacations can be, I don't believe most people get into the leisure mindset for several days after they've left work behind. It takes a while to unwind."

"Then Noah may need a month. He hasn't left work behind yet." His father sent him a chiding look.

"It's harder these days to get away, Dad."

"Sad but true." The pastor gave a rueful nod. "Modern technology and our wired world can make it difficult to untether from work. I do hope you have an opportunity while you're here to—"

The front door opened, and a man in a clerical collar hustled in with Emma in tow and made a beeline for the minister. "Morning, Paul."

"You're late for doughnuts." The minister consulted his watch. "The social hour started ten minutes ago."

"I didn't come for doughnuts."

"You always come for doughnuts between Masses when it's not doughnut Sunday at St. Francis."

"No, I don't. Sometimes I snitch your Danish instead." He gave the minister an elbow nudge, his merry eyes twinkling. "But I'm not here for either today. I'm playing chauffeur to Emma." He drew the young woman forward. "She came to the early Mass. I found her in the meditation garden afterward, and we had a lovely chat. Emma's staying with Bren." He scanned the room, spotted the barista, and lifted a hand in greeting. "Bren was kind enough to take her in while her car is being repaired."

"That sounds like Bren." The minister introduced himself to the young woman. "Welcome, my dear. If you get tired of the good father's long-winded homilies, Grace Christian is at your service."

"Trying to poach my parishioners again, I see. A definite breach of ecclesiastical etiquette." The padre waved a finger back and forth in front of the minister's face.

Emma looked between them as if she didn't know what to make of their exchange.

Noah could relate.

But it was a hoot.

The minister shooed away the priest's hand and changed the subject. "I assume you heard about Fred's accident."

"I did." The man's demeanor grew more serious. "I'm sorry about your injury, Fred. No one doing a good deed should get hurt in the line of duty. Makes you wonder what God was thinking, doesn't it?"

"No." Reverend Baker folded his arms. "Trying to read the Almighty's mind is an exercise in futility. 'As the heavens are higher than the earth—'"

The priest held up his hand. "'So are my ways higher than your ways and my thoughts than your thoughts.' I'm familiar with that verse from Isaiah."

"You knew the source." The minister clapped a hand to his chest in mock amazement. "Praise the Lord."

"I won't dignify that comment with a reply." The padre sniffed. "However, Fred's accident still seems unfair."

"It could have been worse. Noah, meet Father Kevin Murphy." His father motioned toward the priest with his functional arm.

As greetings were exchanged, Bren joined them. "Good morning, everyone."

"Ah, Bren." Father Murphy beamed at her. "Emma told me you've been playing good Samaritan. God bless you."

A faint hint of pink bloomed on her cheeks. "I was happy to

help. Thank you for bringing Emma to me, but I would have picked her up at St. Francis when she was ready to leave."

"I was happy to drive her over. It gave me an excuse to keep tabs on the competition."

"And help himself to our doughnuts." The minister sent him a withering look, but the subtle twitch in his lips took the sting out of the comment.

"That too." The padre winked at them. "Emma, Bren, may I escort you to the fellowship hall?"

"That would be nice. Thank you." Bren adjusted the strap of her purse on her shoulder.

"Noah and I will join you too." His father turned to him. "Unless you want to skip the social gathering."

"Are you sure you're up to mingling, Dad?"

"I can manage to say hello to my friends and have a doughnut."

Noah hesitated, but only for a moment. Anxious as he was to have the delayed heart-to-heart talk with his father about moving, they did have all day for that. And Dad and Mom had always enjoyed the get-togethers after Sunday services.

"In that case, let's stay for ten or fifteen minutes."

They all headed across the vestibule, his dad beside him until a Helping Hands board member waylaid him. With Father Murphy and Emma engaged in what appeared to be a serious discussion, Bren fell back to give them privacy.

That put him side by side with the barista.

Several awkward beats passed as he searched for a topic to throw out.

"Did your, uh, houseguest get her car problem sorted out?" Noah motioned to the duo ahead of them.

"The problems—plural—have been diagnosed. The repairs will take a few days."

"Does that mean she's staying on at the cottage?"

"For a while." Bren lowered her volume. "She's also trying to find a job in town."

Noah stopped. Faced her. "She's staying in Hope Harbor?"

"If the stars align." Bren halted too. "She likes the vibe here. Who wouldn't?"

"Liking the vibe isn't a sufficient reason to put down roots."

"Why not?"

"Because there are other factors to consider when choosing a place to live."

"Such as?"

"Opportunities for gainful employment and career advancement. Cost of living. Access to goods and services. Crime rate statistics. Commuting distance."

"Hope Harbor ticks all those boxes, unless you're intent on climbing the corporate ladder. I don't think that's Emma's priority."

Checkmate.

"Fine. I'll concede that Hope Harbor may be a fit for her—if she can find a job. What is she qualified to do to earn a living?"

"Apparently she's quite a talented baker. She worked in a bakery in Nebraska."

He frowned. "Cupcakes don't pay the bills. Unless there's a bakery in town that wants to hire her?"

"There isn't. She tried that." Bren glanced at the younger woman, who was giving Father Murphy her rapt attention. "I got the feeling the repairs will deplete her savings. I think she may be planning to pay the bill by credit card to buy herself a couple of months to refill the coffers."

"Credit card interest can eat you alive."

"I know."

He squinted at her. Surely this wasn't leading where he thought it was. "You're not thinking about loaning her the money, are you?"

She fidgeted with the strap of her purse. "Maybe."

Bingo.

"Seriously?" He stared at her. "She could be a bad credit risk.

Unless you have a legal document to fall back on, she could skip town and leave you holding the bag."

"She won't."

"Intuition again?"

Her features hardened. "Don't knock it. It's saved my butt more than once."

"From what?"

The question spilled out before he could stop it, and her sudden inhale suggested she was as surprised by it as he was.

But instead of backing off or apologizing for being nosy, he waited. Despite what he'd told his dad, he *was* curious about her background.

"A few . . . sticky . . . situations that could have gone south."

"As a child or an adult?"

Her knuckles whitened on the strap of her purse. "Both."

A faint alarm bell began to ring in the back of his mind. Everyone ran into sticky situations as an adult. Childhood was a different story.

"Bad childhood experiences can have a long-lasting impact." He kept his tone mild, despite the sudden tension in his shoulders.

"That's true." A flicker of pain echoed deep in her eyes, so subtle only someone focused on them would pick it up. "Let's just say I didn't have a dad like Fred. And Mom had other priorities."

A mom with priorities that didn't include her daughter?

A sudden, strong urge to reach out and take Bren's hand blindsided him, and Noah sucked in air. Shoved his fingers into his pockets before he did something inappropriate. "I'm sorry."

"I survived." She offered a stiff shrug.

"Sorry to interrupt, but could I steal you for a minute, Bren?" The woman with the hot-pink streak in her hair joined them, a faint hint of jasmine swirling in the air around her as she bustled over. "Bev Price, owner of Bev's Book Nook on Main Street." She stuck out her hand.

Noah introduced himself as she gave his fingers a hearty squeeze.

"Oh, Fred's son." Her smile broadened. "Nice to meet you. Your father's a wonderful man. One of my regular customers. Do you like to read too?"

"I don't have much time to read for pleasure."

"What a pity. Books are like a magic carpet that can take you anywhere you want to go without ever leaving your armchair. Stop by the store while you're in town. We may be able to find a book that will tempt you to indulge. If not, you can help yourself to the cookie of the day. Your dad's favorite is chocolate chip oatmeal."

"Thanks. I may do that."

"I'll see you around, Noah." Bren turned on her heel and escaped with the other woman, weaving through the crowd that remained in the vestibule. As if she couldn't get away fast enough.

Once the distance between him and the two women increased, Noah took a deep breath.

That had been an unsettling encounter.

No, a stronger adjective was in order. Like disturbing. Unnerving. Alarming, even.

Because he'd come close to touching Bren. Too close. And that would have been a huge mistake, despite the strong—and surprising—protective instinct she'd activated in him. Whatever had happened to her in the past was over. She didn't need his support.

And he didn't need to send signals to yet another woman that could be grossly misinterpreted, either.

Suppressing a shudder, he swiveled away from the two women and homed in on his father.

When their gazes connected, Dad raised a finger to signal he'd be another minute.

After acknowledging the message with a dip of his head, Noah slowly wandered toward the fellowship hall.

But doughnuts weren't front and center in his mind.

That spot belonged to Bren.

And hard as he tried to stem the cavalcade of questions looping through his brain, they refused to be silenced.

If Bren's father hadn't been like Dad, what *had* he been like? What priority would her mother have put above her daughter? And assuming Bren's upbringing had been difficult, could she have left home young too, like Emma appeared to have done? If so, how had she survived? Had someone stepped in and helped her, as she was helping the young woman whose car trouble had caused their paths to intersect, or had she been on her own?

So many unknowns.

Yet as he entered the fellowship hall and wandered over to the coffee dispenser, one thing was clear.

Unless *his* instincts were off, the woman who'd taken up residence in his father's cottage was a survivor. Whatever setbacks and difficulties had befallen her, she'd overcome them. The life she'd created here in Hope Harbor might not be his cup of tea—or coffee—but based on her comment once that she'd lived in quite a few places before settling here, she appeared to have found her niche in this town. And she'd built a life here that suited her.

There was much to admire in that.

Perhaps more than in the success of a man who'd mapped out his life early on and followed the course he'd set with nothing but minor glitches along the way.

Brain churning, Noah took a disposable cup from the stack on the table and stuck it under the spigot of the coffee dispenser. Pressed the lever. Stifled a yelp and jerked back when the hot java gushed out, spattering the side of his hand.

"Sorry about that, young man." A gray-haired woman hurried over, exuding dismay. "Everyone in the congregation knows about this temperamental machine, but we should post a warning sign for visitors. Are you all right?"

"Yes." Even if his skin was smarting.

"Just ease the lever on slow and careful. That'll keep you from getting burned."

"Thanks."

He followed her instructions to the letter after she moved on.

And maybe there was a lesson in that directive for his personal life too. If he continued to ask questions about Bren's background and her story started gushing out, it was possible his admiration for her would not only grow but morph into something more.

Something dangerous.

Like . . . affection.

Which would be bad.

Very bad.

Pleasant as Hope Harbor was, he had no intention of staying. Nor did Bren have any intention of leaving, unless he was misreading her. She came across as too independent and self-sufficient to ever let attraction or romance disrupt the life she'd created here.

So unless he wanted to risk getting burned, he should back off and stop digging for information about the barista next door.

No matter how loud Dad sang her praises—or how much he wanted to learn more about her story.

"This is a quiet corner. Or as quiet as it gets at Grace Christian after a Sunday service." Bev claimed a niche in the vestibule. "Sorry if I misinterpreted, but I was picking up a distress signal back there."

Bren peeked over the woman's shoulder. Noah had disappeared into the crowd.

Good.

"You didn't misinterpret. Thank you for swooping in to my rescue. My gums were beginning to flap, and you know that's not like me."

"No, it's not." A hint of speculation glinted in Bev's irises. "I wonder why."

Bren fingered one of her imperial jasper earrings, the colorful stone smooth against her skin.

She could use a sounding board, and Bev knew more about her than anyone else in town. Not everything, but the bookshop owner had the big picture. And her insights had always been helpful. What could it hurt to see what she had to say about Noah?

After confirming that Fred's son was gone and none of the congregants lingering in the vestibule were within hearing distance, Bren moistened her lips. "I think I can guess."

"I can too. You're attracted to him."

As usual, Bev had nailed it.

"Yes, and that's crazy. As far as I can tell, we're total opposites." She scrubbed her forehead. "This doesn't make any sense."

"Attraction often doesn't."

"But I don't *want* to be attracted to him."

Bev chuckled. "Hormones can be difficult to control."

"You control them."

"Now, yes. Not so much in the past. Otherwise, I wouldn't have my sweet daughter. Beyond unbridled passion, her father and I didn't have anything in common. If he hadn't been killed in the service overseas, I doubt we would have lasted as a couple. But the experience did teach me that I don't need a man in my life. I'm perfectly fine on my own."

"That's how I want to be too."

"Not everyone is meant to go through life solo, dear girl." She leaned closer and touched one of the teardrop earrings. "Imperial jasper is also a reminder of the power of companionship. Don't let a bad experience or two sour you on all men."

"I don't know, Bev. Relationships are risky. Besides, assuming I was willing to consider altering my single status, Noah isn't the right man. He'll be leaving soon. Even if we had a lot more in common than we do, there's no future with him."

"How do you know you don't have a lot in common?"

Bren gave her a get-real look. "He's a CPA. I have a GED. He has a corporate career. I work at a coffee shop. He wears Brooks Brothers shirts. I have purple hair."

The other woman waved all that aside. "Externals don't always reflect what's in the heart. You're also selling yourself short in terms of brainpower. You operate a successful calligraphy business with clients around the country, doing not only the creative work but the marketing and financials. And you built it from scratch. That takes smarts and drive and ambition—and a skill set I'd wager is broader than Noah's."

Warmth flowed through her at Bev's praise.

Was it any wonder she loved this woman?

"Maybe."

"No maybe about it. I bet if you got to know him better, you'd find far more common ground than you expect."

"On the remote chance that's true, it still doesn't solve the distance obstacle. His career is in St. Louis, and I never want to leave Hope Harbor."

"I hear you. I love this town too. But who knows? Our fair little town could grow on him."

"I don't see that happening, but suppose it did. What would he do here?"

"Accounting work, of course. Numbers are a reality of life wherever you live. As a matter of fact, I'd like to consult with him while he's here on a question I have about a business expense now that my accountant in Coos Bay has retired. If I could find a new one closer to Hope Harbor, I'd hire him or her on the spot."

"Tracy at Harbor Point Cranberries does accounting work."

"I've talked to her. With the success of the cranberry operation, she's shedding clients, not taking on new ones. There's definitely a market here for someone with Noah's skills. You may want to pass that on."

Bren didn't try to hide her skepticism. "I can't imagine the work in a small town would be anywhere near as challenging as the types of jobs his firm takes on."

"While that may be true, the trade-off could be less stress. Next time you see him, would you pass on my number and ask him to call me? It will be a paying job, by the way. I don't expect free advice."

"Sure. But don't hold your breath. It may be too small potatoes for him."

"It never hurts to ask. And speaking of finances, are you still thinking about loaning Emma some money until she gets on her feet?"

"I offered, but she doesn't want to take it. I plan to try again." Bren sighed. Shook her head. "I was so like her at that age."

"But you didn't cross paths with a Bren Ryan."

"No. It would have been far easier if I had."

"Except you might not have ended up in Hope Harbor—and wouldn't that have been a shame? We'd never have met, and The Perfect Blend wouldn't be the same."

Pressure built in Bren's throat, and she leaned over and hugged the older woman. "You always put a positive spin on everything."

"It's the only way to live." She returned the squeeze, then stepped back. "We can let the dark clouds in life snuff out the sun, or we can rise above the clouds and stake a claim where the sun always shines. Our choice. Let me know how it goes with Emma. And bring her over to the Book Nook for a cookie and a chat one day."

"I will."

"See you soon." With a wave, Bev strolled away, leaving a trace of jasmine lingering in the air.

As she disappeared, Bren gave the vestibule a sweep.

Fred was nowhere to be seen, so he must have joined Noah in the fellowship hall.

Too bad Emma was waiting for her there. Otherwise, she could duck out and avoid another potential encounter with the father/son duo.

But with Fred's broken wrist, and Noah's obvious concern about him overextending himself, it was possible they'd already left—or soon would.

Best plan? Duck into the sanctuary for a few minutes to ensure the coast was clear before she continued on to the fellowship hall.

And while she was there, it wouldn't hurt to send a request heavenward for guidance.

13

"You're up." Noah closed the fridge and turned as his father appeared in the kitchen doorway, ice pack in hand.

"A man can't sleep all day, even with a broken wrist. But I have to admit I was ready to stretch out after we got home from church. I didn't plan to snooze the afternoon away, though."

"It's obvious you needed the rest. We shouldn't have stayed for doughnuts." The worrisome pasty tint to his dad's complexion as they left the church had been proof of that.

Thankfully, several hours of sleep had restored his normal color.

"Yes, we should. It doesn't feel like Sunday without a bit of fellowship after the service."

"Come on over and sit down." Noah started toward him to offer an arm.

His father waved him off. "I can walk by myself. A bum wrist doesn't make me an invalid."

Instead of arguing, Noah compromised by pulling out a chair for him, then retrieved a throw pillow from the living room and set it on the table. "Elevate that wrist. I'll refill your ice pack."

"You remind me of your mother. She always fussed over every little bump and bruise."

"A broken wrist isn't a bump or bruise. And I'll take your comment as a compliment. Mom fussed because she had a caring heart." He emptied the ice pack into the sink.

"Yes, she did." His dad's expression grew melancholy. "The world lost a ray of sunshine when she passed on. My world in particular."

A perfect opening to introduce the idea of a move again.

"It must get lonely here for you, without her." Noah crossed to the fridge and removed some ice from the freezer compartment.

"Yes, it does. Mostly at night. The house feels too big after it gets dark. But I keep busy during the day, like she would have wanted me to do."

Noah filled the ice pack, secured the lid, and carried it over to the table. After he handed it to his father, he sat. "You know, if you moved back to St. Louis, I'd be close by."

"You have your own life to live, Son. I don't expect you to play mother hen or spend your evenings entertaining me."

"I wasn't planning to do either—but I'd be minutes away if an emergency arose. Like a broken wrist." He tapped the ice pack. "It's going to be tough for you to manage here after I'm gone."

"I'll get by. Are you still planning to stay for the two full weeks you took off?"

What choice did he have at this point, with his father's hand out of commission and no services in place yet to provide the assistance Dad would require for at least six weeks?

"Yes, but that's only a temporary fix. You won't be able to function on your own after I leave."

"I'll be fine, Noah. We help each other out in this town. And speaking of help—I have a favor to ask you. We've run into a snag with a fundraiser for Helping Hands. That's why we had an emergency meeting the other night, and why I got waylaid at church this morning. You may have the skills to bail us out."

They were getting off topic.

"I'll be happy to discuss that, but can we finish our conversation about moving back to St. Louis first?"

"As far as I'm concerned, it's finished."

"Dad. Be reasonable." He linked his fingers on the table. "You're not getting any younger."

His father snorted. "Tell me something I don't know."

"Wouldn't you feel more comfortable having me nearby?"

"I'd be happier, no question about it. So why don't you move out here?"

They were back to that.

"We've been through this before. I've invested years with my firm, and a partnership is on the horizon. It would be crazy to leave now."

"It's not crazy if your priorities change."

"They haven't."

His father narrowed his eyes. "You're not getting any younger either, you know."

As Dad parroted back his comment, Noah braced. "I'm aware."

"Don't you want a family of your own someday?"

"Someday, yes."

"Most men your age are quite a distance down that road."

"I'll catch up when I have time. Serious dating takes effort and energy, and I don't have either to spare at the moment."

"I agree it can be a challenge to find someone you want to spend the rest of your life with. But not always. Sometimes the right person just comes along. Often in a place you least expect."

He was talking about Bren again.

Why on earth was his father fixated on the barista who'd taken up residence in the cottage? Especially since he'd admitted he didn't know her all that well.

But dancing around the inference was silly. They should talk this through once and for all.

"If you're referring to Bren, you'll have to explain why she caught your fancy. You told me yourself you haven't talked to her that much and don't know anything about her background."

"That's true, but I've observed her in action at the coffee shop and at church, and she always has a kind word for everyone. Not only does she remember personal information people tell her, she asks for updates later."

"A lot of people in the service industry cultivate that skill. They know it builds customer loyalty—and tips."

"Now you're sounding cynical again."

"No. Realistic."

His dad shook his head. "It's more than that with Bren. She cares about people. Not at a superficial level, but deep down. I experienced that firsthand. She went above and beyond after your mom died, sitting down to talk with me at The Perfect Blend during customer lulls, asking how I was doing, even dropping cookies off at the house once. She also steps in whenever Helping Hands puts a call out for volunteers. She's always impressed me as a genuine, caring person. Your mom felt the same about her."

"I'm not saying she isn't a nice person. But she's here, and I live more than two thousand miles away. Besides, I doubt we have much in common."

"I can think of one thing." His father's eyes began to twinkle.

Oh, brother.

"Dad." He shot him a don't-go-there glower.

The warning went unheeded.

"I've seen how the two of you look at each other."

Noah gritted his teeth.

He was *not* having a discussion about superficial, hormone-based attraction with his father.

"I think you watched too many rom-coms with Mom. What's the favor you want to ask me?" If his father wouldn't talk about moving, it would be safer to shift the discussion to a more innocuous topic than romance.

After a couple of beats, his dad adjusted the ice pack on his wrist and followed his lead. "One of our board members suggested we organize a 5K run to raise funds for the organization and increase awareness about all the services we offer. We signed on to the idea, assuming he'd lead the charge. But his son in Minnesota was just diagnosed with leukemia, and he and his wife are going out to help with the grandkids for a month or two. None of the rest of us have a clue how to organize a run, nor does anyone on the volunteer steering committee. They're like a ship without a rudder. With your running background, I thought you might be able to get them rolling while you're here."

"Being a runner and organizing a running event are two different things."

"But you run in races, don't you?"

"Yes."

"Then you probably know the basics of how they work."

"Only from the participant side." Although he did have a co-worker who was heavily involved behind the scenes with one particular annual race.

Best not to offer that tidbit, however, if he wanted to steer clear of involvement.

"That still makes you more of an expert than any of us."

"There's another option, you know. Since the event is in the early stages of development, you could postpone or cancel it."

"We talked about that, but we're pretty fired up about the idea from both a civic and charitable standpoint. To generate interest in both Hope Harbor and our organization, we were going to plan a route that took people past sights of interest in the town as well as locations that have benefited from Helping Hands. A tourism boost is always welcome for a little town that relies on visitors for much of its income." He leaned forward. "It wouldn't take up much of your time, Noah—and we'd be grateful for any insights you could offer."

He fidgeted in his chair.

The truth was, he *did* have the time while he was here to sit in on a couple of committee meetings. And he could talk to his coworker, pick the man's brain about what went into planning an event of this type.

It seemed uncharitable to refuse.

"When is this race supposed to take place?"

"October 1."

"That's not a long window for planning. I imagine there are a lot of moving parts. It may be difficult to pull it off in that time frame."

"We won't know unless we try, will we?" His father repositioned his arm on the pillow. "I don't see how it could hurt to have a meeting or two, explore the possibilities."

Noah expelled a resigned sigh. He was stuck. "I'm not an expert, but I suppose I could share what I know with the committee."

"Wonderful." His dad gave him a grateful smile. "Everyone will be glad we don't have to kill the idea."

"Let's not jump to that conclusion yet. You may still have to back off. With my limited knowledge, I can't promise to be of much assistance."

"You know more than all of us combined. I'll let the committee chair know so he can get a meeting on the books ASAP."

"Don't forget to make it clear that my role is purely advisory. I don't want anyone to think I'm—"

Ding-dong.

"Are you expecting someone?" Noah rose.

"No."

"I'll be back in a minute." Leaving his father at the kitchen table, he strode toward the front door. Pulled it open.

An older woman stood on the other side, a shopping bag in one hand, a cake carrier in the other. "Afternoon. You must be Noah. I'm Anna Williams from the casserole brigade."

Noah stared at her. "I'm sorry. What?"

"I'm from the casserole brigade. I took the first dinner slot." She cocked her head. "Didn't you get Adam's message? He said he phoned yesterday afternoon."

Whoops.

That must have been the call he'd ignored while he was pulling out of the urgent care center.

"It's, uh, possible he left a message. I haven't gotten around to checking my voicemail. Sorry."

The woman smiled. "No worries. I imagine you've been preoccupied with your dad. In a nutshell, the casserole brigade delivers dinners and offers other assistance to people who need temporary help, usually after surgery or an injury or if there's a new baby in the family. Someone will come by tomorrow to do a help checklist."

"A what?"

"Help checklist. We take an inventory to see what sort of assistance a person might require. Meals, transportation, help with day-to-day activities, housecleaning, laundry, grass cutting, grocery shopping. Those sorts of chores." She held out the bag and cake carrier. "Enjoy. If you leave the empty containers on the porch, I'll stop by in a day or two and pick them up."

Noah took the items. "Thank you."

"My pleasure. I hope Fred is on the mend soon."

As she bustled back to her car, Noah nudged the door shut with his shoulder and returned to the kitchen.

"Is that from the casserole brigade?" His father examined the bag and cake carrier.

"Yes. You knew about this?"

"Not today's delivery, but I'm familiar with the brigade. Your mom was a regular contributor on the food front. I didn't think I'd be on the receiving end for meals, though. Not with you here. I guess they weren't certain how long you'd be around." He grinned. "Or they assumed your kitchen skills were limited."

Noah set the bag on the counter and began to unpack it. Salad, casserole, green beans, rolls. "This is a full dinner—including dessert."

"Yep. That's how it works. Who delivered it?"

"Anna Williams. She said someone would be by tomorrow with a help checklist too."

"That's always part of the deal. Like I told you, we look after each other in Hope Harbor. You don't have to worry about me being on my own here. I'll be well taken care of after you go back to St. Louis." He sniffed. "That smells delicious. Why don't you dish it up and we'll dive in?"

Noah did as directed, and after his dad offered a blessing, they chowed down in silence until they'd taken the edge off their appetites.

"This is great." Noah scooped up another forkful of chicken tetrazzini.

"Yes, it is. And no cutting involved, if you'll notice. I can manage all this left-handed. The group is thoughtful like that."

Impressive.

Also further proof of his father's contention that he'd be okay in this small community that appeared to take care of its own.

Noah speared a cherry tomato from his salad.

Maybe he *could* leave sooner than planned.

Except suddenly the idea of returning to the stress of the office grind, working long hours, and coming home to a sterile condo and a microwaveable dinner wasn't very appealing.

He popped the tomato into his mouth. Chewed.

Why not stay the full two weeks, whether his presence here was essential or not? His vacation had been approved, and he hadn't taken time away from the office in ages. As long as he logged on every day to ensure nothing fell through the cracks, as he'd been doing all along, no career damage should be done.

Being on-site at headquarters and having face time with the boss were important, of course—but for whatever reason, they didn't seem quite as critical as they had a few days ago.

Which could be bad.

He stopped chewing.

If he lost momentum, allowed his priorities to shift, let his go-getter muscles become flabby, it would be hard to regain his stride.

But surely that was an unrealistic concern. After all, he'd been a man on a mission for years. Had dedicated copious amounts of blood, sweat, and tears to reach a clear destination that was now within touching distance. A stay of two short weeks even in an idyllic town like Hope Harbor wasn't going to divert him from the course he'd laid out long ago.

No way.

Right?

14

Bren was on the 5K run committee?

Curbing an eye roll, Noah paused in the doorway of the conference room at Grace Christian.

Funny how Dad had neglected to mention that yesterday.

Not.

All his father had offered was that someone named John, who owned the Seabird Inn B&B, was the chair of the committee.

He and his dad were going to have a long talk later.

In the meantime, he had a meeting to attend.

Psyching himself up for an encounter he hadn't expected to have, Noah gave the other two members of the committee a quick once-over. John would be the amused-looking man who was watching a thirtysomething red-haired woman gesture emphatically.

But it was Bren who drew his attention.

She was listening to the animated woman too, the colorful earrings she'd also worn to church yesterday swinging as she bobbed her head in agreement. Her gauzy top with silver threads running through it had a bohemian, retro vibe, its purple hue a match for the subtle plum-colored undertone in her hair.

As if sensing his scrutiny, she shifted her attention to him. Offered a smile that seemed strained.

The other two heads swiveled his direction, and the man rose. "You must be Noah." His demeanor was warm and amiable as he walked over and extended his hand. "Welcome. And thank you for coming to our rescue. I'm John Nash."

He returned the man's solid grip. "You may not thank me after tonight. There's a ton of work involved in an event like this."

"The three of us are ready to roll up our sleeves. Right, ladies?" He led the way back to the table.

"Absolutely." The red-haired woman jumped to her feet, energy crackling off her. "Marci Weber Garrison. A pleasure to meet you." She pumped his hand.

"Likewise."

"Marci's the editor of the *Hope Harbor Herald* and runs a PR business." John motioned him into a seat. "If you need publicity or press coverage in this town, she's your gal."

"Both will be essential if you want this event to be a success."

"Reporting for duty." Marci grinned and gave a mock salute.

"You've met Bren, I believe." John sat back in his chair.

"Yes. She gave me quite a welcome the night I arrived." He directed his attention to her. "It actually choked me up."

Bren's lips twitched, and she covered her snicker with a cough.

"Glad to hear it. We like people to feel at home here." John opened the notebook in front of him as Marci dug a pen out of her purse, both of them apparently oblivious to the sizzling current that was arcing between him and Bren—and stalling his lungs.

"We're all ears." Marci uncapped her pen. "Every scrap of information you can pass on is welcome. The extent of my running experience is confined to chasing after three-year-old twins."

"I'm clueless too." John took one of the bottles of water in the center of the table and twisted off the cap. "The only runner among us is Bren."

She yanked her gaze away from his. Cleared her throat. "I'm, uh, not qualified to claim that title yet. As Noah knows, I'm a novice."

True. Her immaculate shoes that first day had been a dead

giveaway, as had the labored breathing she'd tried so hard to control. The attempt to mask her inexperience had actually been kind of cute.

But that was beside the point.

Reining in his wayward thoughts, he opened his notebook. "I do run, but I've never organized anything like this. However, one of my coworkers has. I talked to him today and got a boatload of information. What I discovered is that a running event has a bunch of moving parts."

"We figured it would. That's why we were beginning to panic. If it wasn't for you, we'd be sunk." John gave him a thumbs-up.

"All I'm doing is passing on information. The real work will fall to you."

"Ready whenever you are." Marci positioned her pen on her tablet.

Noah skimmed his notes. "The first question my coworker asked was the purpose of the event. After I explained what I knew, he strongly suggested you have two routes—a challenging one to attract serious runners, and another for people who just want to support a worthwhile cause and have fun."

"That's a smart idea." John took a swig of water. "Your dad tells me you've been running every day here. Is there any chance we could impose on you to help us map out the challenging course?"

He stifled a groan.

That sort of nitty-gritty involvement was beyond the scope of what he'd agreed to do.

On the other hand, it wasn't a huge imposition. His daily runs had taken him in every direction. And it was for a worthwhile cause.

"I can give it a shot, but Dad said you wanted to include town landmarks and locations of Helping Hands beneficiaries. I'll need a list of those, with addresses."

"Consider it done." Marci scribbled on a Post-it note and stuck it to her tablet. "Bren, would you plan the easy route, since you're a beginner?"

146

"I can try, but I'm still feeling my way in terms of what's easy."
She grimaced. "It definitely won't include Pelican Point Road."

"I should hope not." Marci gave an exaggerated shudder. "I get
hives just *thinking* about trying to run up to the lighthouse. I'll
never forget the day my car got stuck at the bottom of the road
and I had to hoof it to our house halfway up. I was gasping. Of
course, being seven months pregnant didn't help." She smirked
and gave Bren an elbow nudge.

"So we have the routes covered. That wasn't too hard." John
set his water down. "In a previous meeting we talked about lining
up sponsors, so that's already underway. What else do we need
to think about?"

"A lot."

For the next twenty minutes, Noah passed on what his coworker
had shared during their call, from creating online registration
forms and a website to designing and writing promotional pieces
like posters, flyers, banners, and press releases.

All three committee members scribbled furiously as he talked.

"I don't know what the budget is, but if you can line up the
sponsors you mentioned, that will help offset costs." Noah flipped
to his next page of notes. "You'll have to buy things like T-shirts,
medals, bib numbers, mile markers, directional signs, and starting
and finish line equipment. My coworker said some of the latter
items can be rented, but he had no idea about sources for those
in this part of the country."

Marci finished writing and looked up. "My head is spinning."

"If it's too overwhelming, you can always postpone this until
the guy who thought of the idea gets back."

As he spoke, the three committee members exchanged glances.

"I think we can pull this off if we recruit a few more people to
help, don't you?" John addressed the two women.

"Yes." Marci gave a definitive nod. "I can handle the publicity
stuff if you two take care of the logistical pieces. And maybe each
of us can solicit one more person for our committee."

"I'm in." Bren raised her water bottle.

"There *is* one more thing." As Noah spoke, they all sent him a wary look. "My coworker suggested that you come up with a catchy name or slogan for the promotional material and T-shirts."

"I can see the merit in that." Marci pursed her lips and rolled her pen between her fingers.

"I can too, but don't count on me for ideas." John held up his hands, palms forward. "I don't have a creative bone in my body—except in the kitchen. The inner chef in me blossomed after I opened the B&B. I'm great at mixing herbs and spices, but stringing words together for clever titles or slogans is beyond my skill set."

"Bren's creative, and I'm decent at headlines. Between the two of us, we ought to be able to handle this. What do you think, Bren?" Marci tossed the question to her fellow committee member.

"I'm willing to give it a try."

As the three of them engaged in a fast-paced discussion, Noah leaned back.

What had Marci meant about Bren being creative? Aside from crafting specialty drinks and perhaps doing foam art, did she have another talent? Or had Marci simply meant that Bren had an imaginative bent?

One thing for sure, his dad's tenant had no lack of enthusiasm. As he watched her interact with Marci and John, her face animated, eyes sparkling with enthusiasm, her distinctive bell-like laugh occasionally adding a musical note to the conversation, a tingle zipped through him.

Which was weird—and discombobulating.

Bren was nothing like the kind of woman he'd expected to find attractive.

Then again, he'd considered Candace a good match, and look what had happened with her.

A shiver rippled through him.

That had been messy. And nasty. An experience dreadful enough to convince him to swear off women for the foreseeable future.

Yet how could any guy not find Bren appealing, with her infectious vivaciousness and kind, generous heart? Add in the intriguing juxtaposition of delicate features with a hint of steel in her eyes, and she was one captivating female.

Bottom line, Bren Ryan seemed like the real deal. A woman who'd found her place in the world and was content there, even if some would assume she lacked ambition.

Him included.

He frowned. Doodled a series of question marks on his tablet.

Was it possible he'd been too hasty in his assessment of her? Too judgmental? Too self-righteous?

While a low-key, slower-paced lifestyle in a small town might not be for him, who was he to say his choice was any better than the one Bren had made?

Truth be told, she appeared to be happier and far less crazed than him on a day-to-day basis. Life could get frenetic back in St. Louis. Juggling multiple and often ridiculous deadlines while dealing with demanding clients was a recipe for stress.

He added more question marks to the string.

What would it be like to wake up in the morning and not have to hit the ground running every single day? To take a real lunch hour, perhaps on a bench by the sea, instead of gulping down a wrap while dashing between meetings? To come home in the evening and enjoy a quiet dinner with a woman who—

". . . done this before?"

As the last part of John's question registered, Noah sat up straighter. Shifted mental gears while the three committee members waited for a response. "Sorry. I was daydreaming for a minute. I missed the first part of your question."

"No worries. We had plenty to talk about and tasks to divvy up while you drifted off. I asked whether we could consult with you during your stay if we run into a snag. Ask you to pass on questions to your runner friend."

"Sure."

"In that case, I think we're finished here for tonight. We all have our marching orders. If you'd be willing, we may want to schedule one more in-person meeting before you leave."

"That would be fine."

"Why don't we all exchange cell numbers before we break up?"

After they took care of that piece of business, John skimmed his watch. "If you all don't mind, I'm going to duck out fast. I have a couple scheduled for a late arrival, and I want to be on hand to greet them."

"And I have twins to put to bed." Marci scanned her phone. "Ben has to deal with an emergency at the hospital in Coos Bay."

"You guys go ahead. I'll shut down here." Bren gathered up her papers.

"If you're sure . . ." Marci was already on her feet.

"Absolutely. Go. Both of you." She stood too and waved them off.

After goodbyes were exchanged, the other two took off, leaving him and Bren alone.

"Can I help you do anything here?" Noah zipped his portfolio shut.

"No. All I have to do is turn off lights and double-check that the door locks behind me."

He was free to leave—even if he suddenly didn't want to.

With no excuse to linger, though, what choice did he have?

"Let me know if you have any questions as you dive into the project. And I'll be happy to review the fun route if you want my input after you map it out."

"Thanks." She flicked him a glance. Swallowed. Dipped her chin and tapped her papers into place.

If there was an electricity meter in here, it would be spiking.

Pulse accelerating, Noah retreated a step. "I guess I'll take off."

"Okay. See you around." She continued to shuffle papers.

He'd been dismissed.

Gripping his portfolio, he pivoted, exited, and walked down the hall, mind whirling.

On a business level, the meeting had gone well. Despite the amount of work he'd outlined, everyone had seemed less uncertain and worried by the time they wrapped up.

If only he could say the same about his heart. Whatever spell Bren had cast on him was wreaking havoc with it.

He picked up his pace toward the outside door.

Being intrigued by a woman with purple hair was one thing. Getting dangerously interested in her was another. Aside from the fact that they seemed to have disparate backgrounds and little in common, geography was against them.

He needed to walk out tonight and forget about her.

Shoring up that resolve, he pushed through the door and strode toward his car as drops of rain began plopping onto the pavement in the deepening dusk.

Where had that come from? The sky had been blue when he arrived.

A quick sweep of the heavens provided the answer. During their meeting, dark clouds had moved in.

No worries. Even if the skies opened, he'd be home soon. Dad's place wasn't that—

He stopped. Furrowed his brow.

Why was his rental car the only vehicle in the lot?

Had Bren walked here?

Very possible. Dad's place wasn't far, and the weather had been clear and sunny earlier.

Noah hesitated.

Any more contact with her tonight wouldn't be wise. Not in light of all the sparks that had been pinging back and forth in the conference room.

But leaving her to the mercy of Mother Nature's whims would be unkind. And the drive to Dad's wouldn't take long.

He turned. Slowly retraced his steps.

Offering her a ride was the right thing to do. Everything would be fine.

After all, how much could happen in the space of a handful of minutes?

15

Noah should be gone by now.

After flipping off the lights in the conference room, Bren peeked out the door.

No sign of him in the hall.

Yes! Her stall tactic had worked.

If the voltage during the race meeting had gotten any higher, it would have tripped a circuit breaker—and an extended one-on-one encounter would have carried a far more potent charge.

Tucking her notes into the crook of her arm, she walked down the hall toward the exit door.

This whole attraction phenomenon with her temporary landlord's son was beyond weird. She hardly knew the man, for heaven's sake. Why was he able to disrupt her equilibrium when no guy in years had done more than generate a fleeting ping of interest on her radar? It wasn't like she was lonely.

Well, not very.

But counting on a man to provide companionship—or anything else—was a mistake. It was much smarter to take control of your life and avoid any sort of entanglements that could lead to dependence and subjugation.

Straightening her posture, she picked up her pace.

A fixation on the past was stupid, but remembering hard-learned lessons was smart. And she wasn't going to—

The outside door opened as she approached, and Noah walked back in.

She halted, heart stuttering.

"Sorry." He paused, keeping his distance. "Did I startle you?"

"Um . . . yeah. I thought everyone was gone."

"I was about to leave, but I didn't see your car in the lot. Were you planning to walk home?"

"Yes. It's not far."

"True. But it's starting to rain."

Dang.

She should have driven here instead of walking.

But better to get a little damp than a lot hot and bothered.

"I'll be fine. It's probably a passing shower."

"I doubt it. The sky's black. I think it's about to pour." He played with his key fob. "Why don't you let me drive you back?"

Share the confined quarters of a car with him?

Her respiration went rogue.

Yet what excuse could she use to refuse? No normal person would choose to risk a drenching if there was an alternative available. Plus, the house wasn't far. Surely she could control the wattage of the attraction on her end. It wasn't like she was a teenager with raging hormones, after all. And even if Noah was also fighting the magnetic pull, he couldn't be any more interested in getting involved than she was. His life was in St. Louis. He'd want to keep a tight rein on his emotions too.

It ought to be safe to ride with him, given the short duration of the trip.

Clutching the meeting paperwork to her chest with one hand, she wiped the palm of the other down her leggings. "Thanks. I suppose that would be the smart choice."

"Yes." Though he didn't sound any more certain about the wisdom of the arrangement than she did.

While she closed the distance between them, he pushed the door open and moved aside to let her pass.

Keeping as much space as possible between them, she edged past him. But a faint hint of his heady, spicy aftershave nevertheless tantalized her nose, disrupting the rhythm of her pulse yet again.

Once outside, a bolt of lightning slashed through the sky and drops of rain dampened the pavement during the short walk to his car.

"This has been a strange summer." She picked up her pace. A discussion about the weather should be innocuous. "We don't usually get much rain in August."

"At least it's cooler here than it is in Missouri."

"By far. I spent a couple of years in KC. The Midwest summers can be brutal."

"When were you in KC?"

She clenched her teeth.

Why did she keep revealing pieces of her background to the man beside her? Yes, this was a harmless tidbit, but Noah already knew more about her history than anyone in town except Bev.

Ignoring the question would be rude, though.

"About eight years ago." She hurried around the back of the car to the passenger side and reached for the door handle.

Noah beat her to it, leaning past her to pull the door open, sending another waft of that enticing scent her direction.

"Thanks." She slid in, focusing on her breathing as he circled the car—in . . . out . . . in . . . out . . . while repeating the same mantra over and over.

Change the subject. Change the subject.

As he slipped behind the wheel and twisted around to put his portfolio on the back seat, she forced up the corners of her mouth. "Where have you most enjoyed running during your stay here?"

If he thought the sudden change in topic—or her slight wheeze—odd, he gave no indication.

"The lighthouse route is my favorite. But I like south of town too." He started the car and put it in gear. "The scenery near Sandpiper Cove is spectacular. And down 101, not far from the lavender farm, there's a quiet byway called Windswept Way that ends at an impressive estate."

"That would be Edgecliff. It was built by a lumber baron. It's a museum and special events venue now." The tension in her shoulders began to ease, and she relaxed back against the seat. If he was willing to confine their conversation to benign subjects for the duration of their ride, she'd be fine.

"Where have you been running?"

"I've been doing circuits around town. On flat terrain. I only plan to run three days a week—Tuesday, Thursday, and Saturday—so I've had a grand total of two sessions to date."

He pulled out of the lot. "Any running program should begin slow and build from there."

"I found that out. How long have you been running?"

"Since high school."

"That's impressive."

"More like pragmatic. It's stress relief from work. And I prefer being outside to spending hours in a gym."

"You must have a demanding job."

"That would be a fair assessment. People don't appreciate mistakes that can affect their bank balance."

"Speaking of bank balances . . . Bev from the Book Nook asked if you'd call her. She has a question about a business expense—and she'll pay for your services."

"I'll be happy to talk to her. No charge." He hung a right on Dockside Drive.

"Oh, look!" Bren leaned forward, lips bowing. "The ice cream truck from Bandon is here."

"You want something?" He slowed as he surveyed the truck

parked along the wharf up ahead, not far from Charley's shuttered taco stand.

The temptation to say yes was strong—but stopping for ice cream would prolong their trip.

Bad idea.

"I'm a sucker for their Fudgsicles . . . but no. I don't need one." Her response didn't come out as definitive as she'd intended.

Noah gave her a scan as he approached the truck. Swung into a parking place that provided an expansive view of the harbor on this rainy evening. "Do you mind if I stop? I haven't been to an ice cream truck in years."

Yes, she minded—but he was the driver. What could she say?

"That's fine."

After setting the brake, he opened his door. "As long as I'm going, are you certain you don't want a Fudgsicle?"

She eyed the truck.

It wouldn't take any longer for him to buy two bars than it would to purchase one. And she didn't often indulge.

"All right. You convinced me." She started to pick up her purse.

"My treat."

Before she could object, he was out of the car and striding toward the truck.

She left her purse on the floor. Arguing about paying would be futile—and it wasn't like a Fudgsicle would set him back that much.

The main priority was to end this trip ASAP.

Except Noah had other ideas after he jogged back in the increasingly heavy rain.

Once he took his place behind the wheel again, he handed her the Fudgsicle, along with several napkins, and began unwrapping his selection.

"Um . . . aren't we taking these home?"

"I'd rather eat mine here. It will be half melted by the time we get back."

Doubtful. They were less than five minutes away, and it wasn't exactly balmy out.

But again . . . he was the driver.

More chitchat was in order.

She peeled back the paper on her treat. "What did you get?"

"An ice cream sandwich. Not very imaginative, I know, but Dad used to buy these for me when I was a kid. There was nothing like it on a hot summer Sunday. It brings back happy memories." The hint of a smile teased his lips. "Did you pester your mom and dad too, whenever you heard the bell on your street?" He bit into his bar.

"No." What would have been the point? Mom might have been willing to buy her a treat, but Dad? Forget about it. And Mom wouldn't have gone to battle over an ice cream bar. Over anything, really.

"For real? I thought that was a rite of childhood." His tone was conversational, his demeanor relaxed, but his eyes were intense. Like he knew there was a story behind her simple *no*.

She took a bite of the creamy chocolate. Let the rich sweetness dissolve on her tongue. "I didn't have that kind of childhood."

As the admission spilled out, her stomach twisted.

What was it about this guy that loosened her tongue?

Could it be those probing baby blues of his, which seemed to discern far more than spoken words conveyed?

Or perhaps it went deeper than that. Perhaps it was because underneath the no-nonsense, businesslike, practical face this workaholic numbers man presented to the world, he appeared to have a caring heart and an ability to sense layers that remained hidden to most people.

"So what kind of childhood *did* you have?"

She caught a drip of chocolate with her tongue as the question hung in the air between them.

If she changed the subject again, odds were Noah wouldn't push. He didn't come across as the type who would trespass into restricted territory once he got the message it was off-limits.

But maybe . . . just maybe . . . she *should* tell him about her past. Perhaps the time had come to air out the closet, own up to the hurt and the mistakes, and then let them go. It wasn't like he was going to shout her story from the rooftops. Besides, who safer to spill her guts to than someone who'd soon be gone, anyway? It could be a cathartic experience.

She balled her shaky fingers in her lap as the Fudgsicle continued to melt in her other hand.

Why not at least test the waters? Get a read on his level of interest by throwing out another comment to see if he'd follow up. "It wasn't like yours."

The rain picked up, beating a steady tattoo against the roof of the car as whorls of fog insulated them from the world in a dry cocoon.

A few seconds ticked by.

"You want to tell me about it?"

He'd followed up.

At his quiet question, she looked over. Swallowed. "I don't know."

His gaze remained steady. "I've been told I'm a decent listener. And I don't betray confidences. If it would help to talk about whatever happened back then, I promise you can trust me. Sometimes giving voice to hurts can help banish demons . . . or disappointments, if demons is too strong a term."

"It's not."

He didn't say anything more as she went back to eating the Fudgsicle she no longer wanted. He simply waited, downing his own ice cream as the minutes ticked by. Leaving the choice about whether to walk through the door he'd opened up to her.

When she got to the stick, she slid it back into the wrapper and wiped her sticky fingers on a napkin. But it was impossible to remove the chocolaty residue without a thorough washing.

Just like it had been impossible to clear away the sticky residue from the memories that had clung to her all these years, refusing to relinquish their hold. Even talking to Bev, helpful as those conversations had been, hadn't freed her from the lingering legacy that still had the power to undermine her peace of mind on occasion. To make her question her self-worth and her choices.

Would Noah perhaps add a new perspective that would help her heal and expel her regrets?

It seemed impossible.

Yet what if he could?

Should she trust her instincts, follow her heart, and take a leap into the unknown?

Or would that be a mistake she'd live to regret?

16

Noah finished his ice cream bar, wadded up the wrapper, and wiped his own fingers as he kept tabs on Bren in his peripheral vision.

She wasn't going to tell him anything more.

And that was probably for the best, despite the odd sense of disappointment welling up inside him. A man who didn't want to get involved shouldn't knock on the door to someone else's heart.

What had come over him, anyway? Minutes ago, he'd been dragging his feet about offering her a simple ride tonight, and now he was trying to elicit confidences?

This was crazy.

He shifted away from her and pulled out his keys.

They should go home and—

"My father was . . . he was a piece of work." The subdued, uncertain voice that spoke from the passenger side of the car sounded nothing like the strong, self-confident woman he'd come to know during their brief acquaintance.

Noah looked over again to find Bren watching him, expression wary.

The ball was in his court. And since he'd thrown out the first pitch—to mix sports metaphors—now what?

Several seconds ticked by as he wrestled with that question. Too many, based on the sudden mask that fell over her face, hiding the revealing hint of vulnerability that had flickered in her eyes moments before.

The corners of her mouth rose, though there was no humor in her smile. "That's fate, right? Some of us get winners, like you did, and some of us get losers. But life goes on." The artificial brightness in her inflection wrenched his gut. "Why don't I get rid of our ice cream stuff? The trash can's closer to me." She reached for his crumpled wrapper.

Instead of relinquishing it, he pulled his hand back. Plucked her trash from her fingers. "I'm already damp around the edges. No sense both of us getting wet. I'll be back in a minute."

He fumbled with the handle on his door. Pushed through, into the rain. Jogged toward the can, berating himself with every step.

Offering Bren his ear had been a mistake. One that could be dangerous. Disruptive. Destabilizing.

Because it was very possible that if he let her tell him about past hurts and traumas, she'd claim more than his ear.

She might also end up infiltrating his heart.

And that would be a disaster.

Bottom line, there was no room for Bren Ryan in his well-planned life. She could divert him from the destination that had been his goal since the day he declared his major in college.

Yet after making his impulsive overture, how could he back away without adding more hurt to those hazel eyes that looked as if they'd seen too much sadness and suffering? In fact, her tentative outreach tonight had no doubt been a giant leap of faith for a woman he suspected didn't trust easily.

Noah tossed the trash in the container and walked back to the car, slowing his pace despite the steady rain that was soaking through his dress shirt, buying himself a minute or two to think this through.

If there was an out, however, he wasn't seeing it.

So he'd have to listen—and do his best to protect his heart.

When he slid back behind the wheel, her stiff lips curved up again. "Thanks for the treat."

"You're welcome." He angled toward her in the dim car, the last scraps of daylight providing only faint illumination. Filled his lungs. Took the plunge. "I'm sorry you didn't have a father like mine."

Her smile faltered. Flattened. "Luck of the draw, I guess." She dropped her gaze. Fiddled with her seat belt.

"Piece of work has very negative vibes."

"It's an apt description." She peeked over at him. "Look, I get it if you've changed your mind about listening to my story. It's not a big deal. No obligation, no offense. Why don't we head back before the rain gets—"

"Bren." Her breath hitched as he leaned over and touched the hand she'd clenched in her lap. "I haven't changed my mind. But I do want to be up front about my concerns." He took a steadying breath. "There's a strange connection whenever we're together. I suspect you feel it too. And both of us know that pursuing any sort of relationship would be foolish—for geographic reasons, if nothing else. I don't want either of us to get hurt. However, I'd like to hear about your dad, if you're still willing to share. We'll just both have to proceed with caution."

The ball was back in her court.

If she chose to tell him her story, fine.

If she didn't? Disappointing—but also fine.

Sort of.

Seconds ticked by as she studied his hand resting on hers. Five. Ten. Fifteen. Twenty.

Finally, she raised her chin and turned toward him again. "I haven't told anyone the details of my past. Bev knows bits and pieces, and Charley has intuited a handful of particulars, thanks to that uncanny perception of his. But I hear you about our . . . connection. Talking about personal subjects could intensify that. It might be safer if we go back to the house."

Yeah, it would.

Especially after her admission that she was thinking about revealing information to him she'd shared with no one else.

Yet that only made him *more* curious about her story.

It also raised a question.

"Why are you willing to talk to me about this? You don't even know me that well."

It was hard to read her expression in the dim light. "It's the oddest thing, but for whatever reason, you feel like someone I can trust." She stared at the drops of rain running down the windshield, her features shadowed, the sadness emanating from her almost as tangible as the odd black stain he'd noticed on her index finger tonight at church. "And I don't trust easily."

Earlier suspicion confirmed.

And the history she was about to share, which she guarded with such diligence, would likely explain why she was hesitant to expose her vulnerabilities.

He retracted his hand. Leaned back in the corner of his seat. Maybe they'd both come to regret this, but he wasn't backing down now.

"So tell me about your dad."

After a moment, she lifted her hand and touched one of her earrings with fingers that didn't appear too steady. "These are imperial jasper. Bev made them. They're supposed to represent peace and comfort and wholeness." She dropped her hand to her lap again. "None of those were present in the house in Kentucky where I grew up."

"Because of your dad?"

"For the most part. But Mom was complicit too."

He frowned. "That's a loaded word." One that reeked of illegal activity.

"I don't mean they were involved in anything criminal, if that's what you're thinking." She darted a glance at him. "On the contrary. Everything was always 100 percent aboveboard. In the eyes of the world, our life was an open book. We were the perfect family during my early years. At least in public."

A red flag began to wave in his mind.

"But not behind closed doors."

"No."

He braced. "Was your dad abusive?"

"Not physically, but he was cold, critical, judgmental, and verbally cruel. He was also a control freak. I was expected to conform to the rigid standards he set, to fit the mold he created for me, and when I rebelled—as I often did once I got older—the punishment was swift."

He wrapped his fingers around the wheel. Squeezed. "Define punishment."

"If I hung out with people who didn't meet his approval, he locked me in my room for the weekend. If he found a speck of food on anything after I washed the dishes, he made me wash every dish in the cabinet. If my room was too messy to suit him, he'd come through and take everything he deemed to be out of place and throw it away. If I wore a skirt he thought was too short, I'd find it ripped to shreds, lying on my bed."

The ice cream bar in Noah's stomach began to curdle. "I consider that abuse."

"Not according to him. He called it discipline. Building character." Acid etched her reply.

"Where was your mother during all of this?"

"In the background. She had her own set of challenges to deal with. He totally dominated her. He picked out her clothes, her makeup, the social organizations she joined. He drilled her on what to say in public, told her how to conduct herself at church, ran background checks on new friends, and forced her to dump them if they didn't meet his exacting standards."

Noah cracked his window and filled his lungs with fresh air.

How could any young person grow up in a noxious environment like that and not be marred for life?

"Why did your mom marry him?"

"She claimed he was different early on. A real charmer was how she described him." Bren's lip curled, and she gave a soft snort. "That may be true, but I only saw the charming side of him in public. He was in politics, and image was everything. In the eyes of the world, he was polished, successful, smooth-talking, personable. It was all a façade, though. And it was disgusting." Her bitterness came through loud and clear.

"Why did your mother stay with him after the charm faded?"

"She said it was simpler to conform than try to live on her own. Mom was a pragmatist. Dad provided her with a beautiful house, expensive clothes, fancy cars, a housekeeper, spa treatments, jewelry. She thought all of that was worth the stress of living with his demands. But the price was too high for me."

"I take it you rebelled?"

"Big-time. As soon as I was old enough to see through the sham, I defied him at every turn. Too much, in hindsight, but it was all about shock value for me at that point. He was focused on image and conforming to societal norms in public, and I was determined to do the opposite."

Ah. Some of the pieces were beginning to fall into place.

"Like having multicolored hair."

"No. That came later. In high school, I went through goth and punk and grunge phases."

"I assume your dad hated all of those."

"With a passion. I ended up keeping my wardrobe in my locker at school, away from him, and I wore it around town to spite him. He also hated the crowd I hung with." She toyed with the zipper on her jacket. "To be honest, the drugs and alcohol they were into weren't my scene, but associating with them was another way to defy him. Unfortunately, my choice of friends came back to bite me on several occasions. I made a few mistakes, had a couple of minor brushes with the law. I regret those now."

"Regrets and mistakes are part of life."

"For some more than others. In my case, the defiance felt warranted to me back then. I couldn't be like Mom and let him control every aspect of my life. And I couldn't handle his constant criticism. No matter how hard I tried in the beginning to meet his standards, it was never good enough. It was always his way or the highway. In the end, I chose the highway."

"When did you leave home?"

"A month after my seventeenth birthday. I'd planned to finish high school and stay until I was eighteen, but I couldn't take it anymore."

Bren's kindness to Emma took on a whole new meaning in light of these revelations.

"Did he search for you? I mean, you were underage."

"Not that I know of. I think he was glad to be rid of the thorn in his side. But I stayed under the radar until my next birthday, on the off chance he would."

"What about your mom? Didn't you think she might try to find you?"

Bren gave a stiff shrug. "I doubted it. She never stood up to Dad. To be safe, though, I did contact her after I left. I also tried to convince her to divorce him, to get out from under his thumb and create a new life. But she wouldn't." Bren sighed. Stared out the rain-streaked windshield. "Looking back, I think she may have been afraid of what my father might do if she left. Maybe that was part of what kept her tethered to him. But she was also hooked on all the amenities he provided." She drew a shaky breath and refocused on him. "Except stuff doesn't bring happiness, you know? Mom had all the material comforts she could ever want, but she was never happy beyond a superficial level."

"Do you stay in touch with her?"

"I did, on and off, until she died five years ago. More off than on in the last two years of her life. We had less and less to talk about as time went on."

Noah did the math. "She must have died fairly young."

"Yeah, she did. In a car accident. I contacted a friend of hers after I tried to call her once and discovered her phone had been disconnected. She told me about the accident."

Shock ripped through him. "You mean your dad didn't even tell you she'd died?"

"No—and I know he had my number. It was in Mom's phone, and he knew she and I talked on occasion." A subtle thread of pain wove through her voice despite the years that had passed.

Noah's throat tightened, and it took every ounce of his will-power to restrain himself from folding her hand in his.

Piece of work didn't come close to describing Bren's father. That required much stronger language.

"I'm sorry. I can't imagine growing up in an environment like that." Or turning out as normal as she appeared to be, given her upbringing—even if her colorful hair and triple-pierced ears had initially thrown him.

"It was tough. And it left me with issues. My self-esteem was in the toilet. So was my trust level. Especially with men."

Making it all the more remarkable that she'd been willing to confide in him.

"I can understand that. What I can't understand is how you managed to survive on your own at seventeen."

Her forehead bunched, and she twined her fingers together in her lap. "It was a challenge."

"Why do I think that's a gross understatement?"

She arched an eyebrow at him. "Because you're a smart man?"

"No. Because I can't begin to imagine being on my own at seventeen. In those days, my biggest worry was prepping for tests, deciding which colleges to apply to, and trying to work up the courage to ask a girl to prom."

She expelled a soft sigh. "College and prom weren't on my radar. I was too busy trying to scrounge up food and find a decent place to sleep."

"How did you manage to do that at such a young age?"

"I figured out early on that fast-food work took care of the eating problem, and I managed to hook up with three other girls who needed a roommate. Once I had a little money saved, I began wandering and taking a variety of jobs. Waitress, receptionist at a health club, barista at a coffee chain, dog walker, laborer at a landscaping company, house sitter. I wandered a lot, searching for a place to call home."

"And you found it here?"

"Yes. In Hope Harbor—and at Grace Christian. And now you know all about me." She played with the zipper on her jacket again. "Sorry to hit you with such a downer of a story."

"Don't be. I'm glad you told me."

And that was the truth—even if the history she'd shared had cracked a door to his heart.

For there was much to admire about the woman sitting beside him. Most people who grew up in the circumstances she'd described would be scarred for life, not kindhearted, productive members of society who took in strangers in need, offered to loan someone their hard-earned cash, and spent time talking to an older man who was grieving the loss of his spouse.

"Seriously?"

"Yeah. Seriously. You're an impressive woman, Bren Ryan."

She shifted, as if the praise made her uncomfortable. And though it was too dark now to see her face clearly, he'd wager she was blushing.

"Don't give me more credit than I deserve. I've made a ton of mistakes."

"I stand by what I said. Plus, your mistakes are history. The important takeaway is that you overcame all the obstacles and ended up in a better place."

"Far better." She peered at her watch in the darkness. "I, uh, guess we should head back?"

"Yeah." Even if he wasn't quite ready for this interlude to end.

But prolonging it would be imprudent. Wasn't he the one who'd cautioned them both to be careful about letting emotion cloud their vision?

And extending this evening any further could do that.

Resettling himself behind the wheel, he started the engine.

As they drove back to his father's place, Bren didn't speak. Neither did he. He had too much to process and absorb.

When he pulled up in front of the house and set the brake, Bren grasped the door handle.

"Why don't you let me walk you to the cottage? It's pouring, and I have an umbrella in the back seat."

She assessed the rain streaming down the windshield. "I could make a run for it."

"You'll be soaked before you get to the gate. Sit tight until I come around."

He grabbed his meeting notes from the back seat, along with the umbrella he'd learned to keep on hand during his visit, and stepped out into the rain.

As he rounded the back of the car, Bren opened her door and rose to meet him, her own notes clutched against her chest.

Tipping the umbrella to protect her, he walked beside her to the gate and pushed it open. As she edged past him, her hair tickled his nose, setting off a tingle in his fingertips.

Not good.

For the remainder of the short walk, he stayed as far away from her as he could without getting soaked.

At the cottage, she fumbled for her key. Slipped it in the lock. Turned to him, the light beside the door casting a golden glow on her complexion.

"Thanks again for the ride—and for lending me your ear." Did she sound a bit breathless?

"Anytime." Did *he* sound a bit breathless?

Probably.

How could he not, with the big hazel eyes of the woman who'd bared her soul to him issuing a subliminal invitation to taste her appealing lips?

And despite the fact they'd both agreed that giving in to the electricity between them would be ill-advised, he found himself leaning toward her, the magnetic pull as impossible to resist as one of Sweet Dreams's luscious cinnamon—

The cottage door opened, and he jerked upright.

"Oops. Um . . . sorry to interrupt. I thought I heard someone out here." Emma looked back and forth between them. "I'll, uh, go inside and—"

"No!" There was a hint of panic in Bren's tone as she spun toward the other woman. "I'll go with you. Noah walked me back with his u-umbrella, but he was just leaving." She shot him a quick glance over her shoulder. "Thanks again."

An instant later, the two women disappeared inside, closing the door in his face and leaving him alone under the umbrella as rain continued to fall around him.

Somehow he managed to jump-start his lungs.

As close calls went, that one had been a doozy. If he wanted to keep his distance from Bren, kissing her would have been the wrong way to go about it.

He slowly pivoted and walked back down the path.

Thank goodness Emma had come to the door. Her timing had been impeccable.

But if that was true, why wasn't he grateful?

You know why, Ward.

At the chiding from his subconscious, he exhaled.

Yeah, he knew.

The truth was, as he'd feared earlier, ice cream hadn't been the only thing in danger of melting tonight.

Because the heart he'd put in a deep freeze after the disaster with Candace was also thawing at warp speed.

And there didn't seem to be a thing he could do to stop it.

17

Emma gulped.

The final car repair bill was even higher than she'd expected.

To make matters worse, not only was she still jobless, she'd run out of places to look for work in Hope Harbor.

As soon as she had her wheels back, she'd have to expand her search.

"I'm sorry about the cost, Ms. Blair." Marv's gravelly voice came over the line, his tone apologetic. "The parts were on the pricey side, and that gasket gave me fits. The whole job took longer than I expected. But I'll have her finished by close of business today."

"Thanks. I'll come by later to pick it up."

As she ended the call, Emma sank onto the couch in Bren's cottage.

Despite her hostess's generous offer to loan her the car repair money, she couldn't accept. The woman had done too much for her as it was.

Nor could she go to Father Murphy for help, despite the assistance he'd offered during their chat in the meditation garden after Mass three days ago. As it was, she'd accepted more charity in the past few days than she'd taken in her whole life.

So she'd have to pay the car bill by credit card and hope she could reduce the balance before too much interest accrued.

But that was a worry for another day. Right now, she needed to pack her bag and be ready to leave as soon as she picked up her car. Imposing on Bren any further would be wrong—no matter how much more comfortable the sofa sleeper in the cottage was than a reclined seat in her car at a rest stop.

After pushing herself to her feet, she trudged down the hall, gathered up her toiletries in the bathroom, and tucked the clothing items she'd taken out of her suitcase back inside.

She also owed Justin a call, but that could wait too. It was getting harder and harder to maintain an upbeat attitude and reassure him they'd be together again soon.

As she finished packing and zipped the suitcase shut, the front door opened. Closed.

"Emma? Are you here?"

Bren was back from her shift at The Perfect Blend.

"Yes. I'll be out in a sec." She picked up her bag, leaned the luggage rack against the wall, and walked down the hall.

"I got us brownies at Sweet Dreams." Bren's words were muffled as she leaned into the fridge and motioned behind her, toward a white bag on the counter that separated the kitchen space from the living room. "While I was there, Alice—" Her gaze fell on the suitcase as she swiveled around. "What's going on?"

"I have to leave, Bren." Emma swallowed past the catch in her voice. "I've tried everywhere in Hope Harbor, and there isn't a job to be had. I can't stay here forever, and Marv said my car will be ready later today." She continued to the door and lowered her suitcase to the floor.

Bren circled the counter, furrows etched on her brow. Pulled out a stool. "Why don't we sit for a minute?"

"Please don't try to convince me to stay. It wouldn't take much

174

to make me cave, and I've invaded your turf longer than I should have." She gripped her hands in front of her.

"It's not my turf. It's Fred's. I'm a temporary resident. And since he was kind enough to offer it to me, it seems fair that I share my bounty with someone else who's in a tight spot."

"I appreciate that more than I can say, but Mom taught me never to take advantage of people."

Bren studied her. "Have you talked to your mom about your situation?" Her manner was cautious, as if she suspected she was treading into a sensitive area.

"No. She died six months ago."

The other woman's features softened. "I'm sorry."

"Me too. We were super close. I miss her every single day."

"Do you have any other family?"

"One brother. He just turned sixteen. I'm going to apply for guardianship as soon as I get settled."

Bren's eyebrows rose. "Who is he with now?"

"Our stepdad."

"And your stepfather would be willing to turn responsibility for him over to you?"

"More than. He only took me and Justin because we came with Mom, and he wanted *her*. At least in the beginning." She swallowed past the bitterness souring her tongue.

After scrutinizing her, Bren patted the adjacent stool. "Please. Sit with me for a few minutes?"

Emma hesitated—but not for long. Despite their short acquaintance, Bren had become a better friend than Denise had ever been.

Slowly she crossed the room and slid onto the stool.

Bren angled toward her, elbow on the counter, sympathy radiating from her. "Is your stepdad why you left?"

"Yes. I waited until I was legal age, then took off. I couldn't stand being in the same house with him. More so after he hooked up with someone else when Mom got cancer."

Bren's expression hardened. "He cheated on her?"

"Yes." Thinking about his infidelity still made her sick to her stomach. "And he didn't hide it from me and my brother. We tried to shield Mom from the truth, though. With all she was going through, she didn't need to deal with that too. In the end, when she was in hospice and slipping away, it was my brother and me who took turns sitting with her. My stepfather wasn't even there when she died." She choked on the last word. Blinked to clear her vision.

"I'm so sorry." Bren pulled a tissue from her pocket. Handed it over.

"Thanks." Emma swiped at her nose. "I walked out on my eighteenth birthday. The hardest part was leaving Justin behind."

"It sounds like you two are tight."

"We are."

"Did you think about staying closer to Nebraska? That way you would have been able to visit in person until you could get guardianship." Bren's inflection was casual. Her intent gaze wasn't.

"Yes. I hate to be this far from him, but I . . . I had to leave."

Bren linked her fingers. "I'm getting the feeling there was a serious reason for that. More than your stepdad's philandering."

It wasn't a question, but the comment invited confidences.

Emma bit her lip.

She'd already divulged more to Bren than she'd ever planned to tell anyone. Should she reveal more?

Maybe.

Because she could trust this woman who'd given her refuge at her lowest point, when she hadn't known where to turn. And perhaps exposing the bad memories to the light would rob them of their power to fuel the nightmares that could sometimes awaken her in a cold sweat.

She ran a finger down the edge of the bag from Sweet Dreams. Caught a whiff of rich, chocolaty goodness as the crimped top slightly unfurled.

In truth, goodness abounded in this room, emanating also from the woman sitting beside her, who lived the Golden Rule.

As the silence lengthened, Bren slid off her stool. "If you'd like to have your brownie now, feel free. I'll get you a plate."

"No." Emma touched her arm. Filled her lungs. "What I'd like to do is tell you why I left Nebraska as soon as I could."

Bren sank back onto her stool. Waited.

"You were right. It was more than my stepfather's cheating. It was also . . . it was how he was with me."

A muscle beside Bren's eye twitched. "I'm not liking the sound of that."

"I know what you're thinking, but he never molested me—or did anything illegal." She fisted her hands. Tight. "But I . . . I always thought he might. From the time I was about twelve, he started looking at me . . . different. And he always found ways to invade my personal space. To touch me. In the hall when we passed, while I was doing the dishes or weeding Mom's garden, during my trips out to the trash cans in the garage. It was uncomfortable and . . . and scary." A shiver rippled through her.

"Did you tell anyone?"

"No. I didn't want to hurt Mom or force her to choose between me and him."

"And this continued until you left?"

"To some degree. It was less of a problem after Mom got cancer and he found other women to take her place. I don't think his current affair is the first time he cheated on her."

"And your mom never had a clue?"

"If she did, she never let on. She wouldn't have wanted to risk rocking the boat." Emma flexed her fingers. Stared down at the indentations left in her palm by her fingernails. "After my dad died, we lost everything. He had debts Mom didn't know about, so she got two jobs to help pay them off, one as a server at a higher-end restaurant. That's where she met my stepfather. She always said it was her lucky day when he walked in, but it wasn't. For her or for me. Except it did take away her money problems."

"But added others."

"Yes." She took a shaky breath. "I tried never to be alone with him, but it's hard to be on edge 24/7, you know?"

Bren's mouth thinned. "Yes, I do—and I can understand why you'd want to put as much distance as possible between the two of you. I'm sorry you had to leave your brother behind for a while."

"Me too. But I'm going to do everything I can to get him out here with me as fast as I can."

Bren leaned forward. Touched her arm. "Do me a favor, okay?"

"I will if I can."

"Stay until you find a job. I'm sure there's one out there for you. If not here, then in Bandon or Coos Bay. And once you have a job, we'll find you a permanent place to live. There are reasonably priced units at Sea Haven Apartments on the north side of town. Please don't go yet."

Emma swallowed. "You make it seem like I'd be doing *you* a favor if I stay."

"You would be. I've enjoyed getting to know you. I also don't want to have to worry about you sleeping in your car—or a homeless shelter—to conserve cash. I know how hard it can be when money is tight, and it's worse if a big bill slaps you in the face."

There was nothing in Bren's demeanor or tone to suggest she was growing tired of sharing her space with an interloper.

Emma's resolve began to waver.

And she knew what Father Murphy would counsel. His reminder on Sunday in the meditation garden, after she'd confessed to feeling guilty about taking advantage of Bren, replayed in her mind.

"Generosity often reaps benefits for the giver as much as the receiver."

She exhaled slowly, some of the tension in her shoulders dissolving.

It seemed she wasn't going to be leaving after all.

"If you're sure about this, I guess I could stay a few more days."

"I couldn't be more sure." Bren leaned over and gave her a

quick hug. "I'd say this calls for a celebration—and I have the perfect treat." She tapped the white bag on the counter. "Oh, that reminds me. While I was at Sweet Dreams picking these up, Alice asked me to tell you she'd like you to drop by tomorrow afternoon before three, if you could. She said the two of you had a nice chat the other day."

Curious that the bakery co-owner would want to see her.

"Yes, we did. But it was brief. Did she say what she wanted?"

"No." Bren slipped off the stool.

"It's not a job, I know that. I asked about one while I was there. She told me Sweet Dreams is a two-person show."

"Yep. Always has been, from what I've heard. I honestly don't think there'd be space in the back room for more than one baker, from the peeks of it I've gotten. And the front isn't too spacious, either. But the clientele is loyal. The shop does a land-office business on brownies and cinnamon rolls alone."

"That's what Alice said. The place is a little . . . dingy . . . though."

"I agree the décor would benefit from an update, but as long as they keep baking brownies, I'll be a customer for life." Bren grinned and picked up the bag. "Why don't you put your suitcase in the hall again while I plate these?"

"Okay. I'll be back in a minute."

She retrieved her bag from beside the door as Bren circled around to the kitchen, then retraced her steps down the hall.

So much for her resolve to leave before the other woman's hospitality ran out.

Yet in all honesty, she wasn't sorry her hostess had managed to convince her to stay. This tiny cottage felt more like home than the house she'd spent the past dozen years living in.

She set her suitcase back on the luggage rack, spirits ticking up.

Maybe her funds were running low. Maybe a job had yet to materialize. Maybe her permanent housing solution was still on the horizon.

But today . . . and for however long it took to find lucrative work and establish a permanent address . . . she'd adopt an attitude of gratitude. Because if her car had to die, it couldn't have picked a better place than Hope Harbor.

As for Alice's request that she stop by?

Perhaps the woman had a lead for her on a bakery job somewhere.

One could hope, anyway.

Especially in a town that incorporated that very word into its name.

18

Whoops.

Bad timing.

Bren came to an abrupt halt as she strode toward the sidewalk after pushing through the gate on the side of Fred's house.

Since when did Noah go running midmorning? Didn't he usually get in his miles much earlier in the day?

The avoidance plan that had been working fine for her after their post–ice cream tête-a-tête three days ago crumbled.

As he turned toward her, his double take suggested he was as surprised as she was by this meetup—and just as leery about further engagement.

Had their almost-kiss kept him tossing for the past three nights, as it had her?

Thank heaven Emma had interrupted, or any further encounters they had during the remainder of his stay would be doubly awkward. As Noah had made clear, he wasn't any more interested in getting involved than she was. That would only lead to heartache, and she'd had enough of that to last two lifetimes.

Soundest plan right now? Carry on as if that charged moment had never happened.

Heck, it was very possible he'd simply felt sorry for her after hearing her tale of woe. That there'd been no sizzle on his end at all.

Get real, Bren. You saw his eyes.

Snuffing out the annoying little voice in her head, she hiked up the corners of her mouth and lifted a hand in greeting. "Morning."

After a tiny hesitation, he descended the two steps that led from the front porch to the walkway and crossed to her. "Good morning."

"Aren't you out and about later than usual today?"

"Yes. An issue came up at the office that delayed my run."

"Ah. This is a working vacation for you."

"That's the only kind I ever have." He gave her neon orange running jacket and tiger-striped leggings a fast scan. Cleared his throat. Slipped on his sunglasses. "So if I'm, uh, doing the math right, today is your fourth running session."

She fiddled with the zipper pull on her jacket. "Your math is solid. I mapped out a potential fun route yesterday in my car to track mileage, and today I'm going to run it to see if it's suitable for a beginner. How's your dad doing? I haven't seen him since church on Sunday."

"He's hanging in. The wrist isn't too painful, and someone came by to fill out a help checklist they'll implement after I'm gone. It sounds like he'll get plenty of attention and care."

"He will. That's how it works in Hope Harbor. And I'm close by too, if he needs anything. Well . . ." She motioned toward the street and retreated a step. "I should get moving."

His forehead wrinkled, and he shifted his weight from one foot to the other. "Would you, uh, like me to tag along and give you my two cents on the route?"

Her pulse stumbled.

Run with Noah?

No way.

Not only wouldn't she be able to keep up, he'd completely

throw off her respiration. It was hard enough to breathe when she ran alone.

"That may not be the best idea." For a bunch of reasons. But she stuck with the most pragmatic one. "I'd hold you back."

"Not necessarily. I could use your route as my warm-up."

If there was a comeback for that, it eluded her.

"Um . . . I guess that could work. As long as you don't mind going slow and staying silent. I'm not certain I can manage running, talking, and breathing at the same time."

"Slow and silent work for me." He seemed relieved by her caveats.

In that case . . .

"Sure. Why not?"

"After you." He motioned for her to precede him.

She led the way to the sidewalk. Once she broke into a jog, he fell in beside her.

For the first mile, he didn't speak—which was fine. The faster-than-usual pace she was setting for his benefit was taking a toll on her lungs.

As they approached the twenty-minute mark, he gave her a once-over. "Let's pull the speed back a notch." Without waiting for her to respond, he slowed his gait.

"Sorry. I told you I'd . . . hold you back." She glanced over at him as she huffed out the words.

"No apology necessary. Like I said, I'm counting this as my warm-up."

"I doubt it takes you three kilometers to . . . loosen up your muscles."

"Not at home. But the scenery here beats the view of city streets any day. I don't mind extending my running time."

If he was trying to make her feel better about slowing him down, he'd succeeded.

She followed his lead on pace as they continued, and once she could breathe again, she looked over at him. "By the way, Marci and I came up with a name and a slogan for the run."

"That was fast. Lay it on me."

"Hope Harbor Coast Busters—Heart and Sole for Helping Hands."

His lips bowed. "Very clever. I would never have thought of anything that catchy."

"Marci's got a gift with words."

"She claims you aren't too shabby with them, either."

"I don't have her credentials. She has a degree in journalism. I only have a GED."

"I'm not certain you can earn a degree in creativity. You've either got that gene or you haven't. I could take creative writing classes until the cows come home, and I'd never be a Hemingway."

"Trust me, I'm no Hemingway either. Take a right at the corner." As they navigated the turn, feet slapping the pavement, Bren gave her unexpected running partner a surreptitious survey.

Good grief.

He wasn't even breathing hard. Nor had he broken a sweat.

As if sensing her perusal, he met her gaze. "You want to take a break?"

Yes.

"No. I'm fine." More or less. "Out of curiosity, how much training does it take to be able to run without getting short of breath?"

He slowed his pace again. "More than four sessions. What's the farthest you've run?"

"However far I got on my ill-fated attempt to run to the lighthouse. And I walked home from there."

"I'll tell you what. Why don't you give me directions for the rest of the course you have in mind, and I'll finish it out before I veer off to the route I had planned for today? I can let you know later whether I think it's suitable for fun runners."

"I should see if I can finish it." But with another mile to go, the temptation to call it a day was strong.

"New runners who push themselves too hard often throw in the towel, which is a shame. Running is great exercise. I'd hate for you to call it quits without giving the sport a fair shot."

He didn't say any more, leaving the decision up to her.

Capitulating felt like failure, but at least her balking lungs would thank her. "You win." She outlined the remainder of the route for him, then motioned ahead. "I'll peel off at the next corner."

"That'll work."

"Where are you going after you finish the fun route?"

"Up 101, toward Starfish Pier. After I'm done, I plan to swing by Bev's Book Nook. See if I can answer her business-expense question."

"I doubt it will be high finance, but she'll appreciate whatever help you can offer. Be sure to check out the tide pools at Starfish Pier while you're out that direction. They're amazing."

"Duly noted. Talk to you later."

He didn't pause as they approached the corner. On the contrary. He picked up his pace, gave her a wave, and zoomed away.

Bren stopped, propped her hands on her hips, and stared after him as she tried to get her erratic respiration under control.

And her breathing wasn't wonky from pushing herself too hard, either. Not at the pace Noah had set for the last half mile.

No, it was all due to the fact that the toned, hot guy who'd come within a few charged inches of kissing her was showing off bunching hamstrings and calf muscles, not to mention broad shoulders outlined by a snug T-shirt, as he sped away.

Whew.

Pulse picking up again, she pivoted and headed for the cottage. Walking, not running. There would be no more ogling for her. What was the point?

In a different world, maybe the two of them could have connected.

But despite Bev's pep talk, they were poles apart in every respect. And Noah's life was elsewhere. He'd made that clear.

So it would behoove her to stop daydreaming about what a kiss from him would have been like and start remembering what she'd told Bev at church last Sunday.

She was perfectly fine on her own. She did *not* need a man in her life. Look what had happened to Mom. She'd been fooled by superficial charm and ended up paying the price for that for the rest of her days.

No, thank you.

Bren skirted a limb that had fallen onto the sidewalk, a casualty of last night's wind, perhaps. Already the vibrant green leaves were losing their color and curling up in defeat. Dying.

That's what happened if you were cut off from the source of your life. From your roots. You withered.

Another reason to avoid Noah.

Because Hope Harbor was where she'd planted roots. It was the place that had rescued her. Offered her solace and purpose and friends. It was her home.

But it wasn't Noah's home.

Someday, if a man came along who shared her values and perspective and was willing to put down roots here too, she might let herself fall in love. Get married. Have a family.

Workaholic Noah, who seemed married to his job, wasn't that man.

And the sooner she reconciled herself to that, the sooner she'd be able to restore the sense of balance and peace he'd somehow managed to disrupt since the night he'd invaded the cottage and activated her defensive mode.

A mode it would be wise to *keep* active until he climbed in his car, aimed it toward the airport in North Bend, and disappeared from her life forever.

What a depressing day.

Emma stopped outside Sweet Dreams. Ran a finger under her damp lashes. Swallowed past the tightness in her throat.

A whole morning spent searching for a job in Bandon, and what did she have to show for it?

Nothing but a raging headache and a bad case of the blues.

Wasn't *anyone* in this part of the world hiring?

She sighed.

Now she had to put on a sociable face and talk to Alice about who knew what. Maybe the woman just wanted to chat about French pastries again.

Whatever conversation the bakery owner had in mind, it was going to be short and sweet.

Pasting on a smile, she entered the shop.

The place was deserted, the display cases bordering on bare at this hour of the afternoon as closing drew near, but the faint chime of a bell in the back announced her arrival.

A few seconds later, Alice pushed through the door that must lead to the baking area. "Ah, Emma. You came." Her mouth curved up.

"Yes. Bren passed on your message."

"I knew she would. She's reliable like that. Why don't we sit?" She motioned to the small table for two in the corner. "Would you like a cup of coffee? I'm not a fan myself, but Joe always has a pot on hand. Says he couldn't function without it, given how early he gets up."

Emma hesitated.

She'd be stuck here longer if she accepted coffee.

On the other hand, caffeine might soothe the throbbing in her temples.

"Yes. Thank you."

"Make yourself comfortable. Cream or sugar?"

"A quick tip of cream."

"Got it. I'll be back in a jiffy."

The woman bustled toward the back room and disappeared through the door.

Emma sank onto one of the chairs and massaged her temples. Skipping lunch hadn't been the smartest idea if she'd wanted to avoid a headache. But it was hard to eat when your appetite had vanished.

"Here you go." Alice reappeared and set a ceramic mug and a paper napkin in front of her. "It's not the high-end brew from The Perfect Blend, but it'll do in a pinch. I hope it's not too strong for you."

"I like strong coffee. Thank you."

"My pleasure." She sat in the chair on the other side of the table. "I imagine you're wondering what this is all about."

"Yes." Emma took a sip of the java. Definitely not The Perfect Blend, but it ought to buffer her headache.

"I don't want to take up too much of your day, so I'll get straight to the point. My husband, Joe, has been dealing with carpal tunnel syndrome for a while now. Apparently it's not uncommon among bakers. Who knew?"

"Yes, I've heard that." Emma continued to sip her coffee.

"Well, he's been putting off surgery because recovery takes six to eight weeks, and we can't afford to close the bakery for that long. So I got to thinking after you and I chatted last Saturday. You appear to have a solid background in baking. I know you'd prefer a permanent job, but Joe and I were wondering if you might be interested in working here for a couple of months to get us over the hump of his surgery. Assuming the two of you hit it off, of course, and we can agree on a fair salary. Plus, we'd want to talk to the previous employer you mentioned."

Emma froze, mug halfway to her mouth.

The owners of Sweet Dreams were willing to consider hiring her?

Her pulse picked up . . . then evened out.

Tempting as their proposal was, a temporary position wouldn't convince a court to grant her guardianship of Justin. He'd be stuck in Nebraska far longer than either of them had planned.

"I understand if you want to think this over." Alice leaned across the table and patted her hand. "Joe and I realize it's a long shot. Most people searching for full-time work don't want a temporary job. But I had to ask. You showing up when you did seemed almost providential."

Yeah, it did.

Should she give some serious thought to signing on for this gig, if they offered it to her? In light of how she'd been striking out everywhere else she'd tried, a bird in the hand wasn't to be taken lightly.

Working here would also give her a chance to investigate other opportunities in the area. Broaden her search up to Coos Bay. Be less rushed and more selective. And the experience at Sweet Dreams would beef up her resume.

She wrapped both hands around the mug. "I do want a permanent position, but they're not easy to find in small towns. My next stop was going to be Coos Bay. But this could be a logical interim step."

"So you'll consider it?"

"Yes." She pulled out her cell and a slip of paper. Called up her contacts and jotted her former boss's name and number and the chain where she'd worked. "This is who you should talk to about my skills. I'll text him to expect a call from you."

Alice took the paper from her. "You'll also want to meet Joe, just like he wants to meet you. He won't be able to do much work after the surgery, but I expect he'll be hanging around here as soon as he can to offer advice and answer questions. We'd want you to work with him for a week first. Sort of a trial run to make certain it's a good fit. Does that sound reasonable?"

"Yes."

"Then come on back and let me introduce you."

The woman led her to the cramped baking area, where the temperature was much warmer than in the front of the shop. A long work counter, part stainless steel and part wood, ran the entire length of one wall. All other wall space was lined with shelving, mixers, containers of ingredients, pan racks, bakeware, dough proofers, refrigerators, and more.

Bren had been correct.

There was barely room in the space for one baker, let alone two.

Reigning over the doughy kingdom was a short, thin man wearing a chocolate-flecked white apron, a baker's cap, and a cheery smile.

"Joe, I think we piqued her interest." Alice drew her forward and did the introductions.

"A pleasure to meet you, Emma." Joe pumped her hand. "Alice told me you worked for four years with a baker who trained in France."

"Yes, I did. Part-time during the school year and full-time in summer."

He grinned. "Our little operation would be a step down for you—but you might be able to add a touch of class to Sweet Dreams."

"It's hard to improve on legendary cinnamon rolls and your delicious brownies."

"We do excel at a few items. Why don't I give you a tour?"

"Okay." Although she could see everything there was to see from where she was standing.

But his real purpose became clear as they made their way down the center of the room and he showed her various pieces of equipment, talked about some of his standard procedures—and asked a ton of questions about everything from best practices for sanitizing the equipment and workspace to the pros and cons of wood versus stainless steel surfaces to how to salvage over-proofed dough.

He was testing her knowledge.

And based on the thumbs-up he gave her at the end of the tour, she passed with flying colors. "You know your stuff, young lady."

"I don't have any formal training." He hadn't asked, but it was only fair to be up front about that. "Just on-the-job experience."

"That's the ideal way to learn this business. If everything pans out, I hope you'll consider our offer, even if it's not a permanent job. The hours would be four to noon, Tuesday through Saturday. The shop opens at seven. Alice comes in at 6:45 and stays until close at 2:30. Did she talk to you about the weekly salary?"

"No. We hadn't gotten around to that yet." The other half of the management team chimed in from the far side of the room.

"Let me throw out a number and tell us what you think." Joe gave her a figure. "If that's sufficient and your reference comes through okay, are you willing to work with me for a week to test the waters?"

The salary wasn't huge, but it was more than sufficient to pay the bills and keep her housed and fed until she found a permanent job with benefits.

As far as she could see, there was no downside to accepting the job if they made an offer after her trial run, other than delaying Justin's liberation.

He wouldn't be happy about that. Nor was she. But any job was preferable to no job, and it would buy her time to be more selective in her search for a permanent position. Plus, changing schools midsemester wasn't ideal. Perhaps they could target December for his move and share Christmas together.

"That seems like a fair amount. And I'd be happy to work with you for a week."

"Wonderful!" Alice beamed and clapped her hands together. "If this comes together, Joe will finally be able to get that wrist fixed. Truly, Emma, you're a godsend."

"I think the timing worked out for both of us. When would you like me to start?"

"Would tomorrow be too soon?" Joe untied his apron and pulled it off.

"Tomorrow is fine."

"I'll see you bright and early." Joe shook her hand again. "Turn in with the chickens tonight."

"I'm used to the early-to-bed drill from my previous bakery job. Thank you for considering me for this."

"We're the ones who should be thanking you." Alice spoke over her shoulder as she led her to the front of the shop and toward the door. "Go around back when you get here in the morning. That door will be open." She took her hand. Gave it a squeeze. "You're the answer to a prayer."

"It's the answer to a prayer for both of us. See you tomorrow."

As Alice locked the door behind her, Emma dug out her cell and struck off down the street toward the cottage. She had to share the news with Justin ASAP.

While this wasn't the kind of job a judge would deem steady enough to grant her guardianship—if they even offered her the position after the trial run—it was a step in the right direction. A fact she'd have to stress to her brother.

Along with a reminder that if all went well, when her tenure at Sweet Dreams came to an end, she'd have another longer-lasting position waiting in the wings . . . and she'd finally be able to put the wheels in motion to fulfill her promise to rescue him from the bad situation in Nebraska. Forever.

19

. . . .

As the melodious jingle of wind chimes announced his arrival at Bev's Book Nook, Noah gave the shop a sweep. From the wicker swing chair in one corner to the macramé wall hanging, pottery lamps, and wind-sculpted driftwood interspersed among the books on the shelves, the eclectic décor created the kind of ambiance a woman with rainbow-hued hair seemed likely to find appealing.

Ditto for the appeal of the owner, who emerged from the back room. Bev's colorful caftan-like garment and that hot pink streak in her salt-and-pepper hair fit right in with the shop's vibe.

It was easy to see why Bren had been drawn to Bev.

"Welcome to Bev's Book Nook." She swept toward him in a swish of kaleidoscope color and floral fragrance. "Thank you for coming by."

He fought the urge to put on his sunglasses as the bright hues assaulted his eyes. "Happy to do it. Bren said you had a question about a business expense."

"Yes, I do. I'm out on a limb now that my accountant in Coos Bay retired. And the only CPA in Hope Harbor is too occupied with her cranberry business to take on new clients. As a matter of fact, I understand she's trying to find a home for her existing customers. So I appreciate your assistance."

"I'll be glad to help however I can."

"Come on back to the office while there's a lull in customers." She led him to the orderly stockroom at the rear of the store, where the office consisted of a laptop, desk, and filing cabinet in one corner. "Have a seat." She motioned him toward the chair in front of the laptop and drew up a stool beside the desk for herself. "Before we begin, I want to be clear that I expect you to bill me for your services."

He waved the offer aside. "There's no charge."

"I don't like taking charity. I believe people should be compensated for their expertise."

"Consider this a favor for a friend."

"We just met."

"I was referring to Bren."

"Oh." The corners of her mouth inched north. "You two have become friends."

Uh-oh. Time to backpedal in case this woman had gotten the wrong impression.

"I used the term loosely. We're new acquaintances. But I've seen her around. I mean, she's living in my dad's backyard. It's hard not to run into her."

"Of course." She offered a solemn nod, though the tiny twitch in her lips was suspicious. "She's a wonderful person, isn't she?"

"Yes. Very kind and generous."

"Indeed. It was a lucky day for Hope Harbor when she joined the community."

"I gather she thinks the reverse is also true."

"As we all do. It's amazing the number of people who've found their way to this special place. Doctors, an attorney, business executives—even a famous actress."

Interesting as that was, it had nothing to do with the reason for his visit today.

He motioned toward her laptop. "Was there a question you wanted to ask, or a spreadsheet you wanted me to review?"

"Yes. I can pull up my spreadsheet if necessary, but you may be able to answer my question without reviewing any financials."

"I'll give it a shot."

"You know about the 5K run that's being planned, don't you?"

"Yes. I'm helping out in a peripheral role while I'm here."

"Kudos to you. It's a wonderful effort. So characteristic of this town. I know Bren is on the committee—not that she has much running experience. Although I did see the two of you running together this morning."

"Yes." And that had been a mistake. He should have let her go off on her own instead of offering to accompany her. *Would* have let her go off on her own if the suggestion hadn't spilled out before he could stop it. "I was checking out the fun run route with her."

"Very helpful of you. I'm sure she appreciated your input."

Keeping this conversation on track was proving to be a challenge. "So is your question related to the run?"

"It is. I opened my shop less than a year ago, and all these months I've been focused on getting the business established. But with everything settling into place, I'd like to begin supporting the community in a tangible way. Bren told me the race committee was thinking about lining up sponsors, and that sounded like an opportunity."

"It could be. Many businesses sponsor charitable efforts."

"I assumed as much, but I have no idea how such things work. If I support the effort, is that a legitimate expense, or would it be a charitable deduction? And what if I donate merchandise instead of cash? Is there an optimal approach for this sort of sponsorship? Anything you can tell me would be appreciated."

Now they were speaking his language.

"Why don't I run you through the basics and then answer any questions you have?"

"Perfect. I'll take notes as you talk." She picked up a pad of paper and a pen from the edge of the desk.

He launched into a business donations 101 spiel, covering 501(c)(3) organizations, the IRS guidelines on charitable deductions versus business expenses, and the different rules for various corporate classifications.

"Bottom line, expenses related to charity are deductible as a business expense as long as you can show a reasonable expectation of financial return commensurate with the amount you paid."

Bev's brow puckered. "How do I do that?"

"It's not too difficult. For example, if a sponsorship fee includes advertising in any of the event's promotional materials, there would be a reasonable expectation that the goodwill generated for your business will win you more customers. A fee like that would be deducted as an advertising expense."

"What about an outright cash donation?"

"Are you a C corporation?"

"No. LLC."

"In that case, no. If you want to give cash, it would have to be a personal gift, not a corporate donation."

She tapped her pen against her notebook. "I'm thinking the sponsorship idea, with an ad, may be best."

"That would be my recommendation. Merchandise is also fine, or a gift certificate to the shop, if either of those would be used by the organization as part of its fundraising effort. Like in a raffle basket or as giveaways for participants. In those cases, you can deduct the fair market value as a business expense."

"My goodness." She blew out a breath. "I had no idea it would be this complicated to do a good deed."

"The IRS doesn't make it simple, I'll grant you that, but those kinds of rules keep people like me in business." He hitched up one side of his mouth.

"Well, you certainly know your stuff. This town could use someone with your expertise."

He let that pass. "If you have any other questions, give me a call. I'll be here another few days."

"Thank you. I'll do that." She stood. "Since you won't let me pay you for your time, let me give you some cookies to take with you."

"That's not necessary." He rose too.

"Yes, it is. No one leaves Bev's Book Nook without a sweet treat." She led him back to the front of the shop and over to a clear cookie jar on the counter. "Today's offering is your dad's favorite. Chocolate chip oatmeal. You can share your bounty with him." She began taking cookies out of the jar with a bakery paper and slipping them into a bag. "I have a book for you too."

"The cookies are more than sufficient."

"I insist. I know you said you don't have much opportunity to read, but maybe this will keep you entertained on the plane ride home."

She finished with the cookies and pulled another stapled-shut bag from under the counter. "Enjoy." She handed everything over.

"Thank you." The bag with the book was on the light side, suggesting the tome inside was a paperback rather than a pricey hardcover. Not that he wanted either, but if it made her feel better to give him a token of appreciation, it would be ungracious to refuse. He could always pass it on to someone at the office.

"You're welcome. How's Fred doing?"

"He's adapting. Not asking for as much help as he should, but that's Dad."

"Ah yes. The blessing and the curse of independence."

Noah grimaced. "I'm in the cursing phase right now—figuratively speaking."

"Fred's making it difficult for you?"

"Let's call it challenging." Like Dad's attempt to shave left-handed this morning that had left him with a slice in his chin. They'd had a spirited discussion at breakfast about the downsides of stubbornness.

"I can imagine. People who are used to being on their own can have difficulty letting anyone get too close or too involved in their life. They're afraid to rely on someone who may not be around long term, or who doesn't live up to their obligations. But often those are the people who most need a caring touch."

Were they still talking about his dad?

The speculative glint in Bev's irises suggested otherwise.

Was she sending him a message about Bren?

But what did it matter if she was? In less than a week he'd be gone. Bren would be history. He'd be back on familiar territory.

Even if that prospect didn't thrill him as much as it once had.

"I'll keep that in mind." He crimped the top of the cookie bag in his fingers.

"You do that." Bev patted his arm. "Give your dad my regards. I'm on the casserole brigade for next week. If he's up to it when I drop off the food, I'll pop in and say hello."

"I'm sure he'd enjoy seeing you." The wind chimes tinkled, giving him an excuse to exit as two customers entered. "Thanks again." He hefted his bags.

"My pleasure. And thank *you* for all your assistance."

As Bev greeted the newcomers, Noah escaped out the door. Stopped on the other side. Exhaled.

That had been a curious encounter. A meeting with two agendas, unless his instincts were off. One related to him and Bren, and one related to the charitable business deductions premise Bev had used to get him to the shop.

No matter. He'd fulfilled his promise and helped out Bren's friend. He could put this meeting behind him and focus on work for the rest of the day.

As long as thoughts of a certain hazel-eyed barista didn't sabotage his concentration.

> Fun run route should work fine for beginning runners and walkers. Sent course suggestion for serious runners to committee members' emails. Also met with Bev.

As Bren read Noah's text, she frowned, finger poised over the keypad on her cell. His clipped, businesslike report didn't invite conversation. A one-word response would suffice.

> Thanks.

She opened her email. Found the promised note from Noah, with an attachment. Opened it. Scanned his suggested route.

Very nice.

He'd managed to incorporate an impressive number of the landmarks and Helping Hands projects from the options they'd provided him.

It ought to be a stellar event.

Setting her phone aside on the dinette table in the cottage, she resumed her work on the latest batch of wedding invitations, response cards, and peripheral material, using the elaborate Spencerian hand the bride had chosen.

This was going to be a profitable job.

She let the pointed nib of her pen flow over the surface of the paper, falling into the smooth rhythm she'd developed over the years, her mind free to wander as she created the beautiful letters that would summon guests to a vineyard in Virginia to watch the happy couple exchange vows and celebrate the beginning of their new life together.

It was satisfying to contribute to someone else's fairy tale, even if she'd never experienced one firsthand.

And perhaps never would.

Much as she loved Hope Harbor, it wasn't teeming with eligible men. Definitely none who'd piqued her interest enough to take a second look.

Except one who was a temporary visitor and not at all suitable for her.

She added a few flourishes—for which the bride was paying extra—to the lettering on the envelope and moved to the next name on the address list.

Paused as a wave of melancholy swept over her.

Funny.

Working on wedding invitations had never depressed her in the past.

Maybe she should put this job aside and switch to the place cards for the high-end dinner in New York that were next on her to-do list.

That might be—

The knob rattled, and a moment later Emma entered, glancing over as she shut the door. "Sorry. I didn't mean to disturb you."

"You didn't. I'm about due to stand up and stretch." She rose as she spoke, tipping her head side to side to get the kinks out of her neck. "Did you stop in at Sweet Dreams?"

"Yes." A smile transformed her face. "They're considering hiring me."

Bren propped her hands on her hips. "For real? I thought it was a two-person show."

"It is. This would be only a temporary position, but it would give me cash flow while I search for a more permanent spot."

Bren listened as her houseguest gave her the lowdown, waiting until she finished to speak. "That's fantastic, Emma. The timing of your arrival here seems almost providential."

"That's what Alice said." The younger woman dropped onto the arm of the sofa. "Justin was bummed by the delay this could cause in my effort to get guardianship, but the experience would beef up my resume and should open more doors. I could also start looking for a place to stay."

"You don't have to rush out of here on my account. I've enjoyed having a roommate." Which was surprising, after more than a decade of contentedly being on her own.

"But I'd have to go to bed super early for this job. Like by eight o'clock. That would be a huge inconvenience, with me sleeping in the living room."

Oh yeah. There was that.

"I imagine we could work something out."

"That might be difficult. Besides, I have to establish a permanent address before I can apply for guardianship. The sooner the better, so I have some tenure there and don't have any delays once I land a permanent job. You mentioned an apartment complex once that was nearby."

"Yes. Sea Breeze. Bev at the Book Nook lives there. I'm not anxious for you to leave, but I see your point about getting an address on record. Let me ask her for the contact information for the manager."

Twin furrows creased Emma's forehead. "Do you think they'll want a big deposit? I don't have much in reserve after the car repairs, and I won't have a paycheck for a week."

"If they do, I can give you a brief loan to get you over the hump."

A sheen appeared in Emma's eyes. "I don't know how I got lucky enough to cross paths with you, Bren, but I'll be thanking God for that every day for the rest of my life."

"Just pay it forward someday, okay?" Bren walked over and gave her a hug.

"I will." Emma squeezed back. "Now I'm going to run over to St. Francis and share the good news with Father Murphy. Let him know his prayers for me may be on the verge of being answered. That will also give you a chance to work without further distraction." She motioned to the stacks of envelopes on the table.

Bren surveyed the pile.

She did need to hunker down and pick up the pace. Her calligraphy schedule was full, and her customers were counting on her to get the elegant lettering for their special events done on schedule.

Yet as she waved Emma off a few minutes later and returned to her chore, it wasn't her young houseguest who proved to be the biggest distraction to the task at hand.

The blame for that fell on Noah.

Because from her seat at the table, she had a clear view of him as he followed his father out the back door, retrieved a shovel from the garage, and proceeded to dig up what appeared to be a dead rosebush in the corner of the yard while Fred supervised.

Setting her elbow on the table, she propped her chin in her palm and watched as he effortlessly took care of the job. Shared a laugh with his father. Rested his hand on the older man's shoulder, his deep love and affection evident in his touch and his expression.

Her throat constricted.

How different her life could have been if she'd had a father like Fred.

How different it could *still* be if she had someone in it who looked at her like Noah was looking at his dad.

When the two men at last strolled back inside, Noah hovered close as Fred navigated the uneven stepping stones, ready to steady him if he stumbled.

That's what love should be all about. Caring. Protecting. Lending a hand and offering support. Sharing a laugh. A touch. A life.

Fingering the imperial jasper earring that symbolized the power of companionship, Bren exhaled.

For years, she'd told herself she was fine going it alone.

And she was. She didn't need a man to survive or to make her life complete.

Yet thanks to Bev's insights—and the arrival of a handsome CPA—she was beginning to admit she might *want* a man in her life.

It wasn't going to be Noah, however, despite the sizzle of attraction that made her respiration go haywire whenever he was near. Even if they had far more in common than she'd initially thought, he'd be gone in a handful of days, back to his demanding job and big-city lifestyle.

She considered the next stack of envelopes for the vineyard wedding in Virginia. Hesitated. Set that project aside and moved on to the place cards for the black-tie event.

It wasn't that she begrudged this bride and groom their happy ending. Not at all. And she'd return to their job in a day or two.

After she came to terms with her sudden case of romanceitis—and figured out how to deal with it when an actual romance was nowhere in sight.

20

· ·

"That was tasty lasagna Bren sent over last night for dinner, wasn't it?"

"Very." As Noah replied to his dad, he set the casserole pan he'd removed from the dishwasher on the counter.

"And there's plenty left for me after you go home next week too. I see some Italian lunches in my future."

Noah removed the bowl for the salad that had accompanied the main dish and put it beside this morning's breakfast dishes waiting to be stacked in the dishwasher.

May as well share the idea that had been percolating in his mind for the past few days. Dad would find out soon enough.

"I've been thinking about asking my boss to let me extend my stay another week. On a remote work basis, not vacation."

"Now that's music to my ears." His father's face lit up. "Though I think your so-called vacation *was* remote work. You were holed up in your room on that laptop most days—and evenings."

"It's the nature of my job."

"How will your boss feel about you staying longer?"

Not happy.

But the closer his departure date loomed, the less inclined he was to leave after only two weeks.

"Remains to be seen." He kept his tone nonchalant.

"May I ask what prompted this change of heart? I got the impression when you arrived that you were champing at the bit to go back."

"I was concerned about my workload." Plus the loss of face time, although now that he'd been away for eleven days, that seemed less important. "But I've been managing to keep up. And with your wrist out of commission, I'd rather hang around a little longer."

His dad appraised him. "I'm coping without too much trouble, and I did fill out the help checklist. Not that I'm discouraging you from staying, but I think I'll be covered after you're gone."

In other words, his father wasn't buying the broken wrist rationale for his son's decision to linger.

He should have known Dad would see through that excuse.

But he wasn't going to reveal the other reason for his change of heart.

Namely, that Bren had gotten under his skin—and he was still trying to figure out what to do about it.

"I have to admit the people here seem to watch out for each other. But it's not like having someone in the house within calling distance 24/7."

"That's true." His dad finished off the last of his morning coffee. "You think your boss will go along with this?"

"I won't know until I ask. I'd call today, but I don't want to bother him on a Saturday. I'll touch base with him early Monday morning."

A twinkle appeared in his father's eyes. "I could groan in the background, if you think that would help."

Noah's lips twitched. "I appreciate the offer, but I expect I can plead my case without sound effects."

His father studied him, concern creasing his brow. "I don't want to cause problems for you with your job, Noah. I really would be fine here on my own, you know."

Yeah, he knew.

And his dad knew he knew.

But concern about his father was the rationale he'd given for wanting to stay, and he was sticking with it.

"I'd just feel more comfortable if you had another week or so to heal before I leave."

"I appreciate that, Son." He rose and waved a hand toward Bren's dishes on the counter. "That casserole brigade is a wonder, isn't it? Thanks to this broken wrist, I've eaten better in the past week than I have since your mom passed on. Tasty food combined with pleasant companionship can stimulate a person's appetite. And that lasagna was top-notch. Bren is quite a cook."

"Yes, she is." Noah tucked their breakfast plates and utensils into the emptied dishwasher.

"Would you mind running her dishes over to the cottage for me? I wouldn't want to trip on the stepping stones while I'm trying to juggle those one-handed."

Blast.

An encounter with Bren hadn't been part of his morning plans, but there was no logical excuse to refuse his father's request.

At least she'd had Emma deliver the food last night, eliminating the possibility of any contact between the two of them during the handoff.

"I can do that."

"Thanks. What's on your schedule today?"

"Nothing special. I got my run in early, leaving me at loose ends aside from a couple of tasks for work. Would you like to take a drive up the coast? I remember how much you and Mom always enjoyed your trips to Shore Acres State Park."

"That would be a treat—but could we defer it until tomorrow? My golfing buddy called last night. He got tickets at the last minute for a talk up at the college in Coos Bay by a paleontologist from Oregon State. The guy's an expert on Jurassic-age vertebrate fossils found in the state. I assumed you'd be working most of the day, so I agreed to go."

"I'll pencil Shore Acres in for tomorrow." His father's social calendar was a sight to behold.

Another indication he'd be fine on his own here—and more proof there was no need to convince him to return to St. Louis.

"Be sure to give my compliments to the chef." His father tapped the edge of the casserole dish.

"I'll do that."

"If you have a chunk of free time later today, you could wander down to Starfish Pier. The tide pools are spectacular."

"Yes, they are. Bren told me about them, so I stopped in during one of my runs."

"A long walk on the beach is always a fine option."

"I'll see how my day looks after I check in at work."

His father rolled his eyes. "Once you sit in front of that laptop, you'll be glued there for the duration."

"Not necessarily." But the probability was high.

"Before you boot up, don't forget about this." Dad tapped the casserole again.

"I'm on it." He picked up the bowl and dish and walked over to the back door. "I'll be back in a minute."

"Don't rush on my account. I'm going to catch up on email. I have a ton of well-wishes I need to acknowledge."

As his dad disappeared down the hall, Noah exited through the rear door, crossed the lawn to the cottage . . . and attempted to ratchet back the surge in his pulse.

Yet hard as he tried to rein it in, his galloping heart refused to cooperate.

Fine.

He'd hand off the dishes, say his thanks, beat a hasty retreat—and keep his distance until he got a handle on why his father's tenant was wreaking havoc on his usual self-control and logical thinking process.

Of course, he could do that just as efficiently in St. Louis as he could in Oregon.

Which made extending his stay foolish and illogical. Likewise for his reluctance to leave.

Another example of how the pretty barista had messed with his brain.

Taking a steadying breath, he paused at the cottage door. Knocked.

"Come in."

At Bren's muffled invitation, he frowned.

She left her door unlocked? And she was inviting an unknown caller in without checking to see who it was?

That was super risky in this day and age.

Brow bunching, he twisted the knob while juggling the bowl and casserole dish and pushed the door open.

As he stepped across the threshold, she glanced up from the dinette table where she was surrounded by stacks of envelopes, her smile of welcome faltering as their gazes met.

"Dad asked me to return these and to give his compliments to the chef." Noah hoisted the items in his hand. "I second that."

"I'm glad you enjoyed the meal." As she pushed back her chair to stand, she bumped the table. A tall stack of envelopes near the edge toppled, spilling onto the floor. "Dang." She dropped to her hands and knees and began gathering them up.

Noah strode across the room, set the casserole and bowl on the island, and joined her on the floor to help collect the scattered envelopes. "Sorry for interrupting you and causing a mess."

"This was my own fault." Tension pinged off her, almost visceral now that he was within touching distance. "You don't have to help me pick these up."

"I don't mind. Being on all fours appears to be my lot when visiting this cottage." Perhaps a touch of levity would dispel some of the nervous energy bouncing off the walls. "Fortunately, on this visit I don't feel like I've been plunged into the bowels of hades."

He was rewarded with an amused snuffle that she quickly smothered. "Sorry. I know it's not funny."

"It is in hindsight. It's the kind of story people tell their grand-kids."

She froze, and his stomach twisted.

Where had *that* stupid comment come from? It was the sort of thing you said to someone you intended to share your life with. To share grandkids with. He and Bren weren't a couple.

She cleared her throat and resumed picking up the envelopes.

"I, uh, suppose that's true." She didn't quite pull off her obvious attempt at a chatty, relaxed tone.

Hard as Noah tried to think of another humorous comeback that would lighten the atmosphere, he drew a blank.

So he continued to gather up envelopes, skimming the front of one as he did so.

Stopped.

Examined a few more of the addresses that were penned in a graceful, elaborate script.

They looked like the kind of envelopes he'd received that contained invitations to friends' weddings.

And there were stacks of them on the table.

His breath hitched.

Was there something he didn't know about Bren? Something his father didn't know about her?

Pulse skittering, he tried to speak past the tightness in his wind-pipe that was restricting the flow of air to his lungs. "The calligraphy on these makes me think of wedding invitations."

"Calligraphy is used for many different purposes, but yes, these are wedding invitations."

His stomach bottomed out.

Bren was getting married.

A shock wave surged through him as he tried to absorb the startling news that was almost as traumatizing as the faceful of pepper gel he'd gotten on his last visit here.

Bren was getting married.

Even as he silently repeated that, it didn't compute.

Hadn't she admitted less than a week ago that she felt the connection between them as much as he did—even if they'd agreed that pursuing it would be foolish?

Why would she do that if she was engaged?

More importantly, why should he care? Hadn't he thought all along they weren't compatible? That a go-with-the-flow woman and a plan-everything-to-the-nth-degree guy could never have a future together? That geography aside, it could never work? Wasn't that why he'd been avoiding her ever since the night he'd almost kissed her?

Yes, yes, yes, and yes.

So he should be glad he wouldn't have to angst about this anymore. As a matter of fact, maybe he ought to return to St. Louis as planned and—

"Noah?"

At Bren's prompt, he refocused. "Yes?"

"Are you all right?"

"Yeah. Sure. I'm fine." He tried without success to clear the rasp from his voice. "Um . . . congratulations."

Her face went blank. "What?"

"Congratulations. On the wedding." He lifted the envelopes clutched in a death grip in his hand.

As understanding dawned on her face, she shook her head. "Those aren't for *my* wedding."

He tried to process that. Failed. "Why else would you have a whole tableful of wedding invitations here?"

"I'm a calligrapher." She picked up a stray invitation that had eluded them, stood, and motioned to the table beside him.

He rose too and scanned the surface.

Behind the piles of envelopes and what appeared to be response cards, there was a desktop easel in a slanted position, several pens, nibs with different tips, ink, a fine paintbrush, and parchment paper.

But the main thing that registered?

Bren wasn't getting married.

She was unattached and available.

His spirits ticked up.

"Sorry. I assumed you were about to walk down the aisle."

She snorted. "The closest I've ever gotten to a walk down the aisle is at the grocery store. That's the closest I ever *wanted* to get."

Understandable, in light of her history. Growing up with a direct window into a toxic marriage would turn anyone off of matrimony.

Which was sad.

So why did the solitary life she'd chosen as a result of her traumatic upbringing make him happy?

More than happy, in fact. It kindled in him an excitement and sense of anticipation similar to what he'd felt on Christmas mornings as a kid while he waited for the all-clear from Dad that Santa had come and it was safe to run into the living room and dive into all the wonderful surprises wrapped in colorful paper waiting for him under the tree.

"So, uh, are you doing this for a friend?" He waved a hand over the table and tried to put a lid on his sudden cheer.

"No. It's a paying gig."

"Yeah?" He surveyed the equipment again. Inspected one of the envelopes.

Her work was beautiful. Flawless. Elegant.

This was not an amateur effort.

"Mm-hmm." She set the envelopes she'd picked up on the table. "How does a person become a professional calligrapher?"

"A ton of practice. Classes. Online tutorials."

"How long have you been doing this?"

She shrugged. "I started to dabble at it in high school. It gave me an excuse to stay in my room and avoid the drama in our household. I was self-taught at the beginning, but after I did a few projects at school, I began to get an occasional paying job. I kept practicing through the years, honing my skills, and after I settled here, I set up an online business. It took a while to get established, but in the past twelve months, I've been inundated with orders."

"So is it like a hobby that pays for itself, or a paying job? If you don't mind me asking."

"I don't mind. It's a paying job. Weddings tend to be the most lucrative because they have multiple pieces that require calligraphy. This one is big." She nodded toward the table. "It will take me two weeks to finish, working part-time. And the pay is excellent."

When she rattled off the tab for the job, he did a double take. "I had no idea calligraphers earned those kinds of bucks."

"If you have a reputation, it can be very profitable. I'm booked six months in advance these days, with a waiting list. My website gets a ton of traffic."

She had a website and a waiting list?

This was a serious business.

"It sounds like you could do this full-time and give up The Perfect Blend."

"I could, but I'm all about balance." She picked up a nib. Examined the tip. Set it back down. "I'd burn out if I did this ten hours a day, every day. And I enjoy the social interaction during my Monday/Wednesday/Friday shifts at The Blend. Calligraphy is a solitary occupation, and while I'm independent and like my space, I'm not built for that much isolation. This gives me the best of both worlds."

Along with an impressive income.

So much for his assumption early on that Bren was content to spend her life making fancy drinks.

What else had he misread about this woman?

"I admire the way you've built a life that suits you."

She tilted her head. "Like you have. Right?"

"I thought so." He fingered one of the beautifully inscribed envelopes. "And I guess I have, career wise. But my job success has come at the expense of a personal life. And a family."

As that admission spilled out, he scowled.

Why on earth had he started down such a personal road?

Of course, Bren followed along. Why wouldn't she, when he'd opened the latch on the gate?

"You have to meet the right person for that to happen."

"Yeah. I imagine that would be tough in a town the size of Hope Harbor." Switching the spotlight back to her seemed like a sound strategy. "Assuming a person was looking."

"Yes. It would be." But she ignored his implied question, about whether *she* was looking.

And he was curious, thanks to the wiggle room she'd left in her answer about not wanting to walk down the aisle. Her use of a past tense versus a present tense could suggest she'd rethought her position on that question.

She folded her arms. "I can't imagine it would be hard to meet the right person in a city the size of St. Louis, though. Assuming a person was looking."

Following his lead, she didn't put *her* implied question into words either as she parroted his comment back to him. But it came through loud and clear.

How to answer?

He could blow it off. Spout a generic comment, as she had. Shut down this conversation.

But in light of his reaction to the news that she wasn't getting married, maybe he ought to tell her about Candace. It would help her understand why he moved with extreme caution when it came to romance. He could also let her know he wasn't averse to falling in love in principle.

However . . . the safest route was to shut down the discussion.

Because it was possible he and Bren had more in common than he'd expected, now that he was getting a peek below the surface and finding the hidden treasure. Like Charley had mentioned that morning on the headland, about Sunrise Reef.

Nevertheless, that didn't mean they could ever be anything more than friends, despite the electricity between them. He was too far along on his career path in St. Louis to switch directions, and Bren had made it clear she considered Hope Harbor her permanent home. That this was where her long search had led her.

Yet even if nothing more than friendship was their destiny, what could it hurt to give her a few insights about his past?

Nothing, as far as he could see.

So if he could summon up the courage to open his heart as she'd done the night they'd shared far more than an ice cream bar, he'd tell her in all its gory detail the dating disaster story that had left him gun-shy of romance.

21

She shouldn't have thrown his comment back at him. If she hadn't answered *his* indirect question about whether she was looking to meet the right person, why should she expect him to answer hers?

Even if it would be nice to know.

"So, uh, where is your roommate today?" Noah glanced around the cottage.

He was changing the subject.

It appeared her curiosity wasn't going to be satisfied.

But you couldn't force people to confide in you if they weren't ready, as she'd told Noah early on about Emma.

Stifling her disappointment, Bren tightened the cap on the ink lid. "At work. Sweet Dreams hired her. She started yesterday." She gave him a quick recap of the good news. "She's planning to rent an apartment next week."

"Did you ever find out what brought her out here?"

"Yes. She and her younger brother were in a bad situation. He'll be joining her as soon as she's established here and can petition for guardianship." The rest of what Emma had relayed had been shared in confidence. But since Justin would be living with his sister for all the world to see, it should be fine to pass on that part of her story.

"I guess your instincts about her were sound."

She forced up the corners of her mouth. "When you've walked a mile in someone's shoes, it can be easier to spot a kindred spirit."

"Yeah." His Adam's apple bobbed, and he shifted his weight from one foot to the other. "What time does she get off?"

"Noon." Bren watched him, trying without success to identify the strange vibes wafting in her direction.

He straightened the pile of envelopes he'd gathered up, aligning all the corners to create a neat, precise stack. "You, uh, mentioned a couple of minutes ago that it shouldn't be hard to meet the right person in a city the size of St. Louis, if someone was looking."

Interesting that he was circling back to their previous subject and venturing into what promised to be more personal territory.

"I assumed there'd be a bigger pool of eligible people to draw from in a large city. Was I wrong?"

"I don't know. I wasn't looking. Like I said, my personal life has always taken a distant second place to my career. But I did meet someone *without* looking earlier this year."

Bren's lungs lurched.

The man standing across from her was involved in a romance back home?

But then . . . why had he almost kissed her? That didn't fit the image he radiated of integrity and honesty and conscientiousness.

Slowly she lowered herself into her chair at the table. "Are you saying you have a significant other?"

"No." His response was immediate and definitive. "May I?" He indicated the chair across from her.

She waved him into it. "I'm a little confused."

"So was I." He sat. Sighed. "To cut to the chase, I had a bad dating experience that left me very gun-shy."

Ah. That explained a lot.

Guys who'd been burned could be more inclined to walk a

wide circle around romance even if a seemingly perfect match showed up. And she and Noah were far from perfect, at least on the surface. Different educational levels and backgrounds aside, there were also the geographic challenges.

No wonder he'd been skittish around her—other than the one lapse at the cottage door.

A surge of high-voltage current zipped through her as the memory of those charged moments replayed in her mind.

Curbing the urge to pick up one of the envelopes and fan her face, she rested her hands one atop the other on the table. "I've had a few of those too. Early on, after I left home, when I still hoped there were some guys out there who were genuine and knew how to appreciate a woman without trying to change who she was. It didn't take me long to see through most of them, though." She exhaled. "It can be easy to be fooled by appearances. Even for someone who knows better."

"I hear you. But as Charley reminded me not long ago, it's what's below the surface that counts." His gaze locked onto hers.

O-kay.

Was he talking about her? Was he saying a romance between an Oxford-shirt-wearing CPA and a barista with purple-hued hair wasn't as far-fetched as it sounded?

Before she could ponder that question, he continued.

"But I fall into the fooled camp with Candace." His forehead crinkled. "It all started when one of my colleagues asked me if I'd be his sister's date for a wedding. I wasn't all that thrilled about the idea, but I did it as a favor for him."

"The date didn't go well?"

"On the contrary. It went very well. She turned out to be buttoned-up and career-focused like I am, well-educated, articulate, attractive, a rising star in her engineering firm."

In other words, everything the Hope Harbor barista sitting across from him wasn't.

"She sounds like a perfect fit." She tried not to let her dejection show in her voice.

"I thought the same. Until she began to get clingy about a month into our dating."

"Clingy how?"

"Dropping hints about marriage. Inviting me to meet her parents. Showing up at my condo unannounced. Expecting me to call her five or six times a day. Sending me dozens of texts with suggestive emojis every day."

"Whoa." Bren gaped at him. "There may be a stronger term than clingy for that sort of behavior."

"I know. Trust me, several came to mind." He forked his fingers through his hair. "I found out later she was in the throes of a major case of rebounditis. If I'd known that, I would never have asked her out for a second date. Or any of the dates that followed."

"How long did you see her?"

"Too long." A muscle in his cheek spasmed. "In hindsight, it feels like an eternity, but it was only about two months. I finally called a halt, which didn't go over well with her—or her brother."

"But the fault wasn't yours. It sounds like her take about your intentions was way out of proportion to your actual interest."

"Bingo. And as far as I know, I never did anything to suggest to her during what I considered to be casual dating that I was ready or willing to get more serious with her. I thought we were in the exploratory stage."

"That's a reasonable assumption. No one should jump to conclusions about a relationship too fast." Even one that generated immediate sparks, like the ones she'd felt for the man across from her. Or an attraction so powerful some might be inclined to call it love at first sight.

Yet letting emotions influence decisions would be imprudent and dangerous. Getting too involved too quickly was a recipe for disaster. Period.

"It may be a reasonable assumption for most people, but it wasn't with Candace—and the situation got worse after the breakup."

"How is that possible?"

"She became vindictive and decided to spew trash talk about me to her brother, who shared it with other people at work."

"Oh, Noah. That had to be incredibly awkward. I'm sorry you ran into someone like her."

"Me too." He scrubbed a hand down his face. "I mean, I suppose I could have been a tad more diplomatic in my breakup speech, but I'd had it. I wanted her to know in no uncertain terms that it was over and I didn't want to hear from her again."

"Did she get the message?"

"Yes. She never contacted me again—but her brother got an earful." Noah picked up one of the envelopes. Rubbed a finger over the thick, expensive paper stock. "I have to admit, the whole experience made me wonder if romance was more trouble than it was worth."

"I can understand that."

"But I'm having second thoughts about that now." He looked at her across the piles of wedding-related material.

Her heart flip-flopped.

Was he suggesting she was the reason for that?

And if so, what did that mean? Because his life was in St. Louis and hers was here. Plus, they hardly knew each other. Maybe all the sparks between them were a flash in the pan. An opposites-attracting phenomenon that would fizzle as fast as it had ignited.

They needed to be sensible about this. And honest. And up front. Talk the situation through like two mature adults.

Bren filled her lungs. Linked her fingers on the table. Took the plunge. "May I ask you a question?"

"Shoot."

"Did I play a role in your new perspective about romance?" Best to confirm that before proceeding.

There was no more than a nanosecond of hesitation. "Yes."

Somewhere in the dark and lonely recesses of her heart, a cheer erupted.

But she tried hard to ignore it. No way was she going to plunge headlong into a doomed romance and make a dumb mistake.

"Noah, I think we have to be realistic and—"

"Wait." He held up a hand, palm forward. "Let me see if I can guess where you're going with this. We met less than two weeks ago. Our lives are based in different parts of the country. Getting carried away by a mutual attraction—assuming I haven't misread that—would be crazy. We're sensible adults who should base any decisions about romance on logic and data and careful analysis. How close did I come?"

"Close. But I wouldn't have put it in quite such methodical terms. I was just going to say we shouldn't let hormones make us do something stupid."

He hitched up one side of his mouth. "I like your take better. It's short, sweet, and to the point."

"So what do we do about this?"

"Give ourselves time to sort it out."

"I like that concept in theory, but time's running out. Aren't you leaving Tuesday?"

"I'm going to try and extend my stay by a week."

Another cheer erupted in her heart.

Nevertheless . . .

"Three weeks still isn't sufficient to make decisions that will affect the rest of our lives." She leaned forward. "You know I love Hope Harbor, and your career is in St. Louis. If we got serious, what are the odds your boss would convert your position into a permanent remote work arrangement?"

His rumpled brow previewed his answer. "Low. The only extended remote work the company ever allowed was during Covid, and management terminated it as fast as possible."

That news wasn't unexpected, but it put what appeared to be an insurmountable barrier on the path to a relationship.

"I don't see how this will ever work, Noah." Hard as she tried to mask it, a tinge of discouragement wove through her words.

"Assuming everything else clicked, geography may be a deal-breaker."

He massaged the bridge of his nose. "I know. And I don't want to start something we can't finish."

"Me neither."

"Let's think about this for a few days, okay?"

As far as she could see, there wasn't much to think about. They were at an impasse, pure and simple.

But giving themselves a few days couldn't hurt.

"That works for me."

"Besides, we may be putting the cart before the horse."

"How so?"

After a moment, he stood and held out his hand. "Walk me to the door while I tell you?"

She gave his outstretched fingers a wary inspection. Holding hands wasn't the best idea if they wanted to be cautious about their situation. Any contact could hike up the wattage and make it more difficult to think logically.

However, the invitation was too hard to resist.

Giving up the fight, she slipped her fingers into his warm, firm grip and tried to ignore the delicious tingle that raced up her spine as he squeezed and tugged her to her feet.

"So explain your cart-before-the-horse statement." Her request came out a tad breathless as she walked across the room by his side.

"We've both agreed that there's serious chemistry between us, but we've never put that to the test with an actual kiss. For all we know, it could fizzle." He stopped by the door and faced her, his mesmerizing blue eyes mere inches away, a heady trace of his aftershave tickling her nose, the barest hint of stubble on his strong jaw begging for a finger graze.

Was he kidding?

How could a kiss do anything but ratchet up the already potent adrenaline that was shutting down her lungs?

"I, uh, think you may be flirting with danger. What happened to let's not get carried away? And basing our decision on logic and data and careful analysis?"

"In my business, we never make decisions without complete information. You can't analyze a situation until you have all the facts, and this is a critical one. Don't you think we should do a bit of research?"

She squinted at him. "I'm having trouble linking the concepts of kissing and research. And this isn't helping my muddled thinking." She lifted their entwined hands.

"My brain isn't all that lucid right now, either. That can happen when a beautiful woman is standing inches away."

At his husky admission, warmth filled Bren's heart. Spilled over, like molten joy.

Hard as she tried to come up with a response, her brain refused to cooperate. All she could do was stare at him, sending who knew what subliminal message . . . or invitation.

In the silence that followed, Noah's features softened. He lifted his free hand. Traced the curve of her cheek. Ran the pad of his thumb softly across her lips.

Her lungs stalled.

If she kissed this man, she was going to be a goner.

But how could she *not* kiss him when she wanted to taste his lips with every fiber of her being?

"You win." The concession came out in a croak.

He eased closer, until nothing but a whisper separated them. Then he slid his free hand behind her neck. Slowly bent down and feathered kisses across her forehead. Trailed them down her cheek . . . close, so tantalizingly close, to her mouth. Lifted their joined hands and settled hers flat on his chest, where the steady, rapid beat of his heart throbbed against her fingertips.

Her eyelids drifted closed, and as she swayed toward him, Noah pressed her close, his hand in the small of her back. Someone whimpered.

Good heavens.

Had that sound come from *her*?

Before she could process that question, Noah's lips were on hers, warm and gentle, exploring and tasting, compelling and coaxing.

But she needed no persuading to dive into the kiss.

And what a kiss it was. Intoxicating, delicious, satisfying, tempting—and filled with enough electricity to light the town of Hope Harbor for a month.

When he at last broke contact and eased slightly back, he was breathing as hard as she was.

"Wow." It was all she could manage.

"Yeah." His response came out in a hoarse rasp, and he cleared his throat. "Based on this research, I don't think we have to worry about the chemistry fizzling."

"No. Not an issue." She struggled to get her respiration under control. "But as far as I can see, this experiment only complicates everything."

"I won't argue with that."

"So what next?"

"Let's not try to answer that question yet. We should give ourselves a chance to come up for air first." He drew back several more inches and took both her hands in his. "If all goes well, I'll buy myself another week here. We don't have to decide on next steps tonight."

No, but they would soon. And until then, how was she supposed to sleep now that he'd whetted her appetite for a romance that didn't seem to have any likelihood of succeeding?

On top of that, this was all moving at a dizzying speed.

"A week isn't very long. I would think you'd want to be super cautious after Candace."

"You're not Candace." He touched the tip of her nose. "And circumstances sometimes force conversations sooner than is optimal. But talking and doing are two different things. We're just at the exploring-the-possibilities stage. Who knows? There may be an answer we haven't thought of." His mouth curved up. "But I'll tell you one thing, Bren Ryan. Wherever this connection between us leads or doesn't lead, you are one amazing woman."

Doesn't lead?

That caveat wasn't promising, despite his flattering comment and their earth-shattering kiss.

But he was a practical man, after all. Focused on spreadsheets and analytics and making sure everything added up. And even with her limited exposure to the kind of stuff a CPA did, she knew that the math with the two of them wasn't adding up, much as both of them wished it would.

"Bren?" He quirked an eyebrow at her.

She summoned up a shaky smile. "Thank you for saying that. You're not too bad yourself, Noah Ward."

"Hold that thought. Let's talk again Monday after I have a conversation with my boss. I promised my dad a trip to Shore Acres State Park tomorrow, which means I'll be tied up most of the day."

"I'm on board with that plan."

He bent down and brushed his lips over hers again in a tender kiss that left sweetness and promise in its wake.

Then he slipped through the door and disappeared.

As he would soon do forever unless they somehow figured out how to conduct a long-distance courtship—and how to reconcile two very different lifestyles and two very different addresses.

22

. . . .

"That's a wrap for today, Emma. Great job."

As Joe sent her a smile while he put away the last of the clean baking sheets, warmth spread through her. "Thank you. You've been very kind and patient these past two days."

"No one learns the routine of a new operation overnight, but you've picked it up fast. And if this works out, Alice will be close at hand, so you wouldn't be totally on your own here."

"That's right. I'm always a holler away." The older woman pushed through from the front of the shop and lifted her cell. "Surgeon's office is on the line. They said they tried to call you, but your phone must be on silent."

Joe pulled out his cell and peered at it. "Yep. That switch has a mind of its own. What do they want?"

"They had a cancellation and can fit you in on Wednesday. Yea or nay?"

He propped his hands on his hips. "Did you ever reach the baker Emma worked for?"

"Just got off the phone with him before the surgeon's office called. He gave her a glowing report."

"That's good enough for me." Joe swiveled toward her. "You ready to take the helm, Emma?"

After only three days working with the resident baker—assuming Joe was even planning to work on Tuesday?

A flutter of panic nipped at her confidence.

And what about the idea she'd hoped to propose if Joe was comfortable with her skills?

"No worries if you don't feel ready, Emma. I've lived with the issue for years. Another six weeks won't hurt me." Joe patted her arm. "But we'll have all day Tuesday to go over any questions you have, and from what I've seen these past two days, I have no doubts about your abilities and your readiness to take this on."

That made one of them.

But she *had* more or less run the show near the end of her tenure at the bakery in her stepfather's grocery chain while her boss was on vacation. Plus, she had four years of experience in a much larger operation than Sweet Dreams.

She ought to be able to do this.

No. That sounded too uncertain.

She *could* do this.

Besides, the sooner Joe had the surgery, the sooner she could move on to a permanent job. A crucial step in her plan to petition for guardianship.

Squaring her shoulders, she gave a definitive nod. "I think you should go ahead and take the cancellation."

Joe turned toward Alice. "You heard the lady. It's a yea."

As the female member of management put the phone back to her ear, she gave them a thumbs-up and returned to the front of the shop.

"Anything else we should talk about before we shut down for the day?" Joe took off his apron.

"Um . . ."

He glanced over at her. "If there's something on your mind, I'm all ears. And I don't bite. Alice will vouch for that." He pulled off his baker's cap.

Go ahead and throw the idea out there, Emma. All he can do is shoot it down. It's not like your job is on the line here.

She inhaled. Crimped her fingers together. "I was wondering if it would be okay for me to add a few other pastries to the case while I'm here. Time permitting, of course—and nothing to compete with your cinnamon rolls and brownies. I just thought it would be fun to offer a treat of the day. Like a special."

"Treat of the day." Joe cocked his head. "I never considered doing anything like that, but I can see the appeal. The cinnamon rolls and brownies are our staples, but adding a bit of variety to my usual cookies and cupcakes and coffee cakes isn't a bad idea. What did you have in mind?"

"Well, I did learn how to make French pastries at my other job, and I have a killer baklava recipe from my mother's side of the family that your patrons might enjoy. I was thinking along the lines of fruit tarts on Tuesday, baklava on Wednesday, eclairs on Thursday. That kind of rotation."

He pursed his lips. "I like the concept, but French pastries are out of my league. After you leave, customers who've gotten to like the fancier fare may be disappointed."

She couldn't argue with his rationale.

Maybe at her next job, she'd have an opportunity to put her more advanced skills to use.

"That's true." She removed her apron and called up a smile. "Forget I brought it up."

He studied her for a moment. "I'll tell you what. Let me talk it over with Alice tonight, get her input. She's always been the brains behind the operation." He grinned.

"I don't want to cause waves. I probably shouldn't have broached the idea this soon."

"Don't apologize for offering suggestions. I've been following the same routine so long I may have fallen into a rut. I'll discuss it with Alice and give you a call with the verdict. And keep a list of any questions that come to mind over the next couple of days."

"I'll do that. Enjoy your days off."

"That's a given, now that I know I'll be leaving the shop in such capable hands."

"Thank you." Emma pushed through to the front of the shop, waved goodbye to Alice as the older woman waited on a customer, and exited into a gloriously sunny day.

Next on her agenda? A visit to Sea Breeze Apartments. Bren's friend at the Book Nook had come through with the contact information, and the manager had been more than happy to set up a tour of the available units for this afternoon.

But first, a call to Justin.

As she walked toward her car, she pulled out her cell and scrolled through her recents. Tapped on his name.

Two rings in, he answered. "Hey, Sis. I've been thinking about you. How's the trial run on the job going?"

"It's not a trial run anymore. They just hired me."

"Awesome!"

"So how are *you* doing?"

"Hanging in."

"Bill giving you any trouble?"

"Nah. He's too busy with his new girlfriend."

She swallowed past her disgust. "What happened to Paula?"

"He must have gotten tired of her. Like he got tired of Mom." Bitterness scored his words.

Stomach clenching, Emma jabbed at her autolock button as she approached her car.

She had to get Justin out of there. Living in the same house with someone like Bill could make a person jaded. Especially a young, impressionable, and vulnerable teen. Bottom line, their stepfather was a bad influence.

And if Bill decided to drag his feet on the guardianship issue for some strange reason, she'd tell that to the court. Not that he was likely to object to her petition. If he had a new woman in his life, chances were he'd be happy to be rid of the responsibility for Mom's remaining offspring.

"Hey. You still there?"

At Justin's prompt, she refocused. "Yes. I'm sorry I can't get you out of there faster, but I do have another piece of positive news to share. I'm visiting an apartment complex today that sounds promising. If it pans out, I may soon have a permanent address. That's a major step toward my court petition."

"So do you think you may be able to pull this off sooner than December?"

At the hope in his voice, she bit her lip.

While making promises she might not be able to honor wouldn't be fair, it was important to keep hope alive.

She slid behind the wheel, stuck the key in the ignition, and composed her response with care. "I'll try to speed up the process if I can. But I want to be sure I have all my ducks in a row. I don't want to sabotage myself before I have everything in place that the court will expect."

"Couldn't I come out for an extended visit until all the paper-work goes through? I bet Bill would sign off on that."

"What about school? I don't think I can enroll you until I have guardianship and this is your permanent address."

"I could drop out. Take a year off and pick up again next fall."

Bad idea. Not only was that illegal in most states, as far as she knew, but a lot of dropouts never returned to school. That's why *she'd* hung in until she'd gotten her diploma.

But try telling that to a desperate sixteen-year-old who'd lost his mother and was stuck with a stepfather who didn't really want him.

"I don't think that's the best choice, even if it happens to be legal here—which I doubt. Can you try to hang in until the end of the first semester? Stick with our plan to get this done by Christmas?"

A sigh came over the line. "I guess. Sorry to put pressure on you. I know you're doing everything you can. I just . . . I miss you and I hate it here."

Her throat pinched. "I wish I could wave a magic wand and make this happen sooner. But I'll touch base every day. And you can call me anytime. Promise me you'll keep hanging in."

"I promise. I'm counting the days until I'm out of here, though."

"I am too." She started the engine. "I've gotta run or I'll miss my appointment at the apartment complex. If I find a unit I like, I'll text you photos."

"That would be awesome. Love you, Sis."

"Love you back."

She ended the call, put the car in gear—and crossed her fingers.

Hopefully an apartment she could afford would be available and wouldn't require a huge deposit.

But if it did, she had Bren's offer of a short-term loan in her back pocket.

Taking any further advantage of the generous women who'd already gone above and beyond for her wasn't her preference, but if that's what it took to help secure Justin's future, she'd bite the bullet and do it.

And she'd also pray that her brother would keep his promise and continue to stick with the plan while she did everything she could on her end to honor her promise to *him*.

That had not gone well.

Gritting his teeth, Noah jabbed at his cell to end the call with his boss.

After all the hours he'd put in on company business during his so-called vacation, asking for a week of official remote work shouldn't have been such a big deal.

But apparently it was.

Per his boss, he was expected back in the office Wednesday morning for a nine o'clock meeting. Meaning he'd have to be out of here tomorrow morning, as originally scheduled.

Giving him twenty-four hours to sort things out with Bren and plan next steps.

He propped his hands on his hips and stared through his bedroom window at the cottage across the backyard.

It didn't help that she'd be at work all morning.

Maybe he could swing by The Perfect Blend, at least say hi. Let her know she was on his mind. Vent a bit about his boss. He could also set up a time for them to get together this afternoon to continue the discussion about where they should go from here— and perhaps share another one of those toe-curling kisses that had kept him tossing until—

At a soft knock on his door, he swiveled around. "Come in."

Dad peeked in. "Morning, Son. I thought I heard you talking, so I assumed you were up. Am I interrupting?" He motioned to the cell.

"No. I finished the call. What's up?"

"Could you do the button on this sleeve?" He entered and held up his arm. "I can't manage it."

"Sure." Noah crossed to him and took care of the chore with a deft flick of his fingers. "You're all set."

"A little accident can really make a person appreciate the blessings of a body with all the parts in working order. And the blessing of a son who cares enough to offer a hand when one of those parts isn't working."

"Unfortunately, I'm not going to be able to offer a hand after tomorrow."

His dad's eyebrows arched. "Your boss didn't approve your request for a week of remote work?"

"No. He expects me back in the office Wednesday for an important client meeting."

"Hmph. Seems kind of unreasonable to me, given how hard

you've worked while you've been here. Not to mention all your years of dedicated service. You don't even use most of your vacation, unless you've been taking trips to Tahiti you haven't told me about."

"No trips to Tahiti." Or many long-weekend getaways, for that matter.

Hard as he tried to suppress his resentment over his boss's hard-nosed stance, it bubbled up to the surface, leaving a bad taste in his mouth.

"Well, you don't have to worry about me after you leave. I'll be fine. I'll call and activate the help checklist today. But I feel bad for you. Other than your daily runs, an occasional beach walk, and sharing meals and a few excursions with your doting dad, this hasn't been much of a vacation for you."

That was true.

Not that vacation had been top of mind for this trip. He'd come for one reason—to convince his dad to move back to St. Louis. Once it had become apparent his goal was not only a lost cause but that his worries about his father's welfare were meritless, however, he'd have gone home early if a broken wrist hadn't interfered.

Yet that injury wasn't what was keeping him here now.

He was dragging his feet about going home because of the barista in Dad's backyard.

And with only a day to figure out what he was supposed to do about the woman who'd managed to infiltrate his heart and wreak havoc on the carefully laid plans he'd made for his life, a major case of panic was setting in.

"May I offer a suggestion?"

At his dad's question, Noah slid his phone back into his pocket and tried to tamp down his escalating anxiety. "Of course."

"Why don't you stop in at The Perfect Blend? Get a fancy coffee and chill for a while. The atmosphere there is always relaxing."

"We're on the same wavelength. You want to come along?"

"I appreciate the invitation, but it may be best if you have space this morning to do some thinking. I'll take a rain check, though. I can't think of anything more pleasant than sharing a morning coffee at The Perfect Blend with my favorite son before he heads home tomorrow."

"Plan on it. You want me to fix breakfast for you?"

"No, thanks. I'm in the mood for cereal today, and I can manage that fine on my own. Now you go on or the crowd will descend and there won't be a seat to be had."

He didn't need further urging. A cup of fresh-brewed java and a piece of that cranberry nut cake were calling to him.

But the *icing* on his cake would be seeing Bren.

Less than five minutes later, he pulled into a parking spot near The Perfect Blend, set the brake, and strode down the sidewalk.

As he approached the entrance, he scanned the saying of the day on the A-frame dry-erase board in front.

There's a very fine line between a groove and a rut.

His step slowed.

A week ago, he'd have seen the humor in that pithy adage. Cracked a smile as he strolled past.

Today it didn't seem all that funny.

Because it somehow felt applicable to him.

Frowning, he jammed his hands into his pockets.

All these years, as he'd toiled as a CPA with an eye toward a partnership, he'd been certain he'd found his groove and was on course to reach his destination.

But this visit to Hope Harbor had chipped away at his conviction that he was on the right track.

Was it possible he was in a rut instead of a groove?

He blew out a breath.

One more conundrum to add to his growing list.

Picking up his pace, he continued toward the entrance of the shop. Pushed through the door. Searched the area behind the counter for Bren.

Zach was there, waiting on a customer, and a fit-looking sixtysomething man was manning the espresso machine. But there was no sign of Bren.

He walked over to the counter. "Morning, Zach."

"Back at you." Zach grinned. "You're becoming a regular here."

"What can I say? You brew amazing coffee."

"We aim to please. Would you like your usual?"

The Perfect Blend crew already had his usual pegged?

Was he that predictable?

Probably. He gave the exact same order on every visit to his coffee shop at home too.

"Um . . ." He skimmed the menu.

A voice spoke from over his shoulder. "I can recommend the café de olla, if you're in the mood to mix things up."

He angled sideways to find Charley waiting in line behind him. "I've never had one of those."

"Then you're in for a treat. Zach makes the finest Mexican coffee this side of the border. I recommended it to your dad not long ago. A hint of cinnamon, a generous dash of piloncillo—" He kissed his fingertips. "Perfection in a cup."

"Sold." Noah gave the offerings in the case a quick perusal. "And I'll try a piece of that lavender shortbread too." If he was being adventurous, may as well go full throttle.

"Another excellent choice." Charley nodded his approval.

"We'll have the coffee up for you in a couple of minutes." Zach bagged the piece of shortbread and handed it across the counter.

Noah pulled out his wallet and inserted his credit card into the machine. "Is Bren here today?"

"No. She switched with Frank." Zach motioned to the older man.

"The owner of the pizza place?"

Zach hoisted up one side of his mouth. "Nope. Different Frank.

This one is retired from the postal service. He plays golf with your dad every week. We'll call you when your order is ready. Charley, what'll you have today?"

"I'll share a café de olla with Noah, if he's willing to let me borrow a chair at his table. Space appears to be at a premium today."

Noah surveyed the shop. Every spot was occupied, but two people at the table tucked into the corner appeared to be getting ready to leave.

Much as he would have preferred to sip his drink in solitude, refusing the request of the affable taco maker would be rude.

"I'll save you a seat at that one." He motioned to the corner and took off to stake a claim.

When Charley joined him a few minutes later, he had two disposable cups in hand. "I got yours while I was up there. Let me know what you think." He sat in the facing chair and set the cups down.

Noah claimed one of them. Took a tentative taste.

Quite a change from his usual Americano, but delicious.

"I like it."

"I thought you might." Charley sipped his own brew. "Those cookies are delicious too. They're one of the most popular items at the lavender farm tearoom south of town."

Noah picked up the heart-shaped cookie. Gave it a cautious once-over. Bit in.

Huh.

For a sweet treat that contained flowers, it was darn tasty. A hint of lemon, a touch of . . . was that mint? . . . and another subtle taste that must be lavender. What an intriguing blend of flavors.

"I'm glad I tried these." He took another bite.

"It's never a bad idea to broaden our horizons." Charley continued to sip his coffee. "You may want to try some of the other items on Zach's menu while you're here too."

He exhaled. "I would if I could, but I won't be here long enough to sample many more. My boss turned down my request for a one-week extension on my vacation."

"That's a shame. Hope Harbor has much to offer. You've barely scratched the surface." Charley glanced toward the counter. "I wonder why Bren had to switch shifts with Frank today. I hope she's not ill. She didn't seem quite like herself when I ran into her yesterday morning at Sunrise Reef."

Was she sick—or more like rattled, as he was?

"Did she have much to say? Give you any clue about what might be going on?" He took another bite of his cookie, watching Charley.

"No. Bren tends to keep her feelings to herself, except with Bev at the Book Nook. The two of them are tight."

Nothing in Charley's placid demeanor suggested he had any insights into why Bren hadn't been quite herself. But his take on her was sound. She did guard her heart. She'd admitted as much the night the two of them had indulged in ice cream bars.

Yet she'd opened that door to him and invited him in.

Which made it all the harder to walk away.

But how was he supposed to fix this dilemma? Hope Harbor and Bren calling on one side, his boss demanding his return on the other. It was an impossible spot to be in.

"Everything okay, Noah?"

At Charley's gentle question, he took a swig of coffee. "I was just thinking about how complicated life can get."

A fan of lines creased the weathered skin beside the other man's eyes. "I tend to agree with Confucius on that subject."

"What did he say?" At this stage, he'd take all the guidance he could get.

"'Life is really simple, but we insist on making it complicated.' And that eminent philosopher Dr. Seuss also weighed in on the subject. According to him, sometimes complicated questions have simple answers." Charley picked up his café de olla and stood. "And now my muse is calling. Thank you for letting me share your table on this fine morning, my friend."

"Thank *you* for the coffee recommendation—and the philosophy." He lifted his cup in salute.

"My pleasure. If I don't see you again before you leave, I hope your journey will lead you safely home."

As Charley strolled toward the door, greeting several patrons en route, Noah sighed. Leaned back in his chair.

A nice parting sentiment—except for the fact that he was beginning to wonder where home was.

Could that have been Charley's point?

No.

The resident artist had no idea what was going on in his life. It had been nothing more than a gracious farewell wish.

But was it possible his muddle about home was one of those complications Dr. Seuss alleged had a simple answer?

Maybe.

If that was the case, however, it was eluding him.

Best plan?

See if he could track down Bren. Perhaps between the two of them they could hash out a solution to a dilemma that didn't seem to have an easy answer.

No matter what Dr. Seuss claimed.

23

. . . .

A flat tire?

Seriously?

As Bren approached the Kia she'd parked in the driveway of her house, a sleeping bag tucked under one arm and a box of kitchenware balanced in the other, she gave the tire a disgusted scan.

Changing a flat hadn't been on her agenda for this Monday morning.

Could she have picked up a nail during her drive to Sunrise Reef yesterday? There *had* been a roofing company trailer parked in front of a house along the road.

A moot point now. Whatever the source of the flat, the damage was done.

Huffing out a breath, she continued to the car and lowered the sleeping bag onto the gravel driveway. Set the box down beside it.

May as well get the job done. The flat wasn't going to change itself.

Resigning herself to the disagreeable chore, she leaned into the trunk to dig out the jack, lug wrench, and spare tire. Paused to pull out her phone when it began to ring.

Her pulse quickened as she skimmed the screen.

Noah.

She put the phone to her ear. "Good morning."

"Good morning to you too. Did I catch you at a bad time? You sound winded."

"More like aggravated." Not a lie, though that wasn't the main reason her lungs were misbehaving. "I'm about to change a flat tire."

"What happened?"

"No idea. One minute it was fine, ten minutes later it was flat."

"Where are you?"

"At my house. I came over to get a few things for Emma to use at her new apartment until she can afford to buy furniture."

"Do you have emergency road service on your insurance?"

If only.

"No. My Kia's been reliable, and I know how to change a tire."

"Why don't you let me do it for you? I've been trying to track you down anyway."

"Why? Did you talk to your boss about extending your vacation?" Maybe there was positive news on that front at least.

"Yeah. It was a no-go."

Her spirits plummeted. "When do you have to leave?"

"Tomorrow morning."

This was *not* shaping up to be a good day.

She propped a hip against the fender and wrapped her free arm around her middle, watching two gulls circle overhead. "That's disappointing." To put it mildly.

"Tell me about it. I'm not a happy camper. We need to talk."

She blinked to clear the sudden mist from her vision. "I don't know, Noah. I've been thinking about our situation. Geography is a huge issue, since neither of us is inclined to relocate if things get serious."

"I'm not ready to give up on us yet."

"Do *you* see a solution to our dilemma?" Because she didn't, and pursuing a lost cause would only lead to heartache. That was the dismal conclusion she'd come to yesterday after her visit to Sunrise Reef and a long, solitary walk on the beach.

The two gulls swooped down and landed nearby, cuddling close as they watched her.

Sheesh. Even birds found partners. Why did it have to be so complicated for humans?

"Not yet. But that doesn't mean there isn't one." A beat ticked by. "I'll tell you what. Give me your address. I'll come over, change the tire, and lend a hand with the stuff you're moving. That will give us a chance to talk in person."

In light of his imminent departure, she should refuse. Hanging around him would just make her yearn for an outcome that appeared to be out of reach. In the interest of protecting her heart, it would be safer to—

"Please, Bren."

At his husky entreaty, she closed her eyes. Tightened her grip on the phone as she tried to shore up her resolve. Failed.

Caving was dumb, and she'd no doubt regret it later, but from a practical standpoint, an extra pair of hands would be welcome with the flat tire.

You're rationalizing, Bren.

She ignored the chiding voice in her head and rattled off her address.

"I'll be there in less than ten minutes." Noah ended the call. Fast. As if he was afraid she'd change her mind.

A valid fear.

Because for a woman who'd once sworn off men, this high-octane thing with Noah was beyond surreal.

Yes, he seemed to be a good guy. And yes, under other circumstances he could tempt her to tiptoe into romance. Bev had nailed it. Not everyone was meant to go through life solo—including a certain barista, as she'd been forced to acknowledge over the past couple of weeks.

Unfortunately, the man who'd managed to breach the defenses around her heart was a short-timer in town.

Sighing, she pushed off from her car and trudged back to the house to gather up another load for Emma.

She had to play this smart. Limit her time with Noah today. Keep reminding herself that he was leaving tomorrow, perhaps forever. There would be no more touching—and definitely no more kissing.

Eight minutes later, when he pulled into the driveway and emerged from behind the wheel, she had her emotions in hand.

Until he walked over and those killer blue eyes softened and warmed, turning her insides to mush. "You look beautiful today."

She tugged down the hem of her *I ♡ Hope Harbor* sweatshirt. "Thanks. And thank you for offering to change the tire." She motioned toward the flat and retreated a few steps before she did something stupid, like launch herself into his arms. "I, uh, set out the tools and the spare."

After studying her for a moment, he nodded. "I'll get on it."

"I'll be inside, gathering up more items." Without waiting for him to respond, she fled to the house.

But once safely inside, she peeked through the window.

True to his word, he'd dived into the chore—and he was handling it much faster than she would have. In a matter of minutes, he had the car jacked up and the flat off and was rolling the spare into position.

Tempted as she was to watch him complete the job, she did have more bits and pieces to collect.

As she rummaged through the closet in her bedroom ten minutes later, a knock echoed through the house.

Shoring up her fortitude, she tucked a pillow under her arm and returned to the living room. Opened the front door.

"All finished." Noah lifted his grease-stained hands. "May I clean up?"

She moved aside and waved him in. "Bathroom's the first door on the left, down the hall."

"Give me three minutes."

As he strode that direction, she carried the pillow and the small stack of towels she'd collected earlier out to the car. Noah had put the sleeping bag and box of kitchen items in the trunk, so she tucked the pillow and towels in beside them and returned to the house.

When she entered, he was in the living room, fists propped on hips, giving her small rental house a once-over.

She gave the space a survey too.

Truth be told, the house wasn't all that great on its best days, and with portions of the walls, floor, and ceiling removed, today it could almost qualify as a disaster zone.

"For the record, it doesn't usually look this bad." She shut the door behind her. "But as I've learned, replacing wiring is a messy job. Fortunately, that part of the job is done. The owner tells me the drywall and flooring people will be in this week to start those repairs. If there aren't any glitches, the painter will be finished by the end of next week and I can move back in."

"How long have you lived here?" Faint grooves dented his brow as he homed in on the chipped Formica and dated appliances visible through the doorway to the kitchen.

"Two years. But I should be able to swing a down payment on a house of my own by next spring. That's been on my wish list for a while." For whatever reason, it was important that he realize she had higher aspirations than this, even if he wouldn't be around to see her move on and up.

He pivoted back to her. "You know, Dad might be willing to let you continue to rent—"

"I'm fine here, Noah." She tipped her chin up a hair. "I'll never forget your dad's kindness to me, but I don't as a rule take charity."

"Giving a friend a break is different than offering charity."

"Be that as it may, I have a lease here. I'm locked in for another eight months." Time to change the subject. "Thanks again for your help with the flat."

After a moment, he took her cue and changed the subject. "Happy to lend a hand. Do you have anything else to haul out to the car?"

"Not much. That card table and folding chairs." She waved a hand toward them. "I'm also going to take a couple of lamps. And maybe an upholstered chair." She walked over to the one she had in mind.

He gave it a dubious inspection. "I doubt that will fit in your car."

"I think I can wedge it in my trunk if I make two trips." It wasn't super light, but she ought to be able to drag it out to her car and lever it in.

"Why don't I put it in *my* car and follow you over instead?"

She hesitated.

That would be easier—and once they got to the apartment, she wouldn't have to worry about being alone with him. Her former cottage-mate would be there.

"If you're sure you don't mind, that would help. Emma signed the rental agreement this morning, and she'll be there. We should be in and out fast."

"No rush on my end. I don't have anything else on my schedule."

"No work today?"

His mouth twisted. "I'm not in a working mood after the conversation with my boss this morning. Besides, I'm supposed to be on vacation."

"In that case, I'll take you up on your offer. Let me help you with the chair."

He crossed to it. Tested the weight. Bent down and picked it up, muscles bunching below the sleeves of his T-shirt. "I've got it. But you could open the door for me."

After complying, she picked up the card table and one of the folding chairs and followed him out.

Within five minutes, they'd finished loading both cars. And ten minutes after that, he was following her into the low-key Sea Breeze apartment complex she'd called home during her first year in Hope Harbor. The efficiency she'd rented had been tiny, but it had been adequate while she decided if she wanted to stay.

Emma's apartment was larger, but not by much. The so-called second bedroom was more like an oversized closet, based on the photos Emma had shown her, but the unit met her needs. She could truthfully claim on her guardianship petition that Justin would have a room of his own.

Bren pulled in beside Emma's Sentra, which was no longer packed to the gills with all her worldly possessions, as it had been since she'd arrived. Noah parked beside her.

Once she slid from behind the wheel, she spoke to him over the roof. "I'll let her know we're here."

"I'll get the chair." He circled around to his trunk.

Bren ascended the two steps to the tiny porch of the unit and rang the bell.

When the door swung open, Emma greeted her with a sunny smile. "Thanks again for offering to loan me a few things from your house until I can furnish my place."

"No problem. I'm not using them at the moment anyway." Footsteps sounded behind her, and she angled sideways. "Noah helped me haul everything over." No sense mentioning the flat tire.

Emma's lips flattened as she surveyed the upholstered chair he was carrying. "I thought you said you were bringing basic kitchen utensils and a sleeping bag. I can't take your furniture too. Especially after the loan you gave me for the security deposit."

She could feel Noah's gaze on her. "You'll be paying that back soon. As for the items I brought over, they're also on loan. I expect you to return them at some point."

Furrows creased her forehead. "I don't know, Bren. I'm not used to taking charity."

"Helping friends out—or giving them a break—is different than offering charity."

As Noah repeated the sentiment he'd expressed at her house, Bren glanced over at him.

If he was hoping to convince her to stay on at his dad's cottage, he was going to be disappointed. Grateful as she was for his father's largesse, she didn't need ongoing help like Emma did. Plus, she had a lease.

But his argument worked with the younger woman.

"I suppose that's true. And I'll return everything—and pay back the deposit—soon."

"I know you will." Bren smiled at her. "Let's grab the rest of the stuff, then we'll get out of your hair so you can settle in."

It didn't take the three of them long to unload her car, yet despite everything she'd brought, the tiny apartment felt bare. Not that it seemed to matter to Emma. From the glow on her face, anyone would think she'd moved into the Taj Mahal.

"I'm going to take pictures right away and send them to Justin." She touched the shade on one of the lamps. "Prove that I'm one step closer to my petition."

"I bet he'll be thrilled." Bren walked over and pulled her into a hug. "You know I'm just a phone call away if you need anything."

"Yes, I do—and I can't begin to tell you what that means to me. I don't think I'd have made it without your help after the car disaster."

"Yes, you would. You're a survivor. But I'm glad our paths crossed. As Reverend Baker once told me, coincidence is a small miracle in which God chooses to remain anonymous."

"I like that thought." Emma gave her a squeeze, then spoke to Noah. "Thank you for helping this morning. And I'm sorry for any concern I caused you when I first arrived. I do understand why you were reluctant to have a stranger stay on your dad's property. I was nervous about the arrangement myself . . . and more than a little suspicious. Bren's offer seemed too good to be true. It's not often you meet someone with such a kind and generous heart."

"I know." The warmth in Noah's voice was impossible to miss.

As Emma looked between the two of them, curiosity sparking in her irises, Bren edged toward the door. "We should be on our way. Let me know how it goes at Sweet Dreams."

"I will."

Noah followed her out to the parking area, and she stopped beside her car. Pulled out her keys and squeezed them tight. She had to be strong about this, and firm. "Thanks again for your help with the tire and the hauling."

"You're welcome." He shoved his hands into his pockets. "It was kind of you to loan Emma the money for the deposit."

"No more worries that I'm putting myself at risk?"

"Not anymore. I trust your judgment and your instincts."

Nice to know—but it didn't solve their impasse.

She moistened her lips. "I should be going."

A hint of desperation flared in his eyes. "Can we at least spend the afternoon together?"

"I have plans for the day. But I'll see you tonight at the 5K meeting."

"A meeting doesn't lend itself to personal conversation. Can you change your plans?"

"No. I participate in a foster grandparent program through Helping Hands, and the woman I visit is celebrating her ninetieth birthday today. Her brother and his family are in town, and they're having a party for her this afternoon. I'm invited." She checked her watch. "I have to go back to the cottage and get ready."

He expelled a breath. Shoved his fingers through his hair. "When are we going to talk?"

"I don't think there's much to say."

"I disagree. I mean, I know there are issues to deal with if we want to explore a relationship. And I know that will be difficult to do long distance. But walking away from this feels wrong."

"It feels wrong to me too, but I can't see how to make this work." She swallowed past the lump in her throat and said what had to be said. "I think we should give ourselves some space, Noah. Return to our lives the way they were before we met and revisit this again in a few weeks. We may have a different perspective on everything that's happened once we're back in our usual routines."

He didn't look like he felt any more convinced about that than she did, but what other choice did they have?

"Can I tell you the truth? At this moment I'm ready to chuck the corporate world and leave St. Louis behind."

Bren quashed the sudden urge to encourage that inclination. A life-changing decision shouldn't be made under pressure or without careful deliberation. Otherwise, Noah could later come to resent it—and the person who influenced him to make it.

Not a recipe for happily ever after.

"That's your heart talking. What's your brain telling you?"

"I don't know. If it's speaking to me, I can't hear it. Nothing is registering except you."

"Which is why distance may be smart while we sort through this. Neither of us thinks too clearly when we're together."

"You're doing a better job of it than I am." He kneaded the bridge of his nose. "This is out of pattern for me. As a rule, I'm able to put emotion aside and be logical no matter the circumstances."

"And I'm the opposite. It's taken me years to get a handle on my emotions. To be honest, I still struggle with that challenge on occasion. Like now. But one of us has to be sensible about this. We aren't going to be able to work out the problem in the next twenty-four hours."

"I guess not." His shoulders slumped. "Will you let me drive you to the meeting tonight?"

She hesitated—but taking two cars would be silly. "As long as we come straight home."

A muscle in his cheek ticced. "In other words, no stops for ice cream. Got it. Six forty-five, in front of the house?"

"That works."

"Okay. I'll see you later." He returned to his car, slid behind the wheel, and started the engine.

Less than half a minute later, he was disappearing into the distance.

Fighting back tears, Bren pried her fingers loose from her keys. Flexed her knuckles to restore circulation.

But the impressions they'd made on her skin would take a while to fade.

As would the impression Noah had made on her heart during his brief but eventful visit to the town she called home.

24

The first day of the workweek had a bad reputation for understandable reasons—and this Monday was doing nothing to change that stereotype.

Noah mashed his lips together and threw the last shirt from the closet into his suitcase.

An uncooperative boss, a stratospheric stress level, and an appealing woman he had to leave behind tomorrow.

This was so not how he'd expected his visit to Hope Harbor to end.

He zipped the case shut with more force than necessary. Other than a few essentials he'd toss in tomorrow morning, he was ready to leave. Physically if not mentally.

At least Bren had agreed to ride with him to tonight's meeting—not that there was much chance they'd find a resolution to their dilemma in the limited private minutes they'd have together.

Maybe because there wasn't one.

A disheartening conclusion Bren may have already reached, based on her comments today.

But he wasn't ready to throw in the towel yet. There had to be a way they could—

At a crash from the kitchen, he jerked. Took off at a gallop down the hall. Skidded to a stop on the threshold.

Dad was standing next to the sink, staring at the pieces of a broken glass bowl on the floor.

"What happened?" Noah crossed to him.

"I dropped your mom's chocolate mousse bowl." He gripped the edge of the sink with his uninjured hand and began to lower himself to the floor.

Noah grabbed his arm. "I'll clean this up for you, Dad."

"No. I can manage. I don't want you to be late for your meeting." He tugged free and gingerly got down on his knees.

Noah did likewise. "I don't have to leave for another five minutes." He picked up a shard of crystal as his pulse slowed. "I remember this bowl—and Mom's Christmas Eve mousse. I used to look forward to it all year."

"Me too. I came across the bowl in the back of the cupboard while I was searching for extra containers for leftovers. I'll ask the casserole brigade to reduce the quantity after you leave, but it will still be more than I can eat." He dipped his chin, cradling a piece of the shattered bowl in his palm. "I decided to wash this and use it for fruit. I knew it would remind me of your mom every time I saw it. Now it's gone too."

At the catch in his father's voice, Noah's throat swelled. "No one can take away our memories, though."

"That's true. And I'm grateful for those, along with all the years your mom and I had together. But it's still hard to let go. Nothing fills the empty place left by the loss of someone you love."

"I miss her too, Dad. No matter what craziness was happening at work, her upbeat attitude always lifted my spirits whenever she called."

"That was your mom. She was a lemonade from lemons kind of woman." His father reached over and laid a hand on his shoulder. "I hope you find a wife like that someday, Son. It's what I pray for every night. Careers are fine, and worldly success is satisfying, but in the end all that really matters is love. Like the Good Book says." He waved toward the door. "Now don't keep Bren waiting. You go on to your meeting."

"I'll help you with this first."

"No. I'd rather do it myself and have a chat with your mom while I'm at it."

Noah hesitated, but only for a moment. If Dad wanted to commune with Mom, he wasn't going to stand in the way. "Okay. I should be back no later than nine."

"Don't hurry on my account. I expect I'll be engrossed all evening in the suspense novel I picked up on my last visit to Bev's Book Nook."

"Call if you need anything."

"I'll be fine." He waved him off and went back to gathering up the scattered remnants of the bowl.

"Are you certain you can get back up with that bum wrist?"

"I'll hoist myself up by holding on to the edge of the counter with the hand that works. Don't fret about me."

A difficult instruction to follow.

"I'll try not to." It was the best he could promise.

Once back on his feet, Noah picked up his keys from the counter where he'd left them earlier and let himself out the front door.

Bren was waiting beside his car as he hurried over.

"Sorry I'm a couple of minutes late. A slight emergency in the house."

"Is your dad all right?"

"Yes." As he opened her door, he filled her in on what had happened. "I felt bad for him. I know it's only a material object, but it's like another piece of Mom is gone. Losing her was hard for me, but it had to have been devastating for Dad. They were best friends as well as spouses."

Bren's features softened. "It must have been wonderful growing up with parents who loved each other that much."

"It was. I took it for granted as a kid, but the older I get, the more I appreciate the importance of a loving home."

"Count your blessings." She slid into the car and pulled the door shut behind her.

She didn't talk much during the short drive to Grace Christian, despite his attempts to draw her out. While she answered his questions about the birthday party, she didn't offer any details. And she remained uncharacteristically subdued during the hour-and-a-half-long meeting that followed.

The other committee members more than made up for her preoccupation, however. There were six now, since each original member had recruited someone else, and all appeared to be enthused.

After John provided a general status report, Marci rattled off everything on her done and to-do lists in such machine-gun fashion, he'd have had difficulty following even if he hadn't been distracted.

In the end, after being peppered with questions he mostly couldn't answer, Noah got his run-expert colleague on the line, put him on speaker, and let the 5K committee members get the information they needed from the source. He joined in when necessary, but for the bulk of the meeting he doodled and watched Bren, who avoided eye contact as much as possible.

As the gathering wound down and Noah ended the call with his colleague in St. Louis, John smiled at him. "That was super helpful. Thanks to you and your friend, I think us neophytes may actually pull this off."

"I'm pumped about it for sure—and I'm not even a runner." Marci grinned. "We've been able to line up a ton of sponsors, both in Hope Harbor and from the surrounding area. And the number of people registering for the run is blowing me away. Where do we stand on the totals, Bren?"

When Bren didn't respond, the woman seated beside her tapped her arm.

After pulling herself back from wherever she must have mentally wandered off to, Bren consulted a sheet in front of her. Provided the number of registrants for both the fun run and the serious route. "If you want my opinion, I think the T-shirt you designed has been a huge draw, Marci."

Several other people seconded that.

"I enjoyed working on it. It was a pleasant change of pace from my usual duties." Marci reached for her purse. "John, are we about done? I have to stop at the market on my way home. Are we the only family that is forever running out of paper towels?"

"I think it's a function of having little ones in the house." John's mouth quirked as he closed his notebook. "Yes, we're finished. Noah, on behalf of everyone on the committee and at Helping Hands, thanks for your willingness to tap your friend's knowledge for us and act as a go-between with him for the many questions I texted you over the past week. We also appreciate your help in planning our routes."

Everyone in the room applauded.

He waved the thanks aside. "I didn't do much. You all clocked the real hours. You'll have to let me know how the event comes off."

"We will. And we'll send you a T-shirt, if you'll give me your address." Marci pulled out her pen again.

"Why don't I buy one instead?"

"Nope. It's on the house." She waited, pen poised.

Rather than argue, he recited his address.

"Got it. I wish you could join us, but that would be a bit of a trek for a short event—unless you had another incentive to come back." She gave Bren a sidelong peek.

If his dad's tenant noticed, she didn't let on.

But apparently the electricity that was obvious to the two of them was also being picked up by others.

"I doubt I'll be able to fit in another trip that soon. I'd be here if I could, though. It would be fun to—"

The door to the conference room cracked open, and Reverend

Baker stuck his head in. "Greetings, everyone. Is the meeting winding down?"

"Yes. Your timing is perfect." John motioned him in.

"Too bad that doesn't carry over to his golf game." Father Murphy leaned around the minister's shoulder, eyes twinkling. "The timing of his backswing and downswing could use some work."

Reverend Baker shot him a disgruntled glance. "If you're going to talk about golf, I could bring up your bounce problem with putting . . . but I won't."

"Thanks for nothing." The padre smirked at his fellow cleric, then addressed the group. "On a more pleasant note, we come bearing gifts." He nudged the minister into the room.

Reverend Baker entered, and Father Murphy followed, bearing a bakery box and a white bag. He set both on the conference table.

"The good father and I took in an early movie in Coos Bay, and with his eagle eye for sweets, he spotted a new dessert shop." The minister tapped the logo on the box. "He insisted we indulge."

"I didn't hear you protest very much."

"In the interest of maintaining harmony between us, I capitulated. However, I have to say the petits fours were very tasty. So we bought a dozen to share, as a thank-you for all your work on the 5K run. Help yourself to coffee too." He motioned toward a coffee maker in the corner of the room, a pod-filled stand beside it.

The meeting broke up in earnest as Father Murphy flipped the lid on the box and pulled napkins and plastic forks from the bag.

Noah tried to mask his impatience.

Socializing with anyone but Bren hadn't been in his plans for tonight, but it would be rude to take off without sampling the treat the clerics had been kind enough to provide.

Bren must have come to the same conclusion, because she selected a petit four and aimed a smile at the two pastors. "These look delicious."

"I can vouch for that." Father Murphy took one too.

"Yes, he can." Reverend Baker arched an eyebrow at him. "That's his third one."

"I wouldn't have gone overboard if we had pastries like this closer to home and I could pace myself. Much as I love Sweet Dreams's cinnamon rolls and brownies, it would be nice to have a few fancier choices."

"You may be in luck."

As Bren spoke, all the heads in the room swiveled her direction.

"What do you know that we don't?" Father Murphy leaned toward her.

"While Joe's out for surgery, Emma's going to put her French-pastry skills to use. She called to share the news late this afternoon."

"French pastries?" John picked up a fork from the table. "That will add a whole new dimension to Sweet Dreams."

"You should all check it out in a week or two, after she settles in." Bren swiped up a dab of icing that was clinging to the crinkled paper cup holding her petit four.

"Count on it." Father Murphy lifted his face heavenward and gave a blissful sigh. "French pastries in Hope Harbor. What a blessing."

"Not for your waistline." Reverend Baker sent him a stern look. "You're supposed to be watching your cholesterol."

"An occasional French pastry won't hurt me. I could buy one to console myself after a bad day on the links."

"In that case, you'll definitely be at Sweet Dreams every Thursday, after our round."

"Ha ha." The padre continued eating.

Noah finished his petit four at the same time Bren did and tipped his head toward the door. Since Marci had slipped out a few minutes ago, there was no obligation for them to linger any longer.

After a nod, she disposed of her napkin and fork and said her goodbyes while he did the same.

He waited until they were halfway down the hall to speak.

"Sorry about the delay. I know you wanted to go straight home after the meeting."

"The treat didn't hold us up for long. But I do have to be up early tomorrow." She tucked her notebook closer to her chest. "What time are you leaving?"

"Also early. I promised Dad I'd take him to The Perfect Blend first, but it will be a quick in and out. On the plus side, it will give me a chance to see you again before I head out." He pushed the outside door open and let her precede him.

"Mornings are crazy at The Blend. About all I'll be able to do is wave at you."

"Then maybe we can say a proper goodbye tonight."

Her gaze met his. Skittered away. "If you mean what I think you mean, that's not a smart idea." She picked up her pace toward the car.

He lengthened his stride to keep up with her. "I've been thinking about our kiss day and night."

"I have too. That's why it's not smart to repeat it."

He stopped at the car, spirits tanking. There went any hopes of another kiss that he could tuck in his memory. "I'd stay longer if I could, Bren."

"It wouldn't matter." She gave a stiff shrug. "Even if your boss had granted your request, in a week you'd leave anyway. Sooner may be better."

"That's not how I see it." He took her hand and searched her eyes in the moonlight. Unless he was misreading her signals, her longing mirrored his.

Her throat worked as she looked up at him. "Don't make me want what I can't have any more than I already do, Noah." Her words came out choked. Anguished. "We need to give ourselves space to think. Kissing will only muddle our minds."

He couldn't argue with her logic.

But he didn't have to like it.

And how could he leave without holding her close once more?

Without burying his face in the purple-hued hair that had gone from off-putting to endearing? Without pressing his lips to hers and—

All at once, she jerked back. As if she didn't trust him—or herself—to resist the temptation to exchange more kisses. "I'm going to w-walk home."

What?

"But it's dark out."

"This is Hope Harbor. I'm more worried tonight about my emotional safety than my physical safety." A breeze ruffled her hair, and she backed up a step. "I'll see you at The Blend tomorrow." She spun around and strode away.

Panic bubbled up inside him. "Wait!"

She paused. Angled partway toward him.

"You'll stay in touch after I go back until we come to some decisions, right? If I call or email, you'll respond?"

"Within reason."

That wasn't much, but it was better than nothing.

"I'll hold you to that."

"I always keep my promises, Noah." Then she pivoted again and disappeared into the night.

Leaving him alone in the darkness, with only the taste of salt from the briny sea air on his lips instead of the sweetness of Bren's kiss.

And unless he could figure out how to deal with his conflicting priorities, the lovely, intriguing woman who'd so unexpectedly entered his life would soon exit it forever.

25

. . . .

Knock, knock.

Sending a glum look toward the door, Bren slumped deeper into the cushions on the couch and clutched the throw pillow tighter against her chest.

It had to be Fred. Who else could it be? Noah was back in St. Louis by now, after his early departure this morning, and no one else had ever come to call at her temporary digs.

Her spirits dropped another notch.

No way was she up to company. She'd have to pretend she wasn't home and run over later to see what Fred—

"Open up, dear girl. I know you're in there."

Bren jolted upright.

Bev was here?

Tossing the pillow aside, she vaulted to her feet and hurried across the room. Pulled the door open. "What's up? Are you okay?"

"I'm fine." Bev gave her ratty comfort clothes that should have been tossed into the trash or consigned to the rag pile long ago a slow perusal. "You, on the other hand, don't look too hot."

"Thanks a lot."

"I'm nothing if not honest, as you know. What's going on?"

No sense pretending with Bev. Her friend knew her too well.

"Noah left today, and I'm bummed."

"I thought that might be the problem. Fred told me he was gone when I delivered my casserole a few minutes ago. He also said the two of them stopped by The Perfect Blend this morning, and that you weren't your usual friendly self. He wondered if you could be sick."

"Only at heart." Bren motioned behind her. "You want to come in?"

"Do you have to ask?"

Bren pulled the door wide, and Bev entered in a swirl of jasmine. But instead of claiming a seat in the living room, she waited until the door was closed, then pulled her into a hug.

As the soothing floral scent engulfed her, Bren clung to the older woman whose nurturing presence, cheerful demeanor, and unconditional friendship had enriched her life beyond measure since the bookstore owner had taken up residence in Hope Harbor.

Pressure built behind her eyes, and Bren sniffed. Eased back as she swiped at her lashes. "Sorry."

"Never apologize for having deep feelings, dear girl. They're what add zest to life."

"They can also add heartache."

"Sad but true. Especially if we care about someone who doesn't care about us in return." Bev took her hand and led her back to the couch. Tugged her down, until they sat side by side. "Is that what happened with Noah?" Her eyes radiated empathy.

"No. He cares. But it's too soon for either of us to have such strong feelings."

"Love isn't bound by clocks or calendars."

"I don't believe in love at first sight." Bren twisted her fingers together in her lap.

"Did you love him the first time you saw him?"

The night she'd sprayed him with pepper gel?

Hardly.

"No, but I started to get interested not long after that."

"Because you began to learn about him. To appreciate his admirable qualities. That's not love at first sight."

"It's close. I only met him two weeks ago, Bev."

"It doesn't take long to spot a gem among stones. Or wheat among chaff, if you prefer a biblical analogy."

"Sometimes it can. My father fooled people who'd known him for years. Most never saw past the illusion he created."

"Are you putting Noah in the same category as your father?"

"Absolutely not. I think he's the real deal. It's just . . . this is happening too fast."

Bev gave a soft snort. "God's timetable doesn't always mesh with ours—and that's the voice of experience speaking, trust me. But beyond timing, do you still think you two have nothing in common?"

A tougher question.

"We're different in many ways, but from what I've learned so far, I think we're on the same page in terms of most fundamentals."

"That's a solid start."

"Not in this case." Bren leaned closer, the taut muscles in her shoulders kinking. "Starting something you can't finish is foolish. He has a career in St. Louis, and my life is in Hope Harbor. This is my home. I've put down roots here, and I can't imagine ever leaving after the long road I traveled to find this place."

Bev gave a slow nod. "That's a major dilemma, no question about it."

"What would *you* do in my situation?"

"Oh, dear girl, I swore off giving advice long ago. My no-holds-barred opining led to a rocky road with my daughter for many years. Thankfully I've learned to stifle my natural inclination to pontificate and to recognize that my way isn't always the right way for everyone else. The only counsel I'll offer is to suggest you listen for direction from the source of all wisdom." She pointed toward the heavens. "But I'm willing to be a sounding board if you want to bounce ideas around."

Bren flopped back against the couch and stared at the ceiling. "I can't ask Noah to give up the career he's worked hard to establish. Especially at this early stage of our relationship. And I don't want to pick up and move again after all the wandering I've done. I love Hope Harbor. I love the life I've created here. The thought of living in a big city has zero appeal. Besides, what if one of us makes a major lifestyle change and the relationship goes nowhere?"

"A long-distance courtship while you test the waters might be a possibility."

Bren twisted her head and squinted at her friend. "I don't know if that's realistic."

"Why not? It worked in the old days, and all they had back then were letters. Between videoconferencing and FaceTime and email and texts, I'd say a modern long-distance courtship has distinct advantages over letters—though I wouldn't rule those out, either. Handwritten notes could have a huge impact in our day and age, since they're such a rarity. That sort of courtship would give you time to get to know each other."

"It still doesn't solve the problem of geography. One of us would have to relocate if we got serious. Unless you're suggesting a permanent long-distance arrangement."

"No." Bev shook her head, her tone definitive. "There are couples who do that, but it doesn't seem ideal. You'd each have your own separate lives for extended periods, with a limited life together. In my opinion, if you love someone, the life together part should predominate. But take that with a grain of salt. As a free spirit who's never had a long-term romantic relationship, what do I know?"

"More than most people, if you ask me. That steady stream of people coming through your shop isn't generated just by free cookies. You could hang out a shingle."

Bev waved the compliment aside. "It's kind of you to say that, but all I offer is common sense."

"Which can be in short supply when it comes to relationships." Bren blew out a breath and hugged the pillow against her chest again.

"Not in your case. You have a sensible head on your shoulders and reliable instincts. From what I saw of Noah, I'd say the same is true for him."

"He wasn't feeling too sensible or levelheaded yesterday. He claimed he was tempted to forget all about his career ambitions and leave the corporate world behind."

"What did you say to that?"

"I told him I thought it was a bad idea."

"Smart. People can regret decisions made in the throes of strong emotions."

Bren sighed. "I agree with you in principle, but it feels more lonely than smart in hindsight."

"Distance can offer perspective, though. It will give you a chance to see how you feel after a week—or several."

"I guess." After all, hadn't she told Noah that very thing? She ought to try to take her own advice. "Besides, what choice do I have?"

"There are always choices, dear girl." Bev patted her hand. "But for now, this strikes me as a prudent one. It can often be easier to see the big picture more clearly from a distance than up close."

"I suppose I'll find out if that's true."

"You'll keep me in the loop, right?"

"Goes without saying. You'll be tired of me bending your ear before this is over."

"Never." Bev stood. "And if I don't hear from you, you'll hear from me."

Pressure built in Bren's throat as she rose too. "What would I do without you?"

"Carry on. From what I've gathered, you were doing fine before I came to town."

"I thought I was. But I didn't know what I was missing until we connected." She shoved her hands into the muff pocket on the front of her sweatshirt. "Kind of like how I feel about Noah."

"See if that feeling lasts." Bev pulled out her car keys. "I expect to hear from you soon."

"You will."

Bren walked her to the door, waved her off . . . and grimaced at the envelopes for the Virginia wedding invitations waiting to be addressed.

But she'd dragged her feet on that job as long as she could. They had to be mailed back to the bride in two days.

Resigning herself to the task at hand, she wandered over to the table. Adjusted her light. Fitted a pen with the appropriate nib.

And tried not to let someone else's happily ever after turn her case of the blues even bluer.

Everything was going great.

Smiling, Emma took off her apron at noon on Thursday and hung it on a hook at Sweet Dreams.

As far as she knew, none of the usual patrons had noticed so much as a blip in Joe's absence. There'd been zero complaints about any of the baked goods she'd prepared based on his recipes—or none that she'd heard. The college student who'd filled in yesterday up front had kept everything running smoothly while Alice stayed with Joe during surgery, and the co-owner was back on duty today with an encouraging report from the surgeon.

Life was good—and getting better every day.

The door from the front of the shop swung open, and Alice peeked in. "Just checking to make sure you were getting ready to leave. I heard you stayed until closing yesterday."

"I thought I should, with both you and Joe gone. I was also

working on a list of ingredients I need to order from your supplier for the treat-of-the-day items we're introducing next week."

"Which are creating quite a bit of excitement, thanks to that fancy sign Bren made showing the daily specials. What a wonderful promotional idea."

"She gets all the credit for that. When she asked me about the lineup over the weekend, I assumed she was being polite. Then she showed up at my apartment with the sign. I was blown away."

"I can see why. It's very classy. I knew she did calligraphy, but that's almost a piece of art."

"I agree." Emma pulled off her cap. "So what have customers been saying about the daily special?" She tried not to sound too eager, but creating those pastries was going to be the highlight of her temporary gig here.

"Mostly they discussed which ones they wanted to try. I'd say the baklava and eclairs are running neck and neck. But the macarons and fruit tarts aren't far behind. And I got a ton of questions about the opera cakes."

"I hope your customers will like everything."

"I think that's a given. This was an inspired idea, Emma. Like I told Joe, even if we only get a temporary boost in sales while you're here, it will be fun to offer something new and different to our customers for a few weeks."

Alice's praise jacked up the heat level on her already warm-from-the-ovens cheeks. "And I'm thrilled to have a chance to keep my skills fresh. It's a win-win all around."

"I wish we had the budget to hire you permanently." Alice planted her hands on her hips. "Joe's not getting any younger, and those early mornings seem earlier every year. Plus, after standing on his feet all day for decades, his back gives him almost as much trouble as the carpal tunnel syndrome. But small businesses don't have the budget for extra full-time employees."

"I understand." The truth was, no matter how much additional business her pastries generated in the short term, there was limited space in the cramped back room. It would be hard to bake and sell them in a quantity sufficient to justify the expense of an additional employee.

"Oh, well, it is what it is. You go on home. There's no staying late on my watch." Alice shooed her toward the front of the shop.

Emma didn't argue. Satisfying as the past two days had been, there had also been a fair amount of stress. A nap was high on her priority list for this afternoon—after a detour to Charley's for tacos. Now that she had a job, she could afford to indulge in a treat once in a while.

A couple of minutes later, she took her place in the queue at his stand, stomach rumbling as the line inched forward. She was going to have to bring more than fruit and yogurt in the future for her midmorning snack. The challenge, though, would be squeezing in a few minutes to eat it. A one-baker shop didn't leave the baker with much free time.

When it was finally her turn to order, Charley greeted her with his usual welcoming smile. "If it isn't Sweet Dreams's new French pastry artist."

"Artist may be too generous a term."

"If I can call myself a taco artist, you can call yourself a French pastry artist. One order today?"

"Yes. But I can't wait to introduce my brother to your tacos as soon as he joins me. I guarantee he'll be a regular here."

"More customers are always welcome." He opened the cooler and pulled out a couple of fish fillets. Set them on the grill. "How's it going at Sweet Dreams?"

"So far, so good." She gave him a brief recap of her first two solo days. "And we've placed the order for the ingredients I need for next week's treats of the day."

"The town is all abuzz about the prospect of fancy desserts close at hand. A dozen or more people have mentioned it to me." He finished chopping some red onion and tossed it onto the griddle.

"I hope they're not disappointed." She motioned toward the

onions as he stirred them. "Until I came here, I don't think I ever had tacos with anything on them that was cooked except the meat or fish."

"One of my little secrets. I like to give the red onions a touch of caramelization. But I don't want them to lose their crunch. Timing is everything, as with so much in life. I believe you're the first person ever to comment on my technique."

She shrugged. "I enjoy cooking as well as baking. Not as much for one, but it will be different after Justin gets here. Once I find a permanent job."

"The experience at Sweet Dreams should help with that. I expect Alice and Joe will give you a glowing recommendation."

"I hope so." She rummaged in her purse for her wallet. "But to be honest, I wish I could stay there. I'd enjoy working with them on a permanent basis. It's a shame the back room isn't bigger and the display space limited. The shop can't handle enough volume to support a third employee."

"The place *is* on the small side. I'm guessing it's provided Joe and Alice with a modest income, but I doubt it's made them rich. Not that wealth was ever their goal. I think they're pleased to have created a town institution. Hope Harbor wouldn't be the same without Sweet Dreams's cinnamon rolls."

"I didn't mean my comments about the size in a negative sense." It was important to make that crystal clear. If Charley mentioned this conversation to someone and Alice or Joe heard about it, they might think she was criticizing their business.

"I didn't take them that way." Charley's demeanor remained pleasant as he turned the fillets and gave them a liberal sprinkle of seasoning from the can on the shelf beside him. "But I bet you have a few ideas about what you'd do if you were in charge there."

She gaped at him.

How could he know she'd been thinking about that very thing? Was the man a mind reader?

"Why do you say that?" She angled sideways to see if anyone

was tuned in to their exchange, but apparently she'd been the end of the line.

Charley set three corn tortillas on the grill and grinned. "You introduced the idea of fancy pastries and a treat of the day after being an employee for a handful of days. That would suggest you have a knack for seeing potential and imagining the possibilities in a situation."

"I do have an active imagination." One of the reasons she'd been able to envision a life free of Bill and lay plans to make that happen.

But she didn't see how that was going to help her at Sweet Dreams, beyond her treat-of-the-day idea. She wouldn't be there long enough to even suggest any of the fanciful ideas her brain had conjured up for spiffing up the front part of the shop and perhaps eventually expanding to an adjacent storefront if it became available.

Maybe the management wherever she landed would be receptive to new ideas and encourage her to be creative, though.

"Imagination can carry a person far in life." Charley pulled a bottle of sauce off the shelf and set it beside him.

"Or compel a person to get carried away. People have to be realistic in their expectations."

"True—as long as they don't set the bar too low. I'm a firm believer in dreaming big. And look at the result." He beamed her another smile as he began assembling her meal. "I was a taco maker who loved to paint, and I ended up finding a creative outlet for both passions. Bren's another example. Not only is she an extraordinary barista, she's built a very successful calligraphy business with customers from around the country clamoring for her services. This beautiful world is full of opportunities for people who keep their eyes open."

It was hard not to be encouraged by Charley's infectious optimism.

"I'll definitely be looking for opportunities in the weeks ahead."

"Those who seek typically find." With a wave, he acknowledged a couple approaching the stand, finished wrapping her tacos in white paper, and slid them into a brown bag.

She handed over several bills.

After counting out her change, he passed it to her across the counter. "Enjoy the tacos. And remember to dream big." He gave her a thumbs-up before shifting his attention to the next customers.

As Emma wandered over to claim a bench on the harbor, her mouth curved up.

Tacos with a side of philosophy.

Not a bad deal for the price.

And it would be smart to keep Charley's advice about dreams and opportunities in mind—just in case this little town where serendipity had brought her had a few more surprises in store.

26

· ·

Hope Harbor felt a million miles and a lifetime away.

And he'd only been back in St. Louis for three days.

Noah set his laptop down on the island in his condo none too gently and continued to the fridge. Surveyed the meager contents, most of which had been there since before he went to visit his dad. A tired head of lettuce. Four eggs. Cheese. An almost empty container of OJ.

It was hard to squeeze in a trip to the grocery store when you spent twelve hours a day at the office.

He pulled out a half gallon of milk and twisted off the cap. Sniffed the contents. Winced.

It had soured.

Kind of like his life.

His stomach growled, and he shut the door to the refrigerator. A frozen nuked dinner would have to do. Nine o'clock was too late to go out for dinner or even order carryout. If his stomach wasn't staging a rebellion, he'd forget about eating and crash.

He pulled out the first entrée he touched, tore off the cardboard packaging, and shoved it in the microwave. It wasn't going to be anywhere near as tasty as the food from the casserole brigade, or

Charley's tacos, or Frank's pizza—but it was an easy, if lonely, meal.

While the microwave hummed, he sank onto a stool at the island and pulled out his phone.

No messages from Bren.

Sighing, he set the cell on the island.

Yes, she'd responded to the couple of texts he'd sent her, but her replies had been brief and impersonal. Nothing in them had captured her vibrant personality or kind heart or the electricity he'd felt in her presence. And she'd initiated no communication.

Was she pulling back? Had she decided he was no longer worth wasting gray matter over and written him off?

Or were her nights as restless as his, filled with longing and uncertainty and conflicting emotions?

Maybe he should call her tonight, instead of waiting until Sunday, as he'd mentioned in one of his texts. It would be easier to get a read on her mood if he heard her voice. Written exchanges didn't capture—

His cell began to vibrate.

Bren?

His pulse picked up—then quickly decelerated when his dad's name popped up on the screen.

Not that he didn't want to talk to his father, but after the last three intense days at the office, a call from his favorite barista would have perked him up more than a chat with his dad.

He put the phone to his ear. "Hi, Dad. I was going to call you later."

"Am I interrupting any social plans? It *is* Friday night."

"Nope. I'm waiting for the microwave to finish heating my dinner."

"Don't tell me you just got home from work."

"Work's crazy busy right now." Like always. "What did *you* have for dinner?"

"Eleanor Cooper sent over beef stew, homemade bread, and a

sizeable chunk of her famous chocolate fudge cake. The casserole brigade is outdoing itself."

Noah's mouth began to water. "That sounds great."

"It was. There was so much food, I invited Bren to join me."

The very person he wanted to discuss.

"Did she come?"

"Yes. We had a very pleasant visit. And a meal shared is twice as delicious."

Noah stood. Paced across the room.

How could he get the information he wanted without activating his dad's matchmaking impulses again?

"Um . . . what did you two talk about?"

"Mostly the 5K and Emma's new job at Sweet Dreams." His father proceeded to give him more details than he cared to know about the latest sponsors for the run and Emma's treat-of-the-day bill of fare. "I told Bren I intended to go to Sweet Dreams on Tuesday and get a piece of baklava, and she offered to take me as a thank-you for dinner tonight."

That sounded like the woman he'd come to know during his stay.

"Are you going to go with her?"

"You better believe it."

The microwave pinged, and he walked over to it. Checked his dinner, such as it was. Reset the timer. "Did she, uh, stay long?"

"No. She was slammed trying to finish a calligraphy order. Bren's a go-getter, let me tell you. But she still manages to have a life and keep everything in balance."

Unlike his son.

Dad didn't say that, but his message was clear.

"You have more flexibility if you work for yourself."

"Very true." The faint background noise diminished, suggesting his dad had walked into another room. "You know, Hope Harbor could use a talented CPA. If someone filled that niche, they'd be able to set their own schedule and make time for runs by the sea every day and a life outside of work."

"They'd also make significantly less money."

"You might be surprised. In any case, there'd be other compensations. By the way, Bren asked me if you'd said anything about when you were coming back for a visit."

That was a positive sign—wasn't it?

"What did you tell her?"

"I said it could be a while, based on past experience."

While there was no recrimination in his father's matter-of-fact tone, it nevertheless niggled at his conscience. Much as Dad and Mom may have wished he'd trekked out to their turf more often, they'd never made him feel guilty for the long gaps between visits.

"I'm going to try to get out there on a regular basis in the future."

"That would be wonderful, Son. And I expect Bren would be pleased too."

His spirits ticked up "Did she say that?"

"Not in words, but a man doesn't get to be my age without learning to pick up nuances and cues. I don't know exactly what happened between the two of you while you were here, but I got the feeling she was missing you."

"She hasn't said anything to me about that."

"Have you said anything to her about *your* feelings?"

They were venturing onto shaky ground.

"Um . . ."

"Sorry to butt in, Son. I try not to be a busybody in general, but I do worry that the parade is passing you by on the romance front. I know you've been keeping your feelings about Bren close to your vest, but the ability I developed to pick up nuances works on you too. And after watching the two of you at The Perfect Blend the last morning you were here, it was obvious you were both lovesick."

Noah hesitated—then proceeded with caution. "Lovesick implies someone is in love."

"Or falling."

"The situation with Bren and me is complicated."

"Does it have to be?"

As Charley's quotes from Confucius and Dr. Seuss replayed through his mind, Noah scrubbed a hand down his face. "I don't know. But if there's a simple solution, I'm not seeing it."

"It's possible you're looking too hard."

Frowning, he propped a hip against the island. "What do you mean?"

"I'm thinking about a story from when you were little. You were running a fever, and your mom sent me to the store to get a bottle of baby aspirin. I searched and searched on the shelf but couldn't find it. I finally had to round up a sales clerk to help me. Turns out the aspirin was right in front of me all along, but because the packaging didn't match the image I had in my mind of what it was supposed to look like, I couldn't see it."

Noah tried to apply the story to his situation. Came up empty.

"Sorry. I'm missing the relevance."

"My analogy may have been a bit convoluted. I was trying to illustrate how the thing we're searching for could be staring us in the face, but if the image ingrained in our mind shows it packaged differently, we can't see it. I know how important your career is to you, and that partnership you've set your sights on, but a CPA is a CPA wherever he practices."

"The nature of the work can differ, though. Along with the rewards."

"True. A CPA job here would look very different, I imagine." His father's manner remained gentle and agreeable. "But in the end, I think it comes down to what you most want to remember about your career when it's winding down. The paycheck? The prestige? The power? The challenge? The stress? Or would it be enough to know you've done good work that helped people but that still left you space for a life apart from your job?"

A faint ache began to throb in Noah's temples. "I thought I knew what I wanted. I had everything planned out."

"People can change their minds. And plans can be altered."

"Not without a lot of effort and disruption."

"Sometimes the payoff is worth it. Are you happy in your job, Noah—and in St. Louis?"

Happy?

That wasn't an adjective he'd often applied to his job. There were days it was satisfying. Interesting. Stimulating. But did he often leave the office feeling happy?

No.

And while St. Louis was a fine city, he'd felt more at home in Hope Harbor than he did in his hometown these days.

"I could be happier."

"In that case, it may be worthwhile to think about alternatives to both the city and the job . . . if you're so inclined. In the end, though, it's your life, and you have to live it in a way that suits you."

"I'm not as certain as I once was about what that should look like."

"Give yourself time to work through it. Rushing big decisions is never smart."

"Patience isn't my strong suit."

His dad chuckled. "Tell me something I don't know. I remember how you always wanted your mom to put her bread into the oven to bake before the yeast had time to leaven the dough. In this case, time may be the leaven that will bring clarity."

"Waiting is easier said than done."

"You can always stay in touch with Bren while the two of you work this out."

"I've tried, but I only get short answers to my texts."

"Have you called her?"

"Once. It rolled to voicemail. I think she may be backing off."

"Or trying to play it cautious and safe. Can't blame her for being careful. You do come across as a workaholic, and she doesn't

274

strike me as the kind of woman who would be willing to take second place in a man's affections to a job."

He couldn't argue with that.

"I hear you." He wandered over to the window. Gazed out into the darkness as the microwave pinged. "On a different subject, how did your wrist look in the follow-up X-ray today?"

"All positive news. The bones are aligned and appear to be healing properly. Is your dinner ready?"

"Yeah."

"Go eat. We can talk more this weekend. You want me to pass any message on to Bren?"

"No. I'll reach out to her again."

"Smart plan. And remember, you're not in this alone. I'm in your cheering section."

"Thanks, Dad. I'll talk to you soon."

"Always happy to hear from you. Bon appetit."

"My dinner isn't worthy of such a gourmet wish, but thank you."

"Love you, Son."

"Love you back."

As his dad ended the call, Noah went to the microwave, removed his dinner, and peeled back the clear film over the container. Grimaced.

Despite the long gap since the wrap he'd wolfed down on the fly at noon, his appetite had deserted him.

Besides, he had more than enough to chew on after the conversation with his dad.

And a major case of indigestion was already setting in.

Noah was calling.
Again.

Why wasn't he sleeping in, like most people did on Saturday morning?

Or was he having as much trouble clocking shut-eye as she was?

Bren tightened her grip on her cell as a breeze ruffled her hair and the first rays of sun topped the hills to the east, gilding the edge of Sunrise Reef. Amazing, as always, how the dark, dull rocks came alive when touched by the sun.

As her cell continued to ring, she caught her lower lip between her teeth.

To answer or not to answer, that was the question.

Answer.

At the prod from her conscience, she exhaled.

Yeah. She should talk to him. Dodging his calls was juvenile and cowardly and rude.

So she'd be mature and discreet—and hope it wasn't super obvious that in her case, at least, absence was making the heart grow fonder.

Because unless the feeling was mutual, and unless they figured out what to do about it if it was, extended contact would only add to her insomnia. Radio silence for a while might be prudent.

Something to think about, anyway.

Bracing, she put the phone to her ear. "Hi, Noah."

A beat ticked by. "You answered."

"Your other call came at a bad time." A slight fabrication. She could have put aside her calligraphy and answered it.

"You didn't return it."

Offshore, a dolphin arced out of the water, its sleek body glistening in the sun as a doleful silver-white harbor seal watched from a rock on Sunrise Reef.

"I returned your texts." Far safer than listening to the mellow baritone that always turned her bones to jelly.

"I've been thinking about you."

"Likewise."

"Dad said you had dinner with him last night."

"Yes."

"In case you didn't pick up on it, he's aware the two of us are interested in each other."

"I picked that up. But he didn't ask me any leading questions."

"He asked me plenty during our phone conversation last night."

She gripped her phone tighter as the sun crept higher, painting the reef with its golden rays. "What did you say?"

"I told him we're trying to sort things out."

"Are you any closer to that on your end?"

"No, but I'm still working on it. Are you?"

"I'm thinking but getting nowhere. Bev suggested we try a long-distance courtship."

"She knows about us too?"

Bren snorted. "I'm getting the feeling that anyone who's seen us together knows about us."

"What do you think about the long-distance idea?"

"I think it could work if one of us was willing to relocate in the event we got serious."

"Meaning me."

She shifted her weight.

Yes, she did. And while it wasn't fair for all the sacrifices to be on his end, she couldn't wrap her mind around the notion of picking up and starting over yet again after searching so long for the home she'd found here.

"You know how I feel about Hope Harbor, Noah. Do you feel as strongly about St. Louis?"

"No. But I do have to think about my job and all I'd give up if I walked away."

"Would job considerations be as important to you if a long-distance courtship led us to consider a serious commitment?"

His brief hesitation was telling.

"I don't know."

Not what she wanted to hear.

But in truth, if he parroted the question back to her and

threw out leaving Hope Harbor as a possibility, she'd have said a firm no.

Impasse, pure and simple.

Which made further contact pointless unless one of them changed their mind.

Time for the radio silence suggestion.

A cloud passed over the sun, momentarily snuffing out the light on the reef as she summoned up the fortitude to do what she had to do to protect her heart. "I have a suggestion."

"Am I going to like it?"

"I doubt it, but I think it's the smart course to follow."

"I'm listening." His cautious tone, however, suggested he wasn't overly receptive.

"I think we should take a communications break. See if lack of contact affects how we feel about each other and our situation."

"For how long?"

"We could try six weeks."

"With no contact at all?"

"Yes."

The sound of a forcefully expelled breath came over the line. "You're right. I don't like it."

"Me neither. But it's safer—for both of us."

"You know what? I'm getting tired of playing it safe." His admission was laced with frustration.

She could relate.

But someone had to be the voice of reason in this conversation.

"Six weeks isn't long in the big scheme of things. And the space will give us a chance to think."

"Can we text?"

"That counts as communication."

"You're killing me here."

"Do you have a better plan?"

Several seconds ticked by. "No. I wish I did. You know six weeks from today is the 5K."

How apropos.

"Maybe a finish line will be in sight for us by then too." Or perhaps just a finish.

But she left that depressing possibility unspoken.

"So this conversation is it for six weeks."

"We'll survive." She hoped.

"Speak for yourself. You've got Bev and Emma and a host of friends, not to mention an ocean view. All I have is work."

"That's all you had before."

"I know. But it doesn't feel like enough anymore."

That could be a positive development—but she wasn't going to get her hopes up. Nor would she encourage Noah to leave the career path he'd followed for more than a decade. If he ever decided to make a change, it had to be his own choice, no coercion involved.

"You've only been back in the office three days. See how you feel in six weeks."

"I *know* how I'm going to feel. Lonely."

"Maybe not. Maybe you'll forget all about me."

"No matter where we end up, Bren, that will never happen. You're not a forgettable woman."

At the husky cadence in his voice, her pulse lost its rhythm for a moment. "You're pretty memorable yourself." Her words rasped, and she swallowed past the lump in her throat. "Take care, okay?"

"You too. I guess it's goodbye for now."

"Yeah." It was all she could manage.

"I'll be in touch six weeks from today."

"Talk to you then. Bye." She ended the call. Closed her eyes. Choked back a sob.

Why, after all these years, had God sent a man like Noah into her world to plant seeds of discontent about her solo life and offer her a tantalizing taste of romance—then put a seemingly insurmountable roadblock in their path?

As if in response to her question, the sun burst through the clouds, bestowing a dazzling radiance on the reef.

But the golden interlude lasted no more than a handful of heartbeats. More clouds moved in, snuffing out the glow on this Saturday morning.

And hard as she tried to ignore the symbolism, Mother Nature's display felt like a visual depiction of her relationship with Noah—and an ominous omen for how it would end.

27

What could she have done wrong?

As the sun beamed down on her at two o'clock on this second Monday in September, Emma parked a couple of doors down from Sweet Dreams and tried to loosen the kinks in her stomach.

They refused to budge.

Because somehow she'd messed up.

Why else would Joe have called her this morning and set up a meeting with him and Alice at the bakery on a day the shop was closed? Especially since she'd see them both bright and early tomorrow morning, now that he was back in the shop almost every day and pitching in where he could with his healing wrist.

And if they let her go, what would she do?

She'd researched area bakeries and compiled a list of contacts. Updated her resume. Written her cover note. This was the week she'd planned to ask Alice and Joe for a letter of recommendation and begin applying for jobs.

But if she was being fired, no recommendation would be forthcoming.

Even worse, she'd once again be without a source of income—and her hopes of a holiday reunion with Justin would be dashed.

At least she'd paid back the loan Bren had given her for the deposit on her apartment. And she wasn't going to go back to her again for any more assistance.

Worst case, she'd talk to Father Murphy and see if she could tap into the church's emergency fund he'd mentioned at their first meeting. Just until she landed a permanent job.

If she landed one, after whatever Alice and Joe had to say today.

She slid from behind the wheel. Squeezed her fingers into tight fists.

As far as she could tell, her tenure at the shop had been flawless—and the treat-of-the-day addition had generated a significant increase in traffic. She'd heard no complaints from anyone.

But she must have made some terrible mistake if the owners had called a special meeting with her.

Standing around outside, however, wasn't going to fix whatever was wrong. May as well go in and face the music.

Forcing her legs to carry her forward, she continued to the door. Twisted the knob. Stepped inside.

Alice and Joe were seated at the single café table against the wall. The folding chair from the back room had been pulled up and was waiting for her. A sheet of paper lay on the table in front of Alice.

"Good morning, Emma." Alice stood and motioned her forward. "Would you like a cup of coffee? I made it under Joe's watchful eye, so it should be drinkable."

The woman's cheery demeanor didn't suggest the axe was about to fall. But what else could have prompted this meeting?

"Thank you, but I had coffee earlier." Besides, her churning stomach wouldn't be receptive to the high-octane, high-acid java Joe favored.

"Then come on over and have a seat."

"I'd offer you a fancy dessert, but our French pastry chef is off today." Joe's smile also seemed welcoming and warm.

What was going on?

Emma approached and perched on the edge of the chair. "Is everything okay?"

"Couldn't be better." Alice squinted at Joe. "You told her we had a proposal to make, didn't you?"

"I think so." His brow creased, and he scratched his head. "But a call came in from Kathleen while we were talking, and after Lisa began clamoring in the background to talk to her papoo, I ended the conversation with Emma pretty quick." Joe transferred his attention at her. "I did mention the proposal, didn't I?"

"No."

"Joe!" Alice sent him an admonishing look. "Can't you see the poor girl is worried?"

"Why would she worry? She knows she's done a stellar job here. Right, Emma?"

The knots in her stomach began to loosen. "I thought I had, but a meeting outside of normal hours did kind of throw me." An understatement if ever there was one. "I wondered if I'd messed something up without realizing it."

"I'm sorry for the misunderstanding, Emma." Joe sent her an apologetic glance.

Alice rolled her eyes. "I should have made the call myself." The older woman patted her hand. "You haven't messed anything up, Emma. Far from it. Business has been booming since you came on board. We're even getting new customers from Bandon who've heard about your pastries. So Joe and I started thinking about how to proceed going forward."

"Actually, the brains of this outfit started thinking." Mouth bowing, Joe hooked a thumb toward Alice. "But I liked her idea. We hope you do too."

"You want to explain it to her, Joe?" Alice slid the piece of paper on the table toward him.

"No." He slid it back. "You're better at business stuff."

"That's true." Alice winked at her and linked her fingers on the table. "I've been watching the numbers over the past three weeks.

Income has increased quite a bit, thanks to your pastries. And those sales are pumping up sales of our other items. Several days this past week the cases were empty before closing. I had to shut down and put a sold-out sign in the window."

"Are you thinking we need to increase output?" Another worry began to form in Emma's mind. She was stretched thin as it was, Joe wasn't yet able to help much, and the baking space was limited.

"That would be ideal to meet demand, but logistically it's not realistic with our staffing and space."

Thank goodness Alice recognized the shop's limitations.

"So what's your proposal?"

"Well, much as we love Hope Harbor and our business here, we miss our daughter and grandchildren. Someday in the not-too-distant future we'd hoped to retire and sell Sweet Dreams to someone who would carry on with the shop. Thanks to your arrival—and the imminent arrival of yet another grandchild—we think maybe that someday has arrived."

As they both looked at her, Emma tried to digest what they were saying.

Were they implying *she* might take over the shop?

Surely not. That would be too fantastic to be real.

"I think she's speechless, Alice." Joe grinned at her.

Emma tried to find her voice. "I'm not certain I understand what you're saying."

"I'll try to be more clear than my partner here." Joe leaned forward. "We'd like to retire and move to Idaho to be closer to our daughter and her family. We want to leave Sweet Dreams in good hands. We can't think of anyone more perfect to take the reins than you."

She hadn't misunderstood.

They were offering her a chance to fulfill her dream of having her own business.

But touched as she was by their proposition, and as hard as she wished she could accept, there was one little problem.

Namely, cash flow.

Emma clenched her hands together in her lap. Swallowed past her disappointment. "I can't tell you how flattered I am that you're willing to trust me with the business you built. And I'd leap at the opportunity in a heartbeat if I could. But I don't have the resources to buy you out."

"We assumed as much. So we put our heads together and came up with a plan we think could work." Alice tapped the sheet of paper. "Would you like to hear it?"

"This beautiful world is full of opportunities for people who keep their eyes open."

As Charley's comment echoed in her mind, a tingle of anticipation rippled through her. "Yes."

Joe let Alice take the lead, and she did a thorough job of explaining the bullet points on her list.

Bottom line, they were suggesting a six-month transition period, during which they would remain active in the shop as mentors while she learned the business side of the operation. After that, they would relocate to Idaho and retain an equity interest in Sweet Dreams, taking a percent of the profits until the agreed-upon price was paid.

"If our offer is acceptable, I'll have the attorney we've used in Coos Bay for many years put together the paperwork." Alice closed the file. "What do you think?"

Emma was fairly quivering with excitement.

This was surreal.

A dream come true.

Wait until she told Justin!

"I think it sounds like a wonderful opportunity."

"Excellent." Alice folded her hands on top of the file. "We'll get the agreement in the works. You should also have an attorney review it. I can recommend Eric Nash here in town. He's top-notch. If we hadn't had a long-term attorney, we'd have switched to him after he moved here. I'll ask our accountant to work with him on the financial terms. That would be Tracy, out at the cranberry farm. First-rate CPA. I hope she has time to take this on. With her farm and cranberry nut cake business booming, she's been cutting back on her clients. You should also have an accountant review the terms and our books. Eric may be able to recommend someone."

"I wonder if Fred's son would do that for me."

Alice's eyebrows rose. "I thought he went back to St. Louis."

"He did, but I could ask Bren to contact him and see if he'd help me. I think they became friends while he was here."

"Whatever works for you is fine with us."

"I'll talk to Bren right away." It was all Emma could do to keep herself planted in the chair while every instinct in her body was urging her to jump up and cheer.

"And we'll loop in our attorney and Tracy." Alice extended her hand. "Here's to a happy and prosperous partnership."

Emma returned her firm clasp. "Thank you."

"Thank *you* for jump-starting our retirement. Saying goodbye to Sweet Dreams may not have been on our radar quite yet, but this opportunity is too perfect to pass up."

"Not that I'm trying to change your mind, but won't you miss Hope Harbor?" Emma encompassed them both in the question. "Hasn't this been your home for many years?"

A touch of melancholy crept into Joe's expression. "Yes. I came here when I was twenty-five, with the dream of opening my own bakery. I doubt it would ever have happened if I hadn't met Alice, though. She's the one who figured out how to do it on a shoestring. We'll definitely miss our shop . . . and this town. Won't we, Alice?"

"Yes." She took his hand. "But one thing we learned after our daughter got married and moved away is that home is more than a place. It's being with the people you love. Living close to our daughter and her family will help make up for missing Hope Harbor." Alice squeezed Joe's hand. "So are we ready to get this show on the road?"

"Yes."

"We'll give you a copy of the agreement to review as soon as it's ready." Alice stood and picked up the sheet of paper. "I'll lock up behind us."

After a round of goodbyes outside the shop, they all headed for their own cars.

Once behind the wheel of her Sentra, Emma reached for her cell. Paused.

Eager as she was to call Justin, it would be wrong to create expectations until she had the agreement in hand. This felt like a bubble that could burst at any moment.

But she was going to pay Bren a visit.

Wait until her benefactor heard this news.

And if Bren could convince Noah to weigh in on the Sweet Dreams books . . . and if everything appeared to be sound . . . perhaps the dream she'd almost given up on was on the cusp of coming true.

As the doorbell at her house rang, Bren finished the last letter on the name of the place card she was working on and set the pen aside.

It wasn't Bev. She'd be manning the counter at the Book Nook.

Must be a delivery. Her latest order of calligraphy supplies had shipped yesterday.

Bren stood, stretched her back, and padded toward the door in her socks. After spending eight hours on her feet at The Perfect Blend with nary a respite in the surge of customers, it was no wonder her toes had demanded release the instant she got home.

She'd been happy to oblige. There was something comforting and homey about wandering around in your stockinged feet—and being back in your own digs, even if they were a step down from Fred's cottage.

Unfortunately, returning to familiar surroundings hadn't eased the legacy of loneliness she'd inherited from the brief interlude in her life that had been graced by Noah's presence.

And the passage of time, and lack of contact, wasn't helping.

If anything, she missed him more now than she had at the beginning.

Propping up her drooping lips, she pulled the door open.

Emma stood on the other side.

"This is a surprise." Her smile broadened. "Come in. And I apologize in advance for the lingering smell of fresh paint and the drywall dust swirling through the air. I hope you don't have allergies."

"No. But I don't plan to stay long anyway. I have news, or I wouldn't have dropped in unannounced." Emma entered, cheeks flushed, eyes sparkling.

"Happy news, I take it." Bren shut the door and motioned her toward the couch.

"Very. You'll never guess what happened today." Emma crossed to the sofa and sat, excitement pinging off her.

"Then I won't try. Tell me." Bren joined her on the couch.

"Alice and Joe met with me today. It was amazing."

As Emma relayed her story, Bren listened without interrupting, delight at the other woman's good fortune chasing away some of her doldrums.

How wonderful that Emma was finding a happy ending to *her* story.

When her unexpected guest wound down, Bren leaned forward. "This is awesome news. I assume you told them yes."

"Of course. It's a dream come true. I do have to review the legal agreement, and the price is a little scary. Not that it isn't fair, but it's a chunk of money to agree to, all on the assumption I can build on the recent sales increase."

"Do you have any doubts about that? From what you said, your treat-of-the-day idea has been a huge success."

"I have plenty of doubts." She wiped her palms down her jeans.

"Not about my abilities or the ideas I have to boost business even more, but it's hard to trust such an incredible piece of luck. I mean, what if there's a pitfall I'm overlooking?"

"That's why attorneys get involved. And I'll vouch for Eric too. I haven't had to use his services, but his reputation is stellar."

"I also need to have an accountant review the financial piece. That's the main reason I stopped by. Do you think if I paid Noah, he might be willing to help?"

Smart choice, with his skills. But . . .

"I don't know, Emma. His job is super busy. It can't hurt to pose the question, though."

Emma played with a button on her shirt. "I hate to ask another favor, after all you've done for me, but I was wondering if you'd be willing to make the initial contact. I don't really know his dad, and Noah was leery about me in the beginning. I don't want to put him in an awkward position, and I thought it would be easier for him to say no through you than directly to me if he doesn't want to help."

Bren leaned back against the couch.

There was almost three weeks to go in their agreed-upon communication moratorium, but positioning this as a business matter should allow her to bend the terms of their arrangement.

And it would help Emma out.

"No problem. If he's agreeable, the two of you can take it from there."

"That would be great."

"I'll text him this afternoon. Have you told Justin yet?"

"No. I want this to be solid first. I'd feel terrible if he got his hopes up and everything fell through. To be honest, it feels too good to be true."

"It sounds real to me—but I understand your concern. I'd feel the same in your place. Are you certain Alice and Joe are committed to this? They've lived here forever. This is their home."

"I asked them about that, and Alice said home is more than a place. That it's being with the people you love. And I know what she means. I won't feel like this is truly home until Justin and I are together again." Emma stood. "Will you let me know as soon as you hear from Noah?"

"I will." Bren rose too and walked her to the door, Alice's comment looping through her mind as she waved Emma off, wandered back to her calligraphy setup, and retook her seat in front of the desktop easel.

The bakery owner's definition of home wasn't one she'd ever considered.

Was Alice right?

Was home all about the people you loved versus the physical place?

If everyone in Hope Harbor disappeared, would this place still feel like home—or would it be just another beautiful spot by the sea?

Probably the latter.

On the flip side, much as she'd miss the residents if *she* left, Bev was the only person she'd let into her heart.

Except for Noah, a visitor who was now back in St. Louis. The place *he* called home.

If they fell in love, would home be wherever he was?

Maybe.

Frowning, she caught her lower lip between her teeth and steepled her fingers.

It would be hard to leave Bev. Likewise for this beautiful place with its sweeping vistas, endless charm, stunning lighthouse, and Sunrise Reef, where she went whenever she needed to be reminded that beauty could be found in the most ordinary places if one sought it out.

But everything about Noah felt like home.

Slowly she picked up her pen.

Instead of reaching for a place card, however, she set a piece of parchment paper on her desktop easel and began to pen a note.

Maybe she'd send it. Maybe she wouldn't. That was a decision for another day.

Yet as the words flowed from her heart, through her pen, and onto the paper, one thing was clear.

Other than a couple of very brief and disappointing dabbles in romance early on, since the day she left home at seventeen she'd been a solo act. Independent. Self-sufficient. Trusting only Bev—and more recently, Noah—with her deepest secrets. Never expecting anyone to help her. Never willing to cede control of her life to another person, or let someone force her to be something she wasn't.

But Noah had never tried to do that.

So if she could wrap her mind around a different definition of home . . . if she could concede that letting someone hold her hand wasn't the same as letting someone hold her up . . . if she could make peace with changing addresses in the name of love . . . it was possible Emma wouldn't be the only one in Hope Harbor to find a happy ending as this summer waned.

28

· ·

This had been the flight from hell.

Noah pulled his carry-on suitcase from the overhead bin and surged down the aisle toward the door of the plane.

Weather delay. Mechanical delay. A passenger who'd passed out in the airless cabin on the tarmac and had to be taken off by paramedics, resulting in further delays.

What else could have gone wrong on the first leg of this journey?

And unless the gods suddenly took pity on him, he wasn't going to make his connection.

Barreling down the jetway, Noah tried not to jostle the other deplaning passengers, but if he didn't catch his next flight, he'd be taking a red-eye to tomorrow's meeting in Cheyenne.

How could a major city like St. Louis offer so few direct flights?

He exited the jetway and took off at a gallop for his next gate—but despite his all-out sprint through the terminal, his plane was taxiing away from the gate when he arrived.

He skidded to a stop.

Blast, blast, blast, blast, blast.

Now he'd be at the mercy of the airlines to get him on a flight to Cheyenne in time for his meeting.

Twenty minutes later, after an intense, bordering-on-heated

exchange with the agent behind the counter at the gate, he secured a flight in five hours. One with yet another connection, which wouldn't get him to his destination until after midnight.

Meaning there was no way he was going to be bright and chipper for tomorrow's eight o'clock meeting.

Grimacing, he tightened his grip on the handle of his suitcase and trekked to his new gate, located at the end of the concourse.

Naturally.

After claiming an empty seat in the departure lounge, he pulled out his phone. Switched off airplane mode. Began checking messages.

He dispensed with the handful of voicemails first, returning the calls that required a response. Moved on to emails.

Good grief.

How could twenty messages have come in while his plane was parked on the tarmac in delay mode and during the flight?

Forty-five minutes later, he finished the last response and dived into the texts. Most were short and easy to respond to, thank goodness. He ought to be able to get through these in—

Wait.

There was a message from Bren? Despite their moratorium on communication?

Pulse picking up, he clicked on it.

> Sorry to bother you, but Emma has an offer to buy Sweet Dreams. She needs someone to review the financial piece of the deal and examine the shop's books. She asked me to reach out and see if you'd be willing. I warned her you were super busy. Don't feel any obligation to get involved.

His spirits dipped.

Bren was texting about a professional matter. Asking him to do a job. Her tone was businesslike and impersonal.

Nevertheless, she'd opened a line of communication. And he'd take whatever contact with her he could get, even if he wasn't ready to pull the trigger on a major life change.

Yet.

He filled his lungs. Exhaled.

That three-letter word said it all.

The truth was, he was getting closer to taking the leap. Especially after a day like today. Because he wasn't loving his job anymore, if he ever had. In hindsight, it was clear it had been a means to an end . . . and that end was looking less and less appealing with every late night at the office, too-short deadline, and stressful travel woe.

And the appeal continued to decline day by day, since it appeared his current career path would give him limited in-person opportunities to find out if Bren could be The One.

So maybe this was an opening to start talking to her again—although how someone in Emma's financial straits could swing such a deal was beyond him.

He put his thumbs to work.

> Happy to help. Sounds like a great opportunity for her. Shall I call you to discuss?

Her response was prompt.

> Not necessary. I'll send you her contact information and let her know you'll be in touch. Thanks.

Thirty seconds later, Emma's phone number and email appeared in a follow-up text without any further message.

He hesitated, thumbs poised over the keypad.

Sighed.

They'd agreed to wait six weeks to resume personal communication. He'd honor that.

Much as he'd prefer not to.

May as well call Emma now, since he'd be sitting around twiddling his thumbs for the next four hours.

She answered on the first ring, sounding both apologetic and a bit nervous as she greeted him.

After reassuring her she wasn't imposing, he got down to business. "Once you have the agreement in hand, forward me a copy and I'll review the terms. But I have to ask, Emma. My understanding was that your finances were . . . slim. I'm not clear how you're going to buy Sweet Dreams. Bren didn't provide any details."

He listened as she explained the arrangement.

"So this will be a gradual buy-in." As she concluded, her excitement crackled over the line.

The setup she'd outlined made sense. It would also be advantageous from a tax standpoint for the current owners to receive payment over time versus in one lump sum.

"Got it. Seems like a mutually beneficial deal. During my review, I'll also want to touch base with the accountant for Sweet Dreams and examine the books. Do you have their contact information?"

"No, but I can get it. Alice said she's a CPA. Her name is Tracy, and she runs a cranberry farm outside of town."

That had to be the same woman Bev had mentioned. The one the bookshop owner had suggested was getting out of the accounting business to concentrate on her farm.

Hmm.

The conversation he was going to have with her might end up serving a dual purpose.

"Why don't you forward her information to me as soon as you have it? I should be able to give you my assessment of the financial strength of the business within a few days. You'll want to factor that into the price they're asking. I don't imagine the shop is a huge moneymaker."

"I don't, either. But I'm not trying to get rich. It would be a dream come true if I could run my own bakery, as long as I can earn enough to cover my expenses."

"You do intend to have an attorney review the contract, don't you?"

"Yes. A man named Eric Nash, here in town."

"If you want to give him my phone number, I'll be glad to talk with him too. I've been involved in a number of deals that include equity arrangements and buyouts."

"Thank you. I'll pass on your contact information. Do you want my address for billing purposes, or do you prefer to email an invoice?"

"There won't be a charge, Emma."

Silence.

"I can't take charity, Mr. Ward."

Mister?

He wasn't *that* much older than she was.

Well, okay, he was almost twice her age—but that didn't make him old.

"Noah is fine. And consider this my apology for being suspicious of you when you arrived in town. I'm sure the attorney will charge you enough for both of us."

A sniff came over the line. "Sometimes it's hard for me to believe how much kindness has been shown to me in Hope Harbor."

"I'm not in Hope Harbor."

"You were, for a while. And honestly, it feels like you belong there."

It did to him too. More and more every day.

Until he was certain of his plans, though, it was best not to respond to comments like that. Besides, if he did decide to move, Bren should be the first to know.

"I wish I was there now. It would be far more pleasant than the airport I'm stuck in. I'll watch for emails and texts from you with the deal documents and contact information."

"I'll get it all to you ASAP. Thank you again. You'll never know how much I appreciate this."

Once they rang off, Noah dug around in his suitcase for a couple of aspirin. The headache that had kicked in as he watched his connecting flight take off was threatening to go full throttle unless he curbed it fast.

The pain meds weren't in his usual spot for such supplies. Not surprising, seeing how this trip had landed in his lap with almost no warning and he'd had mere minutes to throw a few essentials into his luggage before rushing to the airport.

He rotated the case and felt in the outside pocket.

Frowned.

What was that oblong item?

He unzipped the compartment, dug deep, and pulled out a bag.

Ah.

The book Bev had given him the day he'd stopped by to discuss her contribution to the 5K. The one he'd shoved in his suitcase as soon as he returned to Dad's without ever opening it and promptly forgotten about.

He opened the stapled top of the bag, pulled the book out, and read the title.

Leap of Faith.

From the cover art, it appeared to be a suspense novel.

He weighed it in his hand.

With nothing else to do for the next four hours, why not dive in?

Once he located the aspirin and downed them with a swig from his water bottle, he settled back and began to read.

The opening hostage scene hooked him, and the hovering life-and-death danger kept him reading—even after he realized the story also featured a romance.

That wasn't his cup of tea, but the suspense plot was riveting. And there were several uncanny similarities between the romance in the book and his early stage romance with Bren.

Like, the hero and heroine seemed to be totally different at the beginning but found common ground as the story progressed. The heroine loved her work and was a people person, but she had trust issues because of her past. The hero was a workaholic who'd logged several failed relationships, thanks to his job. The two of them lived in different parts of the country, so the only way for them to get together was for one of them to radically change their life.

Of course the story had a happy ending. The guy realized he loved the heroine more than his career, and she realized her soul would be better fed by his love than by her job. Their solution? Relocate and start over together in a new place.

That wasn't going to happen with him and Bren—but had Bev given him this particular book to suggest there might be a solution he hadn't yet found to his dilemma with Bren? To encourage him not to lose hope?

Who knew?

Whatever her motive, the simple truth was that happy endings in novels didn't always reflect reality. That's why books like this were called fiction. They were a pleasant way to pass a few idle hours and—

"Is that seat taken?"

Noah looked up.

An older man was standing beside him, in front of one of the last empty seats in the area now that departure was drawing near.

"No."

The man claimed it, setting his carry-on at his feet. "How was the book?" He nodded to the novel.

Uh-oh.

The guy could be a talker—and garrulous people on planes and in airport waiting areas were the bane of seasoned travelers.

"Entertaining." He tucked it back into his suitcase, angling slightly away to discourage further conversation.

Didn't work.

"My wife always took books with her when we traveled. I never got in the habit, but she said reading helped pass the time in the airport and on long flights. We did a lot of traveling in our day."

The past tense suggested the man could be a widower.

Noah zipped the compartment closed, guilt pricking his conscience.

He ought to cut the guy some slack. Let him talk a little if he needed a friendly ear.

"Where did you travel?"

"Europe, for the most part. She had family in Ireland. But we went to Asia too, and Africa. Spent our fiftieth anniversary last year in Tahiti, at one of those ritzy places with rooms built on stilts over the water so you could watch the sea life from your deck. It was a bucket list trip, and worth every penny." He adjusted his glasses. Cleared his throat. "She passed away real sudden a month after we got home. Here one day, gone the next."

"I'm sorry." It wasn't enough, but no words were adequate when someone was grieving.

"Me too. She was one in a million. I knew that from day one. Took me a while to win her over, though, but what a life we had after I did." A wistful smile touched his lips. "Even though the good Lord gave us fifty years together, I wasn't ready to let her go."

"Do you have children?"

"One daughter. I'm off to visit her and the grandkids now. I think they're going to try to convince me to move closer. And you know what? I don't plan to put up a fight. It's lonely without Clair, and being close to people you love is everything." He cocked his head. "Are you married, young man?"

"Not yet."

"Someone in the wings?"

"Maybe."

"Glad to hear it. I thought I was happy with my work and my outside interests until I met Clair, but after she came into my life, I saw the world through a different lens. One that was brighter and happier. Love can do that for you."

The PA clicked on, and the gate attendant announced their flight.

"I'm in the first boarding group." Noah rose.

The other man stood too. Extended his hand. "Thanks for listening to me ramble, and best of luck with your young lady. If she's the right one, don't let her get away."

Noah shook his hand. "I'll keep that in mind. Enjoy your visit with your daughter."

"I always do. Safe travels, and happy landing."

After joining the queue, Noah lost track of the older man. Nor did he see him board. But the widower could have gotten on while the attendant was taking drink orders in first class.

Nevertheless, the chance encounter had given him food for thought. As had the novel from Bev.

Both had supported everything that already seemed to be pointing him in the direction of making a drastic change in his life.

Before he took such a major step, though, he had some research to do. And he and Bren also needed to have another in-person visit.

So as the plane geared up for takeoff, he focused all his energies on formulating a plan that would allow him to wing back to the Oregon coast as soon as their six-week moratorium was over.

And perhaps find the happy landing the older man had wished for him.

29

As Noah's name flashed on her cell screen, Emma's heart missed a beat. He'd had all the material for the proposed Sweet Dreams agreement for a week, had texted to say he'd talked to Eric and Tracy, and had promised to weigh in as soon as he could review everything.

This must be his verdict.

Emma lowered herself into the upholstered chair Bren had loaned her for the apartment, clenched the arm, and took the call. "Hi, Noah."

"Hello, Emma. Sorry it's taken me a bit longer than I'd hoped to go through everything. Work got crazier than usual."

"No worries. I know you're busy. What's the word?"

"As far as finances are concerned, it's a go."

She closed her eyes. Released her grip on the chair. Started breathing again.

Thank you, God.

"No red flags?" Hard as she tried to control it, a tremor ran through her question.

"No. The books are meticulous, and everything's in order. Tracy is an excellent accountant. As I suspected, the income isn't super high, but you've indicated that's not the deciding factor for you."

"It's not—but how much are we talking in terms of profit?"

When he gave her the number, she exhaled.

Maybe that wasn't high by most people's standards, but it would provide a comfortable living for her and Justin. Besides, once she implemented some of the plans she had in mind for the shop, the income should increase.

"The one suggestion I'd offer is to consider having Eric talk to their attorney about the price they're asking. In light of historic income levels, it's a little on the high side."

She furrowed her brow. "I don't know, Noah. I want to be fair to them, and I don't want any hard feelings."

"There's negotiation in every business deal. Most people's initial price is higher than what they expect to get. I'd suggest a modest counter, but that's up to you. You can discuss it with Eric if you like, get his take. Otherwise, from a finance perspective, you're inheriting a clean operation. No outstanding debts, solid credit rating, well-established operation, steady return on investment, and a loyal customer base. The latter is my own take, based on anecdotal evidence, not demographic data."

"I appreciate all your work on this, Noah. And I'll call Eric today. He only had minor tweaks on the agreement, so once the price is firm, I should be good to go." She tucked her hair behind her ear. Shook her head as her lips bowed. "I can't believe I'm going to own a bakery."

"Not outright. You'll be paying off the debt for years. But for all practical purposes, it'll be your baby. I wish you all the best, Emma."

"Thank you. It's hard to believe this all began with a broken-down car and an unplanned stop at a coffee shop. If I hadn't met Bren, none of this would be happening. She's amazing."

"I won't argue with that."

Emma picked at a loose thread on the chair. "So, uh, are you two still in touch?" Because if they weren't, they should be. The warmth in his voice and the yearning that swept over Bren's face whenever his name came up in conversation were dead giveaways about their feelings for each other.

"Not lately. How is she?"

"Busier than ever, from what I can tell. With the 5K race five days off, she and the rest of the committee are scrambling to get the final pieces in place. Plus, she's swamped with calligraphy orders. The Perfect Blend also seems to be busier than usual. Did you know she's also part of the foster grandparent program through Helping Hands? I just found out about that."

"Yes, I did. She does a lot of other volunteering too."

"If you want my opinion, I think she stays busy to keep from getting lonely."

As the comment tumbled from her mouth, Emma cringed.

She could be overstepping.

Nevertheless, Bren deserved to be happy. And it might not be a bad strategy to suggest to him that he was missed. If he and Bren had feelings for each other, *one* of them had to make a move.

"You may be right." Noah's tone was noncommittal. "Well . . . I'll let you go. Good luck, and don't hesitate to call if you have any questions or I can be of any other help."

"I will. Thank you again."

As the line went dead, she sighed.

Unless her intuition was failing her, he and Bren ought to be together.

But it was going to have to be up to them to make that happen. She could only control so much.

Like the long-awaited call to Justin.

Grinning, she pulled up his number and tapped it in.

"Hey, Em. I've been thinking about you."

"Likewise. And I have a ton of news to share."

For the next ten minutes, she gave him the full download on

everything that had happened with Sweet Dreams, answering all the eager questions he threw at her as she recounted her tale.

"That's awesome, Sis." His excitement crackled over the line. "You're going to get your own business after all."

"It's a miracle. It has to be. There have been too many incidents in perfect sequence for it to be anything else. And there's more. While I was working with the attorney who reviewed the Sweet Dreams agreement, I also talked to him about the guardianship paperwork. He's going to help me fill it out and file it. After he heard my story, he was confident we wouldn't have any issue getting the legalities finished by Christmas. We can be together for the holiday."

"That's amazing! You're the best, Em." Justin's attempt to cover the choke in his voice with a cough was obvious.

"I don't know about that. But I do have the best brother in the world. Can you hang in there until I get everything sorted out here?"

"Yeah. Now that there's light at the end of the tunnel, I can deal with Bill. Having Christmas with you in Hope Harbor will be the best gift ever."

"For me too. Just be aware that I may end up recruiting you to help at the shop with what I hope will be a Christmas rush."

"Count on it. Love you, Em."

"Love you back. I'll call again in a day or two."

As she severed the connection, Emma leaned back in the chair, lifted her gaze, and sent a silent thank-you heavenward for all the wonderful blessings that had graced her life in this tiny seaside town.

Yet even if her stay in Hope Harbor had turned out to be nothing more than a short respite from her troubles and responsibilities, her encounter with Bren would always have been a reminder that hope and goodness lived—and that they could sometimes be found in the most unexpected places and most unexpected ways.

Bren paused outside the Book Nook and took a long, slow breath.

In two days, her six-week moratorium with Noah would be over—and before the two of them talked, she needed a Bev fix. Bad.

She pushed through the door to the cheery ding-a-ling of wind chimes.

From behind the countertop where Bev worked on her jewelry between customers, the owner smiled at her. "Good morning, dear girl. Did you come to see me or to get a cookie?"

"Delicious as your cookies are, the draw here for me is always you."

"Thank you for that. Did you finish the job for the bride in Seattle?"

"Yes. FedEx picked it up half an hour ago." She wandered over to the jewelry counter and inspected Bev's latest creation, a necklace of rough-cut amethyst interspersed with silver beads, an intriguing hint of gold tucked here and there. "What a beautiful piece."

"Thank you."

"But I wouldn't trade it for these." She touched one of her imperial jasper earrings.

"I'm glad they've given you pleasure."

"Also food for thought."

Bev studied her. "How so?"

"You told me once that in addition to all the other qualities this stone represents, it's also a reminder of the power of companionship. I don't know if wearing these was the impetus, but since you gave them to me, I've been thinking a lot about that notion."

"Why do I suspect Noah played a bigger role in your musings than those earrings?" Bev set down the small pliers in her hand, eyes twinkling.

"Because you're smart and intuitive?"

"More likely because I know you." Bev pulled a second stool into place beside hers and patted it. "Why don't you sit with me for a minute?"

Bren circled the jewelry counter and joined her. "Noah and I are supposed to talk on Saturday. That's the end of our six-week moratorium, which was intended to give us both a chance to see how we felt about being apart."

"What's the verdict on your end?"

"I miss him every day. I feel like there's something special between us and that I'll live to regret it if we don't find out where that attraction may lead. But he may have come to a different conclusion."

"You'll know in two days. However, from what I saw while he was here, I don't think his feelings will have diminished, either."

"I don't know, Bev." Frowning, she picked up a silver bead and rolled it between her fingers. "Considering how busy his job keeps him, he may not have had time to think about me."

"If it didn't keep him too busy to help Emma out, I think it's a safe bet he found plenty of time to think about you."

"That doesn't mean he's decided he wants to throw in the towel on his career in St. Louis."

"Have you thought any more about moving there, if no other resolution comes to mind?"

"Yes." But if she decided to take the path she was more and more leaning toward, Noah should be the first to know. "Although I wouldn't relocate without a firmer sense of whether there's real potential between us. That's why I'm going to suggest your idea about a long-distance courtship for a few months, if he's willing to give it a try."

"That sounds like a sensible plan to me."

"I hope he agrees." She set the bead back and rubbed her forehead. "Why do relationships have to be so complicated?"

"In my experience, most things worth having don't come easy—

and there's often a price of some sort to be paid. Maybe that's God's way of making us appreciate them more once we get them."

"I suppose that's one way to look at it. I bet Emma is extra thankful for the bakery contract after the challenges she's faced."

"Is that a done deal?"

"As of yesterday. She signed all the papers, then brought over a treat of the day for each of us to celebrate. I'm happy for her."

"So am I. And I'm hoping there's a sweet ending for you too." Bev touched her hand.

"Thank you. A lot depends on Saturday." Like everything.

"The race will take up most of your day. When are you talking to Noah?"

"I don't know. If I don't hear from him, I'll text him tomorrow and see if we can set up a call on Saturday evening. I don't want to be distracted by race duties during our conversation." The chimes by the door pealed again, and two women entered. "I'll let you get back to work." Bren stood.

"Ladies, I'll be with you in a moment." Bev rose too as she addressed the customers.

"No hurry. We're in the mood to browse." One of the women gave the shop a sweep.

As the two customers began perusing the shelves, Bren settled her purse on her shoulder. "Thanks for being here for me whenever I need a sympathetic ear."

"That's what friends do. And for the record, my ear will always be available, no matter where your life takes you. Friendship transcends geography."

"Thank you for that too." Bren sniffed. Swiped at her nose. "I'll let you get to your customers."

"Will you call me this weekend, let me know how it goes with Noah?"

"Absolutely. Depending on what he has to say, I may have to tap into your wisdom." She leaned over and gave the other woman a hug. "Go sell some books—or jewelry."

"I'm on it." She hugged back. "I'll be waiting to hear from you."

While Bev joined the other two women, Bren crossed the store and exited into the noonday light. If fate was kind, the sunny skies would hold for race day. After all the work that had gone into the event, bad weather would be a real downer.

But the race would go on, rain or shine.

As would her conversation with Noah. That was a given. Surely he was as anxious to touch base as she was.

Twenty-four hours later, however, a wave of uneasiness undermined her assumption about his feelings when she checked messages after her hectic shift at The Perfect Blend ended.

Noah had reached out to her first, and his text wasn't encouraging.

Can we defer our conversation until Sunday morning? I have a packed schedule tomorrow, and I know you'll be tied up with the race. That work for you?

Apparently he wasn't as eager to talk to her as she was to talk to him.

Swallowing past her disappointment, she keyed in a response.

Okay. What time?

You going to church?

Yes. The second service.

How about seven a.m.? My Sunday is booked too.

And clearly a conversation with her wasn't high on his priority list.

This was not looking positive.

But if he'd had a change of heart over the past six weeks, there was nothing she could do about it. Better to find out now than to jump into a relationship with both feet, only to have the romance fall apart after she was even more fully invested. That would hurt worse—impossible as that seemed at this moment.

She typed in a response.

Fine by me. Are you going to call me?

Yes. Talk to you soon.

End of exchange.

"Hey . . . you all right?" Zach halted as he passed by with a mop to begin cleanup duties.

"Yeah. You want me to do that?" She motioned to the mop.

"No. I've got it." He cocked his head and inspected her. "Why don't you clean out the case and take off?"

"Really?" If he was willing to let her cut out early, she wasn't going to argue.

"Yep. I bet you've got a crammed schedule leading up to the race tomorrow."

Yes, she did.

But race duties wouldn't be on the top of her to-do list after she left The Perfect Blend.

That spot was reserved for a good cry.

30

Bren was exactly where he'd expected her to be.

As Noah jogged up Pelican Point Road on Sunday in the pale, pre-dawn glow, the solo figure in a neon green windbreaker popped from the background despite the murky light. She was standing where she'd been the last time he'd come across her here, in the spot that would give her an unobstructed view of Sunrise Reef when the sun crested the hills to the east.

He slowed as he approached the path to the lighthouse, trying to give his pulse a few moments to decelerate after the uphill run.

But in truth, the physical exertion wasn't to blame for his racing heart.

That was all Bren's doing.

Because his future depended on her reaction to what he intended to say to her today.

At the beginning of the path, he stopped. Pulled out his phone. Filled his lungs and tapped in her number.

A second later, she jerked. Put the phone she already had in her hand to her ear. "Hi."

"Hi back." He began walking toward her. "Are you enjoying the view?"

Silence.

His lips quirked as he imagined the twin grooves that would be denting her forehead.

"Um . . . yes. But how did you know I was looking at a view?"

"Turn around."

She swiveled. Did a double take. Clapped her free hand to her chest. "What are you doing here?" She was still talking into the phone.

As he closed the distance between them, he ended the call. "Breaking our radio silence. In person."

She continued to stare at him. "How did you know where I was?"

"I jogged over to your house. When I didn't see your car, I continued up here. Where else would you be?"

"You know me pretty well."

"Getting there, anyway."

"Why didn't you tell me you were coming?" She slowly lowered her cell from her ear.

"I wanted it to be a surprise." He stopped across from her and stowed his phone. "And I thought this conversation deserved to be up close and personal."

She attempted to shove her phone into the pocket of her windbreaker. It took two tries, thanks to the tremors in her fingers. "I was afraid—" Her voice scratched, and she tried again. "I was afraid you'd . . . that you'd written us off."

What?

Frowning, he reached for her hand. Twined his fingers with hers. "Why would you think that? Did I ever give you any indication I'd lost interest?"

"No. But a lot can change in six weeks."

"Not on my end. And I hope not on yours."

"Definitely not. It's just that when you deferred our conversation from yesterday to today, I got worried. I was counting the days until our deadline, and it didn't seem like you were."

His throat tightened, and he squeezed her fingers. "I deferred the conversation because I wanted to have it in person, and with the race yesterday I knew you wouldn't have a spare minute to spend with me. I was here, though. Staying with Dad, who was sworn to silence. I had a few dots to connect first, anyway."

She furrowed her brow. "What kind of dots?"

"Dots that could remove the obstacles on our road to romance. I know the geography issue has been huge, but I couldn't walk away from what I feel whenever we're together without making every attempt to find a solution."

Some of the tension ebbed from her features, and hope sparked in the depths of her irises. "I feel the same."

"I'm glad we're on the same page. I've been giving it a lot of thought, and—"

"Wait." She held up a hand. "Before you say anything else, I have something for you."

Without waiting for a response, she eased her hand free and took off at a trot down the path.

Propping his hands on hips, he watched as she jogged to her car, pulled a flat manila envelope from the front passenger seat, and returned to him at a brisk clip.

Curious.

When she rejoined him, she held it out. "Depending on how our conversation went today, I was going to drop this at the post office on my way home. I had it weighed for postage yesterday. Now I can give it to you in person."

He took the stiff envelope, worked open the flap, and pulled out a calligraphy document done in an elegant hand, replete with ornate flourishes and touches of gold.

It was exquisite.

And the message it contained was even more beautiful.

As he read the note Bren had penned, it was hard to keep his vision clear.

Dear Noah,

If you're reading this, it's because we agreed during our talk on Saturday that whatever this thing is between us, it's worth exploring.

As we both know, geography has always been a huge hurdle, and from the beginning I've been unwilling to consider a move. Hope Harbor is home to me.

But Alice at Sweet Dreams said something to Emma that resonated with me. When Emma asked her how she and Joe could leave a place they'd always called home, Alice said they'd realized that home is more than a place. That it's being with the people you love.

Over these past few weeks, I've come to recognize the truth of that sentiment. And as much as I'll hate to leave Hope Harbor, if we end up falling in love, my home will be where you are. In St. Louis.

So I'm going to follow the advice of the old Irish proverb Zach posted at The Blend last week: "May you always have courage to take a chance."

I'm going to take a chance on you, Noah Ward.

Because if we're meant to be, I believe a future with you could be a taste of paradise.

As he read the last line, Noah's lungs locked.

How had he ever been lucky enough to meet this incredible woman, who guarded her heart and valued her independence and had searched long and hard to find a place to call home, yet was willing to go where he was and give up the life she'd created in the name of love? To put her trust in him.

It was a gift beyond price.

And he was going to tell her that.

As soon as he could talk.

He had to be finished reading her note by now.

But he hadn't said a word.

Heart pounding, Bren clasped her hands in front of her.

Maybe she'd been too open about her hopes for their relationship. Maybe it was too soon to mention long-term commitments. Maybe she'd let herself get too carried away with romantic fantasies.

What if she'd given him a case of cold feet?

Yes, he'd said he was willing to work on the geography issue, but that didn't mean he was thinking the M word at this stage of their—

He lifted his head, and her breath caught in her throat.

Was that a tear welling on his lower lash?

"This is beautiful, Bren. It's the best gift anyone has ever given me."

His hoarse tribute, and the raw emotion in his eyes, loosened the knot in her stomach.

She hadn't shot herself in the foot after all.

"I meant what I said." She wiped her damp palms down her leggings. "I know how important your job is to you. If we get serious, I'd rather move than lose you. And I wanted you to have that in writing."

"You don't have to move to keep me."

She scrutinized him. "What do you mean?"

"I've done a ton of thinking over these past six weeks too. About us, about my job, about what the future might look like if I strayed from the route I planned years ago."

"But what would you do?"

"Same type of work, except here."

"You mean . . . be a CPA in Hope Harbor?" Hope began to percolate in her heart.

"Why not? Tracy at the cranberry farm is the only game in town, and she's been trying to balance the needs of her clients with the demands of the farm for quite a while. She and I have had several long talks, including an in-person meeting yesterday. Based on the information she shared, her part-time CPA work generates a reasonable income. If someone were to practice full-time here, it could be quite lucrative."

"Not as lucrative as your job in St. Louis, I'll bet."

"No—but there would be other compensations." He hitched up one side of his mouth and clasped her hand again.

A delicious zing zipped through her as the warmth of his strong fingers seeped into hers. "But what about all the perks you'd be giving up?"

"There's no better perk than you." He led her to a nearby bench, carefully set her note on the seat, and tugged her down beside him.

She followed his lead without protest, even though it was hard to focus with his achingly tender blue eyes mere inches away.

"Don't you think—" Her voice squeaked, and she tried again. "Don't you think we should talk about how this is going to work? I mean, until we're both sure where this is going, neither of us should make dramatic changes."

"What did you have in mind?" He lifted his free hand and traced the line of her jaw.

It was getting more and more difficult to concentrate. "Um . . . I was thinking we could try a long-distance courtship. Letters, FaceTime, texts, occasional visits."

"For how long?"

"Until we're positive there's potential."

He brushed his finger over her lips, his feather-light touch oh-so-gentle. "Do you have any doubts about that?"

"N-not at this moment. But that's hormones talking."

"There's nothing wrong with hormones." He gave her an un-repentant grin.

"I just want us to be certain about where we're headed before you upend your life."

"How long are you thinking?"

"The end of the year?"

A wince replaced his grin. "Too long. I'd rather be here."

"And I'd rather you be 100 percent confident you're not making a mistake. If our relationship ends up falling apart, I'd feel terrible."

"I wouldn't. My job is losing its luster anyway. Even if it doesn't work out between us, I doubt I'd stay there."

"But you might not move here."

He studied her. "Actually, I might. I like the idea of being closer to Dad, and my research suggests I can earn a decent living here. I don't want you to worry about me, Bren."

"Goes with the territory if you care about someone."

After a moment, he exhaled. "Okay. We'll play it your way. I'll wait until Christmas to decide about pulling the trigger on the job. Fair enough?"

"Yes."

"I'm warning you, though. Be prepared to spend lots of time courting remotely between now and then, supplemented with in-person weekend visits. And block out the week between Christmas and New Year's for yours truly."

The corners of her mouth crept up. "I'll pencil you in."

"Write it in ink."

The sun peeked over the hills behind them, and Bren angled toward the reef. "The show's about to begin."

"Yeah. It is."

She looked back at him, and the passion smoldering in his eyes sent a warm flush coursing through her as she motioned toward the reef. "The rocks will turn gold in a minute."

"Why should I care about rocks when I have gold in my arms?"

Her heart melted.

"Did anyone ever tell you that you have a silver tongue?"

"No. I'm only eloquent with you. And I meant every word."

She looped her arms around his neck as the sun gilded the rocks and two seagulls soared overhead. "I think the time for words is past, don't you? Now that we've resumed communications, there are other ways to connect."

"My very thought."

Without any further conversation, he lowered his lips to hers in a pulse-pounding preview of all she could look forward to as they embarked on what promised to be a courtship to remember.

And all she could look forward to in the years ahead if their romance led to the happy ending she'd never expected to find, here in this little seaside town they would both call home.

Epilogue

"Noah just got here."

As Fred spoke in her ear, Bren swiveled away from the buffet table in the older man's house and zeroed in on the front door. Over the heads of all the people Fred had invited to his day-before-Christmas Eve party as a thank-you for their help while his wrist healed, her gaze connected with Noah's.

Despite his long hours in the air and on the road, he gave her the warm smile that had graced all of their FaceTime and Zoom sessions over the past two months.

But he had to be beat.

What kind of boss scheduled a major meeting the day before Christmas Eve—and refused to let a man leave at a decent hour to catch a flight to visit his father . . . and his significant other, though as far as she knew, Noah had never mentioned their budding romance to anyone at work. Why tip his hand about a potential departure until he was certain he was leaving?

After setting her almost-empty plate of catered hors d'oeuvres on a side table, Bren wove through the crowd toward the man who'd become the center of her world.

He waited for her in the small foyer, and as soon as she was within touching distance, he grabbed her hand and tugged her toward the study. Once they were inside, he closed the door and wasted no time demonstrating how much he'd missed her and how glad he was to see her.

When they came up for air, he rested his forehead against hers. "This beats Zoom and FaceTime any day."

"No contest." She had to coax her lungs back into gear.

"The three days I was here at Thanksgiving only left me wanting more."

"Me too."

"Sorry I'm so late. I was hoping we'd have an hour or two together before the horde descended here."

"You couldn't help the flight delay or the accident that tied up traffic on 101." She snuggled closer. "What matters is that you're here now. And I'll have you almost all to myself for a whole week."

"Almost?"

"You have to spend *some* time with your dad."

"We'll make it a threesome."

"You think he'll be okay sharing you with me?"

Noah grinned. "Are you kidding? He's all for our romance."

"Yeah." She gave a soft laugh. "I figured that out."

"When do you think the party will be over?" He tipped his head toward the living room.

"Hard to say. It's in the winding-down phase, but some people tend to linger. And you look exhausted anyway. Why don't you crash and we'll regroup in the morning?"

"Probably not a bad plan. It's been a long day. But first we have to say goodnight." He pulled her closer again.

"We just said hello."

"Are you complaining?"

"Nope." She smiled up at him and slipped her arms around his neck.

Once again, he dipped his head.

She rose on tiptoe to—

A knock sounded on the door, and Noah groaned. "I knew this party was going to interfere with our reunion."

"We'll make up for it tomorrow."

"I'll hold you to that."

Noah eased back and cracked the door open a couple of inches.

"Welcome home, Son. Sorry to interrupt, but is Bren in there?"

"Yes, she is." She peeked around Noah.

"Emma just arrived with Justin, and she asked about you. I promised to track you down."

"She and Justin must have run into the same traffic Noah did coming down from the airport." Bren turned to Noah. "I should talk to her. She was so excited that the guardianship came through in time for Christmas. Barely. If it hadn't been for Eric making a few calls, I'm not certain it would have."

"I'll go with you. I'd like to meet this brother she's gone above and beyond for."

He followed her out, into the dwindling crowd.

Emma was waiting off to the side in the living room, beside a lanky teen who shared many of his sister's features. Both of them wore smiles that couldn't have gotten any bigger.

When Bren reached them, Noah on her heels, Emma motioned toward her brother. "Bren, this is Justin. I've told him all about you."

She extended her hand to the teen. "And I've heard all about you too. Welcome to Hope Harbor."

"Thank you. I'm glad to finally be here." He squeezed her fingers.

Emma introduced Noah too, but after chitchatting for several minutes, Justin stifled a yawn.

"Sorry." His complexion reddened. "I didn't sleep much last night, and it was a long trip today."

"We should go back to the apartment. I didn't want Fred to think we'd stood him up, so we came straight here from the airport." Emma put her arm around her brother. "But I need to get

Justin settled in. And I have an early day tomorrow. I'm slammed with Christmas orders. Not that I'm complaining."

On the contrary. Her former housemate was glowing, thanks to her well-deserved success.

"I'm about to call it a night too." Bren slipped her arm through Noah's. "We'll touch base again soon."

As sister and brother each fixed a to-go plate at Fred's insistence, Noah once again drew Bren aside, tucking them into a quiet corner in the hallway. "Pick you up for church tomorrow?"

"I'd like that."

"Early service?"

"Yes."

"Dad will be along."

"Fine by me. I like your dad."

"The rest of the day is reserved for us, though. Agreed?"

"Agreed."

"Did you finish the big calligraphy job?"

"I did. It took several late nights, but my schedule is clear for the next week other than my shifts at The Perfect Blend."

"I'll spend those hours with Dad. But the rest of my time is yours. We have a lot to talk about."

"*After* we have a chance to spend in-person time together. You haven't said anything at work yet, have you?"

"No. I kept my part of the bargain."

"Good." She waved a hand toward the coat closet. "Want to walk me to my car?"

"That could be arranged."

He retrieved her coat, waited while she said goodbye to his father, then followed her out and down the street toward her Kia. "It was more convenient when you lived in the backyard."

"You didn't think that the night we met."

"No, but our first meeting led to good things."

Very true.

And as he told her with yet another kiss how much he'd missed her, she was pretty sure that even more good things were on tap for them down the road.

Assuming this week went well.

"Where are we going?"

"It's a surprise." Noah glanced over at Bren in the passenger seat of his rental car. A spot she'd occupied quite a bit during their holiday in-person courting week.

Which was winding down way too fast.

How could it be New Year's Eve already?

"Give me a hint."

"Uh-uh. You're too adept at guessing, as I found out when you and Dad and I played twenty questions the other night. You skunked both of us. Besides, we're almost there." He flipped on his blinker and hung a left onto Pelican Point Road.

She angled toward him. "Are we going to the lighthouse?"

"No."

"But there's nothing else up here, other than the special events center and Sunrise Reef."

"There may be something."

"Not that I've ever seen."

Three-fourths of the way up the road, he turned right, onto a gravel lane that wound through the trees.

Bren looked over at him. "As far as I know, this is a private driveway."

"Yep."

"Do you know the person who lives here?"

"Nope."

"Then what are we doing here?"

"Checking out real estate." He slowed and pointed ahead. "That house in particular."

Bren leaned forward as she examined the modest timber and

stone structure that emerged from the woods. Shifted back to him. "Why are you checking out real estate?"

He parked and slid from behind the wheel. "I'll get your door."

Rather than wait for him to circle the car, she jumped out and met him by the hood. "Why are you checking out real estate?"

He took her hand and drew her toward the house, dangling a key in front of her. "The agent agreed to let us do a walk-through on our own. Want to join me?"

"Noah." She dug her heels in the ground, keeping a firm grip on his hand. "Are you buying a house here?"

"I've been toying with the idea. I can't live with Dad forever after I move back." He started forward again.

"Wait." She didn't budge, forcing him to stop again. "We haven't made any plans about the future."

"I have."

"I thought it was going to be a joint decision."

"It is—about us. However, I've already decided to ditch my job, move here, and open my own accounting business. This is where I want to be." He dangled the key again. "Want to see the house? Because your opinion matters. A lot."

A slow smile curved her lips. "Yeah. I do."

They toured the house room by room, and everything about it lived up to the photos he'd seen. Judging by Bren's expression and comments, she was equally impressed.

But he saved the best for last.

"Let's look at the yard."

She gave the ground outside the sliding door, beyond the deck, a dubious scan. "There isn't much yard."

"This house has more property than you think. Most of it's wooded, though. Come on."

She went without protest, and after following the directions the agent had given him, they emerged onto a rocky outcrop above the sea that offered a stunning vista.

"Wow." Bren drew up beside him. "This is . . ." She paused. Peered into the distance. "That's Sunrise Reef."

"Yes, it is. It caught my eye in the photo in the listing. Seemed like a positive sign to me."

"This place gets my vote." Bren turned to him, eyes shining.

"Mine too. Let's sit for a minute." After leading her to a large boulder that offered a clear line of sight to the reef, he pulled her down beside him. "Here's what I'm thinking. I'll make an offer on this house. Go back to St. Louis and hand in my resignation with four weeks' notice so they don't have to scramble to deal with an unanticipated empty position. While my notice plays out, I get the paperwork going to buy out Tracy's practice, incorporate my own business, and talk to Marci about setting up a website for me like she did for you. I move here in early February, and we resume our in-person courtship. How does that sound?"

She stared at him. "Like a whirlwind." Then her features softened, and she reached out. Stroked a finger along his jaw. "But I'm with you 100 percent."

His pulse picked up at her touch. "Not that I'm trying to rush you, but in the interest of full transparency, it's only fair to tell you matrimony is front and center in my mind."

"It's top of mind for me too."

"So just for the sake of conversation, did you have any sort of timetable in mind before an official engagement?" The sooner the better as far as he was concerned.

"I think six more months might be sufficient."

An eternity.

But at least they'd be in the same town.

"How do you feel about long engagements?" He held his breath.

"Not necessary if there's been a long courtship."

Music to his ears. "Can I say I'm glad?"

"Yes. If I can say I feel blessed." Her irises began to glisten. "I never thought I'd meet a man who could win my trust, but I trust you, Noah Ward. Not only with my heart but with my life."

Pressure built in his throat as he gazed at the woman who'd entered his orbit so unexpectedly. A woman he'd assumed he had nothing in common with at the beginning, who'd disrupted his world and thrown him off his trajectory, spinning him in a whole new direction. Who'd reminded him of a lesson he'd learned long ago and somehow forgotten—that judging a book by its cover is foolish. That when you make the effort to delve below the surface, hidden dimensions and treasures can abound.

Like they did at Sunrise Reef.

"I appreciate that more than I can say, Bren. But the truth is, you've given me far more than I've given you. You made me realize my priorities had gotten messed up, and that what I thought was important pales in comparison to the things that really matter. Like the people who add joy to our lives and enrich our souls. That's why I expect to be asking you a very important question in the not-too-distant future. But in the meantime . . . shall we continue our in-person courtship?" He held out his arms.

She didn't hesitate to melt into them.

And as he claimed her lips once again, he gave thanks.

For the woman who'd won his heart with her kindness and grace—and for the home he would share with her in Hope Harbor for all the tomorrows to come.

Author's Note

If you're new to Hope Harbor—welcome! If you're a return visitor, welcome home. Because truly, visiting this charming little town where hearts heal and love blooms is like coming home.

When the first book in this series released in 2015, *Publishers Weekly* called Hope Harbor "a place of emotional restoration that readers will yearn to visit." Gratifyingly, that has proven to be the case. Last April, when Book #10 (*Sandcastle Inn*) came out, I posted the milestone on my Facebook page. Almost 1,000 readers liked the post, and comments poured in. Among them: "If you want to write another 10, I'm good with that." And "I've read, and loved, them all. I hope the series goes on and on!"

The happy news? There's another book planned, bringing the total to an even dozen. After that, we'll see if everyone still wants more. ☺

Sunrise Reef was especially fun to write because it features a character who's made cameo appearances in a couple of previous books—Bren, a barista at The Perfect Blend. When she first appeared on the scene, I was intrigued—and I had a feeling that someday she'd have her own book . . . if she ever told me her story. Finally she did. And what an interesting story it turned out to be. I hope you enjoyed reading about her (and Noah) as much as I enjoyed telling their tale.

There are three people I thank in every book, because their endless encouragement and staunch support have played such an integral role in my career—my husband, Tom, and my parents, James and Dorothy Hannon. Tom continues to cheer me on every single day, and my parents' legacy of love will always guide my steps, even though they're both gone now.

Thank you also to the stellar team at my publishing partner. Since I signed my first contract with Revell seventeen years ago, it has been a joy to work with such a dedicated, savvy, professional, and caring group.

Looking ahead, Hope Harbor #12 will be on shelves in April 2026. Closer at hand, the final book in my Undaunted Courage series will release in October 2025. And what a finish it will be. Get ready for a wild ride as a century-old mystery, a remote estate, a hidden treasure, a dying language, and suspicious deaths ratchet up the suspense.

Until next time, happy reading!

Love Irene Hannon's writing?
Turn the page for a sneak peek
at the next book in the

UNDAUNTED COURAGE
SERIES

AVAILABLE OCTOBER 2025

Her dream sabbatical was *not* off to an auspicious start.

Easing back on the gas pedal, Cara Tucker frowned at the flashing lights in the distance as she rounded a bend in the two-lane, rural Missouri road.

Why was a police cruiser blocking the entrance to Natalie Boyer's secluded estate—her destination on this early September Tuesday?

Cara coasted forward on the deserted road and squeezed onto the narrow shoulder a dozen yards back from the squad car emblazoned with the county sheriff logo. When a deputy emerged from behind the wheel and walked back to join her, she lowered her window, cringing as a wave of late-summer heat surged in.

"Morning, ma'am." He stopped beside her car. "Can I help you?"

"I hope so. The owner of this property is expecting me. What's going on?"

Instead of answering her question, he posed one of his own. "What's your name, ma'am?"

She passed it on. "Is Natalie all right?"

"Give me a minute." He pulled out his radio, walked several yards away, and angled sideways.

Cara peered at him through the haze of heat. He appeared to be talking, but his words were indecipherable.

Not a surprise, but frustrating nonetheless.

She shut her window, cranked up the AC to compensate for the humidity-laden air that had infiltrated the car, and tapped her fingers on the steering wheel while she waited for the deputy to return.

A minute ticked by. Two. Three.

What was going on?

Had something happened to Natalie?

And if it had, how would she manage to pull off the project that had won her a prestigious fellowship for the fall semester? Natalie and her journals were key to the research.

A sudden prod from her conscience banished those selfish thoughts. The safety of the older woman should be more important than career considerations. Rather than worrying about the feather this project would add to her academic cap, she ought to be saying a prayer for—

The deputy ended his conversation and strode back to her.

Gripping the wheel with one hand, Cara opened her window again and gave him her full attention.

"I just spoke with the sheriff, ma'am. He'll meet you in front of the house. Give me a minute to move my car."

They were letting her in.

Yes!

One hurdle cleared.

While the deputy returned to his cruiser, Cara rolled up her window and put her car in gear.

Once access to the driveway was restored, she rolled forward and swung in, tires crunching on the gravel as she traversed the long lane that wound among the pin oaks, sweetgums, maples, cedars, and white pines that had been left to grow in their natural state on the rolling terrain, with scant room for one car to get through.

Rounding the last curve, she gave the clearing ahead of her a sweep.

The house was just as she'd remembered it from her one visit back in April. Similar in design to the style favored by the Missouri French settlers who'd arrived in the area in the 1700s, it was slightly elevated off the ground, with a steeply pitched hipped roof, wraparound galérie, and a multitude of French doors and windows.

New in the picture were the squad car like the one at the entrance—and an ambulance.

Her stomach clenched.

Natalie had sounded hale and hearty during their phone conversation to finalize all the arrangements, but she *was* in her early eighties. And she did have long-standing physical challenges. While people developed work-arounds for those sorts of things, health-related conditions could create problems on occasion.

Grimacing, Cara pulled to the side of the drive and set the brake. Been there, done that. Experience was an excellent teacher. It also created a deep well of empathy.

Hopefully whatever had happened in this house wasn't as bad as it appeared.

A fit-looking man in uniform exited through the front door, and Cara slid from behind the wheel to meet him in front of the hood.

"Cara Tucker, I presume." He extended his hand. "Brad Mitchell."

She returned his firm clasp. "I'd say it was nice to meet you, but I'm not certain that's the most appropriate sentiment under the circumstances. Is Natalie okay?"

"She claims to be. The EMTs aren't convinced yet."

"What happened?"

"According to her, she felt lightheaded, lost her balance, and fell when she got up after her nap. The housekeeper heard the fall, found Ms. Boyer in a disoriented state, and called 911."

"Did she hit her head?"

"She says she didn't. I told her you were here and she confirmed you were expected. Maybe you can convince her to go to the ER and get checked out. She hasn't been receptive to that suggestion so far."

"I doubt I can change her mind. Our one face-to-face meeting won't buy me much influence."

His eyebrows rose. "I got the impression you were friends."

Flattering, but a bit of a stretch.

"More like acquaintances. My association with her is professional. I'll be spending weekdays here during the fall semester to work on an academic paper."

She left it at that. The sheriff likely wasn't interested in details only someone in her field would find fascinating. Few people outside academia got excited about hundred-year-old journals written in a vanishing language. Even her siblings' eyes glazed over if she went on too long about her research project.

"Are you a student at Cape?"

Her lips twitched in anticipation of his reaction. "No. Associate professor. Historical anthropology."

He did a double take.

Not surprising.

At thirty-four she still looked more like the typical undergrad than a professor.

But the sheriff recovered quickly. "Impressive. What sort of paper are you writing?"

She studied him.

Did he have a genuine interest in her project? Or was he simply being a thorough law enforcement officer and digging for more information about the woman who'd appeared out of the blue in the midst of a crisis?

Didn't matter. A top-line answer would suffice in either case.

"French culture around Old Mines. Natalie has material that will be helpful to me and offered to assist. Since commuting two hours each way every day wasn't practical, she also offered me a place to stay."

"Interesting." A beat passed as he considered her, but rather than follow up on that comment, he motioned toward the house. "Why don't we go in? It's too hot to stand out here in the sun. If you were able to convince her to let you invade her turf, I'm still hopeful you may be able to persuade her to pay a quick visit to the ER."

"Don't count on it."

"You can't do any worse than we have. Shall we?"

He let her precede him up the walkway and the steps that led to the galérie but reached around to twist the knob when she arrived at the door, giving her a subtle whiff of an enticing aftershave.

As she entered the house, it was clear the activity was centered in the living room to her right.

"Ah. Cara." Mouth contorting into a rueful twist, Natalie lifted a hand in greeting from her seat on an upholstered chair. "This wasn't the welcome I had planned for you. I'm sorry for all the turmoil."

"No worries." Cara crossed to her, and the hovering EMTs moved aside. She perched on a chair beside the older woman, whose leg was propped on an ottoman. "Are you okay?"

"I feel fine now. I know Lydia meant well, but she overreacted. The lightheadedness has passed, and my leg will heal."

Cara inspected the woman's exposed black-and-blue knee. "Do you think it would be wise to have a doctor weigh in on that?"

"No." Her tone was decisive. "I've seen too many doctors in my day. And I know my body far better than they do. I can't explain my earlier fuzzy-headedness, but that happened before I fell. I did *not* hit my head. My brain is working fine, and no harm was done to my knee other than a bruise. This is much ado about nothing."

Cara gave the sheriff a slight shrug and telegraphed a silent apology. She was in no position to push the woman, who seemed in total control of her faculties and fully capable of making decisions about her health care.

He acknowledged the message with a slight nod and joined them. "Ms. Boyer, the EMTs will have you sign a form indicating you declined transport and further treatment. Once you do that, we'll leave you in peace."

"Thank you, Sheriff. I do appreciate your prompt response. I'm sorry to have wasted everyone's time."

"To tell you the truth, we prefer calls that end this way." He smiled at her, displaying a killer dimple.

Cara's pulse picked up as she gave him a closer inspection. Broad shoulders that seemed capable of carrying a heavy load. At least half a foot taller than her five-six frame. Toned physique, suggesting workouts were part of his regular schedule. Light brown hair, neatly trimmed. Green eyes the color of imperial jade. Strong jawline. Firm lips, softened now into an appealing flex, that looked like they knew how to kiss.

She blinked.

Where on earth had *that* fanciful notion come from?

As if sensing her gaze, the sheriff transferred his attention to her.

Warmth suffusing her cheeks, Cara shifted away on the pretense of watching Natalie converse with the EMT who'd handed her a clipboard while the other medical technician spoke into his radio. Ogling wasn't her style, even if a man was ogle worthy. Nor was it her practice to dwell on a stranger's physical attributes.

Besides, getting carried away by a handsome stranger was foolish. Her focus this summer needed to be on her research, not on the opposite sex. Just because her sister and brother had both found The One over the past eighteen months didn't mean the same kind of happy ending was in the cards for her. That was a reality she'd accepted long before Cupid came to call on Bri and Jack.

So getting all hot and bothered about a man she'd met mere minutes ago and would have little or no contact with in the future was crazy.

Irene Hannon is the bestselling, award-winning author of more than sixty-five contemporary romance and romantic suspense novels. She is also a three-time winner of the RITA award—the "Oscar" of romance fiction—from Romance Writers of America and is a member of that organization's elite Hall of Fame.

Her many other awards include National Readers' Choice, Daphne du Maurier, Retailers' Choice, Booksellers' Best, Carol, and Reviewers' Choice from *RT Book Reviews* magazine, which also honored her with a Career Achievement award for her entire body of work. In addition, she is a HOLT Medallion winner and a two-time Christy award finalist.

Millions of her books have been sold worldwide, and her novels have been translated into multiple languages.

Irene, who holds a BA in psychology and an MA in journalism, juggled two careers for many years until she gave up her executive corporate communications position with a Fortune 500 company to write full-time. She is happy to say she has no regrets.

A trained vocalist, Irene has sung the leading role in numerous community musical theater productions and is also a soloist at her church. She and her husband enjoy traveling, long hikes, gardening, impromptu dates, and spending time with family. They make their home in Missouri.

To learn more about Irene and her books, visit www.Irene Hannon.com. She occasionally posts on Instagram but is most active on Facebook, where she loves to chat with readers.

Dear Reader,

Thank you for selecting a Revell novel! We're so happy to be part of your reading life through this work. Our mission here at Revell is to publish stories that reach the heart. Through friendship, romance, suspense, or a travel back in time, we bring stories that will entertain, inspire, and encourage you. We believe in the power of stories to change our lives and are grateful for the privilege of sharing these stories with you.

We believe in building lasting relationships with readers, and we'd love to get to know you better. If you have any feedback, questions, or just want to chat about your experience reading this book, please email us directly at publisher@revellbooks.com. Your insights are incredibly important to us, and it would be our pleasure to hear how we can better serve you.

We look forward to hearing from you and having the chance to enhance your experience with Revell Books.

The Publishing Team at Revell Books
A Division of Baker Publishing Group
publisher@revellbooks.com

Revell

Meet

IRENE HANNON

at IreneHannon.com

Learn news, sign up for her mailing list,
and more!

Find her on